Praise for

Unsaid

"UNSAID is an extraordinary story of animals, mortality, and the power of love. I found myself captivated by the world of this book. It will make you remember, rethink, and rejoice in every meaningful relationship you've ever had. Everyone needs to read this novel."

—Garth Stein, author of the international bestseller,
The Art of Racing in the Rain

"Rarely has a novel captured so movingly the deep bonds between people and the animals that share their lives...How each of these vivid characters finds a way to let go and move on is at the heart of this entrancing tale."

—*Parade Magazine*

"UNSAID explores the miracle of sentience in humans and animals, and every character in this story makes heartbreaking mistakes. This compassionate and suspenseful story will remind you to savor every moment of every meaningful relationship you may ever be blessed with—whether human or animal."

—*BookPage*

"UNSAID will really make you think about the relationship between people and animals. I was not able to put it down, and I read parts of it twice."

—Temple Grandin, author of
Animals Make Us Human

"Neil Abramson has written a powerful and imaginative novel. His insights into the animal kingdom touched my heart. My book club will love it."

—Meredith Brokaw, creator and coauthor
of the Penny Whistle books
and *Big Sky Cooking*

"Abramson delivers a touching and dramatic story that is sure to please animal lovers... [A] solid story of loss and love."

—*Library Journal*

"Enjoyed it thoroughly."

—Jeffrey Masson, author of *When Elephants Weep*

"A poignant read on the meaning of life and its priorities—how death and despair can lead to renewal and life, but only if one realizes the interconnectedness of all creatures."

—Irene Pepperberg, author of *Alex and Me*

"A remarkable book."

—Susan Wilson, author of *One Good Dog*
and *The Fortune Teller's Daughter*

"UNSAID, a new novel by Neil Abramson, movingly explores the ways in which animals—including a chimpanzee, Cindy, who communicates with sign language—impact the lives of the humans who care for and about them."

—Michelle Sherrow, blog writer,
PETA Foundation

"This moving and riveting novel beautifully expresses the transforming power of the human–animal relationship. Read it if you share your life with an animal, but more importantly, read it if you haven't."

—Gene Baur, president and cofounder of
Farm Sanctuary, and author of
*Farm Sanctuary: Changing Hearts
and Minds about Animals and Food*

"A suspenseful, heart-throbbing novel exploring the big questions of life, death, sentience, animal rights, compassion, righteous indignation, and what it is all about and why. The surprise twists are like an emotional roller coaster. Read it, weep, grab your chair, and gain insights into the big why!"

—Allen M. Schoen, DVM, veterinarian and author of
*Kindred Spirits: How the Remarkable Bond between
Humans and Animals Can Change the Way We Live*

"In this unique and moving novel, Neil Abramson shows just how strong our relationships with other animals can be, and how we can learn so much from our animal kin, about their needs, their emotions, and respect, dignity, and love. I was continually moved as I read UNSAID and reflected on its important messages about just how important other animals are to us, and encourage you to read this intriguing book and share it widely."

—Marc Bekoff, author of *The Emotional Lives of
Animals, Animals Matter, Wild Justice,* and
*The Animal Manifesto: Six Reasons for
Expanding Our Compassion Footprint*

"A remarkable book, uncanny in that its narrator is recently deceased, but vivid in its development of believable and complex characters, both human and nonhuman. The author embeds in the story important aspects of current controversies over the extent of animal capacities as well as a keen sense of the value of animal lives."

—Susan J. Armstrong, professor emerita,
Humboldt State University, and
coeditor of *The Animal Ethics Reader*

"Upton Sinclair's *The Jungle*, a novel about animal slaughter and the men who perform it, exerted a powerful influence on a much earlier generation. May I hope that Neil Abramson's novel, UNSAID, will have a similar effect on present-day readers and help us understand that animals need us as much as we need them. A riveting tale!"

—George K. Russell, professor of biology,
Adelphi University, and senior
editor of *Orion* magazine

"UNSAID says it all in a lyrical story about humanity's journey from betrayal to reconciliation with our animal kin. A beautiful, wrenching testimony."

—G.A. Bradshaw, director and founder,
The Kerulos Center, and author of
*Elephants on the Edge: What Animals
Teach Us About Humanity*

"This is a story about love, healing, and, even more compellingly, animal rights. The work that Helena and Jaycee did with Charlie and Cindy (both chimpanzees) makes for utterly compelling stories that drive this story and weave all of these characters together in an unexpected way."

—FreshFiction.com

Unsaid

Unsaid

— A NOVEL —

Neil Abramson

CENTER STREET

NEW YORK   BOSTON   NASHVILLE

Copyright © 2011 by Neil Abramson
Afterword Copyright © 2012 by Neil Abramson
Reading Group Guide Copyright © 2012 by Neil Abramson

Center Street
Hachette Book Group
237 Park Avenue
New York, NY 10017

www.centerstreet.com

Center Street is a division of Hachette Book Group, Inc.

The Center Street name and logo are trademarks of
Hachette Book Group, Inc.

The Hachette Speakers Bureau provides a wide range of authors for speaking
events. To find out more, go to www.hachettespeakersbureau.com or call
(866) 376-6591.

The publisher is not responsible for websites (or their content)
that are not owned by the publisher.

Originally published in hardcover by Center Street.

First Trade Edition: June 2012

The Library of Congress has cataloged the hardcover edition as follows:
Abramson, Neil, 1964–
Unsaid / Neil Abramson. — 1st ed.
p. cm.
ISBN 978-1-59995- 410-3
1. Wives—Death—Fiction. 2. Chimpanzees—Fiction. 3. Human-
animal communication—Fiction. 4. Human- animal relationships—
Fiction. 5. Bereavement—Fiction. I. Title.
PS3601.B7585U57 2011
813'.6— dc22
2010034230

ISBN 978-1-59995-409-7 (pbk.)

For my angels—Isabelle, Madeleine, and Amy

Acknowledgments

I am so grateful to many people who have helped make this book a reality.

I was continually amazed at the extraordinary level of skill, genuineness, care, enthusiasm, and integrity of everyone I worked with at Center Street and Hachette Book Group. *Unsaid* could not have found a better home.

At Center Street, profound gratitude to Christina Boys, my wonderful and wise editor; Angela Valente, my daily go-to person, who makes everything run so smoothly; Rolf Zettersten, publisher, and Harry Helm, associate publisher, who believed in this book.

The sales, marketing, and publicity teams have worked so hard and with such passion and creativity. Huge thanks to Andrea Glickson, Martha Otis (and Teddy and Winston), Karen Torres, Chris Barba, Mindy Im, Kelly Leonard, Chris Murphy, Shanon Stowe, Janice Wilkins, Gina Wynn, and Jean Griffin. I am humbled by your talent and moved by your compassion. For his incredible eye, thank you to Jody Waldrup, art director. For his guiding hand, thank you to Bob Castillo, the managing editor, and his terrific team, including my copy editor, Laura Jorstad.

This book could never have happened without Jeff Kleinman

at Folio Literary Management. Seriously. He never gave up on me and never lost his faith in this book. He is brilliant at what he does, but more important he is, as my grandmother used to say, "a good man." And to Celeste Fine and the rest of the gang at Folio, thank you for everything.

My colleagues at Proskauer, and in particular in the great labor and employment department of the firm, have taught me so much more than the practice of law. They have never let me down and, when I needed, actually propped me up. I cannot imagine a better place to practice law or a better group of people to do it with. My very special thanks to Joe Baumgarten and M. David Zurndorfer for putting up with me all these years, being such good friends, and not telling me I was crazy (or at least not about the book). The late Steven Krane, a brilliant lawyer and animal lover, reminded us always that doing the right thing was not merely a process, but an end. I miss you, Steve.

My thanks as well to anthropologist Dr. Barbara King at William and Mary College, the author of *Being with Animals*, for serving as my science consultant. The errors are still mine, but because of her review, there are fewer of them.

Dr. Gay Bradshaw, the founder and director of the Kerulos Center, gave me invaluable information and insight as well as encouragement. Kerulos is doing remarkable work, and I hope their vision is not too long in coming—"A world where animals and their societies live in dignity and freedom in peaceful co-existence with humans."

More thanks to Herb Thomas, a kind and quiet man, who wrote a book called *The Shame Response to Rejection* and changed so many lives, including my own; Roma Roth, who made a remarkable movie about bonobos called *Uncommon Chimpanzee*, gave me the first encouraging words about my writing, and continued to be a source of encouragement throughout this process; and my dear friend Adrian Alperovich, who always gave me good advice.

Thanks and love to my folks, who taught me to love books.

To Skippy and my other animal companions who first opened my heart, I will never forget you.

And to Amy, Isabelle, and Madeleine, who have filled it more than I could have possibly hoped for. There is nothing without you guys. Nothing.

Unsaid

Prologue

Every living thing dies. There's no stopping it.

In my experience—and I've had more than my share—endings rarely go well. There is absolutely nothing life affirming about death. You'd think that, given the prevalence and irrevocability of death, whoever or whatever put the whole thing together would've given a little more attention to the process of exit. Maybe next time.

When I was still alive, a critical part of my job was to facilitate the endings. As a veterinarian, I was a member of the one healing profession that not only was authorized to kill, but in fact was expected to do so. I saved life, and then I took it away.

Whether it was because I was a woman—and, therefore, a life bearer by definition—or simply because my neurons fired that way, the dissonance created by my roles as reaper and healer had been with me since my first day of vet school.

Although I tried to convince myself that I always did the best I could for all in my care, I often worried that every creature I'd killed would be waiting for me at the end. I imagined a thousand beautiful, innocent little eyes glaring at me, judging, accusing, and detailing my failures. I didn't do enough for them, those eyes would say; I wasn't good enough. Or perhaps I gave up too soon. Or maybe, for some, I kept them alive too long when they were in pain—a mere shadow of their former selves—only because that is what someone else wanted for them.

Of these offenses I'm almost certainly guilty. In the end, the responsibility of filling heaven is too difficult a burden for mere mortals like me. Yes, I had cared, but caring is not enough.

As I became more ill, after the cancer traveled from my breasts to my lymph nodes, my worry turned into fear and, at the last, terror. My hands had been the instrument of too many deaths born out of the burden I had asked for but was ill prepared to shoulder. One of these deaths in particular began to gnaw at me until it filled me with such shame that my defenses of denial and rationalization abandoned me altogether.

I came to believe that I could not face these failures without an offering of true and demonstrable repentance. For me this meant not just empty words of apology, but finding meaning in and justification for the decisions I'd made or, alternatively, finally admitting to myself that I wasn't who I believed and that I probably had not mattered at all—not to my husband, my colleagues, my own animals, or those I tended to in life.

In the midst of that search, just as I was beginning to weave some of the discrete threads into a broader tapestry of consequence, I ran out of time. The pain became unimaginable and the morphine drip remained my last best friend until everything just stopped.

And so here I am, unable to retreat and afraid to move onward empty-handed. Instead, I watch and hope that what I see will bring me understanding or at least the courage to move on without it, before everything fades and my pages turn blank. I don't know how much time I have before this happens or the consequence for me if it does, but I don't think it's good.

If you believe my present predicament is merely the product of overreaction or perhaps cowardice, you may be right. But then I only have one question for you.

How many lives have you taken?

1

The irony is that I didn't understand the profound impact that death had on my life until I succumbed to its power. The signs were all there, but I guess I ignored them or had been too occupied with the act of living.

I'd married an orphan—a child of death. In fact, death itself had introduced us.

David had been driving too fast to get to an evening class at the law school. I was driving in the opposite direction half asleep from twenty-four hours at the Cornell vet clinic and completely lost in the memory of a chimpanzee named Charlie.

A large deer suddenly jumped from the woods into the road and froze in the glare of our headlights. I cut my wheel and rolled down a small embankment, stopping near a dense stand of trees.

David and the deer were not as lucky. He stomped on his brakes, but he was too late by seconds. I heard the sickening *thud* of metal against soft tissue and then the sound of his wheels scream as he spun off the opposite side of the road.

I quickly climbed the embankment. The force of the car's impact had thrown the deer into the middle of the road. It was alive and struggling to stand on two clearly broken rear legs. I immediately thought through my options, none of them good.

"Are you okay?" David called to me from across the way as soon as he got out of his car.

I ignored him and ran toward the deer and into the road. The deer's front legs gave out and it collapsed just as a pair of headlights rounded a bend on the hill no more than two miles down the otherwise pitch-dark oncoming lane.

"No!" David screamed. "The cars can't see you!"

I reached the terrified deer in five seconds and tried to move it out of the road by tugging its forelegs. It was no use. The animal was too frightened and far too heavy.

The approaching car was now only a mile away. David reached me and tried to pull me out of the road and back toward his car. "Come on, we need to get out of the road," he shouted.

I pushed him off. "I can handle this."

When I next looked up, the oncoming car was maybe half a mile away. I realized that David was right—because of the steep grade of the road, the car wouldn't be able to see us in time to stop.

David refused to leave me. He yanked off his coat and, after two tries, looped it around the deer's forelegs up by its shoulders. He tied the arms of the jacket into a knot and heaved on the jacket while I pushed, but the deer moved only a few inches.

The oncoming car closed in.

A panicked hoof shot out and caught David on the cheek, carving a deep gash that immediately drew blood. David's eyes glazed over and he stumbled on his heels. For one horrible moment I thought he was going to pass out in the road. I would never be able to move him before the car came through.

"Get out of the road!" I screamed. He shook the cobwebs away, and I saw his eyes finally clear.

He tried to get a better grip on the makeshift sling and said, "On the count of three, okay?"

I glanced at the headlights of the oncoming car. It was too close. I nodded at David, but started to sweat despite the cold.

"One, two, three!" If David said anything else, his words were drowned out by my own scream of exertion and the blare of the car horn.

We pulled the deer clear of the lane and onto the shoulder just as the car passed. Then we collapsed. The car didn't even hesitate as its horn faded into the distance.

The deer struggled to lift her head and blood sprayed from her nose, splattering me and David and mixing with the blood already streaming from the cut on his face.

David slowly got to his feet while I ran back to my car. "Where are you going?" he called after me.

"Stay here." Another car passed, narrowly missing me, as I ran across the road.

I returned two minutes later with my bag and pulled out a deep pink vial of phenobarbital and a large syringe. Death comes in such a pretty color.

"What're you going to do?"

"I'm going to kill her."

"Kill her? But we just—"

"—she's got massive internal bleeding. Her abdomen's already full of blood. I'm a vet. Trust me, she's done."

"When did you know that?"

"As soon as I saw her in the road," I said as I drew the pheno into the syringe like I'd done dozens of times before.

"Then why'd we just almost kill ourselves bringing her out of the road?" David didn't sound angry, just confused.

"Because I want my voice to be the last thing she hears, not the sound of oncoming traffic. I want her to feel gentle hands as she goes, not the force of a car crushing her sternum. I'm sorry, but she deserves that. We all do."

David nodded at my answer. I don't think he understood, but neither did he argue. "What should I do?"

"I can do this by myself," I told him as I turned toward the deer.

David grabbed my arm. "I know you can, but you don't need to. Let me help."

"Okay. Hold her down and as still as you can. I need to go into her neck." David did his best to comply. The doe's eyes were wide with fear and pain. I stroked the doe's throat for a moment to give comfort, but also to find the major vein for the needle. I finally found it.

I took a deep breath, jabbed the needle in, and quickly injected the contents of the syringe. The doe struggled for a moment, and then her lifeless head dropped into David's arms. I took the stethoscope from my bag and listened for a heartbeat. "She's gone," I said.

A tear rolled down David's undamaged cheek as he stroked the head of the animal. His shoulders relaxed, his breathing deepened, and his teeth chattered. Perhaps it was the accident, or the pain from the deep cut on his face, maybe it was the accumulation of the events of his day or simply being witness to the act of taking a life, but this man I didn't know was suddenly known to me.

For that instant, David was again the lonely high school boy who learned that his father was gone, and whose mother left him so soon after. He was the responsible only child who swallowed his pain because there was no one to share his grief. Death had spoken to him in a secret language, and this act of communication had changed him and set him apart. He was both an innocent and damaged by experience.

"I'm so sorry," he whispered into the dead deer's ear.

We called the sheriff's office from the Tompkins County Community Hospital thirty minutes later, reported the deer carcass, and requested a tow for David's car. I held David's hand while they put twenty-two stitches in his cheek and fed him antibiotics and painkillers. You can still see the faint line of a scar when the sun hits his face just the right way.

After that night, without too much discussion and even less fanfare, David and I were together. Period.

Such is the power of death. It can rip apart or fuse together. And now, sixteen years later, it sits on David's chest, slowly squeezing the life out of him.

We lived in a beautiful part of New York State—close enough to Manhattan that David could get to his office in seventy-five minutes, but far enough away that I could pretend I was a simple country veterinarian.

Our house sits in the middle of a clearing at the top of a small hill. The house itself is modest, but the property is very pretty and provided more than enough room for all my creatures.

We bought the house and moved north from the city at my request two years before David made partner at his firm. This was my first real demand during our marriage. I believe it was the right decision—for both me and him. In return for the additional stress of becoming a homeowner and a commuter, David gained a house full of life and love—until, of course, it wasn't anymore.

I hardly recognize our place now. A thin dusting of snow provides the only color to this otherwise steel-gray day. The grounds around the house are a mess—newspapers and small bits of garbage blow across the property. The source of the refuse, a trash bag torn open by a hungry raccoon, lies in the driveway next to two overturned plastic garbage cans. My Jeep is encrusted in snow and ice, its battery long dead. Several unopened FedEx packages marked URGENT and addressed to David Colden line the steps leading up to the house.

I'm reminded by the scene before me that a home is an organism, and no organism gripped by death is particularly attractive.

Right next to the house, a small wood-framed barn and a paddock fill out several acres. My two horses, bored and restless from lack of attention, paw the ground looking for fresh hay.

Arthur and Alice were Premarin foals, unwanted by-products of the manufacture of a drug made from the urine of pregnant horses. We saved these two from the slaughterhouse within a month of our move north.

With Premarin foals, you just never know what kind of horse you're going to end up with, and my two well make the point. Alice, who looks part Morgan and part quarter horse, is shy, sweet, and always up for a good scratch on the head. Arthur, my huge draft horse, is very smart and has little tolerance for any human contact except mine. Even now I believe he senses me; he stares right at the spot where I'm standing and snorts curiously.

A second smaller enclosure abuts the paddock. Several years ago, I placed a large doghouse into the space. Now something moves within the doghouse and pushes mounds of old straw out onto the ground. The creature in the doghouse—a 375-pound pink pig—raises its massive head and grunts in my direction. This is Collette.

We adopted Collette four years ago. She'd been abandoned with her twenty young brothers and sisters in a rotting upstate barn in the middle of winter. When the piglets were discovered, all but three were frozen to the barn's dirt floor. Collette was one of the three.

Collette is a survivor, a champion over death, but her early experiences have left their mark. She is moody and even on good days does not have a vast sense of humor. Today clearly is not a good day.

In the house itself, there is some evidence of life—but just barely. Empty Chinese food boxes merge with condolence cards to form an odd sculpture on the hallway table. A dozen of the cards have cascaded off the table and landed on the floor. Several of these have been chewed to shreds.

The living room curtains are drawn and, but for the glow cast by the dying embers in the fireplace and a dim floor lamp, the room is dark. Loose stacks of unopened mail and used wineglasses cover most of the flat surfaces.

The wineglasses frighten me. David likes wine. In the few times that I've seen him seriously troubled, his wine consumption soared. He was never roaring drunk. To the contrary, the alcohol made him even more subdued and closed off to me. The wine deadens him and that, I believe, is his intention.

I raised this concern with him perhaps twice, but the episode always passed before it escalated. The demands of David's job require that he be 100 percent mentally focused, so his work invariably served as an outer limit for his alcohol intake. But without the daily burdens of the job? I don't know. We've never gone there.

Like the rest of the house, the kitchen is a mess. Empty wine bottles line the counter, and dirty dishes and glasses fill the sink. If this were the city, roaches would be everywhere. Because we live beyond even the borders of suburbia, however, there are no vermin that cannot be rationalized as "wildlife."

I find David in the kitchen struggling to open a can of dog food while my three dogs—Chip, Bernie, and Skippy—wait patiently at his feet. In a dirty pair of jeans, a sweatshirt, work boots, and several days of stubble, he is the house personified. He's lost even more weight and looks so gaunt that the new harsh angles of his face mar his handsomeness.

He is too young for this. Thirty-seven is too young to bury a wife. He still wears our wedding band because even now he cannot believe this is happening to him. I know this because he has the same look on his face as the deer trapped in his headlights so many years ago.

It is more than just the fact that I'm gone. David poured himself into my life. My friends became his friends. My animals became his animals. My plans became his plans. All connections passed through me. That's not a complaint. I was not only a willing vessel for David's life; I found it exhilarating.

In return, David became my rock—steady and dependent, a safe harbor when I became overwhelmed by the accumulation of still, little bodies. He calmed me down when I started to lose it on a difficult case and convinced me to trust my own instincts instead of the textbooks. David's confidence in me was a great gift, and I realize now that I never really thanked him for it.

Up until now, it all worked, didn't it, David? It was a good deal all around, wasn't it? Still, I cannot help but fear that my death has severed your slender tether to this human plane. You are beginning to fade, just like me.

I swear, David, I didn't know. I didn't know it was all going to end this way. It's not like I could've changed things; we met at a crossroads, and the people you meet at the most important times of your life invariably become the most important people in your life. But I do wonder if it would've turned out differently if there had been no death—no Charlie—in the story line. Would I have been available for you when the layers finally peeled away? Would you even have cared if I hadn't been so haunted? Every action is inextricably dependent upon the one that preceded it, like some infinite dance that continues out in perpetuity until one of the partners exits the floor. I know that now. A fat lot of good it does me, though.

David finally manages to open the can of dog food and quickly fills the three bowls on the floor. The dogs look at David, then the food, and back to David. I usually add rice and chicken broth to their dinners, but David doesn't remember this or (as likely) can't be bothered by the extra effort.

Chip, Bernie, and Skippy. My sweet, sweet boys. I miss you so much. I long for the feel of you, to rub your fur, touch your wet noses.

Seeing my dogs again is almost as heartrending as looking at my husband. The always-anxious Chip, the Labrador, was with me the longest. I brought him home soon after our move following one of my monthly vet visits to a nearby mall pet store. When I first saw Chip, the product of some Midwest puppy mill hell, he was only eight weeks old and his face was covered with running sores from a rampant staph infection. I told the asshole of a store owner that I could cure him with a month or so of antibiotics, but the owner complained that the dog would then be too "old" to sell. He demanded that I "put him down" so he could save the cost of the drugs. Chip came home with me that same day and left me only when David drove me to the hospital for the last time.

Bernie, the Bernese mountain dog, is beautiful, huge, goofy, and the sweetest dog I've ever known. He came to us a year later. Bernie had been bred locally to be a show dog. Given Bernie's parents, the breeder had high hopes for "best of breed" at Westminster and then many years of stud fees. Within a few months of his birth, however, it became clear that Bernie's bad shoulders would keep him out of not only Westminster, but any breeding circle that would pay his way.

The breeder requested that Bernie be "put to sleep." I told her that I could easily find Bernie a good home. The breeder insisted that death was the only option that would preserve her reputation; it simply wouldn't do to have a "defective"—her word—out in the world that was traceable to her stock.

I sent the breeder away with assurances that I would take care of it, and then I snuck Bernie home on my lunch break. That was a good day. Chip loved the company, and the two big dogs became fast friends.

Skippy the schipperke, the last dog I adopted in life, was my greatest challenge. He is a small black bundle of thick fur with a beautiful fox-like face and pointed ears. Intelligent, industrious, and energetic, Skippy does not suffer fools lightly. Of the three, he reminds me most of my husband.

I always assumed that Skippy was yet another Missouri puppy mill special, although I don't really know where he came from. Early one winter morning, I went to open my office and found Skippy sitting patiently and alone on the welcome mat at the front door as if he were waiting for an appointment. When I opened the office door, Skippy trotted in with an air of entitlement that I could not question.

I carried Skippy into my exam room and gave him a once-over. Skippy didn't object. He had no tags, no collar, and no visible injuries. I noticed almost immediately, however, that he was breathing too fast for a small dog at rest. When I listened to his chest for the first time, I began to understand why. Skippy had a heart murmur that sounded only slightly less turbulent than Niagara Falls. The sonogram I took of Skippy's heart later that morning completed the sad picture of a heart built wrong. We predicted he had maybe a year of life in that heart before it gave out.

I figured Skippy was a runaway. My staff posted notices everywhere while I silently prayed that no one would come to claim him. That particular prayer, at least, was answered.

Skippy is unaware of his death sentence, or it may be simply that he enjoyed our life together too much to let it go. He is now almost four years old and still going. He's been a great companion and helped keep my own heart open during my last year. I could hold him upside down between my legs or swing him high in the air and he would wag his little stump of a tail and yip with excitement. He would wake me every morning by licking my nose and then run and hide until I found him. After we had our special morning alone time, he would go off and play with the big guys, oblivious to being stepped on or the physiological failings of his heart.

The fact that Skippy has actually outlived me makes me smile.

You just never know with dogs.

"Well, come on then," David says, motioning to the food. The dogs reluctantly move to their respective bowls as David raises a full wineglass in toast. "Cheers."

The doorbell rings and the dogs run out of the kitchen barking wildly. David slowly follows them.

In the darkened living room, David parts the curtains just enough to peek out into the driveway. A silver BMW convertible sits next to the garbage cans.

David trudges to the front door as if he's on a schoolboy's trip to the principal's office. He tries to quiet the dogs and then opens the door. There on the front porch stands Max Dryer.

Max would look like a caricature of an incredibly polished and self-important Big Manhattan Law Firm Rainmaker if you didn't believe his claim that he was in fact the initial model for that caricature. He is fifty-four, tall, thin, handsome, dressed in a custom-made charcoal pin-striped suit, purple tie, and sparkling Allen Edmonds shoes. As soon as he sees David through the screen door—the first time in three weeks—Max pulls out a box of Davidoff cigarettes, lights one with a gold Dunhill lighter, and inhales deeply.

"Max, Max, Max," David scolds and shakes his head. "Those cigarettes will kill you."

Max offers a tight smile. "I'm assuming my clients will get to me first."

"There's always that hope. I guess you want to come in?"

"That's the general idea."

"Fine. Leave the smoke outside, though."

Max tosses his cigarette into the snow, where it sizzles dead, and then he steps into the house.

David, ignoring his visitor, addresses the three dogs. "Fellas, I believe you know Max."

Max bends down to invite the dogs to come to him, but they decide instead to return to their meal in the kitchen.

"Don't take it personal," David says. "As you might expect, they're not themselves. By the way, neither am I. That is your one and only fair warning. Drink?"

"A little early, isn't it?"

David shrugs off the question. "It's some time after Helena's death. That makes it late enough in the day for me. But suit yourself."

"I'll pass for now."

David enters the kitchen while Max heads for the living room. Max opens the curtains and in the sudden light winces at the scene before him. The only part of the room that is not in disarray is the long bookcase that lines one of the walls. The bookcase holds the books I'd read and used for research during my illness. My books still remain as I'd left them. I'm not surprised. Change has been cruel to David in the past, and he has learned to avoid its proof until events overtake him.

Max walks over to the bookcase and scans the titles—*Animal Rights Today; When Elephants Weep; Being with Animals; Kanzi; Animal Behavior and Communication Studies.* Every title concerns animal behavior, animal rights, communication theory, or American Sign Language, but to David they might as well have been in Latin.

David returns with his glass and the dogs at his heels. Pointing to the shelves, Max asks, "All of these Helena's?"

"She read a lot once she became sick. I guess she felt she was running out of time to learn. She was right."

David drops into an overstuffed chair by the fireplace, leaving Max to fend for himself. All the seats by this point have been taken by the dogs. Max tries to make room on the couch next to Chip, but Chip holds his ground.

David enjoys Max's confused discomfort for a minute before calling Chip to join him by the chair. Max quickly takes the open spot.

Max cares about three things—money and women (loved in that order, I believe) and last, my husband. Max, who recruited and trained David from day one, saw him as his protégé. This was a problem for both of them. Although I know David felt a great deal of gratitude toward Max and, when pushed, would admit that he had a deep but inexplicable fondness for his mentor, Max had a recurring tendency to confuse his *c*-words—*care, concern,* and *control.* Max wanted David to be more like him and ultimately replace him on the firm's governing executive committee. The prospect of becoming any more like Max, however, used to keep David awake at least two nights a month.

"So, what is it that gets the great Max Dryer to leave Manhattan on a weekday?"

"You knew I'd need to come to you at some point," Max says. "You don't pick up the phone and you don't return messages. Even my messages."

"Don't beat me up about my communication skills right now."

"I'm not. I was just worried."

David rolls his eyes, a gesture he has perfected around Max. "I can only imagine."

Max glances at the wedding ring that David still wears. David follows his gaze and then self-consciously hides his hand in his pocket.

"Look, I understand how you must feel," Max says.

"Really? Do tell. How many wives have you buried?"

"You know that's not what I meant. You've every right to be bitter, but don't be an asshole."

David looks away as he tries to compose himself. "Sorry, but I warned you."

"It's just that... well, it's been over two weeks since the funeral and four weeks since you've even seen the office." Max once again takes in the disarray that is the living room. "What have you been doing to yourself here? Didn't you have someone coming in to take care of things?"

"She was only a home care aide for Helena. I haven't replaced her yet since..." The sentence hangs between them.

"I think you could use some help around here," Max says while avoiding David's stare.

"You didn't come up here to talk about my housekeeping, did you?"

"No, but you could've made this a little easier."

"But it is so seldom that I get to see you fumfering. It's the most fun I've had since the funeral."

"Lovely."

"So, I'm out of time?" David looks at his watch. "Note to self: The exact duration of the firm's compassion in the event of death of wife. Three weeks, three days, ten hours, and twelve minutes."

"That's not it at all. We only want to know how you're doing. That's not unreasonable."

"I don't really know how to answer that. Seriously, what's the appropriate benchmark? My wife is dead. I can't see her again on this earth. Not today. Not ever. So, how am I doing? I'm doing just great."

"Is sarcasm a sign of healing?"

"What do you want me to say?"

"Let's start with the basics. Do you need anything?"

"Sure. I need a device to go back in time and get back all those nights I spent out with you reliving your greatness, or in the office working on the next draft of a brief that mattered little or not at all, or following you around the country on rainmaking trips. I want— no, I need—all that time back."

Max nods. "I know," he says softly. "If I had the power, I would give it to you."

David looks at Max skeptically at first and then in growing disbelief. "Wow. Do you actually feel guilty? Max Dryer? Is that really you in there?"

"Please stop it. I loved Helena in my own way and subject to my own many limitations—of which I am well aware, thank you."

David searches Max's eyes, but Max quickly looks away. "I think I believe that," David says. And so do I, Max. It's just that you always seemed so proud of your limitations. Perhaps I should've looked at you harder and longer.

"Would you like us to get you a place in the city? Temporary, you know, until you can get your own?"

"The city? Who said anything about moving back to the city?"

"This is me, David. I know you and how you work. I've seen you prepare for trials and I've seen you try cases. How're you going to handle this place? What happens when you're in trial? How can you take care of all Helena's animals?"

Really, David. How can you? I asked him this same question months ago. I was the gaunt woman with the eyes hollowed out by chemo and the scarf wrapped around a bald head. Propped up on pillows in our bed, David's arm around my bony shoulders, I tried to reason with him when all he wanted to do was avoid looking at what I'd become.

"I can tell that you miss it," I told him. "Ordering Chinese food for delivery at midnight, jumping into a cab home instead of racing to catch a train or fighting traffic. Think of how much easier it'll be for you."

"Why are we talking about this? Why is this even relevant?" David asked me, beginning to get upset.

I pulled back from him then, suddenly hot and angry. "Relevant? Look at me. It's the most relevant question we have left, don't you think?"

"Stop it," he begged, turning away from me.

I took David's face in my hands and made him look directly at me while I spoke. "Please don't make me pretend. It is what it is. We both know it. The animals have needs and they're not going to stop having them just because I'm gone. I've given this a lot of thought and made arrangements for placing everyone."

"How could you have decided this without me?"

"Because someone needed to and you won't talk to me about it. Please don't be angry. I'm just trying to be realistic and think of your life."

"This is my family you're talking about, too. You can't just break us up."

"Those are just words, David. Nice words, but just words. We both know the truth. I dragged you up here. You've been great about it all, but you're here because of me. These were never your animals. You're even still afraid of the horses and Collette. You barely know the others. How will you care for them and work sixty hours a week?"

"We've done okay so far," David argued back. "I've made accommodations, haven't I?"

"This isn't a criticism of you. It's really not even about you at all. We knew the demands of your career going into this. But this can't be an accommodation; this is the rest of your life we're talking about. You're not going to be able to count on my friends to take care of everyone forever. People will move on. You will move on. You must."

"It is my decision to make now and I want to keep us together."

"Why? I still haven't heard one reason why."

"Do I really need to say it?" David's voice rose.

"It would be nice if I finally understood what you thought," I said, my frustration and fatigue getting the better of me. "You're a lawyer. You know words. Use them with me for once!"

"Because..."

"Because what? You're still not saying anything."

"Because there is nothing else, okay? There's nothing else," David shouted. "There never was!"

I melted at David's desperation. "I know you feel that way now, honey, but—"

"Don't tell me how you understand! You don't! You can't! I'm the one who's left behind. Again." David rose, but I pulled him back down to me and waited for his breathing to slow.

"Okay," I told him, finally. "You're right. I won't be able to tell you what to do, but I need you to know that you don't have to do this. You've nothing left to prove to me. Just do what's best for them *and* for you. There might come a time very soon when this may not be the same thing."

Now David tells Max precisely what he told me during that conversation months ago. "I'll handle it."

And hearing those words again, I can't help but feel that somehow I failed my own creatures. I should've tried harder to make David understand that their purpose in the world is not merely to serve as proof of his ability to multitask.

"I guess you know best," Max says.

"Yes, I do."

"Any thoughts about when we can expect you back? Just so I can tell the committee."

David sighs. "Tell 'em I need until the end of the week to make arrangements."

Max rises to his feet. "That would be great."

"I know the firm is just grinding to a halt without me."

"Don't underestimate your value. You control a lot of business and the clients love you."

"Only because their alternative is to deal with you." David smiles for the first time since Max's arrival.

"No doubt. Your cases for the time being are being covered, but Chris is spread pretty thin and—"

"—yes, it's an important year for her. I know."

"Actually, I was going to say that they need your special touch."

David walks Max to the front door as he talks to the dogs at his side. "This is the part of the conversation where Max gets manipulative."

"You know me too well, partner," Max says with a shrug.

"It's the ones you sneak past me that I worry about." A light snow is falling again. The two continue to Max's car in silence.

"You don't have to answer this," Max finally says, "and heaven knows, you don't have to tell me the truth, but..."

"Spit it out. I'm cold."

"Did Helena ever, you know, forgive me?"

Poor Max. He does not yet know that seeking forgiveness from the dead is like looking for the wind in a field. But David takes the question with surprising seriousness. He turns his face up to the sky for a long moment. When David looks back at Max, melted snowflakes run down his face.

"It took two people to turn the sad and frightened little boy she met at Cornell into the hard-assed corporate litigator he became. He was not an unwilling pupil. In some ways, you saved that boy as much as she did. There was a cost, though. Helena understood that. Helena also was smart enough to realize the benefits of my employment. This," David says as he gestures to the barn, the paddock, and the wooded acreage beyond, "wasn't going to happen if I was out trying to save the world."

"And so...?"

"So, yeah, I think she forgave you. I think she probably was always a little disappointed at where the elevator let me off. But she forgave you." David wipes the snow from his cheeks.

Max eases his tall frame into the tiny car and lowers the window. "I guess that's something then," he says, gives David a small wave, and drives away.

David watches the red taillights progress down the steep driveway through a screen of ever-increasing snow. "Yeah. Something," he mutters, then jogs back to the house.

David is wrong; I was never disappointed in him.

How could I be? Under Max's tutelage, David soon became very good at being a lawyer. David's success brought financial security to our home, and for this I was grateful. We could not have lived the lifestyle "we" (meaning "I") chose on my salary alone or something too much lower than the absurdly high six figures David's hard work and Max's favorable support at the firm commanded. Because of David, I not only was able to avoid the mayonnaise sandwiches and Cup Noodles of my youth, but also obtained the freedom to create a very special home surrounded by my animal companions.

But it was more than just the money. The job gave David another family—one that could never be taken from him because it lived on and in the insulated world of facts, legal reasoning, and case law. This family helped make up for the history of his profound aloneness and, frankly, took some of the weight off my own shoulders.

So, was I disappointed? No. I just wanted a little more for David, not from him. I wanted him to relax more, to enjoy his life more, to revel in our animals, their antics and little idiosyncrasies, more. I wanted David to feel connected and be in the moment when he was with us instead of distracted by what he'd just left or where he needed to go next. I wanted David to realize that he had succeeded in the practice of law, had mastered the craft of being a lawyer, and now needed to learn the much more difficult craft of creating and living a full life.

I guess I really just wanted him to value what I was able to contribute to our relationship.

I wanted.

Perhaps David's feeling that he disappointed me is understandable after all. Letting someone you love know that you want more for them probably does go into the ear at the same pitch as disappointment.

When David returns to the front hallway of our house, the three dogs are waiting. David walks past them, but they don't follow him this time and instead continue to stare expectantly at the door. It is disturbing to see the recognition that finally crosses David's face.

"It's just me," he says to the dogs. "I'm sorry, but it's now always going to be just me."

The two big dogs eventually give up and move elsewhere. Only my Skippy retains his vigil for me by the front door.

2

The most forceful evidence of the lasting significance of Dr. Jane Cassidy's work to my life is how easily I can find her again in death. I can't seem to see the friends who supported me in my illness or relatives who sent me on my way with grieving good-byes, but whenever I'm not with David or my animals, Jane Cassidy ("Jaycee" to me), Cindy, and the Center for Advanced Primate Studies (known as CAPS) swirl into focus before me. Of course I cannot rule out the possibility that I'm actually only observing false images manufactured by a decomposing brain, but I would hope that the universe isn't that cruel.

Jaycee and I share a painful history. In our final year at Cornell, we became research associates for Dr. Renee Vartag, considered by many (including herself) to be one of the more brilliant minds of her generation in the field of primate immunology.

Our work for Vartag involved caring for a long-term test subject—a bonobo or pygmy chimpanzee named Charlie. Charlie had been born in captivity and was four years old when we met him.

Bonobos, like their chimpanzee relatives, are commonly used in immunological research because their immune systems are nearly identical to those of humans. At the time, that was the full extent of my knowledge of chimpanzees, pygmy or otherwise. Unfortunately, I soon learned more.

Charlie lived in a twenty-by-twenty indoor/outdoor enclosure that had been built to Vartag's specifications. Vartag had given us only a few responsibilities for him. We fed him, made sure he always had fresh water, cleaned him, and gave him (as specified in one of Vartag's many terse memos to us) "no less than sixty minutes of human interaction a day."

We also were required to give Charlie his "supplements"—a carefully measured cocktail of natural and synthetic vitamins and nutrients that we added to his food. According to Vartag, Charlie had been receiving his supplements since he was two and they were specifically designed to improve his immune system against disease or infection. We collected urine and fecal samples every day and sent them to the lab for analysis, presumably to measure the results of Vartag's hypothesis.

Although Jaycee and I were only obligated to spend a daily hour with Charlie, that quickly became a meaningless guideline. Charlie was a remarkable creature—curious, playful, intelligent, and very aware. If you've never looked into the face of a chimpanzee up close, you simply cannot imagine how human-like and expressive they can be. But it was Charlie's hands, not his face, that I remember most; they were not only incredibly dexterous, but also soft and warm and vulnerable, like a child's hands. I soon found that I was spending whatever free time I had with Charlie in his enclosure. When he saw me arrive each day, he would point at me and his face would light up.

Whenever I went to visit Charlie, Jaycee was already there. If I was smitten with Charlie, Jaycee was singularly absorbed by him. When I was with the two of them, I sometimes felt like I was the third wheel eavesdropping on a jealously guarded love affair.

Three months into our relationship with Charlie, we received in our mailboxes a new memo from Vartag decreeing that the oral supplements would stop and injections would begin.

Vartag assured us that the shots were merely a potent combination of vitamins B_{12} and C—harmless. She also told us that we were only required to give one shot to Charlie every other day. Finally, she told us that if we were not prepared to follow her harmless protocol, then we didn't get to keep our jobs. It was that simple—"No shots, no Charlie."

I could walk away from the money without any qualms, but abandon Charlie? We convinced ourselves that if we didn't do it, someone who cared less about Charlie would take over and hurt him. As far as we know, rationalization is a uniquely human defense mechanism. I was lathered in it.

Pygmy chimpanzees actually are not much smaller than regular chimpanzees, and they are about as powerful. If Charlie had fought us on the shots, we never would have been able to administer the supplements without anesthetizing him. But Charlie trusted us by now, as Dr. Vartag clearly understood. She counted on that trust.

I remember so clearly the look of hurt and betrayal on Charlie's face when I first jabbed him with a needle. Instead of a source of play and joy, I had suddenly and unexpectedly become an instrument of sting and fright. It was just a quick shot, and probably didn't even hurt that much, but I swear he never looked at me the same way. Although a few treats and toys seemed to placate Charlie and we moved on to happier things, I never again saw that look of unfettered vulnerability in his eyes. The guarded gaze that replaced it grew only more distant as the shots continued.

We tricked, cajoled, and sometimes begged Charlie in order to give him his shots, but toward the end he simply submitted to the puncture by extending his arm and looking away. Seeing this exercise in learned helplessness was the worst of all for me by many orders of magnitude.

In my work with Charlie, I had ignored one important aspect about the field of immunology—the most important aspect, actually. How do you really test the strength of an immune system? You try to make someone sick.

When Charlie's lab tests evidenced the correct number of T-cells, proteins, prions, or whatever marker Vartag was looking for, she injected him with blood contaminated with hepatitis C. We didn't know.

The diarrhea hit Charlie first and hard, then the bouts of vomiting, refusals to eat, lethargy, and the bone-racking fevers. Before my eyes in a matter of days, Charlie went from an animated bundle of activity to the type of being you would expect to see in late-term hospice care.

And still the supplement shots continued. Now, however, Charlie was more apt to turn away from me when he saw me and offer me his thigh or behind for the injection. More and more often, when the shot was over, Charlie would not turn to face me. Even Jaycee was unable to get him to rise. She spent hours just stroking his fur.

Charlie knew something was different, that he felt ill, but he had no sense of causality. The why of it was beyond his comprehension, except that it had something to do with our appearance in his life. One day he chased a ball, and the next day he couldn't.

In the world of Charlie's narrow radar screen, only one thing had changed—us. And he was right.

When we learned about the contaminated blood, Vartag was amused by our outrage. "Did you think you were going to spend your careers curing puppies of parasites and mending butterfly wings, ladies?" she challenged.

I called her unprofessional. Jaycee called her a number of other things.

Our reward for confronting this international legend in immunology was swift and decisive—she summarily fired us.

We pled our case to anyone at the school who would listen—the dean, the president, the provost, the university's Animal Care and Use Committee. At this point, we didn't care about the job or the money. We just wanted to nurse Charlie, or at least to be there for him as he died. Everyone nodded politely as we told our story, took notes, assured us that they would look into it, and promptly did nothing.

The only faculty member who at least recognized that we had been used and that Vartag's conduct was inappropriate was my faculty adviser, Dr. Joshua Marks. He tried to intervene, but Vartag was too powerful. I never saw Charlie again.

I told David this precise version of the events surrounding Charlie's death on that very first night we met in Ithaca after we returned from the hospital. I've repeated this version in my own mind a hundred times since. If only repetition could make it true, then perhaps I wouldn't be locked in this colorless expanse, deafened by echoes of doubt and desire as they bang against the emptiness of my future. Only Jaycee knows the truth, and at this point she has no reason to tell.

After Charlie, Jaycee and I went in very different directions. I wanted nothing more to do with primates—not ever. Jaycee, however, wanted to understand Charlie and what she felt had existed between them. Her work and her passion concentrated on one issue—whether the great apes possess the heretofore uniquely human state of mind we call consciousness.

I don't believe in coincidence. So when, a few days following my initial diagnosis, I happened to open up the Cornell vet school alumni magazine (a magazine I generally make it a point not to read) and saw an article on Jaycee and her work on primate sentience, I knew I needed to call her.

Jaycee's quest had led her through a number of areas of study—zoology, psychology, biological anthropology, and applied linguistics. She had never stopped learning. When I found her, she was working on a four-year grant at CAPS. She immediately invited me to witness her work firsthand at the CAPS campus.

The campus sits on twenty beautiful wooded acres north of Manhattan on the Hudson River. Once I arrived on that first visit, I found it difficult to leave. I visited her a dozen times thereafter, until my body made the trip impossible.

Jaycee's work was compelling. I learned more from her in that final year about the complex relationship between the human and non-human mind than I had in all five years of vet school and subsequent small-animal medicine practice combined. Jaycee had crossed a significant barrier between "us" and "them," and I quickly came to believe that my voracious desire for overdue answers could only be satisfied on the other side of that barrier.

You need to understand that CAPS was designed to be a "show-piece" facility for "non-invasive primate study." In fact, CAPS doesn't even have a surgery suite. Instead, most of the primates (rhesus monkeys, macaques, baboons, bonobos, and chimpanzees) are generally permitted to live in social colonies, largely unaware that they are the subjects of study in the fields of psychology, sociology, and anthropology.

CAPS is the kind of place that its parent body, the National Institutes of Science, can invite congressmen to tour as an example of its progressive dedication to "humane research techniques" whenever one of the other twenty "invasive" NIS primate study facilities gets into hot water for doing things like infecting chimpanzees with hepatitis or failing to provide post-surgical pain management. In short, although the facility could never duplicate how the primates would have lived in nature, if you are a captive primate in the employ of the federal government, CAPS is the place where you want to do your time.

Because CAPS is a well-financed facility with little controversy associated with it, it also is able to attract some preeminent primate researchers, like Jaycee. These researchers obtain the ability to do very advanced work on the government's nickel. NIS in turn obtains the right to tout these big names with their important-sounding studies when they go to Congress for their annual budget appropriation. Generally, it all works as long as everyone does what they're paid to do and they keep their mouths shut.

It is impossible for me to think of Jaycee now without also seeing Cindy, a seventy-five-pound chimpanzee who has lived at CAPS since her birth in captivity four years ago. CAPS is the only home that Cindy knows, and Jaycee is the only mother Cindy has ever had.

Jaycee's research lab, a large room filled with digital video cameras, flat-screen monitors, and computers, occupies the first floor of one of the buildings on the CAPS grounds. The middle of the lab is dominated by a twelve-foot-by-twelve-foot steel-and-Plexiglas enclosure—half cage, half fishbowl—that Jaycee calls the Cube.

I'm able to see the lab quite clearly now. Although the Cube door is wide open, Cindy sits patiently in the structure and shows no interest in jumping out. A large keyboard is anchored to the interior of the Cube for Cindy's use. A mirror runs one entire wall of the enclosure, and Cindy has one eye on her reflection as she moves about.

The keyboard in the Cube is unlike anything you have in your home. The keys are quite large, but not alphanumeric. Instead, each key is marked with a symbol or a series of symbols.

Cindy wears black gloves on her hands; these are wired to a small electronic box belted to her large bicep. The big LED screen that hangs on the front of the Cube and the digital camera that has been directed at its opening complete the gadget-rich environment.

Jaycee sits just outside the door to the Cube at a computer console. Although her keyboard is normal size, the symbols on the board match those on the board in the Cube.

Jaycee designed Cindy's project to determine the depth of human communication skills that a captive-born chimpanzee could develop if the primate was completely acculturated in human language from birth. While you can disagree with the merit of doing so, you can't dispute the fact that human language has always been a scientific benchmark for sentience; the presumption—correct or not—has always been that those who can effectively communicate with us necessarily are self-aware and think like us. With that premise as her foundation, Jaycee finally chose the science of interspecies communication as the instrument to prove her theory that not only did certain primates possess this Holy Grail of mental states called consciousness, but primate consciousness is pretty damn near to our own.

I watch now as Cindy pushes several buttons on her large

keyboard and immediately follows this by making specific gestures with her gloved hands. These gestures look as if they correspond to the hand movements that form the basis for American Sign Language. The words JANE. I AM HUNGRY NOW! instantly appear on Jaycee's computer screen and the large LED screen affixed to the enclosure.

Jaycee reads the message on her screen and laughs. As Jaycee signs back to Cindy, she says in a firm but gentle tone, "It is not mealtime, Cindy. Please continue." Cindy carefully watches every nuance in Jaycee's signing.

When she is certain that Jaycee is finished, Cindy makes several additional gestures with her hands and punches a few more keys on her board. Jaycee's screen now says I WANT TO PLAY WITH MY DOLL NOW! Cindy looks toward Jaycee and sees Jaycee frown. After a small hesitation, Cindy pushes two more buttons. As a result, the exclamation mark is replaced with a question mark.

Jaycee signs her answer to Cindy, this time making no effort to hide her frustration. "No Cindy. Time for work. Play later." Cindy watches Jaycee until the last sign and then turns away from her board and drops her head to her chest in an unmistakable sulk.

Jaycee looks over to the enclosure and tries very hard to suppress a smile as she signs, "You're being very stubborn today."

Cindy makes a fist and twists it back and forth. The words POTTY, POTTY, POTTY appear on the screen.

"You just went to the potty," Jaycee says and signs.

Jaycee's senior research associate, Frank Wallace, a man in his late twenties, observes the interplay over Jaycee's shoulder. "Maybe we're putting too much pressure on her," he whispers.

"Then give me another damn option, Frank," Jaycee snaps. "The grant is nearly over, I've got Jannick questioning my methodology, and the one presentation that could get us an extension is just days away."

Frank takes a step backward. "All I'm saying is—"

"—I know." Jaycee sighs. "I'm sorry. You're on my side."

Cindy steals a glance toward Frank and Jaycee to see if they're noticing her unhappiness. Jaycee briefly makes eye contact with Cindy, and the chimpanzee quickly turns away again.

"Whatever the reason," Jaycee says, "today's pretty well shot."

Other chimpanzees before Cindy have demonstrated an ability to communicate with humans on their own linguistic turf through gestures based on American Sign Language or symbols that represent words, called lexigrams. Washoe, Loulis, and Kanzi were the best-known examples, but there were scores of others with varying degrees of language competence. Up to this point, however, the discoveries about what these creatures could learn didn't change the world—either for primates generally or for their human cousins. Too many remained unconvinced; the threat to the long history of invasive primate experimentation was too great. Highly educated and well-respected scientists challenged the research, and even the merit of conducting the research at all, belittling decades of language work with primates as either well-intentioned mistakes or, worse, no more than complicated "circus tricks," the product of hidden cues, wishful interpretation, or data manipulation.

And still, the invasive primate experiments continued.

According to Jaycee, some chimpanzees who had been taught to sign a limited human vocabulary were even returned to the general captive primate population when their experiments were shut down for lack of funding or interest. The chimpanzees were then confined to small cages in cold labs where they were experimented on, operated on, and infected with diseases. These animals continued signing to the end of their lives—words like *key, out, hurt, no, stop, end*—but their new handlers and fellow captives were not trained to understand them and so the pleas literally went unheard.

Jaycee was working to find a new way to eliminate any legitimate doubt by combining the hard work that had come before with technology so new and advanced, it was evolving daily in her lab. In the process, something else entirely had passed through all the wiring, keystrokes, and megabytes of data between tester and subject, and as a result Jaycee swore that she would never let Cindy suffer the same fate as some of those earlier unfortunate non-human souls. After I'd spent time with Cindy, I took that same oath. Thankfully, Cindy remained secure in Jaycee's hands, and I never needed to make good on my promise.

Jaycee walks to the door of the Cube and turns off the camera. Cindy spins around at the sound and leaps into Jaycee's arms just like a child greeting a parent after a long absence. Cindy begins stroking Jaycee's hair.

"Okay, okay." Jaycee laughs despite her worries. "Stop buttering me up. You win. Playtime." Jaycee hands Cindy a small cloth doll with the shape and the face of a little human girl. Cindy hugs the doll to her chest.

I know that doll. I brought it to my first meeting with Cindy. Jaycee had suggested that I bring something for Cindy as an offering of friendship. I laughed at first at what I thought was Jaycee's joke. Once it was clear that Jaycee was serious, I searched frantically around the house for something that might be appropriate. The only thing I could think of was a cloth doll David had given me on some long-past Valentine's Day. He told me it looked like me—and it did.

Cindy loved the doll, and that act of giving for some reason allowed me quick entry into her tiny inner circle of trusted humans. Jaycee tried to convince me that it was all about me and not the gift, but I never really believed her. That, however, was the only thing I ever doubted about Jaycee or her work.

Others, I now know, do not share my conviction. This knowledge comes too late for me. I can do nothing to uphold my oath.

3

By the time of my death, Joshua Marks had evolved from my faculty adviser, to residency adviser, to mentor, to dear friend and veterinary practice partner. Although Joshua is only twelve years my senior, his sorrow always made him appear much older.

There is a saying that I heard somewhere: "God can warm in his hands for a thousand years those who have buried a child and still they will not feel the glow of his countenance." Whoever wrote that must have had Joshua in mind.

Within two years of the death of his five-year-old boy, Joshua and his wife were divorced amid rumors of infidelity and prescription drug abuse, Joshua had left (or was kicked out of) Cornell, and he had moved to this tiny hamlet. The practice he took over was the very first place he had worked as a teenager, cleaning out cages and feeding the animals. That's where I had joined him.

Joshua had returned to his beginning I assume in the hope of finding some higher meaning for what had happened to his family. I'm certain that Joshua believes he has yet to find it. Instead, he remains prepared to accept the events in his life as merely the congregation of separate circumstances with no more meaning than an entry in *TV Guide*. That is where his vision fails him. With a move a few inches to the right or the left, he could be scratching his head in wonder and, perhaps, even hope. Maybe he still will be able to do that for himself before, like me, his time runs out.

The animal hospital where we worked together is a cozy old converted farmhouse. Joshua always kept the office clean, but no matter how often he turned over the cages, the back room (and therefore the entire hospital) always had a faint odor of anesthesia, alcohol, dog feces, and cat urine. It is that familiar smell that draws me here.

The hospital is unusually crowded for a Wednesday. Four dogs on short leashes, two cats in porta-crates, and their owners wait impatiently in the reception area. The yowls and meows of animals who are anxious or in pain contrast sharply with the happy, carefree dogs and cats in the advertisements for veterinary products that adorn the walls. I don't recognize any of the animals in the room, which is just as well.

A name plate on one of the walls by the reception desk identifies DR. JOSHUA MARKS and DR. HELENA COLDEN as the two vets of the practice. Joshua hasn't yet taken my name down. Like my husband, he's not good with that kind of change.

Joshua's examination room is decorated with photos of patients and holiday cards. Two small framed photos—one of a Newfoundland and the other of a Siberian husky—occupy the spot on his desk usually reserved for family pictures, disproving the myth that all dog owners eventually begin to look like their dogs.

When I find him, Joshua is palpating the abdomen of a large mutt with the help of Eve, one of our vet techs. The dog clearly is uncomfortable and will not remain still for Joshua's probing fingers.

But Joshua never loses his patience and tries to comfort the dog as best he can with soothing noises he has never uttered to another human being.

"How much food did they say was in the bag that Misha got into?" Joshua asks.

Eve looks at the file before answering. "It was almost full. So twenty pounds or so, I guess."

"I think it's moving," Joshua notes as he continues his exam. "No bloat, but let's do an X-ray and keep him overnight to be sure."

The exam room door bangs open. Beth, our other full-time vet tech, carries in her arms a small whimpering mess of blood and dog fur. I know too well that wounds of this magnitude can only be caused by a car striking animal flesh and bone. The dog will soon go into shock, if it isn't there already.

"Sorry Dr. J," Beth says in her usual unflappable calm despite the blood dripping onto her scrubs. "This one just came in. Police found him by Wingate Road. Compound leg fracture. No tags."

The receptionist buzzes Joshua on the office intercom. "Dr. J, your two thirty and your three o'clock are both waiting. And your three fifteen just walked in. What should I tell them?"

Joshua rubs his head in frustration and then barks at Beth. "I'm already half an hour behind on my appointments. See if Helena can take the emergency. Tell her…" I almost blurt out that Beth should bring the dog to my office with a suture kit and a saline bag, but then I remember.

Beth and Eve gape at Joshua. From the looks on their faces, he realizes his error. "I'm so sorry," he says. In exhaustion, embarrassment, or both, Joshua covers his face with his hand. "Eve, can you please take Misha for his X-ray? Beth, just give me a second and then I'll see the fracture."

Beth backs out of the office with the dog in her arms and Eve follows with Misha. Once they're gone and Joshua believes he is alone, he grabs a handful of pencils from a jar on the desk and, one at a time, slowly begins to snap them in half.

The only other animal hospital that services our area is about as far removed from our type of practice as you can get. Dr. Thorton's Animal Medical Center occupies a large, modern glass-and-metal structure off Route 100, right smack in the most affluent area of the community. Thorton runs a twenty-four-hour operation with four full-time vets and a large support staff of technicians and helpers. He even has his own lab and lab techs on premises. This means Thorton has a great deal of overhead and he freely passes these costs on to consumers—whether they can afford it or not.

Over the years that we worked together, I saw Joshua spend hour after hour on a particularly difficult case, researching each option, calling experts from the Animal Medical Hospital in Manhattan and humbly asking them for advice, all for the price of the same office visit—if even that. He would send blood or urine out to the lab for testing only when necessary and only at cost. At the end of all this work, Joshua would present his conclusions and recommendations to the nervous clients with the type of compassion and understanding that only comes from having been on the receiving end of unfortunate news.

This approach is not part of the Thorton economic model. For the same type of case, Thorton instead runs a battery of expensive diagnostic tests irrespective of the animal's symptoms. Since he owns his own lab, the markup on even the most mundane blood test is huge and goes directly into his pocket.

At the end, after all the tests have been exhausted, Thorton reaches a conclusion predicated largely on the process of elimination (what he would call in his most pompous tone, and with a sheath of test results in his hand, "the differential diagnosis"). He then communicates his conclusion to the waiting family while checking his watch frequently.

Thorton is not a bad vet—I imagine that he often reaches the right medical conclusion—just not a particularly nice person. He turns away clients who blanch at his estimates (50 percent due at the time of service) or question the necessity of a costly liver scan for a dog with normal liver enzymes. I know this about Thorton because these clients invariably ended up at my door and then stayed long after.

I think the thing that bothered me most about Thorton was that he always left the families to their grief before the tears came. Joshua never did that and, more often than not, added his own. I'd like to think that my own clients believe Joshua trained me well at least in this respect.

Sally Hanson is one of Thorton's techs. I dealt with Sally only infrequently over the years, but I saw her around town. Once you meet Sally, it's hard to forget her. She is one of the few African Americans in our "community," and at the age of thirty-six, with high cheekbones, dark copper skin, and a tall, slim build, she looks like she got off at the wrong train station for some Ann Taylor photo shoot and just never left.

I don't know how or why Sally decided to work for Thorton, I just know that she did. I try not to judge, lest I be required to justify my own conduct to whoever controls access to points beyond. Circumstances and context can often explain a great deal.

I can't think of any reason why I should be able to see Sally now, but here she is before me, running into the operating room to give Thorton a surgical clamp.

"Finally!" Thorton, short, fat, and bald with sausage-like fingers and glasses much too large for his head, shouts at her. Between them on the OR table is a large golden retriever with a silver muzzle who has been opened up for some type of thoracic surgery. I'm guessing the surgery isn't going well.

"Damn it, Hanson, what do I need to do to get you to give me some suction here," Thorton yells. Sally immediately complies, but the cavity quickly fills again with blood.

Out in the crowded waiting area, Sally's son, Clifford, sits quietly drawing on the sketch pad in his lap. Clifford looks like he is nine or ten. He's even more beautiful than his mother, with his giant brown eyes, long eyelashes, and rounded features.

Although I can't see what he is drawing, Clifford's pencil strokes are not the hesitant stray marks of a doodler. With his tongue extended from the side of his mouth in concentration and his brow furrowed, he draws as if his subject is evanescent and he must get the image out of his head and on the paper as quickly as possible.

It takes me a moment, but I finally understand what is missing from this waiting room. There are no barks, whines, yeows, or screams coming from the dogs and cats waiting for treatment. Where there otherwise should be the noise of panic, fear, and hurt, there is only stillness and the scratch of a pencil point against heavy sketch paper. When I look more closely, I see that every animal eye in the room is focused on the boy and his pad of paper.

Besides the boy, the only other person in the waiting room without an animal is an older woman with starched white hair and a nervous habit of chewing on her thumbnail as she paces in front of the reception desk. That must be her dog in the OR.

As I watch, a drastic change comes over the boy. He stiffens in his chair, drops his pencil, and then grimaces in pain. The dogs nearest him begin to howl.

The boy slowly rises to his feet, places his pad on the seat, and moves toward the operating room. Dr. Thorton nearly knocks the boy over in his rush to get to the surgical supply cabinet located on the far side of the reception area. The boy doesn't appear to register Thorton's presence and instead enters the OR suite.

Sally, struggling to stop the blood coming out of the unconscious dog's chest, doesn't notice her son until he is almost upon her.

"Clifford, you can't be here," Sally tells him sharply. "Go back to the waiting room."

Clifford ignores her. No, that's wrong. He doesn't even seem to be aware of his mother. He approaches the dog on the table with an affect that is so flat, it cannot be faked.

"Clifford! Not here!" Sally quickly looks to the entranceway of the OR to make sure they're not being observed. "Please," Sally begs him. "You need to get out!"

Clifford lowers his head onto the head of the dog and closes his eyes. Then, in a sweet, light, clear, and beautiful voice, Clifford sings out, "Grass grass grass. Grass for all to see. I love the green green green grass grass grass." Clifford's smile is so wide and his face is filled with such open joy that Sally is speechless. "I knew it," Clifford says to no one in particular. "Grass and trees and...can you smell the air? It's been so long since I've smelled air like that."

Thorton bangs back into the OR. "What the hell is going on in here?"

Thorton's outburst shocks Sally into action. "I'm getting him out, Dr. Thorton."

"He can't be in here," Thorton says.

"Grass grass grass," Clifford sings again with his eyes squeezed closed. "I knew there'd be grass."

"I understand, Doctor," Sally says in near panic. "I'm sorry. But I just can't pull him away or he'll—"

"Well, either you do it, or I will," Thorton threatens as he takes a step toward the boy.

"No! Please, don't." Sally steps between Thorton and Clifford. "You don't understand. He—"

"What's that boy doing to my dog!" It's the white-haired woman from the waiting room. She must've heard the yelling. "Dr. Thorton, what in God's name is going on?"

"It's quite okay, Ms. Pendle," Thorton says in his most assuring tone.

"Mother of God. All that blood. Is that from Archie?" Ms. Pendle asks, her face sheet white.

Before anyone can answer her, Clifford breaks out into a joyous yell: "BennieBennieBennieBennieBennieBennieBennieBennieBennie." Tears stream out of Clifford's closed eyes. "I knew you'd make it for me, Bennie. I knew it'd be you. No cane, too!"

Ms. Pendle stumbles backward and steadies herself on a nearby countertop. "No cane?" she repeats.

A small crowd of staff forms by the entrance of the OR. "Jennifer," Thorton commands to a vet tech in surgical scrubs, "please show Ms. Pendle to my office." Jennifer gently eases the confused woman out of the room.

Once Thorton checks to be sure that the client is gone and the door to the OR is closed, he turns on Clifford. "That's enough," Thorton shouts at the boy and grabs him by the arm, trying to pull him away from the dog.

Clifford screams as if Thorton's hand is made of acid.

"NoNoNoNoooooooo!" Clifford tries to pull his arm away in agony. "Bennie. They're taking me."

Sally jumps to her son's aid. "Get your hands off him," she shouts as she rips Thorton's hand away. "Can't you see he's not even here?"

At the sound of his mother's voice, Clifford's eyes flash open and he bolts upright. He looks around the room and finally appears to recognize his surroundings. The anguish on Clifford's face—on any face that young—is horrible to see. Fresh tears pour down his cheeks, this time as far removed from joy as possible.

"I'm sorry MamaI'm sorry MamaI'm sorry MamaI'm sorry Mama." Clifford repeats these three words over and over without inflection and as he does so, he begins to draw in the air with the pencil he no longer holds in his hand.

"It's okay, Cliffy. It's okay." Sally puts her arms around the boy's shoulders and slowly moves him toward the entrance of the OR.

Thorton listens to the dog's chest with a stethoscope. "The dog's gone," he confirms in disgust and then throws his stethoscope across the table.

Sally ignores him. To Clifford she says, "Let's get your pad and pencil." Sally looks like she's aged years in seconds.

Clifford allows himself to be walked out of the OR, but will not make eye contact with his mother. "I'm sorry MamaI'm sorry Mama."

"I know," Sally says.

Thorton shouts at Sally's back, "My office in ten minutes."

Fifteen minutes later, Sally sits in one of Thorton's exam rooms with Clifford on her lap. The boy is almost composed, except for the occasional snuffle. Sally tries to rock him, but his hands are in constant motion, drawing with the pencil and pad Sally retrieved from the waiting room.

A knock on the exam room door is so tentative I almost don't hear it. Ms. Pendle, her eyes rimmed with tears, walks in on Sally and Clifford. The boy takes no notice of her.

"I'm very sorry for your loss, Ms. Pendle," Sally says. "I deeply regret the confusion in there."

Ms. Pendle nods. "How is your son?" she asks in a voice choking back grief and uncertainty.

"He'll be fine."

"May I ask..." Ms. Pendle searches for words that will not offend.

"He has Asperger's syndrome. The wiring in his brain is a little different from the rest of us. When he gets upset..." Sally lets her sentence hang and nods toward the operating room.

"I see. I'm so sorry."

Sally searches Ms. Pendle's face for some evidence of condescension and sees only what I see—an old woman now alone in the world trying to find some solace in the part of being that she doesn't understand.

"Thank you. Clifford generally manages pretty well—except when he's upset."

Ms. Pendle hesitates before she next speaks. "Your son mentioned a 'Bennie' in there. Is that someone he knows?"

Sally shrugs. "It's not a name I've heard before. No one we know."

"Do you know why he might've chosen that name?"

"When he has an episode, his brain is firing on all cylinders. He could've picked the name up anywhere—TV, a book, someone at school. The doctors say the words probably don't mean anything. Like his drawings—hypergraphia, they call it," Sally says, pointing to the paper Clifford is transforming with his pencil. "Just regurgitations from somewhere in his brain. He probably won't remember any of this by the time he calms down. He never does."

Ms. Pendle clears her throat and then turns away from Sally to straighten some jars on the countertop that do not need her attention. "My husband loved Archie. Sometimes I think that dog was the only reason he wanted to live after his stroke. He hated that cane."

"I'm sorry?" Sally asks.

Ms. Pendle turns to face Sally, and again her words fail her. "You see . . . it's just that . . . well, my husband's name was Benjamin. I was the only one who called him Bennie."

"Oh." I can literally see Sally's growing discomfort with the road this conversation has taken. Her journey has been too hard and too long. Sally's lips press into a razor-thin line as her eyes narrow in suspicion. Behind those eyes, just for an instant, I see a woman who believes in nothing except the need to care for her son and the hope that, with the right education and training, he will learn to be independent from her in some way that matters in the world. I see a woman who believes in no one except herself because everyone else has failed her or Clifford. I see a woman who has long since put away the glass slippers, the pretend ball gowns, and any dream that some glitter-winged fairy godmother is going to "bibbity-boppity-boop" away her responsibilities.

But Ms. Pendle's face is so hopeful and vulnerable right now that I fear Sally's response. To my great surprise and relief, however, I see Sally's defenses momentarily soften. "My husband once told me that animals were put on this earth to help redeem us," she says. "That must be hard work, but they never give up on us. It would make sense to me that, when it's all over, they finally get to just enjoy the fruits of that labor. Don't you think?"

Ms. Pendle squeezes her eyes shut and nods gratefully. When she opens them again, she mouths a silent *thank you* to Sally and backs out of the room, leaving Sally alone with her son and his now completed drawing.

Clifford's picture is so finely detailed that it looks like a black-and-white photograph.

In the drawing, Archie and an old man without a cane walk side by side through an ancient grove of trees.

In the CAPS lab, Jaycee runs Cindy through her finger-spelling exercises. I've seen them do this before. Jaycee first speaks and signs a word, then waits for Cindy to copy her gestures with her gloved fingers. Jaycee confirms that Cindy has matched the sign correctly by checking that the word appears on her computer screen.

In the five minutes I've watched them so far today, Cindy got almost all the words correct. When the computer reflected an error, however, Jaycee gently molded Cindy's fingers until the correct word appeared. Every correct response elicited Jaycee's excited praise and a squeal from Cindy.

They are just finishing the word *apple* when a man with thinning gray hair that matches the color of his suit thunders into the lab.

"You had no right!" he shouts at Jaycee.

"Nice to see you too, Scott," Jaycee says as she quickly returns Cindy to the Cube. Cindy curls her lips back against her teeth, a sign that she does not like either this man or his tone.

"You could've at least given me the common courtesy of telling me that Congressman Wolfe was coming," he says, his voice only slightly less booming.

"Why? So you could convince him not to come?"

"No, because I am the director of this facility and I make those decisions."

"His committee is the only shot I've got for an extension of funding, and you won't help me. I did what I had to. Sorry if it doesn't fit within your little political protocol."

"I'm attempting to save NIS and yourself from what will be a terrible embarrassment. You've no idea the situation—"

"—just because you don't trust my work, doesn't mean it's not valid."

"Actually, as far as the funding for this project goes, that's exactly what it means."

"Professional jealousy is not an attractive quality on you."

"Jealousy? That's what you think this is about?"

"I don't see a lot of other reasons."

"How about the fact that you can't replicate your results? Those gloves and this computer program only seem to work for you. She won't converse with anyone else. Why is that?"

"That's not true. I'm not the only one she's responded to."

"Who else, then? I know she won't do it with Frank. Show me just one other person. Bring him here and show me."

Jaycee doesn't take the offer.

"That's what I thought," he barks. "No one but you. That's prima facie evidence that she's not responding to language at all; she's responding to your cues—whether they are intentional or not. Congratulations—you've turned her into Pavlov's dog! That's why no respected peer-review journal will accept your work. And if you weren't so close to this and"—he points to Cindy—"to her, you'd see that I'm right."

Cindy becomes more agitated as the argument continues. She paces the length of the Cube, whimpering every few moments.

"I don't think Wolfe will see it that way," Jaycee says. "And we both know that's really what you're afraid of, isn't it, Jannick?"

Jannick throws his hands up and heads toward the door. He turns to Jaycee one final time. "You've really lost yourself in this, Dr. Cassidy. It's sad that we've gotten here, but it convinces me that my initial decision was absolutely correct. If you can't replicate your test results with someone else asking the questions, then this project will end regardless of the dog-and-pony show you put on for Wolfe."

Once Jannick is gone, Jaycee opens the door to the Cube and Cindy jumps into her arms. She calms Cindy with the soothing sounds and gentle strokes that I imagine a mother would use to assure a frightened child.

I know why Jaycee is unwilling to present the other person that Cindy spoke with. She can't.

That person is me.

4

The passage of another few days has David looking slightly more human. He has shaved and dressed in a pair of khakis, a button-down blue oxford shirt, and Sperry loafers.

He paces nervously around a living room that likewise appears to have received a few minutes of attention since Max's visit; there is still a mess, but now it has the broad outlines of a shape and the food remnants, at least, are gone.

As David paces, he reviews the notes and questions he's written to himself on a yellow legal pad. Chip, Bernie, and Skippy follow David's movements from their places on the floor—four steps to the right, stop, turn, and then four steps back.

David pauses for a moment and peers down at the dogs. "I need you all to be on your best behavior." The dogs return David's look as if they not only understand him, but are prepared to comply. But David doesn't know them like I do.

Soon enough, the doorbell rings and the dogs obediently follow David to the front door. Behind it, waiting on the porch, is a small, pencil-thin woman in her early forties. Her steel-gray skirt and starched white blouse are ironed to perfection. Her hair is combed into a tight bun the likes of which I've only seen in magazine advertisements from the 1950s for kitchen products.

David opens the door. "Please come in," he says. The woman extends her bony hand, and David shakes it gingerly.

"I'm Margaret Donnelly, but you may call me Peg."

"Peg it is." David waves her into the house.

"What a charming piece of property you—"

As soon as Peg crosses the threshold of the house into the hallway, Bernie can no longer control his excitement. He lets out a joyful "woof" and jumps on her. The unexpected force of Bernie's two forepaws on her slender shoulders knocks poor Ms. Donnelly square on her ass. Although unharmed, Ms. Donnelly, apparently not a dog lover in the best of circumstances, begins to scream for help. Chip and Skippy now bark wildly at her, joining the game. The more the dogs bark, the more Ms. Donnelly screams.

"Peg—Ms. Donnelly—just please calm down!" David yells at her as he tries to pull Bernie away.

"They're attacking me!"

"They're not attacking. They think you're playing."

Amid the shrieking, Chip and Skippy can resist no longer and join the fray. Ms. Donnelly and the three dogs form a heap in the middle of the hallway. David tries to separate canine and human, but it's like trying to remove a fly from a bowl of oatmeal—there's no way to do it without taking some of the oatmeal, too. In the process of reaching and pulling, David accidentally grabs Ms. Donnelly's breast. At this perceived violation of her person, Ms. Donnelly lets out a primordial shriek only a Saturday-morning cartoon character could replicate.

I start to laugh. It is such an odd feeling that at first I don't recognize what's happening to me. But then I hear myself. I put my hand over my mouth to keep the sound inside. That doesn't work. I feel the need to turn away even though I'm somehow sure that no one can hear me. I run out the front door almost doubled over in laughter.

Suddenly Ms. Donnelly catapults out of the house. Her hair has been ripped from its neat bun, her blouse is covered with paw prints, and her skirt is so askew it is turned nearly all the way around. She runs down the front steps while pulling dog hair from her mouth.

In her panic, Ms. Donnelly nearly trips over Henry, my huge orange tabby cat, who is cleaning himself on the front steps. Henry pauses only for a moment with annoyed interest to watch Ms. Donnelly race sobbing to her Ford before he returns to his more important business. Ms. Donnelly, once safely entombed in her car, screeches down the driveway.

Inside the house, David, his arms folded sternly across his chest, stares at the three dogs. Chip and Bernie are now quiet and contrite under his gaze. I could swear, however, that Skippy is smirking. "That was your best behavior?"

David grabs the legal pad off the table in the hallway and scratches out Ms. Donnelly's name so hard his pen gouges the paper.

My definition of a bad day is one spent trying to pound square pegs into round holes. Measuring David's subsequent five interviews against that yardstick, David has had a very bad day.

When Congressman Wolfe arrives at the lab for Jaycee's presentation, he is accompanied by a staff aide, a photographer and—to Jaycee's obvious alarm—Scott Jannick.

After brief introductions by Jannick, Wolfe says, "You've got thirty minutes, Dr. Cassidy. Then I need to head back to the city. So, show me what Cindy can do."

Jaycee clears her throat and then begins her well-rehearsed remarks. "As I explained in my letter to you, we have known for decades that chimpanzees are capable of acquiring and using human language. The problem is that physiologically, they are not capable of producing human speech sounds. So we've always had to use a substitute for human speech—principally American Sign Language and lexigraphy. But both those forms of language have their problems. Lexigraphy is far too limiting and rigid. ASL is preferred because it is more flexible and allows for spontaneous conversation except it requires advanced manual dexterity. Unfortunately, the chimpanzee hand was not made for the nuances of ASL. Chimpanzee ASL work before ours was criticized on the grounds that the chimpanzee gestures or attempted gestures allowed too much room for interpretation or manipulation by the tester.

"So, that's the bad news. The good news is that there have been some extraordinary advances in technology and computer modeling in the last few years. We believe we can now overcome those limitations and literally unlock the language potential of the chimpanzee."

Wolfe shifts impatiently in his seat as Jaycee continues. "My research assistant, Frank Wallace, was working on his PhD in a relatively new field called computer-assisted linguistics when I co-opted him for my research. Basically, the theory is to develop computer models for those with speech impairments in an effort to augment the speaker's own capabilities. For example, a stroke victim wants to say 'give me the apple,' but may only have the physical capability to say 'gif ma aal.' By mapping the individual's specific impairment against a normal speech function, we can then plug that into the computer model so that it compensates for the gaps between what the speaker wants to say and what he or she is physiologically capable of saying. This is called interstitial linguistic programming or ILP. And yes, that is a mouthful."

Jaycee hands the congressman a thick PowerPoint presentation book. "This describes in detail the theory and programming behind ILP and how we applied it here."

Wolfe passes the book to his aide without looking at it. "My staff will read the documentation later. I suggest you just tell me what you think I need to know so we can get on with the demonstration, Dr. Cassidy."

"Of course. We began with the idea that we could use ILP for other parts of anatomy besides the vocal apparatus. We modified the ILP for Cindy by treating the differences between her hand and a human hand as an impairment. We created a computer model of a human hand and then superimposed a computer model of Cindy's hand over it. There were obvious differences. We programmed the ILP to compensate for the differences. Then we had a pair of gloves tailored for Cindy's hands and wired the gloves with the ILP program.

"You'll see that she uses the gloves in conjunction with a specially designed lexigraphic keyboard that we taught her to use. The board supplements the signing and can give us the type of information that normally would be provided by the ASL speaker through what we call non-manual markers—like facial expressions, head movement, gaze direction, or mouthing. Once we run the gloves and her keyboard answers back through an ASL translation program, Cindy's signs are almost instantly converted into English words that appear on a computer screen."

"And for my little non-scientific mind, what does that all mean?" Wolfe asks.

"We converse. In English," Jaycee says and then lets her answer sink in for a moment. "And you can read Cindy's words in real time as she uses them without me trying to tell you what Cindy is saying."

"Seeing that would be well worth the trip," Wolfe says. "Why don't you show me that now."

Jaycee calls Frank on the office intercom. "We're going to proceed with the demonstration now. Can you bring Cindy in?"

In less than a minute, Frank enters the lab carrying Cindy. She is already wearing her gloves. Frank places Cindy in the Cube, next to her keyboard, and then joins Jaycee and the others near Jaycee's desk.

The photographer snaps a few pictures of Cindy. The flash momentarily startles her, and she shakes her head to get rid of the afterimage.

Jaycee waits until Cindy is resettled and then says, "I'm now going to engage Cindy in a conversation. Her answers will appear in English on this computer screen here." Jaycee points to the screen next to them.

"Do you mind telling us what your first question will be?" Jannick asks.

"I was going to begin by asking Cindy to tell us her name and to say hello to the congressman, but there is no prearranged format. I can ask her any question that would be appropriate for a four-year-old."

"Four?" Wolfe asks. He makes no effort to hide his skepticism. "You mean to tell me that this chimpanzee has the language skills of a four-year-old?"

"Correct," Jaycee says proudly. "Cindy has the cognitive age equivalent of a four-year-old human girl. Perhaps the congressman would like to give us a question for Cindy."

"Indeed, I would," Wolfe answers. "Let's ask her to name her favorite food. That seems about right for a four-year-old."

Jaycee smiles. She's asked Cindy that question hundreds of times and the answer is always the same—peanut butter. "Of course. First, I will sign the question for Cindy and then you will be able to see her response."

"Actually," Jannick interrupts, "if you don't mind, Jaycee, I'd like to be the one to sign the question to Cindy."

Jaycee and I both see the trap Jannick has set at precisely the same time—and way too late. This was why he didn't try to stop Wolfe; Jannick wanted Wolfe at the demonstration so he could make his point about Cindy to the one person who could kill any further discussion of the project.

"That's not the demonstration protocol, Scott." Jaycee struggles to keep her voice calm.

Jannick will not be put off. "But surely the person who asks the question shouldn't matter if the language has been learned. The words are, after all, the same words regardless of who says them. I still sign pretty well, so it shouldn't be an issue."

Jaycee glares at Jannick. "This is my study. Cindy is familiar with me. You can't just step in and expect to be able to divorce the act of communication from the underlying relationship." She turns to Wolfe and says, "Dr. Jannick has never worked with Cindy. It would be most appropriate for me to be the one to lead the interaction."

Wolfe's aide whispers into his ear and Wolfe nods. "Perhaps Scott is correct," Wolfe decides.

Jannick doesn't wait for further discussion. He takes three steps toward Cindy in the Cube. Cindy watches him closely. "Cindy," Jannick says at the same time he signs, "what is your favorite food?"

Cindy just stares at him.

"Let me try again," Jannick tells Wolfe. "What is your favorite food?" Jannick asks as he signs, this time more slowly.

Still no response from Cindy.

"Hmm. Did I get the signing right, Frank?" Jannick asks. "Did I ask her what I intended?"

Frank, who looks like he would prefer to be anywhere but here, simply nods.

"How about another question, then," Jannick says. "A simple yes or no. Cindy, do you like peanut butter?" Jannick asks and signs.

Cindy is painfully silent.

"Perhaps she just doesn't like you," Wolfe tells Jannick half jokingly.

"I guess it wouldn't be the first time I was rejected," Jannick says. "But we do know she likes Frank, right? He's worked with Cindy since the beginning. What do you say, Frank? Give it a try?"

Frank looks to Jaycee for guidance. They both know that Frank will be no more successful than Jannick. "This is very disruptive and unfair, Dr. Jannick," Jaycee says. "Cindy has no reason to use your language with you."

"How about because I asked nicely?" Jannick asks. "What's the magic word? Please? Okay, Cindy." Jannick turns back to Cindy and says and signs, "Please."

Jaycee's face turns bright red. "When you are done hijacking my demonstration, Scott, I would like to show Congressman Wolfe—"

"—that your work cannot be replicated?" Jannick scoffs. "That you've spent the last four years of the government's money creating a technology that no one else can use and, therefore, is proof of nothing? I warned you about this, Jaycee!"

Jaycee spins on Jannick, forgetting Wolfe and the demonstration. "She speaks to me! Why isn't that enough?"

Jannick pulls out a folder and waves it in front of Jaycee's face. "Because the grant agreement you signed says it's not enough. Because the testing protocol *you* designed to ensure the validity of the experiment requires more. You can't change the rules at the end of the game."

Wolfe's aide whispers to him again, and Wolfe examines his watch with exaggerated deliberateness. "I'm going to need to get back to the city, Doctors. It's been an interesting experience and I assure you, Dr. Cassidy, the committee will give your materials a careful vetting when I return to DC. Why don't you join me for the drive down, Scott, and we can review budget issues."

Wolfe's aide escorts him out of the lab and into his car before Jaycee has the chance to protest.

In his now empty and silent office, Joshua begins the process of closing for the day. He does a last check of the animals in the back cages to make sure that everyone has enough food and water for the night and that all the post-surgical cases are stable. Then, moving to the front of the office, Joshua shuts down the computers and one by one turns off all the lights.

Prince, an enormous tortoise-striped tom tabby, follows him around the office. Prince was the tiniest of strays when Joshua first found him. He was so sick looking and scrawny that no one wanted to adopt him. The fact that he had lost one ear and an eye in some street battle didn't help his adoption chances, either.

After a while, Joshua stopped trying to place the cat and accepted the fact that Prince was a fixture of the office. Every night before he left, Joshua put out a clean litter pan, a bowl of dry cat food, and a dish of fresh water and gave Prince roaming rights through the office. This arrangement apparently was agreeable to the cat, as he soon became a feline behemoth able to push open the heaviest of the office doors.

Prince meows and rolls on his huge back on the reception desk. Joshua obliges him with a belly scratch for a few moments, but then something by the door catches Joshua's attention. His hand freezes in midair. There it is, staring right at him, illuminated by one last, small light—the office name plate.

Joshua walks over to it and, with a slow shake of his head, slides the wooden slat engraved with my name from its spot.

With my name under his arm, Joshua turns off the remaining light and quickly walks out into the heavy shadows of a November evening.

Prince meows loudly after him.

Still dressed from the day that ended many hours earlier, David sits on the edge of our bed with the dogs and several of my cats asleep nearby. Although he grips a photograph of the two of us walking on the beach, he stares at the television, which is tuned to a station that has long since signed off.

Our bed was a good place for us. Of course there was sex, but almost more than that, it held so many moments of non-physical intimacy because I was often already in bed by the time David got home. It was also the place where David was the least serious and defensive, and where his work life was the farthest from his mind.

So bed was where we had late-night conversations about nothing more significant than which flavor of ice cream is the most difficult to make and which melts the slowest, shared laughter at a TiVoed sitcom, or debated which one of us would get up in the middle of the night to let a cat in through the bedroom window and then, only minutes later, back out again.

These are all the small interactions that fill the many, many hollows of married life.

But David is not thinking about these memories tonight. I can tell that he's not because there's not even a hint of happiness recalled around his eyes. Perhaps he is thinking of a different bed—my hospital bed. There are no great—or even good—memories of that bed.

By the time I was back in the hospital for the final time, I was mostly unconscious, hooked up to monitors that precisely measured the life leaving my body. We didn't really need the machines to tell us what was happening. My pallor and sunken features spoke clearly that the time for hope had long since passed.

David, pale and exhausted from lack of sleep, sat beside me hour after hour. He was supposed to share this vigil with Liza, my college roommate, closest friend, and champion, but more often than not he asked to be alone with me.

Throughout our marriage, Liza's contradictions had always irritated David. She smokes cigarettes before and after her yoga class, drinks wheatgrass juice with lunch and cosmopolitans with dinner, and can quote extensively from the Old or New Testament (she was a religious studies major before she became a psychologist), but would have a hard time identifying the governor of New York. And when it came to romantic entanglements, of which there were many, Liza had all the self-restraint of squirrel in a bag of peanuts. Still, she was fiercely devoted to me—and by association, my husband. Despite her idiosyncrasies, whatever comfort David found toward the end, he found in her.

On my last day, Liza summoned David into the hallway outside my hospital room. David was on the brink of tears. "She's still hanging on," he told her. "This is torture."

"But that's what you've been asking of her," Liza said gently. "It's all been about the fight to stay here with you. She won't abandon you."

"That's over now."

"Is it? Is it over for you?"

"Do I have another choice?"

"I think before she goes, she needs to know that you'll be okay. Give her your permission to stop the fight and let go."

"Come on, she's not even conscious. Don't start with the new-age crap. I can't do the *Touched by an Angel* thing right now."

Liza put her hands on David's shoulders. "You need to say good-bye and release her."

David's eyes flashed. "But it's a lie! It's all a damn lie!"

"I know, honey. But sometimes lies are the only truth you've got." David backed away from Liza, and her hands dropped uselessly to her sides. "I'm going to smoke. You need to go say the words and take care of business." Liza kissed David on the cheek and walked away.

I passed in silence four hours later.

I was hoping that our good-bye would be an instrument of the understanding that had eluded me, that something would pass between us in those final moments. I was praying for the epiphany of closure—that we could be each other's last, best teacher. Instead, as David sat next to me, I could almost hear his internal dialogue of doubt, fear, and self-deprecation—all the *I should have*s and *I can't*s. I was unable to redirect him and so having him there with me, especially toward the end, was nothing short of agony. I became just another hard and futile ending.

You never know who will turn out to be your greatest teacher until it all ends. In belated retrospect, I now realize that the most important lesson I'd ever learned about saying good-bye actually came from a six-year-old girl.

A yellow Lab, humorously misnamed Brutus, had been brought to my office with a fractured pelvis—the consequences of his run-in with a Volvo SUV. I advised the dog's family—a pleasant single mom and her young daughter, Samantha—that I probably would be able to repair the fracture but that there was a chance of serious post-operative neurological damage. I also told the mother that, in light of the cost of the surgery, the dog's age, and the prospect that the dog might not fully recover, euthanasia also was an understandable option.

The mother explained that Samantha had witnessed the accident that nearly killed the dog and that her husband had died two years earlier in a head-on car collision.

"If there's any way that Samantha's last memory of Brutus can be something other than the accident," she told me, "then I want to try to do that for her."

The orthopedic part of the surgery went well. Samantha and her mother came to visit Brutus at the hospital every day for at least a few hours. I can't tell you precisely what the dog was feeling during these visits, but anyone who observed the dog when Samantha lifted his head and put it in her lap well understood that the visits were neither unappreciated nor unimportant. Anyone who says otherwise is either cruel or stupid.

Unfortunately, my initial diagnostic hunch of nerve damage was spot-on. Brutus had no control over his back legs. Worse than that, he also couldn't pass body waste on his own. This meant emptying his bladder with a catheter every three hours and subjecting him to an enema every twenty-four hours. For a large dog who has lived an independent life, the inability to pass waste on his own is something I can only describe as humiliating. You can see it in the downcast eyes, the ears that refuse to perk up, and eventually, in some cases, the refusal to eat or drink.

On the fifth day post-surgery, Brutus stopped eating. On the sixth day, he stopped drinking.

When Samantha and her mom came to visit on the seventh day post-surgery, I took the mother into an empty exam room to discuss options while Samantha stayed with Brutus in the holding area.

"Yes, I can keep him alive with IV fluids," I answered the mother's question. "But you've got to start asking yourself toward what end."

The mother started to cry. "It's not so much about Brutus. I just can't tell Samantha that she's going to lose something else that she loves. She's been through—"

We were interrupted by a knock on the door. It was Samantha. Her eyes were wet, but her voice was clear. "I think Brutus wants to die," she said. "I think he wants to die so he can go to heaven and run again." Samantha then turned on her heel and left the room, leaving her mother and me staring at each other.

Samantha's mother decided that her daughter didn't need to see or know about the act of euthanasia. We ran through a short script of what I would tell Samantha later that day after I had ended Brutus's life. Before Samantha and her mother left, that little girl hugged her dog as if she knew it would be for the last time.

When I called a few hours later, Samantha answered the phone. I told her, "The angels came and took Brutus to heaven."

There was a pause of a few seconds. When Samantha spoke, there was a tremor in her voice. "You think he's running again?" she asked.

"Yes," I said, holding back my own tears. "Like a puppy."

Samantha began to cry. "Then that's good. That's real good."

After that day, whenever I picked up the file for a terminal case, I prayed for better angels, for the truth, wisdom, and mercy that Samantha had found in opening the gates of heaven for Brutus. I guess during those last days with me in the hospital, David's fear of being alone again forced him to pray for something else entirely.

Four hours. Two hundred and forty minutes. Fourteen thousand four hundred seconds. I waited for David as long as I could. I suppose perhaps I still am.

In our bedroom now, David drops the photo on the bed and reaches for the phone. I assume that, like me, he's looking for contact, for sound, anything to stop the white noise that rings in his ears. He dials a number he now knows by heart. It rings a few times before Liza's sleepy voice comes on the line.

"David?" Liza yawns into the phone. "You okay? Never mind, don't answer that."

"I'm really sorry to be calling so late."

"Don't even. What's keeping you up?"

"I never told her it was okay, you know? I never said good-bye."

Liza takes her time before answering. "I know, honey."

"Maybe I should've listened to you."

"I said it for you, not for Helena."

"Still..."

"Have you slept at all tonight?"

"It's too quiet."

"I'll get someone to phone in a scrip for something in the morning to help you sleep."

"Thanks, but I don't think I really want to sleep."

"Bad dreams?"

"No. It's just that every time I wake up, it starts all over again...
the newness of her being gone...Does that make any sense?"

"I think so. But if you don't start sleeping, you'll start circling
the drain. Trust me. There's a reason why sleep deprivation is a
method of torture."

"I'll let you know. What I really want—" David stops himself.

"What?"

"I just want to be able to cry until there's nothing left—until I
can't feel a damn thing anymore. It's like if I could stick my finger
down my throat and make myself vomit, it would all come out and
I wouldn't be sick anymore. But I can't get there. I haven't cried
since the funeral, but I feel everything. I know it sounds stupid."

"Not stupid. It just sounds like you're wound pretty tight right
now. I think if you can just get some sleep—"

"—I heard you the first time, dear."

Liza knows that it's time to get off the subject. "How's the house-
keeper search going? Did you find someone?"

David laughs. "You don't want to know."

"C'mon. Tell me."

"I wouldn't trust any of them to wash Collette's fruit, let alone
take care of Skippy."

"Skippy can take care of himself. It's you I worry about, doll.
You're going to need to choose someone."

"This I know." David hesitates. "When do you think..." His
voice trails off.

"When do I think what?"

"Nothing. I should let you get back to sleep."

"You want to know when I think it gets to be okay?"

"Smart girl."

"Do you want me to answer you as your friend or as a shrink?"

"Which answer will I like better?"

"I'll give you both and you can decide."

"Good. I like the illusion of having a choice."

"As a shrink I'd tell you that it takes time to heal, and that over time you'll be able to learn to objectify the loss you've experienced. Objectification is the first step; it will provide the context that will allow you to deal with the loss."

"I hope your answer as a friend is more helpful."

"Not so much. Look, I still reach for the phone to call her two or three times a day and then I remember she's not there. I can't even begin to imagine what you're feeling. So I think 'okay' is still a ways off. If five years from now you're waking me up in the middle of the night and we're still having this same conversation, I would say that you probably have a problem. Anything short of that, I just don't know. There are no rules for it. I'm sorry."

"Don't be. That actually was pretty helpful," David says.

"That helped? Then you really are bad off." They both laugh at that. "You let me know if you want that scrip, okay? Better living through chemistry."

"Thanks for listening."

"Anytime."

"Same here, okay?"

My friend and my husband exchange their good nights and hang up their phones. David turns off the TV, gets undressed, and climbs beneath the covers. I lie down next to him.

We both stare at the ceiling of our bedroom until the alarm clock goes off in the morning.

5

In the cold darkness of a mid-November dawn, David rises from our bed and carefully removes a suit, dress shirt, and tie—his work uniform—from the closet. He places these items on the unused side of our bed as the dogs watch with interest. He throws on a pair of jeans, work boots, and a sweatshirt and heads out of the bedroom with the dogs a short step behind.

I follow David as he does the morning chores. He feeds the dogs and all the cats quickly and without incident. I feel some of his tension ease as he enters the flow of a routine with growing confidence.

Then he walks outside to face the pig and the horses.

If you haven't lived with a pig, forget everything you think you know about them. They are not slow in thought or movement unless they choose to be. Neither are they subtle once they decide what they want or don't want.

David approaches Collette's pen warily, a bucket of food in his hand. Collette, covered in hay and straw, appears to be sleeping in her house, which is a good three feet from the gated entrance of the pen.

David tries to slide the thick metal bolt on the gate into the open position, but the bolt sticks about halfway. That's a bad start to things. Collette stirs in her house, but David, focused on moving the bolt, doesn't seem to notice.

My first serious boyfriend in college had a sky-blue Triumph TR7. I didn't really care for the boy, but I loved the car. What can I say in my defense except tell you that the car could go from a dead stop to sixty miles per hour in less time than it took me to move his hand out from under my shirt. The car didn't just move—it charged.

Collette this morning would have put that TR7 to shame. Just as David manages to slide the bolt open, Collette is on her feet and rocketing toward the gate. David sees the blur of her huge form heading toward him, but it is too late for him to do anything except jump out of the way as Collette blows through the gate.

Collette is free, but she doesn't move far; there's still that bucket of food to consider. Because Collette is a member of the porcine family, she is genetically predisposed to eat. She has never shown either the willpower or an iota of intention to contradict her genes. For Collette, food is not only king, it is the entire damn kingdom. Although David has had very limited contact with Collette since she came into our household, I know he is aware of at least this much.

I can see David calculating his options—pig, food, David, gate—like it is some law school logic puzzle.

David shakes the bucket of food to get Collette's attention and then takes a few careful steps toward her. The ground near the pig-pen is slick with a thin sheet of ice, and David slips and slides as he attempts to maneuver. The pig grunts at him suspiciously.

"Come on, Collette. Time for breakfast," David says in his most soothing tone as he shakes the bucket again.

David makes the rest of the distance to Collette without her moving off, but it clearly is a *Be careful what you wish for* moment. In his logic game paradigm, David has successfully joined the objects of "pig," "food," and "David," but now he is farther away from the "gate."

David tries to nudge the pig ever-so-gently in the desired direction. Even though it is only the slightest hint of physical contact, Collette immediately drops to the ground with a loud squeal as if she's been shot in the head. David pulls his foot out of the way just in time to avoid her zaftig rump, but he slips and lands facedown right next to Collette's head.

David lifts himself on his elbows and Collette turns her face to him. They are now eye-to-eye at ground level, only a few inches away from each other. She yawns in David's face.

In the end, it takes far longer than it should have—and certainly more time than David allotted—but to his credit, he eventually succeeds in joining "pig" and "food" with "David" on the correct side of the "gate." Collette eats and her world, if not entirely fulfilled, is for the moment at least sated.

Twenty-five minutes later, David emerges from the house dressed for work under a black Brooks Brothers overcoat. He checks his watch as he heads toward his Jeep and the long drive to his office.

Just before he gets into the car, David looks back at the house and our large backyard surrounded by chain-link fencing. Chip, Bernie, and Skippy stand by the fence watching him leave. Before today, this play was repeated thousands of times in one form or another over the course of our marriage. I call it *Dogs Watching David Go to Work.*

Before today, the dogs would have waited outside until David's car had gone. Then they would come inside the house for the real start of their day with me. On most days this meant that the three of them would jump into my old battered Jeep for the quick trip to my office. Skippy would take the front passenger seat so he could watch the world through the windshield. Bernie and Chip would fall asleep almost immediately in the back of the car. I would stop at the Dunkin' Donuts drive-through so I could get a decent cup of coffee and give each of the dogs a bagel. They would be my companions at the office, as comfortable there as at home.

When you live with animals, there are many such plays—expectations stated, responses given, and behavior modified. Companion animals, almost without exception, thrive on the familiar and routine.

The plays we had performed with my creatures are over now, locked away behind a door to a room that David and I can never again enter. The horses seem to know this reality. The dogs, however, take longer to get there. This is not because they are less intelligent or unaware, but only because dogs believe in the inertia of good things.

David starts walking toward the dogs to give them one final good-bye when a powerful and angry *BANG* from within the barn spins him around. I can see it suddenly dawn on David that the horses are still locked in the barn from the night before. In doing battle with Collette, he completely forgot about the horses. Before he can depart, David still must release Arthur and Alice from their stalls into the paddock and give them fresh hay to tide them over until dinner. David has no choice; he must enter the barn.

David and I always felt very differently about the barn. I loved the place. The mixture of manure, fresh hay, and molasses feed is the smell of the living. In the summer, the concrete floor and high ceiling keep it cool; in the winter, the heat of the horses combined with the insulation provided by bundles of wood shavings keeps it warm. When the horses are out in the paddock, field mice and birds compete in a delicate dance on the barn floor for the remnants of grain and sweet feed.

David, on the other hand, always viewed the barn with anxiety. Because the barn contained large animals in a relatively small and confined space, in David's mind this meant danger. It was not as if a horse had ever actually hurt David. Perhaps that was the problem—real actions have tangible, measurable consequences that can be ameliorated; actions that reside only in the mind are capable of forever escaping rational attention.

There is also one important fact about horse barns that David today apparently has forgotten: It is impossible to remain clean in one, even if you're standing completely still.

Once in the barn, David gingerly removes several flakes of hay from a nearby stack and holds them carefully away from his body to prevent the slightest incidental contact with his black overcoat. The coat, like the 100 percent merino wool suit underneath, is a magnet for hay.

David steps outside of the barn for a moment and tosses the hay through the slats of the horse fencing and into the paddock. He quickly confirms that he has remained hay-free throughout the process and returns to the barn.

David takes hold of Alice's halter and carefully moves the horse from her stall into the paddock through a doorway at the rear of the barn. Alice, smelling the fresh hay and morning air, cooperates with David's inexperienced hands. She is out and snacking in less than three minutes.

David exhales a breath of relief and then sets his sights on the towering form that is my horse Arthur. He reaches for Arthur's halter just as he did Alice's only moments ago. That's David's mistake; Arthur, as David should know by now, is what we call head-shy, meaning that he does not like to have his face touched—particularly by men.

Arthur ducks and bobs his large head to avoid David's hand—a tactic that works for several minutes. David finally grabs hold of the halter and tries to pull the horse through the back of the barn and into the paddock. Arthur, however, chooses to remain where he is.

In the face of Arthur's obstinacy, David starts tugging on the halter, cursing under his breath. Arthur doesn't welcome my husband's hostility. While David still holds the halter, Arthur whips his head around, sending David tumbling into the nearby hay bales.

When David rises unsteadily from the barn floor, he reminds me of Ray Bolger in *The Wizard of Oz*. His knee joints wobble and hay sticks out of his hair, topcoat, pant legs, and even his socks and shoes. When he walks, hay drops out of his pants as if the hay somehow has become his very essence.

Arthur whinnies his amusement and then, halter half off, saunters to the back of the barn, through the gate, and into the paddock where Alice waits for him.

David, very late now, runs for his car as he pulls hay out of his hair.

By my count, the score is Horse 1, David 0.

Seventy-four minutes later, David stands before a soaring office building in Midtown Manhattan amid the crush of workday morning bodies. He looks to the very top of the glass-and-chrome structure as people brush past him. Then he squares his shoulders, tightens his tie, and walks inside.

David passes his identification card through the security gate and then, together with a handful of other people dressed just as he is, heads to the elevator bank servicing the top fifteen floors of the building.

In accordance with some established rule of morning Manhattan elevator etiquette, communication is kept to a bare minimum. David looks at his shoes as the elevator tings each floor between thirty-three and forty-three. When the doors open on forty-three, a small woman of sixty passes him to exit. She gently squeezes David on the elbow and whispers her condolences. David offers a weak smile in response. A few others murmur their sympathy as they, too, leave the elevator.

David stays on the elevator until the forty-eighth floor. The elevator doors open and David reenters the world of Peabody, Grossman and Samson, the world that gave us money and him a successful law career, but that also so often took David away from me physically and in ways that mattered even more.

A young blond receptionist stationed behind a huge marble desk with subdued modern lighting speaks quietly into a telephone headset. She spots David, smiles, and mouths *Welcome back* as he passes and proceeds through a set of glass double doors etched with the letters PG&S.

The relative quiet of the reception area gives way to the frenetic sounds of a large Manhattan law firm. Phones ring, fax and copy machines whir, and snippets of conversation sound from all directions.

As David advances down the central hallway of the law firm, many of the secretaries call out to him in welcome while a few of the attorneys wave to David through the glass walls of their offices.

David soon arrives at Martha's workstation. When he was first assigned to Martha, it was only because the partner for whom she had worked for the prior decade left the firm literally in the middle of the night with all his client files. Although the partner never confided his plans to Martha, the leaders of the firm had always assumed (but could not prove) that she was aware of the traitor's scheme. As punishment for her failure to drop a dime on her boss, Martha was demoted to secretary to the bottom rung of all Manhattan law firm professional life—a first-year associate.

Martha at first declined to speak to her new charge and David, who can be quite obstinate and arrogant when challenged (yes, even back then), didn't help matters. This situation continued for over a month until Martha's beloved cat became ill with early-stage kidney cancer. David, seeing a potential opening to their impasse, volunteered my services.

When Martha walked into my office at the Animal Medical Hospital in Manhattan for the first time with her cat, I was astounded by the disconnect between the mental image I had formed of her from David's stories (old, crotchety, matronly with perhaps a broom hidden somewhere under her desk or, more likely, sticking out of her ass) and her true image (tall, fit, only in her late forties, with bright blue eyes).

Following our brief but polite introductions, I examined Smokey and confirmed the initial diagnosis. I also explained to Martha the somewhat limited options available. After listening to my litany of pros and cons of treatment, Martha rocked Smokey in her arms and said simply, "We never had children."

On that day, Martha and I agreed that we would do whatever we could for Smokey, but also that we would never let his quality of life suffer. Martha made me promise—and I did so willingly—that if I ever thought she was holding on beyond an appropriate time, I would slap her out of it.

That moment came five months later on a cold day like today when Smokey stopped eating. I arrived at Martha's apartment that evening with my kill bag. Martha's husband, a small, older man with a kind face, greeted me warmly at the door and ushered me in. Before I even was able to remove my coat, Martha asked, "Can't we feed him by tube?" She took one look at my face and answered her own question. "It's time, isn't it."

"Yeah," I whispered. Martha nodded, tears beginning to spill down her face. She held Smokey while he passed. By the end, despite all my efforts to maintain my air of professionalism, I was crying almost as hard as she was. I believe that Martha loved me for that.

Martha was my first real proof that an act of caring for another's companion animal creates a bridge that one must work very hard to ignore or destroy.

Martha soon became not only David's real secretary, but also his chief protector and principal defender at the firm. She understands who at the firm kisses and who turns their cheek to be kissed.

When Martha notices David's return this morning, she jumps out of her chair and gives him a long, warm hug. "Let me have a good look at you." Martha slowly turns David around and picks off a few flecks of hay from his shoulder. "Well, you look like crap."

"Thank you." David smiles at her.

"Seriously, you look awfully pale. And thin. How do you feel?"

"I'm fine." In response to Martha's look of skepticism, David adds, "Really, I am."

"Good thing you practice law better than you lie."

David and Martha walk together into David's large office. His desk is completely covered with neat stacks of files and lists, and this is where David's attention is first drawn. He shakes his head in disbelief.

"Don't worry," Martha says. "It's not as bad as it looks. The most important thing is that you're back."

David moves behind his desk and into his chair. Once seated, his eyes cannot avoid the photo he keeps on his desk of the two of us in Paris.

"Can I get you anything?" Martha asks in the mounting silence.

David shakes his head, eyes on the picture.

"It'll get easier," she says.

"Really? When?"

Martha shrugs off the question. "I've divided your phone calls into condolence, business-related, and urgent business-related."

David finally picks up the lists in front of him. "Thanks. What else do I need to know?"

Martha chews her lower lip.

"Just tell me. I'm going to find out anyway."

"Well, you're scheduled to pick a jury in the Morrison case before Judge Allerton in three weeks." Martha quickly blurts out this last part as if by saying it fast perhaps David won't really focus on what she's just said.

"What?" David closes his eyes and shakes his head. "Chris was supposed to get an adjournment."

"That is with the adjournment."

"He only gave me one week? Allerton's granted longer extensions for hangnails."

"It's not about you; it's the thing he's got with Max."

"Well, whatever it is, it's not very fair."

"You've been away too long if you think fairness actually matters. You can always make another run at him in person."

"You mean beg."

"It's only begging if you whine," Martha says. "There's a fresh pack of toothpicks in your top drawer. And I also told Max that if he got stupid with you, I personally would go into his address book and e-mail all his girlfriends each other's phone numbers. So don't let him push you to do anything you're not up for yet."

This is why I love Martha. She knows almost everyone's personal weakness at the firm, but only exploits that knowledge for the deserving few. David smiles at the thought of Max squirming. "Maybe Max will surprise us both," he says.

"Sure. And maybe flaming pigs will fly out of my ass."

David grabs a toothpick from his top drawer and drops it into the corner of his mouth. "Unless you've got more happy news, can you find Chris for me?"

"That I can do. One last thing. You're still scheduled to do your annual presentation to the first-years tomorrow on ethics. I should get someone else to cover it."

"No way. That's the one where I get to tell the kids about the oath and all the horror stories about what happens to lawyers who go to prison for perjury. I always look forward to that one."

"Let someone else do it this year. You've got enough on your plate."

"It's only an hour and it's one of the few things I do around here that matters. First-years need to understand the importance of telling the truth. Keep it on my schedule."

"As you wish," Martha says as she backs out of the room bowing to David before she closes the door behind her. This gets a smile out of him.

David picks up the top sheet of paper from a pile. Before he makes it through the first paragraph, there's a single loud knock on the door and then Max bursts into the office.

"Man, it is good to see you back behind that desk," Max says. "How's it going so far?"

David waves to the stack of papers and phone messages on his desk. "I just got in. I'm feeling a little overwhelmed at the moment." When Max doesn't respond, David repeats the word *"overwhelmed"* with an exaggerated slowness. "Surely you've at least heard the term before, no?"

"Come in when you need to; leave when you need to. Delegate the crap to your associates," Max says.

Chris Jerome, David's favorite senior associate, walks in at that moment and stands behind Max. Max at first doesn't notice her, and continues, "The truth is a trained monkey could do most of it."

Chris clears her throat and Max turns to greet her. "See? Perfect timing," he says. You might think Max would be at least slightly embarrassed by the fact that an associate overheard his comment, but then you don't know Max; he would've proudly said the same thing directly to a room full of associates.

"Vince Lombardi's got nothing on you when it comes to inspiration," Chris tells him. "You know, Max, even monkeys get to go home and have a banana every once in a while."

Max rolls his eyes. That's partner-speak for "Associates don't know how good they have it; when I was an associate they wouldn't even let us wear shoes until we had made it past our fifth year, and it wasn't until our sixth year that they took the razor blades out of them," or something like that. "I'll pick you up later for a quick lunch at Marconi's," Max tells David.

"As usual, you don't listen," David says. "I'm swamped."

Max waves away the objection. "You still need to eat." As Max passes Chris on the way out, he whispers something to her and then closes the door behind him.

"So, what'd Beelzebub say?" David asks her.

"What do you think? He wants me to watch over you and make sure you're okay." Chris takes one of the two seats opposite David's desk.

"Just be careful with Max. He can be a good friend at the firm—"

"—as long as you know he's standing in front of you," Chris finishes. "I know, I know. You've told me a hundred times before."

"And I know you've been working eighteen-hour days to stay on top of my cases. Thank you. I promise I'll make it up to you."

"Don't keep score, okay? I'm still running at a deficit."

Chris could easily be every wife's worst nightmare—attractive, smart, only thirty, and required to spend long hours with their husbands.

I admit that, even though Chris was married and David, during the life of our marriage, had never given me cause for real worry (he often joked that he was too tired to satisfy me, let alone a second woman), there was a time several years back when I had my own doubts about her. Chris started calling David at home during all hours of the night. It didn't help that most of the partners at the firm—male and female—are on their second or third spouses and most of these are former secretaries, legal assistants, or associates.

Before I had the chance to confront David about my concerns, he came to me for my advice. David often did that about interpersonal issues—the aspect of his life where he always felt the least prepared and the most vulnerable. I loved that he trusted my judgment; it made me feel like we were allies.

It turned out that Chris had been receiving inappropriate, unwelcome, and increasingly frequent advances from a very senior partner (what kind of first name is Whitney for a man anyway?) whom she'd been working with to prepare for a trial. Chris went to David to discuss what she should—and could—do without impacting her career.

David, ever loyal to his favorites, wanted to speak to "Whit" and, if that didn't stop the jerk, report him to the executive committee. Chris rejected that suggestion; no amount of assurance could convince her that David's actions would be career-neutral.

As the situation spiraled downward and Chris considered leaving the firm, David decided he would need to report the situation, notwithstanding Chris's wishes. This is when he laid out the situation for me. I was so relieved at his explanation for all the Chris intimacy that I blurted out the first solution that came into my mind.

"Castrate the little bastard."

David first looked at me with that *Can you please be serious* expression he occasionally threw my way, but then I could see the thin tendrils of an idea take hold of him. He broke into a wide smile.

"Castration. Of course. Thanks, honey." He kissed me briefly on the lips and then spent most of that evening talking on the phone.

In the end, David got Chris to agree to wear a microcassette recorder during all interactions with the offending creep. By the end of only one week, Chris had recorded enough of Whit's comments about her physical appearance and invitations to out-of-town "educational seminars" (this last said with an audible smirk) to fill two tapes. She then handed David the tapes with disgust, as if they were something she'd found floating in a subway toilet.

David played the tapes for Whit that very evening. When he was finished, David told Whit that he not only would have the tapes played at the next partners' meeting, but would also deliver copies to Whit's (second) wife. The price for David's silence was relatively cheap: an immediate cease and desist of the behavior and a well-deserved "excellent" review for Chris.

Three years later, Chris is now only nine months away from being voted on for elevation to the exalted status of partner, the tapes are secured somewhere in our home, and Whit is Chris's biggest cheerleader (a result that may coincide with the fact that David sends Whit a blank microcassette tape through the interoffice mail about once a month).

Sitting in David's office now, Chris pulls out a folder full of notes. "Are you ready?"

"Do I have a choice?"

Chris shrugs. "Probably not one consistent with your remaining a partner at the firm." Reading from the file, Chris recites a long list of matters and their status. David tries to stay focused, but I can see the struggle; his eyes keep sliding toward our picture on his desk.

To my vestigial ears, Chris's voice soon merges with the phones ringing and conversations taking place in the other offices until all these elements become simply a wall of overwhelming noise that forces me from the building.

There were many things that made me devoted to Joshua Marks once he left the ivy-covered buildings of Cornell and became, like me, just a small-town vet. His loss had made him less certain about himself and his world. He took his patients and their well-being seriously, but no longer viewed himself as anything more than a journeyman veterinarian—"another schmo riding the bus," he would say. Now Joshua listened more, said little (and nothing about himself at all), and chose his words much more carefully. I felt comfortable in the silences that existed in the ever-growing gaps between his sentences. I was not the only one.

Jimmy Rankin, a fourteen-year-old boy in a football jersey, waits for Joshua in our reception area. The office has not yet officially opened for the day, so the waiting room is empty except for the boy and the large cardboard carton in his lap.

Jimmy has dark hair, bright blue eyes, a warm smile, only one ear, and a deep scar that cuts through the left side of his face. He lost the ear and gained the scar in the car accident that took his older brother's life two years ago.

After that accident, Jimmy somehow became a magnet for all types of stray animals. He found them—or they found him—in the most unlikely of places. Almost all these strays have found homes either through his own efforts or through the persistence of (okay, the guilt inflicted by) the people at our office. Invariably, Jimmy names every creature he finds—dog, cat, squirrel, raccoon, or bird—the same thing; he calls them all some variation on *Pete*, the name of his dead brother.

"Any luck, Jimmy?" Joshua asks as he emerges from an exam room and greets the boy with a handshake.

"Not so much, Dr. Marks. A lot of lookers, but no takers."

Joshua nods in knowing sympathy. "Well, keep trying. Everyone doing okay in there?" Joshua peers over the side of the carton and sees eight small kittens crawling over one another and a hot-water bottle.

"I think so, but the little guy, Tiny Pete? He's not taking to the dropper so well."

"Let's have a look," Joshua says as he gently pulls the smallest kitten out of the box. Joshua checks Pete's eyes and mouth and gently squeezes the kitten's belly. The kitten gives a little squeak in response. "I think he's basically okay, but why don't you leave these guys with me today and I'll watch them while you're at school."

"That'd be great. I really didn't want to leave them home alone. You know how Mom can be."

Jimmy's mom hates the strays. After the death of her son, she hated anything that asked for attention—including, on most days, the disfigured son who survived. The fact that every stray is named Pete probably doesn't help.

"Thanks, Dr. Marks. You're a real lifesaver."

"Nope," Joshua says as he places Tiny Pete back in the box containing his brothers and sisters. "You are."

A timid knock on the front window interrupts them. Sally Hanson motions through the glass for Joshua to unlock the door, and he quickly complies.

"I'm sorry to catch you so early," Sally says as soon as she steps inside, "but I needed to see you."

I always assumed that Joshua knew the other veterinarian's employees in town as I did—by face perhaps, but not by name, and certainly not by first name. In fact, I don't ever recall Sally or any other employee of Dr. Thorton visiting our office socially or otherwise.

Joshua introduces Jimmy as his "friend," and I can see that Jimmy beams at this description.

For one brief moment, Sally pauses over Jimmy's scar before she catches herself and extends her hand. "Very pleased to meet you, Jimmy." Sally forces her eyes away from the boy's face and to the box of kittens. "Those are some very cute-looking critters," she tells him.

"Jimmy found this brood behind the high school."

"Do you have any animals, Ms. Hanson?" Jimmy asks.

"Not anymore. I've outlived them all, I'm afraid."

"How about a new beginning then?" Jimmy lifts Tiny Pete from the carton and gives Sally his most dazzling smile. "You could have one. Just promise to give him a loving home."

"Oh, I wish I could. I really do."

"Please? Pete needs someone like you. He's so small."

Sally's eyes plead with Joshua for a rescue from the hard sell.

"It's time for you to head off to school, pal," Joshua says.

Jimmy nods his understanding. He's not a stupid boy. He puts on his coat and collects his book bag. "Well, I expect these guys may be around for a while, so if you should change your mind..."

"I just may do that," Sally tells him, but he knows that she doesn't really mean it. "And thank you for your work," Sally adds. "It's good to know that you're out there."

Jimmy shrugs off the compliment. "Anyone else would do the same thing."

I know Sally would disagree. I can tell it by the look on her face when she hears Jimmy's words. She knows that it's not really like that out there. She knows that you can pass a hundred people on the street and not one of them would have done the same thing. She knows that Jimmy's affection for the creatures he saves will be a weakness in dealing with his own kind, when they laugh at his ear, stare at his scar, and ridicule his compassion. Sally knows— personally and painfully—that his love of animals can never ever inoculate him against malice, guile, or judgment.

Sally and I are sisters in this knowledge. I could never bring myself to warn Jimmy in life. Sally apparently cannot, either, and tells the boy only, "Let's hope so. But you actually did it."

Joshua turns to the boy. "Why don't you come in the back for a minute and help me get these guys settled." To Sally, he adds, "I'll just be a few."

Once in the back, Jimmy and Joshua divide the kittens into cages. Jimmy holds Tiny Pete so they are eye-to-eye, gives the kitten a gentle kiss on the forehead, and then places him in with his brothers and sisters. "Do you think she'll come around?" Jimmy asks.

"Not sure. I think she's already got a lot on her plate. What do you think?"

"I think sometimes good people need a second chance to say yes."

Joshua looks at Jimmy's upturned, beautiful, disfigured face searching for evidence of a deeper agenda in his statement and sees only honesty and the need for approval. Joshua smiles at the boy. "I do believe you're right."

After Jimmy departs, Joshua brings Sally into his office, where they sit facing each other across Joshua's worn desk.

"It's been a while," Joshua begins. "How've you been? How's Cliff?"

"Thorton just fired me," Sally says without a hint of emotion. Joshua doesn't say anything for a long few moments. "The words you're searching for," Sally offers, "are *I told you so.*"

"Don't you at least know me better than that? I told you at the time that I understood."

"So you said, but—"

"Thorton was offering you a salary and benefits that I couldn't match."

"You still think that was the only reason I left?" Sally asks with a mix of bitterness and sadness.

"I'm not too good at reading between the lines, as I think you may recall."

"Oh, I think you can read between the lines just fine."

"What happened with Thorton?"

"Clifford had a bad episode."

"I'm sorry. How is he?"

"He's been doing fine. The program he's in here has just been terrific for him. It's been worth any sacrifice to keep him in the school district. But recently his episodes…they're different. I'm afraid he's finally going to explode with puberty, or when the next big event happens in his life, and all those years of lost emotions will…" Sally's voice trails off, as if she's realized that she's said too much.

"I take it Thorton didn't respond well."

"It wasn't Clifford. I got scared, made a scene."

"Knowing Thorton, I can guess the rest."

"And so, bottom line"—Sally looks away in embarrassment—"I really need a job. I know you know how difficult it is for me to come here and ask this. I wouldn't if I had another option."

"I know. It's just that…" Joshua closes his eyes and rubs his forehead.

"I'll work whatever shifts you need me, I'll go back to cleaning cages—"

"It's not about that. You don't—"

"You can cut my pay, I don't care. I just need full-time employment within the school district so Clifford can stay in the program. Whatever it—"

"Sally, just listen to me for a minute." Joshua stands and turns to face the window. "I'm sorry, but I'm not going to be able to help you."

Sally slumps in her chair. "Wow. I've got to say that you're the last person I would've expected to put personal feelings above the needs of a child."

Joshua spins back to face her. "I'd forgotten how cruel you could be when your feelings are hurt."

Sally rises to leave. "Well, I can see this was a complete waste of time."

"I'm closing the practice," Joshua says to her back.

This stops Sally where she stands, and she turns to face Joshua. "What?"

"That's why I can't help you. I'm sorry."

"May I ask why?"

"A bunch of reasons. I'm tired, Sally. It's always been a two-vet practice here. I don't want to train someone new. It won't be the same and, honestly, I don't really want to try."

"When will you lock the doors?"

Joshua shrugs. "Very soon. My staff doesn't even know yet. I want to try to place as many as I can."

"That means Thorton will be the only game in town."

Joshua nods. "For now. Someone else will come along. They always do."

"Not always. And certainly not someone better."

"Whoever it is will have something more to give."

Sally chooses her next words carefully. "I think I understand. I'm sorry for what I said. I'm just scared out of my mind right now about what I'm going to do next."

"I don't blame you."

"If you can think of anyplace else, please let me know."

"Actually, I think I may have another idea, if you can keep an open mind."

Sally laughs, but it has the edge of someone who has learned to expect little. "I'm looking at stock clerk at the Agway at the moment, so I'm open to any suggestions you have."

In the research lab, Jaycee types at her computer terminal while Cindy sits on the desk next to her. Every few moments, just when Jaycee appears deep in thought about what's on the screen, Cindy reaches over and presses a few keys on Jaycee's keyboard. Jaycee attempts to ignore Cindy's petulant demands for attention, correcting without comment the chimpanzee's errant keystrokes. This goes on for a few minutes until, undeterred, Cindy thrusts her doll into Jaycee's face, blocking Jaycee's view of the screen. Jaycee bursts into laughter and swats playfully at the doll, but Cindy pulls it out of the way just in time.

"Cindy, I've got to get this letter out to Wolfe today. Now stop goofing around."

Cindy drops the doll back into her lap and looks as if she's ready to comply. Jaycee leans toward the computer screen, but as soon as she does, Cindy shoves the doll back in Jaycee's face.

Jaycee calls out to Frank at the other end of the lab. "Can you keep Cindy busy for ten minutes while I finish this?"

"Sure," Frank says.

In the time it takes Frank to walk the fifty feet between his workstation and Jaycee, Cindy's entire world changes. The world can be very mercurial if someone owns you.

Frank sees a dark blue Ford Explorer through the small lab window. Three men emerge—Jannick and two young and very large security guards. Both guards have sidearms. The guards lead the way to the entrance of the building.

"Get her in the Cube," Frank yells to Jaycee as he runs to the nearest computer terminal.

"What's wrong?" Jaycee jumps to her feet with Cindy in her arms.

"Just go!"

Jaycee drops Cindy into the Cube and hands her the doll. Cindy starts to protest, but Jaycee ignores her and slams the Cube shut. Agitated by Jaycee's unusually brusque treatment, Cindy begins to pace in her enclosure.

The three men step into the room without a knock or the slightest indication that they are unwelcome intruders. They enter as if they have that right.

Jannick whispers something to the two guards, and they quickly proceed to the computer terminals and secure the keyboards.

"Don't do that," Jaycee yells at them. "You'll lose files." The guards ignore her.

Jannick steps toward Jaycee. "It's over."

"But the extension—"

"—is not going to happen."

"You can't do that," Jaycee says, her voice starting to rise.

"It's no longer up to me."

Cindy's movements in the Cube become more agitated. She begins to whimper as she paces.

"You're a real bastard, Jannick."

"This really shouldn't come as a surprise to you. I've been saying it for the past three months. I really did try to help you. For someone who studies communication, you just don't listen."

"At least give me the week to put my work in order."

"You know the rules. You can't continue to have access to the NIS computer system. Besides, this space is already committed. I promise you that we'll carefully pack everything and send you your personal possessions."

"Be reasonable."

"We tried that, remember? I didn't want this, but you tied my hands, Jaycee."

"This is because I went to Wolfe, isn't it?"

"This isn't punitive and it's not personal," Jannick says. "It's because the grant is over and NIS needs to make transitional arrangements."

"What about all my work from the project? I want copies."

"Your work belongs to NIS. It always did."

Jaycee starts toward the computer on the nearest table—an act of defiance. One of the security guards steps in front of her.

"I told you before, I won't just abandon Cindy," she says.

Cindy now runs from one end of her enclosure to the other, shrieking every few seconds.

"She'll be cared for, I assure you," Jannick says.

"How? By putting her back in the general primate pool?" Jaycee shouts in part to be heard above Cindy. She moves toward the Cube to comfort Cindy, but the second guard blocks her path. Cindy sees this and erupts into full panic.

Jaycee stretches her hand out to Cindy around the guard. Cindy reaches through the bars and briefly touches Jaycee's fingers before the guard puts his hands on Jaycee's shoulders and moves her away.

Frank shoves the guard. "Get the hell off her."

The guard unsnaps the safety on his holster. "Please don't do that, sir," he says in a voice so calm that it is frightening.

Jannick steps between them. "Not necessary," he says to the guard.

Jaycee takes Frank by the arm. "This isn't going to help any-thing." She turns on Jannick. "This isn't over. We'll be back." Then Jaycee calls to Cindy around the guard's shoulders as she signs, "I'll be back for you, Cindy. I promise." But Jaycee's words are nearly unintelligible over Cindy's screaming.

At the doorway of the lab, Jaycee looks back to Cindy one more time. Cindy wraps her hands around the bars of the Cube and pulls, but of course the bars don't move. They never do. The Cube has become just another cage.

Cindy throws her head back and screams.

I will never hear my own child calling for me. I always thought there'd be more time to convince David that, his past notwith-standing, he wouldn't lose everything he loved. Now I'm grateful I didn't really try. It is actually a great comfort to me that David need never answer those questions asked in the timid voice all children use when they're experiencing a pain that they don't understand— "Where's Mommy?" "Is she coming back?" "Can I talk to her?"

I don't need to forget the sound of my own child's voice. But as long as I retain the smallest smattering of sentience, the terror of Cindy's scream will stay with me.

6

Many hours later, when the sky has turned dark, I find David still in his office staring absently at a document on his computer screen. Several paper coffee cups litter his newly disorganized desk, and our photograph is now buried under pages of memos and faxes.

In all our time together, I never fully understood what David's day actually involved. It's not that he kept it from me. I think it was more that I was afraid to see how hard and cold he could be to others.

Today, this is what I discovered. David:

Took thirty-two phone calls;

Made twenty-one phone calls;

Attended four meetings within the office;

Lost his patience with three associates and one paralegal;

Apologized twice;

Received five faxes;

Sent four faxes;

Argued with Martha three times;

Ignored several calls from Max;

Revised, but did not finish, two briefs;

Interviewed a potential expert witness by telephone;

Read 146 e-mails (excluding spam, which he deleted without reading);

Sent 134 e-mails;

Forgot to return a call to Joshua;

Ate lunch at his desk;

Chewed through twenty-three toothpicks;

Looked at our picture seven times;

Picked up the phone and dialed our home number three times, each time remembering only after the first ring that I wasn't there.

I would've liked to see some evidence of internal struggle, to be able to observe that David was working hard to hold it together on his first day back. I say this not out of narcissism, but because of my concern that David will fall into his old patterns of allowing work to take over his life to the exclusion of any meaningful emotions at all. It is only in the interstices of David's day that he will know remembrance, grief, sorrow, and, finally, healing. Pain explains a great deal of human conduct, but the fear of pain even more. I worry that David's fears—of loneliness, the new silence of our home, the needs of our animals, and probably twenty other things hanging off in the shadows—will drive him to fill any void with the work he knows and does well.

Thinking about the hollowness of David's day suddenly draws me back to Cindy. It's a vision that I've been fighting against for hours because I know I'll never be able to unsee it.

Trapped in her Cube and alone now in the cavernous lab, Cindy stares at the door that has been key-locked from the other side. People have entered the lab to feed and observe her, but none of them was Jaycee and so none of them mattered to Cindy. Her enclosure looks much smaller to me in Jaycee's absence.

Cindy peers nervously around the empty lab and, still holding my doll in one hand, moves over to the board in her Cube. She slowly begins to tap on the symbols.

The words PLAY NOW appear on Jaycee's computer screen across the room, but no one is there to read them. Cindy continues to type and the words CINDY BE GOOD NOW appear on the screen.

Finally, Cindy gently puts the doll down, bends over the symbol board, and slowly, clumsily, taps buttons with the index fingers of both hands. The words SORRY SORRY . . . SAD . . . OUT NOW appear on the computer screen.

When she realizes that no one is coming to answer her, Cindy picks up her doll and moves to a corner of the enclosure. She catches a glimpse of herself in the mirror and quickly looks away.

Then she makes herself as small as possible and, hugging her doll, rocks on her feet.

It was always extremely rare when the very distinct worlds of my husband's work and mine collided other than through our direct intervention. So I'm understandably shocked when Jaycee knocks on the door to David's office just as he is preparing to leave for the day.

"Can I help you?" David asks with the disinterested tone he probably reserves for people who have come to his office in error.

Jaycee enters with her hand extended. "I'm Jane Cassidy."

David stares at her blankly for a moment. "I'm sorry, but I think you're in the wrong place."

"You're David Colden, right?"

"Yes, but..."

"Helena's husband?"

"Do I know you?"

"I saw you at the funeral."

"Sorry, but there's not a lot I remember about that day."

Jaycee finally lowers her hand. "I understand. I was a friend of Helena. We went to vet school together." In response to David's blank stare, she adds, "We worked together on chimpanzees."

Still nothing from David.

"Charlie? Cindy?" Jaycee adds hopefully.

I can see that David is searching his memory. "Charlie, yeah. Something about HIV research, right?"

"Close. Hepatitis C."

"Right, right. There was another research assistant with Helena, right?"

"That was me."

"Wow." David is taken aback. "That was, like, fifteen years ago. How did you find me? How did you even know that Helena had passed?"

Jaycee stumbles over David's ignorance. "Helena didn't talk about any of the work she was doing with Cindy?"

"I vaguely remember Charlie because she was so upset by it, but I've never heard of any Cindy, Ms. Cassidy."

"Jaycee, please. My friends call me Jaycee."

No, Jaycee. He doesn't know about you or Cindy—because I never told him. I wasn't even sure I should risk bringing you into my present, but I needed answers that you seemed to have found. I was confident that our story together would end with me. There was no reason to believe otherwise. There was no nexus, no loose ends. You were never supposed to be here.

But here you are.

"Okay, Jaycee," David says. "I'm sorry, but I've really got to get home. It's only me, you know? So..."

"I need to speak to you about my work with Helena. It's all sort of complicated. Can I buy you a cup of coffee so I can try to explain?"

David looks at his watch again. I can tell he's getting annoyed. "Can this wait? I can schedule a meeting with you tomorrow or the next day—"

Jaycee suddenly looks on the verge of tears. "I've waited as long as I can. Please, Mr. Colden."

David is unable to refuse this plea made in my name. "David," he says with a sigh. "Call me David."

Seated at the Starbucks around the corner, Jaycee opens a folder and removes a black-and-white close-up photo of a chimpanzee. She slides the photo across the table to David.

"This is Cindy. After four years of intensive work, Cindy has acquired significant human language communication skills—she can ask and answer questions, make requests, and engage in conversation. All in English."

David looks at Jaycee skeptically. "Ms. Cassidy...Jaycee, this is all very interesting, but, one, I have no idea what you're talking about and, two, I have no idea what it's got to do with me, or even Helena."

"I'm getting there. Just bear with me for a few more minutes. Based on her language skills, I can prove that Cindy has a cognitive age equivalent of a four-year-old human," she says proudly.

David leans forward, uncertain of what he's just heard. "I think I missed that."

"Yes," Jaycee says, smiling. "Four years of age. And growing, we think. Cindy's learning curve appears to be exponential, just like the language-acquisition rate of a human child."

"You're pulling my leg. Look, I've seen some interesting news stories about chimpanzees that have learned some sign language, but a four-year-old? No one has ever said that."

"Correct. No primate has ever tested this high."

"So, what're you saying? There's been a sudden evolutionary surge in the last few years? Chimps have just gotten smarter? That doesn't make any sense."

Jaycee laughs for the first time. "You're looking at the wrong side of it. It's not that chimpanzees have suddenly evolved. The primates are the same, but the science and technology are different… so much better than what other researchers had, even just a few years ago. The new computer simulations, training modules, and computer-assisted analysis are allowing us to tap into aspects of the primate mind in ways we couldn't even dream about a decade ago. We can prove things now that a stone's throw in time behind us were just hypotheses."

David steals a glance at his watch. "Okay, let's just pretend that I understand everything you've just said. What's it all got to do with my wife?"

"At first I think she was just curious to see what I'd been doing after all this time. Then she met Cindy, and…Are you sure she never mentioned any of this?"

"I don't remember it. Honestly, though, between work, her illness, and the animals, I can't swear that I was listening as hard as I should've been." David shrugs. "She did say that she was working on some research. I thought it sounded like a good way for her to keep a positive attitude. She didn't mention the subject, and I didn't ask."

"Well, actually, she became a critical part of the team. We'd reached a plateau with Cindy's language development. We became too insulated. Then Helena started making her trips—"

"Trips? As in plural?"

"Yeah. At least a dozen over the last year. Of course they tapered off when…"

David is visibly shocked. "I'm sorry, but you must be wrong about that. I would've noticed that many trips." David studies his coffee, as if he may be trying to remember my absences during that period, but the truth is he wouldn't have noticed a pink bulldozer parked in our living room at that point in our lives. He shakes his head. "Really, you're mistaken."

Jaycee doesn't push him on it. "Whatever the actual number was, she made a unique connection with Cindy. There were only two people Cindy actually communicated with—me and your wife. For whatever reason, no one else was able to establish the bond that Cindy requires for the use of language."

"Are you telling me that Helena signed with this chimpanzee?"

"Yes. You did know that she could sign, right?"

"Sure. She has a deaf cousin, but—"

"—and then Helena began doing her academic research. She was always much better on that end of things than I was. It was Helena's idea to put the mirror in Cindy's enclosure, so Cindy could actually watch herself sign. After that, Cindy actually began using non-manual markers—"

"Non-manual whats?"

"Markers. Body language to augment meaning. The mirror was simple, but brilliant. I should've thought of it, but I didn't. It really was a breakthrough for Cindy—probably raised her CAE by over a year."

"I get it now," David says. "You'd like her research notes, right? I haven't found any yet, but whatever I find I'd be happy to give you."

"I wish that was it, but it's not. We're at the end of our grant. I applied for an extension and was turned down."

"I'm sorry to hear that. Have you tried another source? Perhaps if—"

"I've gone everywhere and talked to everyone. Even Washington. Believe me, it's not for want of trying." Jaycee struggles to keep it together. "I was kicked out of CAPS."

"I see. So where's Cindy now?"

"She's waiting at CAPS at the moment. NIS is required to obtain approval from the US Department of Agriculture before they transfer primates between facilities. It's supposed to allow the USDA to track the primates to ensure that a chimp infected with something like Ebola isn't moved by accident to a facility that doesn't have the correct level of biohazard containment. It can take up to a month to get the approvals, maybe less if there's someone making the right phone calls. I have someone at the DOA who is keeping an eye out for the application for Cindy, but we can't even be sure that NIS will follow the regulations."

"And once Cindy gets transferred?"

"She gets shipped out of CAPS and goes back into the NIS general population at another facility."

"And that means...?"

"Invasive primate biomedical research—bloodborne pathogens, tuberculosis, seizures, organ transplantation, and developmental surgical techniques. Once she's transferred..." Jaycee can't bring herself to finish the sentence. I know that in her own career, Jaycee has seen too much of the horrors Cindy will face.

"Why don't you just try to buy Cindy?" David asks. "I know it might be a chunk of money, but I can contribute some and get others to—"

"I tried that, of course. Cindy's not for sale. A signing chimp out there in the real world where people can see what she can actually do? NIS isn't going to let that genie out of the bottle. It's the same reason why they won't give me back my research notes so I can finally publish the journal paper."

"So for now?"

"She waits."

"Why don't you go public. Take it to the *Times* or something."

"If I do that, they'll just go ahead and transfer her now. By the time I find her, it'll be too late to do anything for her except grieve."

Jaycee removes a photograph from her folder and lays it on the table in front of David. In the picture, Cindy holds Jaycee's hand and they both look directly into the camera. Jaycee is smiling.

Jaycee then takes out a short stack of memos and research reports and pushes the documents toward David. Some of these documents bear the NIS insignia and others the crest of the US government. "This is what I was able to recover about my work before I was thrown out."

David ignores the stack. "I'm sorry about your situation, but I still don't understand what you think I can do to help."

"I need you to help me get Cindy out of CAPS before she gets transferred. I need you to get a court order."

David leans back in his chair. Even before he answers, he begins to shake his head.

Jaycee jumps in before David finds his voice. "I know it's a lot to ask after what you've been through, but I just thought you knew about Helena's work with me and you'd want—"

"I'm sorry. I wish I could help, but I can't."

"But I don't have much time. Once Cindy is transferred—"

"It's just not possible for me for a host of reasons. I can't even think of a legal basis for what you're talking about. Every first-year law student learns the rule—animals are chattel. Cindy legally is property. She's no different under the law than the chair I'm sitting on—and she's not even your chair."

"That's the whole point. She's not property. She's got a thinking mind, chairs don't."

"That's a lovely sentiment, but it's not the law. Not today, anyway. There isn't even a valid forum to bring that kind of claim and no law you can use to bring it under."

Jaycee removes a thick spiral notebook from her bag and hands it to David.

"What's this," he asks without opening it.

"Helena's research notebook."

What David had told Max in reference to the books lining my living room wall was basically correct. I'd read them—devoured them, really—as my illness progressed and my work with Jaycee continued. I read to find information useful to Jaycee's work with Cindy. But that was only part of it. I also was hoping for some private message in all the printed words to halt my growing anxiety that when I finally succumbed, I would face a series of dark and hostile rooms or, worse, just a note that said, "Life is a struggle and then you die. The end."

So I not only read, I made notes—pages and pages of notes in the notebook David now holds. I recorded quotes and chapter abstracts, thoughts about what I'd read, ideas for future research, sketches of Cindy, summaries of my interactions with her, and suggestions for improving the assumptions embedded in the computer programming. I know I left blank pages at the end of the book for the lightning bolt of understanding that never came.

Jaycee waits for David to open the notebook and look at the last-ing evidence of my own hand, as if she believes that will compel David to offer his help. I didn't realize until this moment how little Jaycee understands the pathology of fear. David places the note-book on the table unopened between them.

"Couldn't you just look at the issue?" Jaycee pleads. "Make some phone calls, write some threatening letters? Buy me some time until I can figure something else out? I have money saved. I can pay you."

"I can't do it. It's not about money. I'd need to get it approved by the firm, and they won't. And even if they would, I'm just not the guy... not now. My plate's got too much on it as it is."

"But Helena—"

"—never mentioned this to me at all. She never asked for my help with it when she was alive."

"But she—"

"—is gone." David's sharp tone reminds me of a dog emitting a low growl when someone gets too close to his food bowl—a warning before the bite. David lets out a deep breath, and when he speaks again, he is slightly more kind. "I know this is important to you. I see that. I can try to get you a referral, but..." But it is a losing cause and the only lawyers who would take it are those Jaycee wouldn't want. David doesn't need to finish the sentence. Jaycee gets it.

"I see," she says, defeated. She begins collecting her papers when the first tears finally come. "I'm sorry," she says as she wipes them away. "I didn't plan on the waterworks. I know you've got your own grief."

"There always seems to be enough to go around." David rises.

"I'm sorry, but I really need to get home now. I've got all of Helena's animals waiting for me. If you give me your card, I'll e-mail you if I have any better ideas."

Jaycee offers David the folder, but he hesitates. "It's just a copy," she says. "My contact information is in the file." David takes the folder without further protest. "Please pass it on if you think of anyone. Anyone at all."

"I will."

Jaycee slides the notebook over to David. He stares at it for a moment and then places it into his bag.

They shake hands and then David leaves for the parking garage and his long ride home. By the time he gets to the highway, David's head is filled with work and he has completely forgotten about Cindy.

I'm not as lucky. I've no distraction that is equal to the task of excising from my mind the image of Cindy alone and afraid in her cage.

I know this image. I've seen it before. It is of despair and of learned helplessness. It is, I am certain, one of the images that bind me to this time and this place.

David arrives home two hours late. The expectations of my animals after having waited this long for human companionship and food are now too high and David is beyond tired.

The dogs see the car headlights coming up the long driveway and begin to bark from the backyard where they've been confined for the last thirteen hours. By the time David parks, the barking has crescendoed into a wall of noise.

David opens the backyard gate and the dogs pounce on him

with their wet and muddy paws, yapping (in Skippy's case) and woofing (that's Bernie and Chip) for his undivided attention. To David's credit, he doesn't reprimand them; he even tries to sound excited to see them, but I can tell it's an act—he's got the voice right, but his face gives him away.

After a few minutes with the dogs, David brings them inside to feed them. Chip, true to his breed, is the only real food hound, but tonight all three eat as if they should've eaten hours earlier, which is precisely the case.

The food settles the dogs down for now, but David still has a long way to go before he can even think about resting. He opens a bunch of cat food cans and places them on the floor without even bothering to empty them on a plate.

None of my six cats is prickly. They are all former strays who have suffered through human cruelty or indifference. I believe they are grateful for our warm, comfortable home even though they must occasionally remind the dogs that *c* comes before *d* in the alphabet. They have come to trust that they will be treated with respect and kindness—clean litter boxes, fresh food, clean water, and space on our bed.

Now, however, my cats stare at the open cans in what I imagine is hurt and disappointment before giving in to hunger and licking the contents.

Ignoring the cats, David changes into old clothes, slips on a pair of rubber boots, and trudges back outside into the moonlight to tackle the big animals.

Collette is the first stop, and she has some choice words for my husband. Her water trough is frozen over, which means that the heating element designed to keep this from happening must be replaced. David knows how to do this about as much as he knows how to fly the space shuttle. Instead, he tries to fill the trough using the hose hooked up to the water pipe in the barn. This could have worked, except David forgot to drain the hose following its last use and it is now filled with ice. In the end, David is forced to carry buckets of hot water from the house to melt the ice in the trough, a task made more time consuming by the fact that he spills about half of each bucket on himself during each trip.

Finally, David comes to Arthur and Alice. They are still out in the paddock. David at least remembers that he must bring them into the barn for the night. We have coyotes and even the occasional bobcat in the woods surrounding the house. While direct confrontation is unlikely, Arthur in particular spooks easily and I've seen enough of equestrian medicine to know that panic causes injuries that can kill a horse.

David opens the gates connecting the paddock to Alice's stall so she can walk right in to the bucket of horse food that David has placed there for her. Alice is more than happy to follow the well-worn routine and get out of the night. She is chewing even before David slides the bolt of the stall door closed, locking her in.

Arthur also chooses to come into his stall from the paddock. David's relief is palpable—one more fight he can avoid.

At the moment Arthur enters the barn and begins to eat, the shrill ring of David's cell phone shatters the relative quiet. Arthur startles at the noise for a moment, but settles down as soon as David answers the phone.

"Yes?"

Cell phone and BlackBerry service on the property—whether at the house, in the barn, or in the woods—quite simply sucks. There were times when I would walk in on David contorting himself into poses that Gumby and Pokey would envy in order to receive e-mails on his BlackBerry.

The signal tonight is no different—only one bar—and David strains to hear Chris on the end of the line. "Where are you?" Chris asks.

"I can barely hear you," David shouts into the phone. Chris says something unintelligible. "Say again?" David asks as he moves around the barn to try to increase signal strength.

"I said that we have a problem. Those assholes in the Morrison case filed a motion in limine."

"What are the grounds?"

Chris's answer is garbled.

"Hold on a sec. Let me find a better spot." David, his eyes fixed on the signal strength indicator, stands at the barn entrance, where the reception is slightly better.

"Okay," he says into the phone. "Start over. What are they seeking to exclude?"

"Any trial testimony of our experts."

"What the hell? Our expert testimony is the case. When is the motion returnable?"

"They moved by order to show cause. Our papers are due day after tomorrow."

"This just keeps getting better. What basis?"

"They say we didn't turn over all the notes of the experts."

"That's absurd. Of course we did," David says. There is a long pause as David waits for Chris to assure him that at least this part of his life remains safe. When she doesn't volunteer, David finally asks, "Didn't we?"

Chris blows out a breath as if her next words are physically painful. "I thought so."

David takes the phone from his ear and looks at it for a moment as if it has betrayed him. When he speaks again, his voice has an unpleasant edge. "You thought so? Did I hear you right? You thought so?"

"I'm sorry. I had to delegate the production on this to a first-year. I guess there might have been a mistake."

"Allerton will hang me for this. I'll be labeled a liar. That'll be it for me!" I hear in David's voice a growing panic that is alien to his usual work personality. "I won't be able to fix this, Chris."

"I know. We're checking everything now, but it's going to be hours. So far, we know that—"

"Know what?"

Chris doesn't answer him.

"Tell me."

More silence from Chris. David checks the phone and sees the SIG-NAL LOST message blinking back at him. "Crap." He's about to redial when Arthur comes charging out of the barn and into the night.

I'm not sure how Arthur released himself from his stall. I assume that David didn't push the bolt all the way in and Arthur worked it open with his huge lips. He's done that a few times with me. It was a plaything between us; I'd give him a little extra grain or a rub around his ears and he'd go back into the stall a little less jumpy for the attention.

But this time Arthur isn't playing.

Arthur runs about four lengths from the barn entrance and then turns toward David, snorting angrily. Released from the small confines of his stall, awash in the spectral glow of the moonlight with plumes of smoke streaming from his nostrils, Arthur is the picture of raw power unleashed. He is now animal life freed from the constraints of human influence.

David is frozen in place by the vision of Arthur and forgets the phone. He forgets Chris, motions in limine, and even, I think, me. Horse and human stare at each other, radiating hostility. I can imagine what they see: David sees in this animal an unknowable adversary composed of an incomprehensible combination of flesh, blood, and bone, while Arthur sees in this human an unknowable adversary composed of an incomprehensible combination of muted color and ungainly appendages.

Arthur shakes his giant shaggy head from side to side as if trying to erase the image. This movement seems to bring David back to his immediate situation. He runs into the barn, quickly fills a plastic bucket with feed, grabs a lead rope, and jogs back outside.

Holding the lead rope behind him and out of view, David takes a few tentative steps toward Arthur as he shakes the bucket, rattling the food inside.

"Come on, buddy," David says in a poor attempt at a soothing voice as he inches toward the horse. "I've got a snack for you." Arthur's eyes never leave David.

David continues to creep forward a few steps at a time until he's within five feet of the horse. Then David slowly lowers the bucket of food to the ground and, keeping eye contact with Arthur, makes a large loop out of the lead rope behind his back.

I have absolutely no idea what David thinks he's going to be able to do. A horse isn't a dog; it's not like you can throw a leash around it and drag it against its will. Still, David appears to have a plan, or at least he thinks he does.

Arthur isn't having any of it and he springs backward out of David's reach. Startled by Arthur's sudden movement, David stumbles and almost falls to the ground. In frustration, he kicks the food bucket and it takes flight, spraying grain everywhere before it lands on its side fifteen feet away from him and directly in front of the horse.

Arthur takes the final few morsels of grain from the bucket, careful never to lose sight of David. The bucket rocks back and forth under the pressure of Arthur's insistent mouth.

Over the creaking of the bucket, I hear a different noise echo off the trees. At first I can't place the sound—it is too low, too soft, like a whisper. Then I begin to discern syllables. There are three. I finally recognize my own name—"He-le-na."

David calls for me, repeating my name over and over, the volume growing in rage and desperation until my name becomes a curse. Finally, mercifully, David shouts out my name one final time into the darkness where it breaks into something weak and mournful.

Exhaustion finally overcomes him. He trudges back up to the barn, leaving Arthur where he stands. At the entrance, David turns toward the horse, gives him the finger, and slowly drops to the ground.

David awakens on the hard, cold ground two hours later to see that Arthur has returned to his stall. Holding his breath, David walks up to the stall, closes the door, and slides the bolt all the way this time.

Only after David secures the bolt with a clip for good measure does he allow himself to exhale and make eye contact with Arthur. He mutters one word—"bastard"—and then retreats to the house.

Horse 2, David 0.

7

The next morning, David rises in shadows, races through the chores (he throws Collette's food over her fence and leaves the horses in their stalls with enough hay and water for the day), and starts his drive to the office. It's as if he's trying to escape our house as quickly as possible to get to his real home—his law firm.

It is still dark when David turns onto an empty Route 33. Route 33, the local road that connects our little town to the major highway south to Manhattan, is surrounded by deep woods on both sides for about ten miles until the highway junction. It is ridiculously winding and unlit, but nevertheless has an unreasonable posted speed limit of fifty-five miles per hour. It is this confluence of woods, winding, darkness, and speed that has made Route 33 famous in our community as "Route Road Kill." Deer, coyotes, rabbits, opossums, raccoons, foxes, dogs, cats, and turtles all regularly find a violent end on this particular piece of road.

Sometimes, they aren't quite yet dead. Ever since that deer strike in Ithaca the night we met, David knew that I had one rule when I was in the car either as the driver or the passenger: If it was still moving and if I could get it in the car, it was coming with me. Period. David didn't argue with the rule (although I did hear him once or twice pray for the road to be clear). I mean, seriously, how could he argue? What's the importance of making it to a movie on time compared with ending the suffering of a raccoon with a broken back?

What did David do when I wasn't in the car with him? I'd often reminded him about Route 33 because he usually drove on it before the sun had risen or long after it had set. He would nod at me obediently. But when I would take Route 33 to my own office a few hours later, I couldn't help but wonder whether any of the mangled carcasses I saw were the product of David's inattention or distraction. Even worse, had any been alive when David drove past? He never said and I never asked him.

As David searches the radio stations for this morning's traffic report, I hear the small, tragic *thump.*

David quickly checks his rearview mirror. An opossum lies in the road.

"This isn't happening," he says and stops the car. He waits there on the deserted road, his eyes glued to the rearview mirror. The opossum twitches. Once, twice. The animal is probably still alive and in need of medical attention and now David knows it.

"Sorry," he mutters as he shakes his head. David takes his foot off the brake and drives away.

I don't believe what I'm seeing. David just drives away. My David. If there is more concrete proof of the inconsequence of my life on this earth, I cannot think of it.

I can't even bear to look at David anymore as he continues on to the lone traffic light before the highway junction.

When the light turns green, David slams his hand against the dashboard and then does a screeching U-turn. He drives until he returns to the spot in the road where he last saw the injured animal.

The opossum is gone.

David puts on his hazards, takes a flashlight from the glove compartment, and exits the car. He walks a few steps down the center of the road, swinging the flashlight in a slow arc. "C'mon. Where are you?" he grumbles. There is no blood or fur on the road.

An oncoming car slows and flashes its brights at David. He waves it on.

In the restored quiet, David turns his flashlight toward a rustling among the fallen branches on the shoulder. Yellow eyes gleam back at him.

"You okay, pal?"

In apparent answer, the opossum scampers into the brush and then climbs the nearest tree with ease.

David finally allows himself a smile, gets back into his car, and drives off.

Ninety minutes later, David walks under the bright lights of the hallway leading to his office. Although he wears an expensive suit and a tie that would pay for a month of pig feed, the overall effect is wrong; his cheeks are too hollow, the circles under his eyes are too dark, his hair barely brushed. He looks rumpled from the inside out.

Martha spots him. "You're late."

David grumbles an inaudible response.

"You okay?" she asks.

"Swell. Can't you tell?"

"You look like crap. Something happen?" Martha sniffs the air around David and grimaces. "And what's that smell?"

"Don't ask. Find Chris, please."

"You're already late for the partners' meeting," Martha says as she picks up the receiver and dials.

"Don't care." David's tone cuts off further discussion, and he walks into his office.

Chris is at his office in seconds. She's wearing yesterday's clothes. Before David can open his mouth, she tells him, "I've been trying to call you for the past two hours. Those bastards did get all the notes. I checked it all over again twice last night."

David slumps into his chair in relief and finally offers Chris a smile. "Then we should have one hell of a response."

"Already working on it."

"I'm sorry I snapped at you last night. I should've known better."

Chris waves David off, already beyond the incident. "You can grovel for forgiveness later. We've got work to do."

"Who's doing the papers with you?"

"One of the newbies. Dan something or other."

"Any good?"

"Really smart, but . . ."

"What?"

Chris shrugs. "You'll see." Chris leans in toward David and suddenly crinkles her nose. "What the heck is that smell?"

"The cats peed on my shoes," he answers.

"And you still wore them?"

"They peed on all my shoes." David buzzes Martha on the intercom.

"Yes, O cranky one?" Martha answers through the speaker.

"Can you find Dan something or other and get him to come into my office? And I need a wet rag and some soap."

Within moments, a breathless twenty-four-year-old clearly in need of more exercise and less cookies fills David's doorway.

"You called for me?" he gasps.

David waves him in. "Daniel, right?"

The kid enters, gives a shy, obviously lovestruck hello to Chris, and then takes the seat next to her. "Yes."

"I hear you've been working hard. Thank you," David says. Daniel steals a glance at Chris, looking for guidance.

"You're okay," she tells him. "Just think of what a normal person would say and try to say that."

Daniel thinks for a moment. "I love this work," he gushes to David with a smile that makes his shiny face look even younger.

Chris shakes her head in dismay.

"What's wrong? Did I say something wrong?" Daniel asks.

"I said 'a normal person.'"

"But it's the truth."

Chris nods. "And that's what's so very sad."

"C'mon, leave him alone." David comes to Dan's aid. "Enthusiasm is a good thing. It reminds me of—"

"Don't say it, David," Chris orders.

"It reminds me—" David begins again.

"Don't say it!"

"—of Chris here," David finishes with a grin.

"Argh!" Chris moans. "You really suck."

Daniel turns to Chris with renewed confidence. "Like you? Really?"

"No, not really," Chris spits.

David quickly catches Dan's eye, winks at him, and then gives him a barely discernible nod. "It looks like you're going to have another late night. Here's what I'd like you to do..."

David ticks off ten other tasks that I do not understand either because I never did in life or because it is becoming too hard to hold on to the knowledge of such narrow things.

Cindy is awakened by the sound of the lab door being unlocked. For a moment, her eyes show excitement, as if she believes this may be the instant of Jaycee's return.

But it is not Jaycee who appears. It is Jannick. Cindy grunts in warning.

Jannick moves to Jaycee's desk and turns on the computer terminal. Then he sits in Jaycee's chair and positions it so he faces the Cube.

"Just you and me, Cindy," Jannick says. "No show, no tricks, no distractions." Jannick takes out a notepad and a pen. "Now, what is your name?" he says as he signs.

Cindy watches, but does not respond. After a few seconds, Jannick repeats the question. His voice is surprisingly gentle, but he might as well be talking to a stone wall.

"Okay," he says. "How about your favorite food? What is your favorite food?" Jannick asks slowly as his hands form the words.

Again, Cindy shows no indication of understanding or any intention to respond.

"Do you want peanut butter?" Jannick pulls a small jar out of a bag he's brought and moves toward the Cube, holding the jar before him as an offering. As Jannick gets closer, Cindy's lips curl around her teeth. Jannick opens the jar and gingerly places it in the Cube.

Cindy takes the jar and pushes it back out of the Cube and onto the floor, where it rolls to Jannick's feet.

"Just give me one word," Jannick says, his frustration mounting. "Any word. Anything close to a word. Just use your hands. Show me I'm wrong, damn it!"

Cindy is either unwilling or unable to respond. She turns in the Cube so that her back is now facing Jannick.

Jannick stares at the Cube in silence for several minutes, finally throws his hands up, and then walks out of the lab.

Still in a suit and tie from his long day of demanding clients and scheming adversaries, David has fallen asleep on our couch.

He used to be a remarkably deep sleeper. It was something of a running joke between us. The dogs could be barking at the cats sleeping on his head while the phone was ringing, and still he would slumber on. It was as if he knew I'd be there to deal with these interferences so that no one would come to harm. It was my joy to know that he trusted his life with me enough to believe that it would support him even when he wasn't paying attention to it. Now that he is alone, however, every squeak or bump robs him of whatever peace he finds in the darkness behind his eyelids.

It's been so rare to see him asleep that I can't stop myself and I lean over him to try to take in his relaxed features, his eyelashes, the top of his lip, his smell. I miss the feel of his face against mine.

The doorbell rings and somewhere in another part of the house, the dogs begin to bark. David's eyes try to open, but he is too tired. "Helena? Thank God," he murmurs. "I dreamed that you had..."

Somehow, in a way I do not understand, in this minute of this hour of this day of this month of this year, I'm again in David's physical perception of this world. I begin to panic because there's so much I want to share with him before the opportunity is lost. I move to kiss him, to tell him about Charlie and Cindy, and to assure him that everything will work out—which is precisely what I pray for him to tell me.

But I'm too late. His eyes have opened and now he's looking through me. I'm already gone for him.

David mumbles my name uncertainly and then, jolted to full consciousness by the doorbell and the barking dogs, he rises and shakes away the cobwebs of his memory of me.

He glances at his watch. Eight forty-five PM.

At the front door, David finds Chip, Bernie, and Skippy trying to scratch through the wood to get to the person on the other side. He attempts to quiet the dogs but by now they're too worked up.

David opens the door and Sally, dressed in a winter coat, gives him a small, awkward wave. "I hope I'm not too late, Mr. Colden."

"No, not at all." David gestures her inside. She offers her hand, and David takes it.

Once Sally enters the house, Bernie makes a move to jump on her, but she puts her hand out, palm down. "No sir," she says in a clear firm voice. Bernie obediently sits on his haunches, as do the other two dogs almost in unison. Sally gives each dog a small bone-shaped cookie that she pulls from the pocket of her coat. "Easy now," she cautions Bernie, and he takes the treat most gingerly from her hand. "I hope you don't mind, Mr. Colden. I like to praise jumpers that keep all four on the floor."

I can see that David is impressed. "As far as I know, nothing bad ever came from giving a dog a cookie."

"Hmm. I like that."

David brings Sally to the living room and they sit across from each other. The two big dogs settle down quickly. Skippy, however, takes up position directly in front of Sally's chair and stares at her with mild suspicion. Sally moves to scratch Skippy's ears, but he's having none of that and retreats to a spot a few feet away.

I'm vaguely pleased this woman has not so quickly won over my dog.

"I'm guessing this is Skippy," Sally says.

"He is. I take it you're okay with the dogs, cats...?"

"...pigs, horses, sheep, cows. Animals have never been the problem. Not the four-legged kind, at least."

"For what it's worth, Helena always thought Thorton was a jerk."

"Thanks. I wish it had worked out differently."

"But then you wouldn't be here. Joshua tells me you have a son."

"Yes. Joshua's filled you in on my situation?"

"Yeah. He said you wanted me to have the whole picture."

"I find the truth works best for me; I'm not smart enough to keep all the lies straight in my head anymore." Sally laughs at herself. "My son can be engaging, charming, even normal, but sometimes he's not. I love him with every fiber, but I'm his mother. He can be frustrating to be with, particularly if you're not expecting it."

"It must've been hard, working full-time and being there for him."

Sally shrugs. "You do what you need to do. It's only hard if you think you've got a choice in the matter. Once you realize that you don't, well, it all becomes pretty clear, doesn't it?"

"I guess."

"You don't sound convinced."

Now it's David's turn to laugh at himself. "Is it that obvious?"

"After your loss, you're entitled to your doubts, Mr. Colden—"

"—David, please. When I hear Mr. Colden, I always feel the urge to turn around and look for my father."

"David it is. I'd prefer Sally."

"Good. Me, too."

Sally pats her lap for Skippy to come closer, but he declines. "So, David, do you have thoughts about how you'd like this to work—if, I mean, you decide to hire me?"

"Honestly, I'm not even sure what to ask you. I guess it comes down to the fact that my wife's animals are used to a lot of attention from her and I can't do that for them. I need to get back to work and regroup. Is this something you can and want to do?"

"Yes," she answers without hesitation.

"I'm a little concerned that you might find some of the day-to-day stuff a step backward for you."

"What? Beneath me?"

"I suppose that's one way of putting it."

Sally laughs again. "I started out cleaning kennel cages. I'm a vet tech, not a neurosurgeon. I'll take care of all the animals—dogs, horses, pigs, cats, whatever you've got. You don't need to worry about them. I can also do housekeeping and cooking for you. I have my own car and will do shopping and make sure you have clean clothes and food in the fridge. I can even stay over if you're stuck in the city, as long as my son can stay, too. I also would like to be able to have him come here after school, if you don't mind. He's very well behaved. I assume that's okay."

"Sure. But I don't know anything about Asperger's, other than the little bit Joshua told me."

"In Clifford's case, the disease causes impaired non-verbal communication. That's pretty typical. He can't read non-verbal cues and doesn't express them well. He's been tested and has above-average intelligence and verbal development, but struggles to relate in social settings; he can't make the verbal and non-verbal fit together. He wants to get through to people so much that he gets tied up in his own head."

"God, that sounds awful."

"We're working on it. He's in a really excellent program now. They try to train these kids to recognize and understand non-verbal communication. For you and me, we don't even think about what a nod of the head means; Clifford has to learn that through repetition and exercises—like someone learning to play the piano or sign language."

"Anything I need to be careful about with him?"

"Not really. He doesn't like loud noises. He draws a lot when he's anxious. Hypergraphia is the name for it. Children with Asperger's sometimes are blessed with an exceptional skill. In Clifford's instance, he's very talented with a pencil and paper."

"Really? What types of things does he draw?"

"Not a lot of rhyme or reason to it; whatever pictures he sees in his head. I think maybe it's his way of trying to compensate for the gaps in his communication."

"He'll be okay around the animals?"

"Oh, my, yes." Sally laughs. "If God's made the animal that can bother my son, I haven't found it. He's going to love your animals, feels comfortable around them. I wonder sometimes if he just sees the world the same way they do."

"I'd like to meet him," David says.

"You will. With all the animals you've got, I doubt wild horses could keep Cliff away."

"I told Joshua that I'd match what Thorton paid you."

"That's certainly one of the reasons why I'm here."

"Money's not the issue for me. I just need someone I can trust with everyone here. I need someone I can count on."

"I understand completely. I won't leave you hanging. You respect me and I'll respect you. Don't take advantage of me and I won't take advantage of you."

"That seems fair." David nods and breathes a sigh of relief. "I really didn't know what I'd do if I didn't figure something out."

"Yeah, well, me neither."

"By the way, you wouldn't happen to know how to stop cats from peeing outside the litter box, would you?"

"As a matter of fact..."

David and Sally spend the next hour discussing the nuts and bolts of running my home—who gets fed what and when, who can eat next to each other, who can be "difficult," where the fuse box is located, and how to placate half a dozen angry cats.

I stop listening after a few minutes; it is far too painful for me to overhear the details of the living.

Following the meeting with my husband, Sally returns to her small but clean and ordered apartment. A young woman meets her at the door and signals for her to be quiet.

"Clifford put himself to bed. He said he was tired of waiting," the woman says quietly.

"Did he behave?"

"My Cliffy? He was the perfect gentleman. He even helped me fold laundry."

Sally's shoulders drop in relief. "Thank you so much, Annie. Cliff feels comfortable with you."

"It was no problem, really. How'd the interview go?"

"Good. I can have the job." At this news, Annie lets out a squeak of excitement and gives Sally a hug.

"That's a relief."

"You're not kidding."

"What's the husband like?"

"He seems nice enough. Tired, struggling to put one foot in front of the other."

"So, you're going to take the job, right? I mean, what've you got to lose?"

"Yeah, I'm going to take it," Sally says with some weariness. "But I'm not fooling myself. There's always something more to lose."

After Annie leaves, Sally sits quietly at her dimly lit kitchen table and sips a cup of tea. Notwithstanding her brave words to David, I can tell that she, too, has her doubts about choices she's made and whether some consequences were avoidable or at least foreseeable. Lost in those thoughts, Sally rises from the table and walks into what I assume qualifies in her house as "the living room." Several framed photographs line the wall, and she moves toward them.

In one picture, a younger, joyous Sally dressed in a wedding gown holds hands with her new handsome husband in military uniform. Sally kisses the tips of her fingers and then touches the man in the picture.

Sally next moves to a photograph of her husband holding two-year-old Clifford in front of a brightly lit Christmas tree. Sally grins at the memory of a happy holiday long past.

Sally's gaze then lands on an older black-and-white photograph of a young girl sitting in the lap of a stern-looking man while a pretty young woman looks out from behind the chair. No one in that picture is smiling. The young girl looks just like Sally. I'm assuming from the resemblance that the man and the woman are her mother and father.

Sally touches the image of her father, but quickly pulls her hand back as if the picture burns her fingers.

8

By your actions, so shall you be judged.

In the three days that Sally has worked for my husband, her actions have been true to her words. She's taken care of everything for David so that when he finally arrives home at night, he doesn't need to acknowledge that he lives with my animals. Even the dogs no longer try to get his attention. They sense what I already know: The wall surrounding David now is just too high.

Sally, on the other hand, is well along in gaining the trust and affection of my dogs, at least Bernie and Chip. This largely has been a function of three things. First, Sally is extremely kind to them in word and demeanor. She has not raised her voice—even when Bernie, in a fit of enthusiasm, knocked over the dry-cleaning delivery man, or Chip stole (and then ate) a new loaf of bread off the kitchen counter. Both times Sally laughed. Dogs love laughter; I think to their ears it is the sound of safety and acceptance.

Second, Sally is confident. Her movements with the dogs are smooth and deliberate, as if she has a plan and they're a part of it. Frightened people do frightening things. Dogs do not like to be with frightened people.

Third, Sally makes it a point of cooking for the dogs. She'll add rice or scrambled eggs to their dog food. One dinner, she cooked a pound of ground turkey and dished it out to them in chicken broth. My dogs generally are not finicky eaters, but they love flavors. They like people who give them flavors.

The cats are still a little wary of Sally, Arthur barely acknowledges her (but neither has he tried to hurt her), Alice does as she is told, and Collette is, well, Collette.

Skippy, however, seems to me to be most like my husband at the moment—he still grieves. Skippy, more so than the other two dogs, knew the nuances of my day, my words, and my touch. We shared lunches together frequently off the same plate. When I cried over losing a difficult case, I believe Skippy tried to comfort me. When I was angry or frustrated, his antics amused me. When I spoke to him, I often used the same terms of endearment as I did with my husband—*honey, sweetie, handsome.*

Grief doesn't leave a great deal of room for new people or new experiences. I don't believe for a moment that Skippy dislikes Sally. I just think he's too weary to start all over again with another human who may disappear forever for reasons he can't control and doesn't understand.

If that description of my relationship with Skippy strikes you as too anthropomorphic, then you have both my apologies and my pity.

Clifford arrives at my house late in the afternoon of Sally's fourth day of work.

Standing on the front porch, he holds tightly to his mother's arm with one hand and his sketch pad and pencil with the other.

I can hear the dogs barking from the backyard. "There's nothing to be scared of, Cliff," Sally assures him.

"Are you sure?" Clifford asks in his cold monotone.

"I am." Sally kisses his forehead. Clifford relaxes his grip just a bit, enough for Sally to open the front door, and they step into the house.

Chip, Bernie, and Skippy scratch and bark behind the sliding glass door at the back of the house, desperate to come in and see the new boy. If Clifford feels something about the dogs, it doesn't show on his face; he just stares at them with his head slightly lowered and tilted to one side. The barking suddenly stops.

Sally ignores the dogs for the moment. "I'll make you a snack and then you can say hi to them," she says and leads Clifford to the dining room table. Clifford sits in one of the chairs and opens his pad to a clean page while Sally heads off to the kitchen.

Clifford's eyes seem to take in every detail of the dining room. He picks up his pencil and is poised to draw when the telephone in the kitchen rings. The effect on him is immediate and painful to watch—he squeezes his eyes shut and the pencil in his hand quivers. Sally answers David's call before the second ring. "Yes, he's here now...So far..." The words fade as I return to watch the boy.

Clifford drops down from his chair and walks to the large sliding glass door that separates him from the dogs. The dogs are instantly alert in anticipation as Clifford reaches for the door handle.

I know what will happen next because it is the same exact thing every time. Once the door is opened, the dogs will charge into the house like lunatics and run around for a few minutes before beginning to settle down. Bernie, Chip, or both will almost certainly jump on Clifford in a playful greeting. Skippy may nip at the cuffs of his jeans to show this new person that he is still alive. No harm will be done, but the boy may be frightened by the paws and the noise.

None of this, however, actually occurs this time.

Instead, Clifford slides the door open perhaps eight inches and squeezes his small frame through. Once outside, Clifford holds his arms stiffly down at his sides with his hands open and palms turned outward. He's completely still, but smiling at something off into the distance.

The dogs at first seem stunned that this strange boy has chosen to come out to see them. Then they sniff his offered hands. Chip licks Clifford's fingers and then, tail wagging, lies down on his stomach and whines.

Sally finds Clifford moments later. I thought she might be angry at the boy, but she isn't. She slides the door open a crack to speak with her son. Clifford is turned away from her so she cannot see his face. The dogs no longer are interested in coming inside or doing anything other than being with the boy. "You've made friends," she says gently.

"Why are they so sad?" Clifford asks.

"Someone they liked very much has died."

"Oh. Like Papa?"

"Yes, Clifford. Like your papa. Now please come inside. It's too cold for you without your coat."

"Can the dogs come in, too?"

"Of course."

"I like them."

"I know you do. Come inside now, please."

"Okay, Mama," Clifford says as he turns toward Sally and the door. "Mama?"

"Yes, honey?"

"There are still no telephones in heaven?"

"No. I'm sorry."

"Do you think he knows I think of him?"

"I'm sure he does."

I don't know what to make of this remarkable child who cannot understand human vocal inflection but somehow senses the loss felt by my animals who have no human voice. There's no meaning without context, and for Clifford I have no context. ·

I do know what I see, however, and in Clifford it is a gentle soul, old beyond his years and free of judgment. My animals take to him immediately, none more so than Skippy, who follows Clifford around the house as if they are old friends reunited following a long absence. Candidly, while I might have been jealous if the human partner to this love affair had been Sally, I feel only gratitude for Clifford and the grace he has brought to my house.

Max's sudden decision that it is "absolutely imperative" that David meet a new "whale" (firm slang for someone controlling more than seven figures in potential legal fees) results in David pulling into the driveway at nine forty-five PM.

David enters the dark, silent house and I can begin to feel some of his loneliness. What is it he was rushing to get home to anyway?

Bernie and Chip—who both look like they've just been awakened—give a few halfhearted barks in David's general direction. David tries to generate some canine enthusiasm for his arrival, but soon gives up. The two dogs return from whence they came, probably the bedroom floor. Skippy is nowhere to be seen, which by itself is not unusual as he has taken to guarding my side of the bed.

David heads to the kitchen eager for a note from Sally or some other evidence of another human presence in the house, but finds nothing. The sink is empty of dishes. Cleaned dog and cat food bowls lie on the counter. It looks like everyone has eaten and gone to bed. This is precisely what David believed he wanted when he hired Sally—someone to deal with all the life in his house.

David pours himself a glass of wine from an open bottle in the fridge and then moves his attention to a stack of mail on the kitchen table. He quickly flips through the letters and stops at a large, thick brown mailer envelope addressed to him from Grumberg Architects, Inc. I can see from David's face that he knows exactly what's inside, although I've never heard of the group.

David rips open the package and pulls out a letter and several large folded sheets of paper. He reads the letter first.

Dear Mr. Colden:

With many apologies for the delay, enclosed you will find the final blueprints for the garden you have requested. We have been in contact with the stonemason and the contractor and are happy to advise you that they believe they can obtain the quantities of the particular stone you requested in time to begin construction after the new year. The garden could then be finished in time for May plantings.

We do hope you like the design. We have carefully studied the blueprints for several historic English country gardens and have tried to come up with something that reflects the same general feel (on a reduced scale, of course). Please call me after you have had a chance to review the plans.

> Very truly yours,
> Arthur Grumberg Jr.
> Enclosures

David drops the letter onto the table and moves to the folded pages. He opens them slowly, almost as if he's frightened of their contents. I assume this is all some mistake. David cares about gardens as much as I care about attorney billing rates. But I see David's hand tremble as he opens the last corner of the final page.

There, spread out on the kitchen table, is the blueprint for a large garden set within a circular stone wall.

I know this garden. This is my garden.

David passes his hand over the blueprint, imagining the texture of the stones. Beyond that, I cannot see because my eyes are filled with tears.

Sally steps quietly into the kitchen and watches David in respectful silence for a few seconds. She does not want to interrupt him, but also does not wish to spy. Finally, she clears her throat.

Startled out of his thoughts, David spins around. "I didn't think you were still here. Did something happen?"

Sally shakes her head. "Sorry. We were in the back room watching some TV and we all fell asleep."

"I got delayed. I should've called."

Sally waves him off. "There was no need."

"How was your son's visit?"

"Great. Clifford would move in if he could." Sally looks at the blueprints over David's shoulder. "Are you planning to have some work done around here?"

"No. Not anymore. I was going to surprise Helena for her birthday. She always wanted a garden like this."

I can't believe he remembered. We were in my Ithaca apartment late one night a month after we'd met, curled up in bed together, warm against each other while the wind howled outside. *The Secret Garden*—the original 1949 version with Margaret O'Brien—was on the local television station. The movie was in black and white, except for the scenes where the garden came back to life. The transition in the movie to color—to life—took my breath away. I leaned my head against David's shoulder then and said, "I'd love a garden like that someday and we can sit together among the trees and the flowers and forget the rest of the world." My words came out before I'd thought to stop them. It was too much too early, too into the future for a boy burned so thoroughly by the past.

But to my relief David didn't withdraw. "Then I will make one for you," he whispered back. "And on cool summer evenings we will sit among the trees and flowers and look for fairies in the moonlight."

It was one of those moments when I was able to see into that well-guarded part of him—the part that really longed to be carefree and fun and part of something and, I guess, loved.

I knew I loved him then.

I know I still do.

Now, in the cold kitchen of the home I used to share with him, David stands in mute, solitary anguish, examining the garden that will never be.

Sally puts on her reading glasses and looks through the blueprints more carefully. "Wow. That's some present."

"It was at a point when we believed the disease was going to mean surgery, and recovery. I thought the garden would be a good place for her to sit and heal. Both of us, I guess. We got that wrong. I never called the architect to cancel the plans after...you know..." David's voice drifts off.

"I'm so sorry. This would have been beautiful to see."

Skippy enters the kitchen, his little nails tapping on the floor. Clifford follows a step behind. Both Clifford and the dog give big yawns.

"Clifford, this is Mr. Colden."

David bends down slightly to get into Clifford's field of vision. He speaks slowly. "Nice to meet you. How was your day?"

Clifford looks first to his mother, who encourages him. "It's okay," she says.

Clifford's eyes focus at a spot above David's head and he smiles. "I like your home," he says in his unyielding monotone. "I like all the animals, but I like Skippy most of all. He is a good dog."

"Yes, he is, and you're welcome here anytime."

Skippy trots back out of the kitchen, and Clifford follows him.

"Can I get you something to eat or anything before we go?" Sally asks.

"Looks like Skippy's made a new pal," David says.

"You've no idea. They've been inseparable all day."

"Obviously it's up to you," David says, "but it seems kind of silly to go home tonight just to turn around and come back in the morning. You two can have the spare bedroom and I'm sure I've got extra toothbrushes and things."

"I don't want to impose."

I only now get how desperate David is to avoid being alone in the house. "No imposition at all," he says. "I need to be up and out before you get up anyway. C'mon, I'll show you where everything is." David leads Sally out of the kitchen and back toward the den and the spare bedroom.

"That certainly makes sense, but I don't know if Clifford will be okay with it. He's got his routines and, well…" David and Sally stop at the door to the den. Clifford is curled up on the couch under a throw rug with Skippy resting between his legs. Bernie and Chip sleep on the floor next to the couch, and a few of the cats sleep precariously balanced (as only cats can do) on the arms of the sofa.

"Like I said," Sally says, finally allowing herself to feel a small measure of relief, "I'm sure Cliff will be fine staying here."

Four hours later, when the house is in the deepest part of sleep, David rises from our bed, throws on a bathrobe, and returns to the kitchen. He pours himself a snifter of cognac, picks up the blueprints, and brings them and the liquor to the dining room. Skippy waits for him there.

"Why are you awake?" David asks. I know the answer, even though David does not. Skippy wakes up every night at this time and wanders the house looking for me. Tonight is no different, except perhaps that his apparent sense of urgency is diminished. He seems more tired or, perhaps, resigned.

David sits down at the table, pats his lap, and Skippy jumps up. The three of us sit in the dining room poring over the details of the blueprints until the cognac is gone and the first sliver of light appears in the eastern sky.

9

The following day, David, Chris, and Dan appear in the courtroom of Judge Arnold Allerton to explain why they should not be sanctioned.

Allerton is a federal judge and that means, as David once explained to me, he is appointed for life. I know from David that Allerton was a Yale Law School classmate of Max and that because of some incident from those days, Allerton is barely civil to Max to this day. It is for this reason and one other that David always tries to step lightly in Allerton's courtroom. The other reason is that Allerton has absolutely no patience for the gamesmanship that is the bread and butter of all litigation. He is one of the few judges whom David both fears and respects.

Across the aisle from David and his team sit two particularly smug-looking lawyers. The older one looks like a woodchuck I raised in vet school and this makes his scowl difficult to take seriously. No one shook hands when they entered the courtroom and they will not do so when they leave today. There is no pretense of cordiality. Instead, all the lawyers wait impatiently for Allerton to enter the room and take the bench.

Within moments, there are two loud raps on a closed door behind the dais. The door flies open and a short rotund woman in her mid-forties yells, "All rise!" The lawyers are instantly on their feet. Judge Allerton enters holding a stack of documents and drops into his throne-like chair with a huff.

It might be the fact that he is on a raised dais or that he is covered in a black robe, but Allerton seems larger than everyone else in the courtroom. He is completely bald, which makes him look ageless and somehow angry.

"Be seated," the court clerk calls. The attorneys again follow the instruction.

Allerton peers down from the bench. "Someone want to tell me what this is about?"

Both David and the woodchuck are instantly on their feet like racehorses jockeying for position out of the gate. Allerton rolls his eyes. "Okay, children, let me hear from the movant first."

The woodchuck begins a Dickensian tale of woe about his client's repeated attempts to discover critical information from and about David's key expert who is expected to testify at trial only a few short weeks away and about David's delays and, finally, the coup de grâce, David's failure to turn over a set of documents "absolutely essential" to the trial.

David jumps up to respond but Allerton shoots him down. "Not yet, Mr. Colden. Precisely how much delay was there, Mr. Jared?" Allerton questions David's adversary.

"Excuse me, Your Honor?" Jared asks.

"You said that Mr. Colden delayed in getting you documents. Quantify that for me. Weeks? Months?"

"Well the exact time...I...ur...I don't really think..." Jared's colleague hands him a note and he quickly reads it. "Four days, Your Honor."

"And at that time Mr. Colden had requested an extension, had he not?"

"I believe so, Your Honor, but—"

"You 'believe so,' Mr. Jared? 'I believe' is for the tooth fairy and Santa Claus. We're here because of your sanctions motion. That's a very serious motion. I think you'd better do a damn sight more than 'I believe.' Did he request an extension or not?"

"Yes, he did," Jared answers. Jared clearly didn't expect things to go this way, and he isn't happy about it.

"And did Mr. Colden tell you why he wanted the extension?"

"I'm not sure."

"Oh, you can do better than that, Mr. Jared. Do you know or not?" The word *not* echoes in the otherwise quiet courtroom.

Jared's colleague hands him another note. Jared scans the note quickly. "I believe—"

"Pardon me?" Allerton snaps.

"I mean, yes, we know he stated that he needed more time because his wife had died...unfortunately." Jared then turns to David. "My condolences, of course, for your loss." The woodchuck's offer of sympathy, made for the first time during a proceeding to sanction my husband, is almost comical.

Allerton apparently doesn't see the humor. "You are correct in your facts, Mr. Jared. Mr. Colden's wife died following a long and cruel illness. And so he asked you for a brief extension and you said what?"

"Mr. Colden is part of a very large firm, Your Honor. Surely there are other capable lawyers who could have—"

"I asked you about your response to him, sir. Did you under-stand my question?"

After several seconds of hesitation, Jared answers weakly, "We declined the request."

"Why did you do that, sir?"

"The schedule was—"

"I see. And then there's the matter of the documents you say Mr. Colden is withholding, correct?" Allerton asks as he picks up a document from the pile in front of him. "What document in par-ticular was missing?"

Jared slides into a well-rehearsed response. "Mr. Colden's office would be—"

"Are you aware of the existence of a specific document that has been improperly withheld or not?" The frustration is dangerously clear in Allerton's voice.

"I think…Not a specific document, no," Jared finally concedes.

"The reason why I ask, Mr. Jared, is because I have an affi-davit here from a Ms. Jerome that includes her sworn statement that they have reviewed everything again and double-checked with the expert and—get this—there are no other documents. Period." Allerton flips through the pages of Chris's sworn statement. "Have you seen this affidavit, Mr. Jared?"

Jared looks at his younger colleague, who nods slightly. "Yes, we've seen it," Jared admits.

"Well then, is Ms. Jerome just lying? Are you accusing her of perjury?"

"I believe she is mistaken," Jared answers.

Allerton makes a show of looking through the papers on his desk. "Well then, where's your answering affidavit? Where's the document where you lay out your proofs why you believe she's wrong—or worse, has committed perjury? I can assure you, if you have proof that Ms. Jerome has lied to this court, then I will not rest until she's disbarred. I've done it before. I will not abide liars in my courtroom. Just give me the proof."

"We just received the affidavit last night. We have not had time—"

"According to the fax stamp on the document, you got the affidavit yesterday at three twenty-two PM. That's not night."

"I was out of the office at another engagement when it came in and I didn't see—"

"But you're part of a very large firm, Mr. Jared," Allerton answers. "Surely there are other capable lawyers who could have drafted some response." Even Jared knows enough at this point to keep his mouth shut. "Now, I also have before me Mr. Colden's application to adjourn the trial date in this matter."

"We oppose that application because—"

That's as far as Jared gets before Allerton snarls, "I think I've heard enough from you today, sir." Jared sits down reluctantly. "It seems to me, Mr. Jared, that with all of your 'I believes' and 'I thinks' you might be well served with some additional time to learn the ins and outs of your case. I wouldn't want to deprive you of the opportunity to present every learned argument to the court."

The woodchuck pops up again, and I'm reminded of the arcade game Whac-A-Mole. "But Your Honor, the trial date is set. We have witnesses flying in from all over the world. My client expects—"

Allerton shoots Jared a chilling smile. "I understand," he says. And then—whack! "Perhaps you'd like to bring your client into my courtroom, Mr. Jared. I'd be more than happy to explain to him the rationale for my ruling and the role your conduct played in it. Shall we adjourn until noon then, so you can get your client?"

Jared's face could not be any redder. "That won't be necessary, Your Honor. I'm sure my client will understand that the court has a very busy calendar."

"I had thought so. I'm putting the trial over for three months. My clerk will issue a revised scheduling order. Good day to you all."

The clerk calls, "All rise," and then Allerton is gone. Jared and his colleague race out of the courtroom—either to share the bad news with their client or to avoid having to face David in his victory. Chris, David, and Daniel watch them scurry out. "Like big rats, don't you think?" Chris asks.

"Not like rats," David answers. "Once you get past the tail thing, rats are actually okay."

David gives congratulatory handshakes to his team, but in light of the win he just obtained, his mood seems subdued. Although David's work life just got a whole lot better, I'm not at all certain he really wanted the luxury of empty time. The pressure of a trial would have been just the thing to perpetuate the fantasy that it was all business as usual. Now there would be more freedom from which David would need to escape.

Chris must sense the same reserve. "That was priceless. You can smile now."

"Let me buy you guys lunch at Rizzo's," David offers. "Go on ahead and order appetizers. I need to make a few calls first."

Chris searches David's face with concern and then shrugs. "Don't be too long." Chris and Daniel quickly pack their materials and leave. As they walk out, I can hear Dan enthusiastically recapping the blow-by-blow of the proceeding to Chris as if she hadn't just seen the whole thing.

David, now alone in the courtroom, collapses into his chair—partly in relief, partly in exhaustion, and partly in sadness. He just sits there, his eyes moving from the judge's bench, to the jury box, to the now vacant opposing counsel table, and then to his wedding band. It's like he's trying to connect dots that refuse his desire for order and symmetry.

In a few minutes, Judge Allerton, this time dressed in just a suit, returns alone to the courtroom. David instantly jumps to his feet and starts collecting his papers. "I'm sorry, Judge. I'll be out of here in a moment."

"No need to get up, Mr. Colden. I'm just getting a few pleadings," Allerton says as he moves toward the bench and starts shuffling some pages.

David remains standing. "I want to thank you for...you know...being understanding of my situation."

Allerton looks up from what he's doing. "Please don't thank me for treating you like a human being. I would've hoped that our profession had not sunk so low that common courtesy is actually shocking."

"Perhaps not shocking, but certainly appreciated."

Judge Allerton nods in understanding. "August 12, 1997, ten thirty-seven PM."

"Excuse me?"

"August 12, 1997, ten thirty-seven PM. The exact time my wife died."

"I'm sorry. I didn't realize."

"I can tell you that it does get better. Not a day goes by when I don't think of her, but it does get better."

David's lips begin to tremble. Judge Allerton looks away and quickly pulls together his papers. "Good luck to you, Mr. Colden. And do try to settle this case. I'm sure you now have better ways to spend your time."

"Thank you, Judge," David whispers back as Allerton exits through the door behind the dais.

At about the same time that David leaves the courthouse, Sally enters Joshua's examination room carrying Skippy under her arm.

"This is a nice surprise," he says. "Everything okay?"

"Everything's fine."

"How's it working out with David?"

"I take back every horrible thing I've ever said about you."

"I wasn't aware of any, but that's good to know."

"I owe you a big one."

Joshua shakes his head. "You deserve to have something work out for you for once."

"I will give you an 'amen' to that."

"So, what can I do for you?"

"I was wondering what you can tell me about this guy," Sally says as she gently places Skippy on the exam table.

Joshua takes Skippy and playfully lifts him into the air. Skippy seems to enjoy this. "You know about his condition, right?"

"I know it's an issue with his heart, but David was a little fuzzy on details."

Joshua nods. "I was there the day Helena found him and worked him up." Joshua takes the stethoscope from around his neck and listens to Skippy's heart. Skippy sits patiently through this; he's been examined by Joshua many times. "His left ventricle is about half the normal size."

"Is there maybe something more I could be doing? Clifford's getting very attached to him."

Joshua returns the stethoscope to his neck and checks the color of Skippy's gums as he talks. "It's structural. He's doing the best with what the Lord gave him. I'm sorry, Sally."

"And so, as he gets older..."

Joshua's examination moves on to Skippy's ears and eyes. "Yes, his heart will get weaker. It's already enlarged—trying to do the work it can't do. He'll eventually go into heart failure. We'll be able to up his Lasix and increase his digitalis for a while at that point, but it's a losing battle."

"No surgical option?"

"No, not even if he were human. Too much damage. He'd never survive."

"Of course Cliff would've had to pick a dying dog," Sally mutters.

"I'm not surprised. There was always something a little bit special about him," Joshua says as he rubs Skippy's lush black fur. Joshua accidentally touches Sally's hand and he quickly moves it away. "Helena said he was the perfect little husband."

"It's his eyes," Sally offers. "There's an intelligence there that's hard to ignore, don't you think?"

"Yeah, I do."

"How long do we have with him?"

"He keeps surprising me. Today he looks pretty good, but I guess he can turn quickly. In the end, it will be a quality-of-life decision," Joshua says, unable to keep the sadness from his voice. I know Joshua dreads the thought of having to make that decision yet again. "I only hope Skippy will make it clear when it's time."

Sally lifts Skippy off the table onto the floor, where he sits at Sally's feet, watching the conversation. "I'm so damn tired of having to say good-bye."

"I understand." At this moment Joshua must be thinking of his own good-byes—to his marriage, to me, to his little boy.

Sally searches Joshua's face and settles on his eyes before he turns away again in embarrassment. "Yes," she says, "I believe you do."

"For whatever small consolation it's worth, I don't think Skippy shares our conception of his disease. I bet he feels today pretty much like he felt yesterday and the day before. He gets up, eats, plays, maybe chases a chipmunk or two. That's his day. He's living. He's not waiting."

Just then a giant Newfoundland blasts through the door and bounds into the exam room with a harried Eve close behind.

"I'm so sorry, Dr. J," Eve says breathlessly. "He just got away from me."

The Newfie jumps on Joshua and they are nearly face-to-face. The dog lets out a deep "woof" and then licks Joshua's nose. He giggles like a little boy and his entire face opens up. Sally laughs, too. Skippy, though, is not amused at the intrusion, and he growls.

"It's okay, Eve. I've got him," Joshua manages to say as he struggles to get the big dog's paws off his shoulders.

"It looks to me like the other way around," Sally says, still laughing.

"Let me introduce you to Newfie Pete. Another of Jimmy's rescues."

"Is he looking for a home, too?"

"No way," Joshua says as the dog gives his face a good coating of drool. "You're never leaving me, right, buddy?" Joshua hugs the dog's huge head.

Moments later, calm is restored and Joshua escorts Sally and Skippy out of his exam room. They pass the "holding room"—a wall of cages filled with cats and dogs in various states of injury or distress. The kittens that Jimmy had found are huddled together in a few cages.

"Tiny Pete?" she asks.

"You even remembered his name?"

"It's been tough to get that one out of my mind."

"He's doing pretty well."

"And?"

"And what?"

"And what about the hard sell. How he needs a home, how he shouldn't have to spend any more time in a cage. You know the routine."

"I wouldn't do that with you. I figure if you're not taking him, then there's a good reason."

Sally walks with Joshua and Skippy to the front entrance of the hospital in silence. Her face is a mask. She may be thinking of other cats and dogs she has known and buried over her life, or her husband, or Clifford, or she may simply be thinking about lunch. I just can't tell. I get the sense that, somewhere along the way, Sally has become truly expert at hiding what is most important to her just in case someone may be watching from the shadows.

At the front door, Sally turns her focus again on Joshua and gives him a knowing smile. "Oh, you are good, Joshua Marks. I'll give you that. Oh, yes, you're very good. The 'no-sell' sell. Almost had me, too."

"Apparently not good enough, though," Joshua says with a mischievous grin and a suggestion of hope in his voice.

"We'll see." Sally waves good-bye and walks with Skippy to her car.

Joshua watches her go. "Happy Thanksgiving," he calls after her, but Sally is already in the car and doesn't turn back.

10

Thanksgiving. I completely forgot about it.

Thanksgiving for us had always been something of an odd holiday. My father died in my last semester of vet school, and my mother joined him during the second year of our marriage. David's parents were long gone by the time I'd met him. With no children of our own and no parents, David and I couldn't even pretend we had a "family" in the "Hallmark Thanksgiving" sense.

There was never a roast turkey at our table because I was a vegetarian and David, out of respect for me, did not eat meat in the house. During the first few Thanksgivings of our relationship, I tried every type of fake turkey, even going so far one year as molding fermented tofu and mashed potatoes into the form of the giant bird. The reality, however, is that meat tastes like meat and nothing else does, so eventually I gave up. Instead, Thanksgiving dinner at our house was all about carbohydrates—mashed potatoes, stuffing, yams, bread—a vegetable or two, and very good wine.

Depending on their plans in any given year, we would force this carb-fest on Joshua, Liza and whoever she happened to be with at the time, Chris and her husband, Martha and her husband, and any single junior associate on David's team who had no place to go. These were humor-filled gatherings that made us feel like our house was full of life. It was that feeling of life that made us thankful.

Eventually on Thanksgiving night, once all the guests had left, we would clear the table and do the dishes together, giving the dogs, cats, and Collette whatever remained of the food. Exhausted and wine-buzzed, we would settle into the den with the dogs and watch *Homeward Bound*—that sappy movie about two dogs and a cat who get separated from their family and must overcome perils and obstacles to find their way home.

Homeward Bound was our *It's a Wonderful Life*, our *It's the Great Pumpkin, Charlie Brown*. We knew all the dialogue by heart and could repeat every scene. No matter how late it was, no matter how tired we were, regardless of whether David had to be at work the next day or I was on call, we would sit through all eighty-four minutes of the movie surrounded by our creatures. For this, too, we were thankful.

Seeing David enter our house now, looking weary and preoccupied, I'm certain that he also has been thinking about Thanksgiving. My husband, though, faces the Thanksgivings of his widowed future while I dwell on the Thanksgivings of our married past.

David gives the dogs a perfunctory greeting. Sensing his mood, they soon move off to other areas of the house. In the kitchen, David grabs an open bottle of wine from the refrigerator, pours himself a full glass, and skims through the mail. He skips through the bills and correspondence and pulls out a magazine—the jumbo "Thanksgiving Issue" of *Food and Wine*.

Taking his wine and magazine to the living room, David drops onto our couch and begins paging through the glossy images of the family gatherings and beautiful holiday tables he believes he will never see.

Sally emerges from the back of the house. "How was your day?"

David manages a smile. "Fine." The smile quickly becomes a smirk. "You know, people yelling at each other about money. Yours?"

"Great. No yelling and certainly no conversations about money, although I think Collette might be pushing us soon for a new house for her. How about some tea?"

"I'm good, thanks," David says, gesturing to his glass. Sally is about to tell David of her trip to see Joshua, but the look on David's face, the glass of wine in his hand, and finally the magazine in his lap make her think better of it. Instead, she starts collecting her bag and coat for her trip home as David watches her over his magazine.

"Clifford's not with you?" David sounds a little disappointed.

"No. He was tired, so the sitter put him to bed."

"How'd you pull him away from Skippy?"

"With difficulty."

"Big plans for Thanksgiving?" David asks her, waving the magazine in the air.

"Clifford and I are expected by my father and his wife. It's sort of a tradition."

David nods and takes a long drink from his glass. "I didn't realize your father was still with us."

"Alive and kicking. He remarried after my mother died."

"Does Cliff like her?"

"Not really. She's not my favorite, either. But she's a gracious host and treats Clifford well."

"Sounds like you've got a good plan then. If you're done early, you're welcome here. Our friend...my friend Liza will be coming over. And probably Joshua this year."

"Joshua? Does he really ever leave the hospital?" Sally asks.

"On Thanksgiving, at least, after he makes his rounds."

"Well, the offer is very thoughtful, but we probably won't be back until Friday morning. Will you be off from work?"

"Officially, yes. But I may go in. Still lots to catch up on."

"Well, I'll be here if you need to go, so don't worry."

"Thanks." David downs the rest of his wine as Sally puts on her coat. "Sort of odd, you know?"

"What's that?"

"Did you ever see *Rudolph the Red-Nosed Reindeer*?" he asks.

Sally smiles. "Every year."

"Remember the Island of the Misfit Toys? That used to be our house on Thanksgiving—the place where everyone with no better place could go and feel welcome." David refills his glass in the kitchen, and Sally waits for his return. "Now I guess I'm just another broken toy."

"It's hard. I know," Sally offers.

David clears his throat and tries to sound casual when he finally asks Sally, "So how long did it take you to...you know...with your husband...?"

Sally quickens her pace to leave. "I'm really the wrong person to use for comparison. I was young, with a child. It's just different."

David knows where he's not welcome. "I'm sorry. I didn't mean to pry. I just thought..."

"It's okay," Sally says as she concentrates way too hard on the act of putting on her gloves. "I'd better get going." As David walks her to the door, Sally mumbles something just below audible.

"Excuse me?" David asks.

Sally sighs, knowing that her plan for a quick getaway has failed. This time I understand her. It has failed mostly because, although Sally wants to believe she is hard and therefore immune from further hurt, she is anything but and just as vulnerable as she ever was. For her this means that when the next hurt comes—and she knows that it always does—she will not be able to wish it away or ignore it. Instead, she will need to live through it, and she's already done so much of that type of living.

Sally turns to face David straight-on and then gently places her hands on his shoulders. "The first holiday is by far the hardest. Try to stay out of the house until it's time to go to sleep. Distract yourself with whatever you can find that you won't feel bad about in the morning. No one—and I mean no one—will be able to understand, so don't ask for it, don't expect it, and don't be angry when you don't get it. Their perfect words will fail you. And so will yours. Understand?" Sally's voice trembles with memory.

She releases David's shoulders and gives him a quick peck on the cheek. "It's not my business to tell you how you should manage your pain," she says. "And God knows I don't have any good answers. But one thing I can tell you is that looking at your own grief is a lot like looking at the sun. You can't do it for very long before it screws up your vision. Sometimes permanently."

Without further comment, Sally turns up the collar of her coat against the cold and walks out of the house into the night.

Liza arrived at our home a little after two PM on Thanksgiving Day. Thankfully, she came without a date, but holding a pumpkin pie. The pie was a running joke. The three of us hate pumpkin pie. It is Collette's favorite, though.

The wine came out immediately, and Liza and David drank quickly—one glass, then another and then a third, all before the food made it to the table. The last several months have increased David's alcohol tolerance. Liza, however, was always something of a lightweight to begin with, and three glasses of wine in quick succession without any food took their toll on her. I guess that was her intention.

"You know," David says, taking a big gulp from his glass, "I think you may have a drinking problem."

Liza laughs into her glass. "Well, *there's* a pot, kettle, black thing if ever I heard one." She clinks David's glass with her own. "Besides, I can't have a drinking problem; I'm a mental health professional."

"I know it's not easy being here."

"Not easy, no. But at least with you I don't have to pretend." Liza slowly takes in the living room and then all my books still where I'd left them. "It's just that it's the first time I've been in this house without her being here. I've been avoiding it."

"Really? I didn't notice," David jokes.

They make small talk for an hour about David's job, Liza's patients, her new love interest of the moment (who "has the kids for the holiday"), Sally, and of course the animals. There is, however, a large white elephant in the room—and I am it and I hate being it. I become larger and whiter as their wine buzz begins to fade.

"Do you want to talk about how you're really doing?" Liza finally asks as the two of them sit down to a dinner from the small gourmet store in town—mashed potatoes, roast asparagus, stuffing, cranberries, and spinach.

"You first."

"C'mon now. Stop playing around. I'm worried about you."

"You said I had five years," David says as he makes himself a plate. "It hasn't even been two months."

"You have as long as you need. It's not a race."

"But ... ?"

"But the only difference between a rut and a grave is the depth and the grief. Moving on doesn't just happen. It takes some work, too."

"I thought I was working."

Liza makes a sweeping gesture with her arm toward the bookcases. "Nothing's been moved. I don't see a single box."

"So?"

"This house was all about Helena, and it still is. I bet if I went into the bedroom and opened up her closet, I'd still find her clothes."

"That's a pretty good bet. So what?"

"Doesn't it hurt every time you see her things?"

"Of course, but wouldn't it hurt more to get rid of them?"

"Sure, at first. It's called catharsis." Liza reaches out and touches David's hand. "It's why we bury people and have funerals instead of hanging the bodies from the ceiling. It hurts really, really bad and then the wounds scab over."

"Can we talk about something else? It's Thanksgiving, after all." David reaches for the wine bottle.

"Sure." Liza moves the food around on her plate for a few tense moments. "Who do you like for governor?" she says with smile.

David almost passes a mouthful of wine through his nose. Liza has never voted in any election and believes the capital of New York is Manhattan. When he finally composes himself, David asks, "Are you, you know, working past it?"

"I'm not a fair comparison. I mean, I knew her longer than you, but she wasn't my wife. I didn't share a bed with her. And besides, all joking aside, I do have five years of training in emotional objectivity, coping mechanisms, and grief counseling, and a dozen years of private practice in psychotherapy. You don't have any of that background."

"So, is that a yes or a no?"

Liza shrugs and looks down at her plate. "Both."

David pushes back from the table and rubs his hands together. "Enough shop talk. I've got something for you."

He leaves the room and returns a few seconds later with a small box wrapped in Christmas paper. He goes to the couch in the living room and pats the spot next to him. Liza joins him.

David hands Liza the package. "An early Christmas present, since you'll be in Mexico with what's-his-name."

She opens the paper to reveal a small square jewelry box. "You proposing to me?"

"Just open it, you moron."

Liza lifts the lid on the box. Her eyes widen and her breath catches. "Oh, my," is all she can manage before the tears come.

Like most women, over the years I'd accumulated several drawers of jewelry. Very few pieces actually had meaning to me and, of these, two mattered the most. The first, a pendant consisting of all the tags of the dogs I had loved and lost, was cremated with me at my request. Those tags had meaning only to me, so I thought that was fair.

The second item was an antique platinum-and-sapphire ring David had found in Paris during our honeymoon. Liza always loved the ring and jokingly (long before I knew I was sick and never after) asked me to leave it to her if I died first. This is what David gives to Liza now.

"I know Helena wanted to be sure you got it after…"

"That bitch," Liza sobs as she throws her arms around David and buries her face in his shoulder.

The doorbell rings and the dogs bark at the intrusion. "You better get the door," Liza says into David's shirt, but she shows no intention of letting go.

Before David can extract himself, Joshua lets himself in and, followed by the three dogs, finds Liza and David in the living room. David offers Joshua a weak smile.

"Is everyone all right?" Joshua asks over the sound of Liza's sobs.

"Just fine," David answers. "Our professionally trained and emotionally objective friend over here is just having a moment." Liza punches David on the shoulder. "Ouch."

"You're such a wuss," Liza says as she wipes her eyes. "Happy Thanksgiving, Joshua." Liza gives Joshua a kiss on the cheek. "Excuse me." Liza heads for the bathroom, leaving David and Joshua alone.

"I was beginning to wonder whether you were ever going to come over," David says.

"I know," Joshua says. "I wanted to be able to...I couldn't find the..."

David lifts himself off the couch. "I understand. I wouldn't be here, either, if I didn't live here."

"I didn't mean that." Joshua stops himself, closes his eyes and takes a deep breath. "Maybe I did."

"Doesn't matter." David hugs him. "You're here with me now."

Liza, a little more composed and blowing her nose, makes a noisy return.

David lifts his glass to Joshua and Liza. "Welcome to my home," he says. The emphasis on the word *my* is painfully clear.

"Now you just need to start filling it with your own things. Don't you think?" Liza turns to Joshua in the hope of extracting some moral support.

Joshua is a smart man. He's seen the house. "How does that poem go again?" Joshua asks. "The one about home?"

"'. . . bereft of anyone to please . . . ,'" Liza starts.

"'. . . it withers so,'" David finishes and then swallows the remains of his wine.

Barely five miles from David's house, Sally and Clifford finish their own modest but happy Thanksgiving dinner in their tiny dining room.

"Thank you, Mama. That tasted very good," Clifford says. It is precisely what a normal, polite, and well-brought-up nine-year-old would say at this moment, except that his voice is devoid of affect or warmth; it is like a compliment coming from the voice synthesizer of a computer.

Sally smiles back at her son. "You're very welcome. What did you like best?"

"Stuffing. You make the best stuffing."

"Well, thank you, Cliff. Would you like another piece of pie?"

Clifford rubs his stomach. "No thank you, Mama."

"You know that I'm very proud of you, son." For an instant, Clifford's eyes show understanding, but then he cocks his head to one side just like a dog in the face of something it doesn't comprehend. "I know you work very hard on your exercises and at school and I want you to know that I'm just so proud of you. You never forget that, okay?"

Clifford's face holds the same blank look. "Do you think Skippy's sleeping right now?"

Sally works hard to maintain her smile. For just one moment, she had allowed herself to believe that they were a normal family having a normal conversation that lasted more than one precise question and one specific answer. She had permitted herself to imagine that Clifford could verbally acknowledge her love for him.

"I suspect Skippy is asleep by now, honey," Sally answers. "Would you like to see him tomorrow?"

Clifford doesn't answer the question. He's already moved on to something else. "Can I watch television now, Mama?"

"Yes, you may," Sally says. "Only one of your DVDs, okay? It's already set up for you." Clifford hops down from the chair and runs into the adjoining room. Within seconds, I can hear the muffled sounds of the television.

Even with the noise, the apartment is remarkably still and quiet. This is what loneliness sounds like.

The phone in the kitchen rings. Sally stares at it like it is a downed power line—inherently dangerous, capable of causing great pain, and unpredictable. She finally answers it. "Yes?"

"Hi, Sally. It's Joshua. I'm not disturbing you, am I?"

"Nope."

"David said you were up with your father."

"Yes, well, I'm home now. Were you with David?"

"For a little while."

"How was he?"

"About what you'd expect, I guess."

"It was nice of you to go. It's a hard holiday to grieve."

"Yes, it is," Joshua answers from too-personal knowledge. "How was your holiday with your father?"

Sally laughs bitterly. "Not what you'd expect, I think."

"Oh?"

"Really long story," Sally says, closing off further inquiry.

"Well...," Joshua stammers. "I just really...um...I want to wish you and Clifford a happy Thanksgiving."

"Can you do me a favor?"

"Sure." Joshua braces for something rejecting.

"Let's you and I give each other the gift of three minutes of honesty. Tonight I'm just too old and too tired for anything else."

"Okay, starting when?"

"Right now," Sally says. "Why did you really want to call tonight?" Joshua pauses in his answer. "No thinking now," Sally commands. "Just tell me."

"Okay, here goes...Okay, now."

"I'm aging here, Joshua. Just get it out, man. Why did you call?"

Now Joshua's words come out in a rush. "I was thinking about you. Since you've reappeared after all this time, I find myself thinking about you. I don't really know why or what it means. But I'd like to take you out for an evening and see what happens?"

"Wow," Sally says. "That was good."

"Now your turn," Joshua says.

"No way," Sally says, laughing.

"But...but you said," Joshua stammers.

"I lied," she says, still laughing. "But I will accept your invitation for an outing. You can call in the IOU for your three minutes then."

"You're a cruel, cruel woman, you know that?" Joshua says, but his tone is lighthearted.

"I may be cruel, but I'm not stupid. And here's a down payment—you made me laugh tonight. I needed that. Thank you."

*   *   *

As the shadows outside my house deepen and finally—thankfully—turn to dark, David finishes the Thanksgiving dishes. Having Liza and Joshua over may have been a good thing for him, but I know he was happy to see them go so he could face the white elephant by himself.

David eyes my books on the shelves in the living room and Liza's parting words echo in his ears—"This house was all about Helena, and it still is." David nods to himself. "Okay," he mutters. "But just not tonight."

My husband lifts his glass of wine off the dining room table and takes it into the den, where the dogs and several of the cats are already asleep.

David turns on the television, pops a DVD into the player, and picks up the remote control. He presses a few buttons and watches the screen. Within moments I see the familiar beginning of *Homeward Bound*.

David drops into the recliner in front of the television. As soon as he gets comfortable, Skippy jumps into his lap and turns so that he, too, is facing the TV. Skippy's alert eyes watch the movement on the screen.

David falls asleep in a matter of minutes. He's made it through his Thanksgiving.

There is a picture of me on a small table next to the recliner. In the picture, I'm walking through the woods of New Hampshire on a beautiful autumn day. I hold a younger Skippy in my arms. I'm laughing at some face David is making behind the camera. I remember that day; I may have had a day when I was happier, but if so, I can no longer remember it.

Skippy adjusts himself on David's lap so that his head now rests on the arm of the recliner, staring at that picture. Skippy's eyes show recognition and then he makes a sound. Perhaps it's my imagination, but to me it sounds like a sigh.

While David slumbers, Jaycee parks her red Jeep in the woods near a gap in the chain-link fence surrounding the CAPS facility. She slides through the fence and heads toward her old lab.

National holidays are not a good time for animals in government captivity. Exercise periods are suspended and a skeleton custodial staff ensures only that the animals have enough food and clean water until the next check-in twelve hours later.

Jaycee must have counted on this, because the entire CAPS facility appears abandoned for Thanksgiving. I don't see another human and there's only one car—marked CAPS DEPARTMENT OF SECURITY—in the large parking lot.

Jaycee makes it to her lab building without incident. She ignores the front door and instead moves to a side window. She pushes on the window, but it doesn't budge. "Bastard. That bastard," she mutters.

Jaycee crouches down and takes out a small sheet of paper and a penlight from her coat pocket. In the narrow beam of the light, I can see a crudely drawn picture of her lab building. One of the windows is marked with a large red *X*. Jaycee laughs quietly.

She puts the paper and light back in her pocket and moves to the next window. When Jaycee pushes on the base of this one, it opens easily. I can hear her exhale of relief.

Jaycee climbs through the opening and into the darkened lab. She takes a minute to orient herself and then jogs to the Cube in the middle of the room. Cindy is curled into a ball in the corner.

"Cindy," Jaycee whispers. "It's me. Wake up."

Cindy doesn't stir at all. In that moment, we both fear the worst. "Cindy!"

Jaycee unlocks the Cube, opens it slightly, and reaches in for Cindy's hand. It must be warm to her touch because Jaycee relaxes, but still Cindy doesn't move.

Jaycee checks the clipboard affixed to the outside of the enclosure. There it is on the first page. Cindy has been given a dose of ketamine large enough to tranquilize a horse. "Damn it all." Jaycee clearly hadn't planned on trying to carry seventy-five pounds of deadweight. She quickly scans for something to assist her, but the room has been stripped of all equipment by this point.

"Looks like we do this the hard way." Jaycee reaches in and pulls Cindy toward her. With a groan, she lifts Cindy out of the enclosure and into her arms. She holds the chimpanzee as you would a child, her two arms making a bridge under Cindy's bottom.

Jaycee heads back toward the window with Cindy, struggling under her weight. At the same time, the two security guards begin their routine perimeter check. Jaycee finally manages to pull Cindy back out through the window as one of the guards spots Jaycee's Jeep near the gap in the fence. He immediately radios his partner and then the police.

Cindy begins to stir in Jaycee's arms at the worst possible time. "It's okay, Cindy. It's me. We're getting out of here." Jaycee's words, however, only seem to make Cindy more animated.

The first guard is about to commence a building-to-building search when he notices movement and sound in the darkness. He takes off in Jaycee's direction, radioing his partner as he runs.

Jaycee is five hundred feet from the perimeter fence when the first guard spots her. "Stop where you are!" Jaycee ignores him and runs toward the fence.

"I'm armed, Dr. Cassidy," the guard shouts. "This isn't a tranquilizer gun." Jaycee hesitates at the use of her name, but only for a moment.

"This is your last chance," the guard yells. "Stand where you are and lower the specimen to the ground!" Jaycee keeps moving.

A shot rings out, and Cindy jerks in Jaycee's arms.

It was a warning shot, fired into the air, but it brings Jaycee back to reality. She looks to the fence and her Jeep even farther beyond. In that moment, she knows that she won't make it, and even if she makes it to the Jeep, she won't get far. The second guard comes into view on the other side of the fence with his handgun drawn and confirms her conclusion.

Jaycee stops and slowly tries to lower Cindy. But by this time, Cindy is awake enough to recognize her rescuer and refuses to let go of Jaycee's neck. "It's okay, Cindy," Jaycee tells her and tries to break the chimpanzee's powerful grip.

With his handgun out, the first security guard carefully approaches Jaycee. "I said to lower the specimen."

"I'm trying."

"Do it, or I'll do it for you."

"Don't hurt her, please," Jaycee begs.

"Lie facedown on the ground."

I begin to hear the police sirens. They're coming for Jaycee.

Jaycee does as ordered, and Cindy loosens her grip. The chimpanzee turns toward the first guard and shrieks in terror.

The second guard grabs Cindy by the arm and begins to pull her away from Jaycee. Cindy fights against him. She bites the guard's hand and draws blood.

He screams and then backhands Cindy in the face. She falls to the ground, momentarily stunned by the blow. Cindy quickly gets back to her feet and, howling like a creature from the mythology of nightmares, makes a straight line for the guard who hit her.

This time there is no mistaking where the guards are pointing their weapons.

Jaycee screams and then dives toward Cindy, tackling her. Jaycee tries to pin Cindy's body with her own, both shielding Cindy and preventing her from rising.

Jaycee signs the same words over and over again until Cindy stops struggling beneath her.

I recognize the words—*Forgive me.*

David awakens with a start to the rolling credits of *Homeward Bound* and the sound of whining. When I see the look on his face, I know that he has dreamed and that he has not dreamed well.

He checks his watch—only eleven thirty PM—and quickly reorients himself. Skippy is still asleep on his lap, but Bernie and Chip, the source of the whining, clearly both need to go out. David gently lowers Skippy to the floor—an act Skippy accepts with great annoyance—and rises from the chair.

"Come on, guys." Still groggy, David moves slowly toward the front door. Chip and Bernie follow him. Skippy watches them for a moment and then decides to join.

David reaches the door as the dogs begin to bark in anticipation. He swings the door open and the dogs instantly bound out and down the front stairs. They give chase to something in the darkness, something huge and vaguely familiar.

"Wait! Wait!" David yells at the dogs, but it's a useless gesture. David squints into the night, trying to make out the shapes. "What the hell is that?"

Then he hears Arthur's angry whinny.

David throws on a pair of shoes and runs after the dogs. He finds them by their barks and by the sound of hard hooves pounding on frozen ground.

The dogs playfully run in and out of Arthur's legs, oblivious to the fact that Arthur isn't playing.

I finally catch sight of Arthur's eyes, and what I see makes me very afraid.

Arthur is no longer angry.

Arthur is no longer my horse.

Arthur is now simply prey. He is chased by wolves, or monsters, or whatever primordial demons horses fear the most. With the darkness taking away his ability to see an escape, Arthur stomps, kicks, and bucks at the smaller creatures underfoot. David yells for the dogs to come back to him, but they're having too much fun.

It is here that David makes a critical error in judgment. Dogs have an almost inexplicable ability to avoid a horse's hooves. They dodge, spin, and duck out of harm's way with eyesight and reflexes that are so much better than ours, they make us seem like caricatures of animate objects. Dogs generally can fend for themselves even among the most panicked of horses; not so humans.

David enters the fray grabbing for any dog collar he can find, still calling for them to come to him.

I hear the blow in the darkness—hoof against flesh—followed by a sharp gasp of pained breath. It is a sound I've heard before, a lifetime ago, on a dark and winding Ithaca road.

11

By the dawn of the following day, David has twelve stitches and a huge bruise on his right cheek and a stomach full of painkillers. He is as down as I've ever seen him. No one was at the hospital with him to hold his hand, no one was waiting for him when he got home, no one tenderly kissed his stitches.

By the late morning, two men are at the house attempting, without success, to force Arthur out of the barn and toward a truck and horse trailer. The men, whom I now recognize as employees of the large horse farm in town, are pulling hard on the two lead ropes attached to Arthur's halter. They succeed only in moving him a few feet out of the barn. Then Arthur rears up in panic, pulling the men with him. I'm torn between willing Arthur to fight this abduction and to surrender peacefully.

Sweet, gentle Alice screams for her stablemate from her stall. The dogs, watching from behind the backyard fence, bark continuously at the noise and activity.

David turns away from the pandemonium. He doesn't notice Sally's car pull up the driveway.

Clifford is out of the car in seconds, racing toward Arthur with his eyes squeezed shut and screaming, "They are killing him! Stop them!"

Sally runs after him. "Clifford, stop. You're going to get hurt."

Clifford is about to run right into Arthur when David reaches out and grabs him by his shirt, bringing him as gently as possible to the ground. Clifford continues to struggle. "Stop them! Stop them!"

Fearing for Clifford's safety, the workers allow Arthur to retreat completely into the barn and his stall. One of the men quickly steps forward and locks the stall door.

Arthur and Alice, united once again, nuzzle each other quietly, while Clifford whimpers on the ground. David and Sally help him to his feet. "I'm sorry," David says. "I thought he was going to get trampled."

"I know," Sally answers while hugging her boy. "What's going on here? And what the hell happened to your face?"

"I'll explain later. Why don't you take Clifford inside? Skippy's waiting for him."

"Don't let them take the horse, Mama," Clifford pleads, his words filled with all the inflection and desperation so often missing from his speech. "They're going to kill him, Mama."

"Nobody's going to kill anything, Cliff. Don't you worry about that. Right, David?"

My husband doesn't lie. "I think you should take Clifford inside." His tone has the beginning of an edge to it.

The boy finally opens his eyes. "They are going to kill that horse. It's in my head, just like before. I saw it, Mama," Clifford says.

"That's not going to happen," Sally tells him, but I can see that she is less certain now. "You go into the house so I can speak to these men, okay?"

"You promise?"

Sally hesitates, but there is no other way to get Clifford into the house. "You bet." Clifford walks stiffly toward the backyard without looking back. The dogs greet him joyfully and follow him into the house.

One of the men approaches David. "I don't know what the hell just happened here, but that kid has got to learn he can't just run up to an angry horse like that. He could've been hurt."

"That kid," Sally snaps, "is my son and he is disabled, so maybe you can back off a little."

David turns on Sally. "These men are doing me a favor, okay?"

"I'm sorry, miss," the man says. "I didn't mean any disrespect. But, Mr. Colden, I think it'd be safer if we tranquilize him to get him into the trailer."

"Why are you trailering him?" Sally asks.

"Give us a minute," David tells the man, who moves to a respectful distance, leaving David and Sally alone. "Arthur almost killed me last night. I can't deal with him anymore."

"What are those men going to do with him?"

It's as if David doesn't even hear the question. "It's all hard enough without having to worry about being trampled to death, you know?"

"Where are they taking him?"

"Away. They're taking him away. They'll find him a home someplace else, maybe someone who can work with him."

"That's a lie and you know it. Who's going to take that horse the way he is now?"

"Actually, I don't really give a rat's ass where they take him or what they do with him, as long as he's not here."

"Please, David. You're angry now, but it's got nothing to do with this. Don't do this. We can still figure something out."

David shakes his head. "I'm really done trying to figure things out. I'm just done, okay? I thought I could do this, but I can't."

"Just let me help you."

"Why do you suddenly care so much about this horse anyway?"

"It's not about the horse at all," Sally says. She struggles for a moment to find her next words, but when they come, they come fast. "Sometimes, I try to think of what it must be like to see the world as Clifford does—nothing filtered or distorted by grief or envy or anger or inadequate words, everything is exactly what you see and what you see is exactly what everything is. It must be frightening and overwhelming, yes, but also so beautiful." Sally puts her hands on David's shoulders and turns him—but not gently—so he faces the barn. She points at the horses. "Can you see it?"

The two horses face each other across their stalls, their necks almost touching.

"Look, I'm not Helena. I can't be her. I don't need to be reminded."

"You still don't get it."

"Then try talking in English."

"Last week you asked me about grief, about how long it takes to recover. I should've told you then, but I just couldn't. You're asking the wrong question. It's not the recovery you should be worrying about. It's the decisions that are born out of your grief that will haunt you. Some decisions, once you make them, you can't make any better—"

"Don't try to tell—"

"Please let me finish," she barks at him. "You just live their consequences again and again. That's why grief is so damn powerful— it has one fierce ally and that ally is regret. Before you know it, you've become that bitter shadow that people who used to love you cross the street to avoid. It's not about horses, or Helena, or Clifford, or me. This is all about you—just you."

"Really, mind your own damn—"

"So I'm asking you—please—to look right there, look into that barn and tell me the truth. What do you see?"

Before David can answer, the man returns. "Mr. Colden, I hate to interrupt, but we're on a tight schedule here."

David nods to him to proceed and then turns toward Sally, his face red with barely controlled rage and frustration. "I see a horse. Just one stupid, angry, miserable horse. You're not my conscience, you're not my therapist, and you're obviously not my friend. So please go into the house and do what it is I pay you for."

Sally gasps as if she's been slapped in the face. "You know what I think, Mr. Colden?" Sally asks through clenched teeth.

"No, surprise me, Miss Hanson."

"I think you're a damn liar and a coward." Then, with her head down and fists clenched, Sally moves toward the house.

I follow Sally. I just can't be near David right now.

Thirty minutes later, I find David sitting on a bale of hay next to the barn, his head in his hands. David holds Arthur's old halter in his lap.

The truck and trailer slowly pass me as they head down the driveway. I try to steel myself for a final good-bye to my damaged Arthur.

But the trailer is empty.

Once the truck and trailer are gone, David, pale with exhaustion and pain, gets into his car and drives away.

Sally watches David's departure from the kitchen window. When she is certain he's gone, Sally begins to pack the few belongings she and Clifford had brought to the house. Her movements bear witness to the same fatigue I saw in David moments ago, except I imagine that Sally's weariness emanates from that place near the heart where hope is temporarily shielded against harsh reality.

Clifford comes up behind her. "I'm sorry, Mama."

Sally drops to one knee so she can be sure that she has Clifford's attention. When she speaks, her voice is firm but warm. "You never need to apologize for trying to save something that deserves saving. Not ever. You understand me, son?"

"Yes, Mama, I understand," Clifford says as he struggles to maintain eye contact. "But I don't know how to save anything."

"Well, maybe you just did."

After leaving our house, David ends up at the Bronx Zoo a few hours before closing. He still holds Arthur's halter and has that bewildered look of someone suddenly aware that he has gotten to someplace on his own power, but with no recollection of how it happened.

The zoo was one of my favorite places. Here, just a few blocks from the type of demoralizing poverty most of us will never know, children and those adults with open hearts can stand eye-to-intelligent-eye with a chimpanzee, see the true majesty of a lion who does not sing and dance to Elton John songs, and hear the plaintive howl of the North American timber wolf.

The crowds today are thin because of the cold and the holiday. David makes his way to the Congo exhibit and his final destination—the gorilla pavilion. That is the place within the zoo where I spent the most time by far. I'd often dragged David to this one spot, pointing out the different gorillas by name while he looked on with mild interest. David could never keep the names of the gorillas straight and each time quickly lost interest in doing so.

There are less than a dozen people in the entire pavilion at this time of day, and David easily finds a seat in front of the large glass window with the most expansive view of the gorilla community.

David doesn't take notice of the nine-year-old Hispanic girl silently weeping several feet behind him. The girl wipes her eyes with her sleeve and takes a few steps toward him.

"Excuse me, mister," she says in an impossibly small voice.

When David turns to face her, he cannot avoid the red eyes, the runny nose, the sniffling, or the look of sadness that is much deeper than her tears. What he sees is enough to lift him from himself if only for a moment. "Can I help you? Are you okay?"

"Can I use your cell phone? It's just a local call."

David unsnaps the phone from his belt and hands it to her. "Can I call someone for you?"

"No thanks. She'll freak if you call."

"Who's that?"

"My mother. I need her to pick me up."

My knowledge of Spanish is minimal. My ability to comprehend the conversation is further hampered by the girl's machine-gun speed and the fact that she shouts most of her words. I can make out something about a cat, a man called "Alberto" and *"la herida,"* a word she uses over and over again, which if faint memory serves means "a wound."

The girl suddenly snaps the phone shut and hands it back to David. "Thanks. Sorry if I was too long," she says with embarrassment as she wipes her eyes again.

"No problem. Is your mother at the zoo? Can I help get her?"

"No thanks. She'll pick me up in a little while." The girl laughs at herself. "No point in running away if there's no one home to notice."

"Running away? Sounds serious," David says. The girl just shrugs and then takes a seat next to him. They both watch the gorillas for a while.

Other patrons walk through the pavilion, probably assuming that David and the girl are father and daughter.

"You ever run away?" the girl finally asks.

"Once. I was nine."

"Why?"

"My parents told me we were going to move. I didn't want to go."

The girl nods in understanding. "What happened?"

"I didn't get far, and then we moved, so I didn't really change much. What happened to you?"

"My mom's new boyfriend is allergic to cats, so she gave my cat away without telling me."

"Wow. That's bad."

The girl looks at David to make sure he's not making fun of her and sees that he isn't. "She says that it's just a cat."

"Boy or a girl?"

"Girl. Cielo. It means 'sky' in Spanish. She gave the cat to my cousins. She says I can visit it whenever I want. But..." The girl shrugs again and her eyes water.

"But it's not the same, is it?" David asks sympathetically.

"No. And I keep thinking how scared Cielo must be. She sleeps all day on my bed until I come home from school. Then I go to school on Wednesday and the next thing she knows she's someplace else with people she doesn't know and I'm not there. What happens when she starts to look for me in the middle of the night and I'm just not there?"

"Well, for what it's worth, I can tell you that I have six cats and they deal with changes pretty well. I'm sure she'll miss you a lot, but when you see her and explain it to her, I bet she'll understand and she won't be too scared anymore."

I can see the girl thinking about what David has said. "You have six cats? Really?"

"Yup. And horses, dogs, and a pig, too."

"How'd you end up with all those animals?"

"That is a very long story."

"You're very lucky."

David thinks for a moment. "I guess that's right."

"But if you have all those guys to play with at home, what're you doing here?"

David looks at the girl for a few long moments and then smiles kindly at her. "That's a good question."

David and the girl sit there talking for the next twenty minutes. They talk about cats, dogs, and gorillas (David points at each gorilla, telling the girl their names from memory until the girl knows them all). The girl laughs at David when he tells her about Collette and nods respectfully when he honestly answers her questions about the bandage on his face and the troubled horse that caused the deep gash underneath.

Minutes before her mother arrives, David makes her promise that she won't try to run away again, whatever the reason. The girl makes David promise that he'll tell all his animals about her—even the horse that "broke" his face.

The girl's mother—a wisp of a woman carrying a handbag

almost as big as she is—runs into the pavilion, sees her daughter, lets out a screech of relief, and throws her arms around the girl. David quietly moves to the other side of the room where a few other patrons stand watching. He gives the girl an assuring nod and the thumbs-up sign. After a moment's hesitation, the girl returns her mother's embrace.

"I want to show you something, *mi loco corazón*," the mother says through a heavy accent. She takes the large bag off her shoulder and opens the zipper.

A pretty calico cat pops its head out of the bag.

"Cielo!" the girl screams. The girl takes the cat out and nearly crushes it in her arms. The cat doesn't seem to mind at all. "But Mama, what about Alberto's allergies?"

The mother hugs the girl again, this time with the cat between them. "Alberto?" the mother says softly. "He can take pills or he can sneeze."

He can take pills or he can sneeze.

I really do love the zoo.

12

It is near dark by the time David returns home from the zoo. He finds Sally sitting at the kitchen table with Skippy in her lap and Chip and Bernie at her feet. Her eyes are closed and she hums an unfamiliar tune.

"Just saying my good-byes, David," Sally says without opening her eyes. "I'll be out of your way in a moment." Sally kisses Skippy on the side of the face and gently places him on the floor.

"You didn't get me to keep that damn horse just to leave me, did you?"

Sally finally looks at David. "I wasn't going to quit the best job I've ever had. I just thought, you know, the job was going to be the price."

"Price for what?"

"Doing what I thought was the right thing this time. I'm still living with echoes from the last time I screwed things up. I just can't carry any more of that weight."

"Echoes. Yeah, I know that word, too." David slumps into the kitchen chair next to Sally. "You asked me what I saw in the barn? Well, I saw her. I see Helena in every bale of hay. In the saddles and the curry combs. I hear her voice in every bark, in every purr, and every whine. These animals that I'm now surrounded by? This life? They were her life. I thought I could adopt it as mine, you know, to give me something to continue with. But no matter what I do, I find that they're just the echoes of her life and I fight every day not to resent the hell out of them. And her, too."

"I understand," Sally says, but David gives her a doubtful look. "You don't think so? Ah yes, I almost forgot. The arrogance of pain."

She rubs David's arm affectionately then rises from the table. Sally prepares two mugs of tea and then returns with them to the table.

"If my son were wired a little bit differently, he'd be able to tell you quite a lot about being treated like an echo. And the consequences." Sally takes a sip from her mug. "Better yet, ask my father—he was an eyewitness to that piece of history and would be more than happy to tell you about my failure. That's what I was trying to warn you about."

"Your father? I don't understand. You just spent Thanksgiving together. How bad could the relationship be?"

"I haven't spoken to my father in over five years."

"But—"

"I know, I know. I lied. But in my defense, I think it was more to myself than to you, believe me. Every year I think maybe this time I'll get invited or he'll call. Or maybe I'll get up the nerve to ask for an invite. But we carry our rejections with us. They become a part of us so that they shape everything we do, like some disease of the blood that can be managed, but never quite eliminated."

"What happened?"

"The details don't matter. They rarely do. I grieved the death of Clifford's father too hard and for too long. Self-pity, self-involvement, self-destruction—the screw-cap kind—and a whole lot of navel gazing about the 'why' of it all. That didn't leave much for a two-year-old boy who even then was very different. My father took him and I let him. He and my mother gave Clifford the stability and attention that I just couldn't find at the time."

David searches for something comforting to say, but all he can manage is a nod of encouragement.

"It took about a year, but one day I finally realized what I'd lost. I missed my son and wanted him back. I cleaned myself up, dried myself off—literally—and knocked on my dad's door."

"Your dad refused?"

"That's an understatement. My mother was on my side, but my father is a highly educated and hugely stubborn man who prides himself on his many academic accomplishments. I, on the other hand, had fallen in love and didn't even finish college. Then we had Clifford before we got married. It didn't take a lot to confirm my father's presumption that I was a failure; I gave him more than enough ammunition for that judgment when Clifford's dad passed. Honestly, I'm not certain my father was even wrong at the time.

"But I finally did get Cliff back and found the best program in the state for his condition. It happened to be here in this school district. And he's thriving. I'd do anything for him now. But it all did come at a huge price."

"Your father."

"He can't abide being wrong. And that a judge told him publicly that he was wrong is more than he can bear. Then my mother died and my father turned his grief against me. He's shut Clifford and me out ever since."

"That's so unfair."

"Maybe. Maybe it's too hard for him. I like to think he's doing it for Clifford, that he thinks in the end I won't make it and I'll give Clifford back with a termination of parental rights and he and his new wife can then undo any damage I've done to the boy."

"But if he just saw you and Clifford..."

"That's the point, David. It'll never happen. Even if he was in this kitchen and looked right at us, he'd never see us. That's the blinding nature of his own sense of loss."

David is silent for a long moment. "I hear what you're saying, but if there's a message in that for me, I don't follow you."

"Really? There's a very bright line between an echo and a legacy. These animals that you're surrounded by had a life before the funeral and they sure as hell have one now. One thing they're not is just an illusion of your grief. It would be a great sin if you treated them that way just because you loved your wife."

Sally takes out a folded sheet of sketch paper and slides it over to David. "Clifford drew this. He wanted you to have it. To be honest, it's the only time I can remember that he wanted to give away something he's sketched."

David opens the folded paper and reveals a minutely detailed and uncannily accurate picture of me leading Arthur through a canopy of ancient trees. I have to look hard at the drawing to make sure that it's not a black-and-white photograph. The picture takes my breath away and I can see that it has the same effect on David.

"How...how does he know what Helena looks like?" David stammers.

"I guess from pictures that you've got around the house. He's like a sponge with visual images."

"I had no idea. He's really brilliant."

"Very gifted, yes. Still, I'd trade it all for him just to understand intuitively what a smile means without having to process it through whatever codes he uses to understand human beings."

David can't take his eyes off the drawing. "Where is he now?"

"Up at the barn."

David jumps out of his chair. "He's up there with that horse by himself?"

Sally grabs David's arm. "Relax. Clifford's fine with the animals. They treat him like one of their own. That's his other gift."

"Still, I—"

"Would you feel better if we took a look?"

David nods and is already halfway out the door before Sally follows him.

David stops just short of the entrance to the barn, allowing Sally to catch up. She motions for him to stay quiet with a finger to her lips.

Whatever Sally once was or did, she now clearly knows her son. Clifford stands before Arthur's stall door with a flake of hay in his hand. The huge horse leans over the door and gently takes mouthful after mouthful from Clifford's offering. I could do this with Arthur, but I was the only one.

Sally softly calls her son's name. "Are you all right?"

"Yes, Mama," Clifford says without turning around. "Do we need to leave this place now?"

"No, Cliff. Everything's fine."

"Okay," Clifford says, but his voice contains no hint of relief or happiness at the news. Clifford finally turns around and sees my husband. "Thank you, Mr. Colden. I like it here."

David, now embarrassed and drained by his earlier outburst and the events of the day, can only manage a smile.

"I was thinking about something, Mr. Colden," Clifford says. "When the car would take me to school, every day I would pass a farm and there would always be a horse standing by the fence looking at the car pass. I would see this horse every day. One day when I passed, there was no horse, just a mound of dirt." Clifford is speaking very fast now, with almost no pause between his sentences, like he has the whole script written out in his head and he's just trying to get it out. "My mother told me that the horse must have died and that mound of dirt was where the horse had been buried underground. The horse was dead, I guess. They had buried the horse in the spot where I had always seen it when the car used to pass."

"I remember that, Clifford," his mother says. And then to David, she adds, "That was at least two years ago."

"It was before I understood about being dead, except I knew that my father was in heaven and that is where the dead go, so I knew a little about it. I thought that since I had seen that horse every day, that I had been the one to make it be there. And then when I didn't see it every day, I thought that I had been the one to make it not be there. I thought that seeing something was also the same as making it do something. I understand more now." Clifford drops what is left of the flake into Arthur's stall. "I think Arthur is like I used to be. He thinks that the difference between seeing and not seeing is something that he made happen. It makes him feel bad."

"I don't under—" is all David gets out before Clifford, having voiced the words in his head, exits the barn.

David turns to Sally for guidance, but she just shrugs. "I'd let it go for now," she says.

David touches his wound and then shakes his head. "Okay. I'm going to take more Advil. Do you know if we have any food? I've only had popcorn."

"Of course. Why don't you go to the house and I'll make something."

"You don't mind?"

"Not at all."

"I don't suppose you and Clifford would like to join me?"

Sally smiles at my husband. "I think we would. I think we'd like that a lot."

David smiles back until he winces because of his stitches and then walks toward the house.

In the barn, Sally tries to stroke Arthur on the nose, but he quickly pulls his head back. "Okay. Too much."

She then takes in the rest of the barn and the items that had once been mine—an antique silver curry comb that David bought for me in Paris, a saddle, a pair of muck boots. She touches a pair of reins just where I'd held them in my own hands. All these items lay where I last left them, like they wait for me.

Sally shivers for an instant and then walks out into the darkness.

13

Max enters David's office to find him typing away at his computer. David's face has gotten better over the last two weeks—still a bruise, but not the broad cotton bandage that had made him appear so vulnerable and that had given Max so much fodder for his "move back to the city" campaign.

David looks up from his work. "You have that look on your face, Max."

"What look?" Max raises his hands to protest his innocence.

"That look," David says, pointing. "The last time you had that look, you were trying to convince me that back-to-back trials were good for my marriage."

"Ah, back in the days when you listened to me."

"I was young and stupid."

"No, you were almost brilliant. And who knows, you may have that chance again. You'll never guess who just called."

"Satan. He needs you back at the office."

"Would you be serious please?"

"I don't want to play. I've got a set of papers to get out the door."

"Simon."

"Dulac?"

"That's the one."

"I thought he was forced to retire."

"He's risen phoenix-like from the ashes. After all these years, he got his revenge. He bought the company that bought his company. Now he wants to retain us to do all his work."

"Great for you. You're wonderful, as usual, okay? Now can I get back to work?"

"He also asked for you to be his chief consigliere."

"Me?"

"And, as you might expect from Simon, he needs quite a bit of advising."

"I lost his last trial. What would he want with me?"

Max shrugs. "He says he trusts you. Can you meet with him?"

"It's your relationship. You've known him forever. You don't need me."

"Actually, need and want. Simon was quite insistent."

David shakes his head and motions toward a stack of papers on his desk. "It's not a very good time."

"There's no better time, really. I'll give you half the credit for all the work."

"It's not about that. It's not always about money."

"I'll overlook the fact that you said that." Max hesitates for a moment and puts a finger to his lips in concentration. "Hmm. Nope. Sorry. Can't overlook it. Of course it's always about the money, you moron. This amount of new business will give you real power to control your life. That's what you always wanted, isn't it?"

"'Always' seems kind of stale to me right now."

"It'll be a nice fresh start for you. New memories on new cases."

"Max..."

"At least just meet with him."

David closes his eyes and bangs his head against the headrest of his chair. "Okay. If you leave me alone, I'll meet him."

"Great. Paris will be cold, so dress warm."

"Paris?"

"Simon had a stroke several years back. Didn't I tell you? He's in a wheelchair. Obviously it's very difficult for him to travel here." Max quickly heads for the office door before David can argue.

David is on his feet. "You really suck. I have responsibilities now. I can't just drop everything. And Paris of all places? You know better!"

Max turns at the door. The look on his face confuses me. For just one moment, I think he's going to say something meaningful, something understanding. He opens his mouth and I want to smack myself for being so foolish. "A lot of people have honeymooned in Paris. But it's just another city—a city with business."

Max departs, shutting the door behind him. David throws the Scotch tape dispenser at the door where it leaves a small dent before dropping uselessly to the floor.

At the animal hospital, Joshua gingerly removes a bandaged cat from one of the cages lining the back room as Sally looks on, sipping tea from an old cracked mug.

"Thanks for coming with me tonight," Joshua says. "It's nice to have the company of a human."

Sally smiles as she rubs the cat on the ears. "And what's the story with this one?"

"Stray," Joshua answers. "Probably a fight with a dog or another cat."

"So who pays for the care?"

"If someone adopts her, they'll probably offer me something toward it. Otherwise, it's just the cost of doing business."

Sally looks at all the cages, each with a dog or a cat receiving some type of medical attention. Many of the cages are marked FOR ADOPTION. Sally notices Tiny Pete and a few of his brothers and sisters in two of the cages.

"From the looks of things," Sally says, "I'm guessing you haven't paid off that X-ray machine yet."

"Are you kidding? We've got money rolling in."

"Well, that explains the fancy car you picked me up in. The '96 Honda Civic is a classic."

Joshua returns the cat to the cage and opens another. A small mutt runs out onto the floor. Joshua and Sally play with the dog as they talk about Clifford, David, me, Joshua's plans to close the practice, and the passage of time.

Finally, Joshua asks the question that I can tell has long been on his mind. "What really happened with us? At first we were pretty good."

"Are you using your three minutes?"

"If I need to."

"That one's easy. I don't know. It just started feeling like we were two raw wounds rubbing together."

"But what changed?"

"Nothing did. I think that was the problem. We both have a couple of long stories in us. They define who we are, but we never spoke about them. In the end, we couldn't get past them or through them."

"I'm tired of being afraid," Joshua says quietly.

"Me, too. I assume there are worse things, but I'm not aware of them at the moment."

"At some point you've got to say 'what the hell' and take the chance, don't you?"

"Otherwise nothing ever changes," Sally agrees. "We can't keep blaming our silence on the absence of an understanding ear."

"So, whatever the other person does with it—"

"Right, that's just about them."

They let the silence between them grow for a few seconds. Then, finally, Joshua says, "I once had a son."

"I'd like to hear about him."

Joshua swallows hard. "He was sick. Near the end he was in excruciating pain. I needed to stop that for him. No one else was going to do it, so I made that decision for my little boy. After we buried him and I had to go back into the world, I did some awful things to people who cared about me."

"Do you still love him?" Sally whispers.

Joshua can hold back his tears no longer and nods. "He was the last, best of me."

"I don't believe that."

And so, Sally and Joshua pass part of their evening together in the telling of stories. To themselves their stories, once spoken aloud, are shameful if not completely beyond the realm of human forgiveness. But to each other, the tales—told tentatively at first and then in the rush of a completely unexpected unburdening—are far too familiar in tone to permit judgment.

I choose to honor their confidences in each other. My discretion is really the only gift I've left to give them.

Later that night, when Joshua drives Sally back to her house, there is a troubled silence between them that comes from their vulnerability. The evening has had too much intimacy shared between two people who've not yet laid the supporting foundation of trust.

Joshua pulls the car in front of Sally's apartment complex. He glances over at her as he begins the same sentence for the second time, "I want to thank you for...," and then stops.

Sally waits a few seconds for him to continue. When it is clear that Joshua is paralyzed by his own thoughts, Sally leans over to him, says, "What the hell," and kisses him full on the mouth. Joshua, unprepared at first, quickly recovers and gently holds her face in his two hands.

Sally finally pulls away and searches his eyes. "The most I can tell you is that I really will try not to do anything to hurt you. Hope you'll do the same for me."

He smiles his answer. In that instant, I can imagine what Joshua looked like when he was thirty or perhaps younger, before death forced him to learn about true sadness.

Sally reaches into the backseat and takes hold of a small portable kennel with two little kittens inside. One of these is Tiny Pete.

"Let me help you with those," Joshua offers.

Sally playfully smacks his hand away. "Don't you touch my kittens."

"May I walk you to your door?"

"I think we should end the night on a high note before one of us screws it up." After Sally exits the car with the portable kennel, she sticks her head through the car window. "You can think of me, though." Sally jogs up the steps, quickly unlocks the front door, and vanishes into the house without a backward glance.

14

I'm disappointed but not surprised to see that the house is devoid of my usual Christmas decorations even though the holiday is only a week away. There is no evergreen roping around the horse fencing, no wreath on Collette's house, no candles above the fireplace, no Christmas cards on display in the dining room. David appears to have either forgotten about or purposefully ignored the year's end on the calendar.

He's in our bedroom now, attempting to pack a small suitcase while several cats watch from the bed. His resistance to this Paris trip is evident in his apparent inability to find anything—and I do mean anything—that he claims he needs.

"Sally," David yells, "have you seen my passport?" This is his fifth request to Sally and his second for the passport—a document that she has never seen (as she told him just moments ago) and that sits in the top drawer of his dresser.

"Nope," Sally calls back. "I'll help you look—"

The doorbell cuts her off. Sally breaks into a smile and quickly heads for the door, quieting the barking dogs along the way. She must expect that it is another surprise visit from Joshua—the third for the week.

Sally opens the door not to Joshua, but to Jaycee. Jaycee is bundled against the cold and stamps the snow off her feet. She looks awful.

"Can I help you?" Sally asks while holding Bernie back by his collar.

"Yes. I'm looking for David Colden. Is this the right address?"

"Who shall I say is asking?" Sally's tone is polite, but cold.

"Jane Cassidy—Jaycee."

"Regarding?"

Jaycee clears her throat. "Regarding trying to keep me out of prison."

Sally raises an eyebrow at this response, but doesn't comment. "Please wait here for a moment," she says and then abruptly closes the door on Jaycee.

She finds David still in the bedroom. "Was that the UPS guy with my documents?"

"No, it's a woman," Sally says with a hint of suspicion. "She says she wants you to keep her out of prison."

This gets David's attention. "What? Did she give you a name?"

"Jane Cassidy."

"Jaycee?"

"Should I let her in?"

"You left her out on the steps?"

David heads to the front door, and Sally follows him. He opens the door and steps aside to let Jaycee in. "Sorry about keeping you out there."

Chip and Bernie sniff Jaycee for a moment and then, finding

the situation of little interest, return to their resting spots. Skippy, however, watches the scene warily from a place next to Sally's shoe. "Sally said you mentioned something about prison. I'm assuming that's a joke?" David takes her coat, but she clings to the backpack she carries.

"It's no joke. I'm in real trouble." She sounds weak, like she's been awake for days.

David walks Jaycee to the dining room and puts her in a chair. Sally scoops up Skippy in her arms. "I'll be in the back if you need me."

David takes the chair next to Jaycee. "What happened?"

"I couldn't get anyone to take my case," she says.

"I'm not surprised."

"I couldn't let it just happen. I needed to do something."

"So you...?"

"I tried another way."

I can see David's mind at work, thinking through the range of possible actions that could have gone bad and brought Jaycee to his door—she launched a sit-in at CAPS, she refused to leave her congressman's office until he saw her, she posted something defamatory on the Internet. "What do you mean by 'another way' exactly?" he asks.

Jaycee takes a breath and then drops the bomb. "I bribed a custodian to leave a window unlocked and I broke in and tried to free Cindy."

"You what?" David stares at Jaycee in disbelief.

"I tried to free Cindy."

"By breaking into a federal facility? That's a federal crime. A felony."

"I know that."

"And of course you got caught."

"On the way out, with Cindy in my arms."

"Are they pressing charges? Maybe they don't want the publicity, or—"

"They did and they are. Apparently, I'm to be made an example of the NIS 'zero tolerance' policy for criminal trespass. I was arrested at the facility and then booked and processed for, let's see"—Jaycee counts on her fingers—"breaking and entering a federal facility, breaking and entering with the intent to steal federal property, theft of federal property, and criminal trespass. I went before a judge and now I'm out on bail."

"What about the bribery? Did they charge you with conspiracy?"

"No. They don't know about the custodian."

"Good. Maybe you can give him up for a deal," David says, thinking through the options. "Please tell me you didn't enter a plea yet?"

"Not guilty, of course."

"Damn. Why didn't you call?" David answers his own question. "You tried, didn't you?"

"Oh, yes. You and several other lawyers."

"Who's the assistant US attorney assigned to the case?"

"I don't know."

"I guess it doesn't matter. We know people in that office. I'll make some calls and get you a deal to avoid a trial and any jail time...maybe probation and community service."

"I'm not doing that. I didn't do anything wrong. I'm not pleading guilty."

"Reality check, Jaycee. You broke into a federal facility in an attempt to steal federal property. The fact that the property is alive doesn't matter. In the eyes of the law, what you did is no different than breaking into a post office to steal stamps."

"But it is different. Cindy is different. I broke into a lab to save a sentient being from a life of torture."

"We've been through this. It's a great story for some mass mailing for one of the animal rights groups, but Cindy's abilities are a complete irrelevancy under the law."

"It shouldn't be that way."

"And Helena shouldn't be dead. So what. 'Shouldn't be' doesn't change a damn thing."

"You said the last time that there was no place to make the claim that Cindy is different from a chair. I've just given you a place—it will be at my trial; that Cindy is a being with the right to be free from torture will be my defense."

"No judge is going to listen to that as a defense. No judge will let you present it to a jury."

"Why not?"

"Because it doesn't matter to the law you violated."

"Necessity is a defense to unlawful entry," Jaycee says with a law school professor's assurance.

"What?"

"In New York, an action taken out of necessity to protect life is a defense to the crime of unlawful entry, including criminal trespass," Jaycee recites confidently.

"How do you know that?"

She digs into her backpack, takes out a copy of *New York Criminal Law in a Nutshell,* and drops it onto the table between them.

I know from David's law school days that the Nutshell books— an endless series covering virtually every law school subject—are a distillation of the so-called black letter law regarding the titled subject. Law school students use the books to prepare for finals, which cover half a year, sometimes even a full year, of material in one grueling four-hour exam.

"Page one sixty-seven," Jaycee says.

"You can't plan an entire defense around one sentence in a Nutshell. You have no idea what you're talking about."

"I know. I need a lawyer. I'd like it to be you."

"You still don't get it. The defense of necessity to save life applies to human life only. End of story."

"What about Matthew Hiasl Pan?"

"I've never heard of him. Is that going to be your expert witness?"

Jaycee takes out another paper from her backpack, a *Science News* article, and hands it to David. "He is a twenty-six-year-old chimpanzee in Austria. The Association Against Animal Factories brought suit in Austria to have him declared a non-human person. They took the case all the way to the Austrian Supreme Court. What if we make the same argument—Cindy is a non-human person?"

David glances at the article. "Yeah, I remember this. And how did that all work out for Matthew?" David asks, but from his tone it is clear he knows the answer.

"They lost."

David shoves the article back to Jaycee. "Of course they lost."

"But at least they tried. And Matthew couldn't even sign. Let me show a jury what Cindy can do."

"The judge won't let you try. And even if I thought this would have a chance—and I don't—I don't do criminal defense work. You need someone who specializes in that."

"I'm willing to take my chances with you."

"But I'm not. You're not even making sense. Why me?"

"Because Helena once said you were—"

"Don't do that! Don't use my wife in this."

"I'm not. You asked me why—"

"Stop it." David leans forward, his accusatory finger out and pointing. "Did you plan this whole thing? Break in, get caught, just to make your case that Cindy should be free? To argue that she's a 'non-human person'? Was this all just to further the cause?"

"I'm not here for a cause. They're using my break-in to expedite the Department of Agriculture's approval of Cindy's transfer. I don't really care about any other case or any other chimpanzee. This is about Cindy. I've raised her from a baby. I bottle-fed her. I taught her how to speak. She calls me by my name. Do you understand that? Even now she calls for me." The raw emotion in Jaycee's voice sends David back into his chair. "I've got the death of one chimpanzee on my hands. And now I'm going to have another." Jaycee doesn't even try to hold back her tears. "If I can get the jury to find my actions were justified, you know, get them to know Cindy as more than just a piece of property, then maybe I can make her too hot to transfer."

David takes a deep breath in an effort to calm himself. "I'm sorry. I really am," he says quietly. "There are excellent criminal defense lawyers and I will get—"

Jaycee waves David's offer away before he even makes it. "Did Helena ever tell you what it was like to watch Charlie die?"

No, Jaycee, don't do this.

"The chimpanzee you and Helena worked with? What's that got—"

"Right. Worked with and then killed."

No, no, no.

"C'mon now," David says. "Isn't it time to get over that? Helena beat herself up about that damn chimp for a long time. And for what? You guys didn't even know what that professor was doing. You were deceived by an egotistical jerk, okay? It's time to let that one go. Find another demon."

David's answer stops Jaycee dead in her tracks. I know what's coming and I can't do anything to prevent it.

"Is that what you think? That we didn't know?"

"Of course you guys didn't know. That's what Helena said. She'd never purposefully destroy a healthy animal. Did you even really know my wife?"

"I did. Did you?" Jaycee asks. "We knew what was being done to Charlie every step of the way. It was a hep C study. Helena and I injected him—"

"—with some kind of super-nutrients to strengthen his liver."

"Yes," Jaycee says, almost in a whisper. "And we also injected him with the hepatitis virus to test the efficacy of the supplements. Make no mistake: We knew exactly what we were doing. We watched him die when the supplements did nothing to repair the damage we—me and your wife—had caused. That's when I decided to learn all I could about chimpanzees, when I vowed that I'd never let another primate suffer the same fate if I could help it."

"You're lying. Helena would never have done that. And she certainly wouldn't have lied to me about it."

I know precisely what David is thinking because I feel exactly the same way: How could it have been a lie? How could it have been a lie when I confessed my story to you while warm in your arms after the accident that first night? How could it have been a lie when you comforted me afterward and then never left me? What kind of creature could maintain for so long a fable so fundamental to the creation of us and to the myth of me? You looked at me our first night together and thought you saw grief—an emotion you know too well. But what you really observed was my guilt, and you were too innocent to know the difference.

"All I can tell you is that we thought we could save him. We thought—"

"How dare you!" David shouts. "You come into my house trying to manipulate me. And when that doesn't work, you try to throw Helena under the bus so I'll take your case?"

"It's not like that."

"Of course it is. You can get out now."

"I'm sorry. I thought you knew. Helena was my friend and she learned from this mistake and so did I. We can't correct that one, but we can save this life. I know we can."

"You don't care who you hurt, do you?"

"I didn't come here to cause you more pain. I came because you understand what it's like to lose someone you love."

"Get the hell out of my house!" Even as David yells these words—his defense of me—I know that the seeds of doubt have been sown in his mind. He's too good a lawyer not to consider Jaycee's story a real possibility.

But Jaycee has no choice and nothing left to say. She grabs her coat and walks out.

I tried a hundred different times at the beginning to tell you the truth, David. I wanted you to know what I'd done, because I wanted your absolution. But each time my courage and then my words were lost to me. As time went on, it just became easier to hide the truth than to tell it. And then, when the end for me became visible, when I had to face the reality not only of my own mortality, but of my weaknesses as well, I was too scared. I just couldn't do it.

Instead, I sought out Jaycee. That was not only a quest for understanding, but candidly also for the punishment I believed I deserved. Every interaction I observed between Jaycee and Cindy was another reminder of the life I'd taken and the debt that I still owed.

I can't tell you, even at this late date, all the reasons I decided to take the job with Vartag knowing the true nature of my responsibilities in her study. Much of what I'd confessed to you during that first evening was true. It was an honor to be selected to work with her and she really made you believe in her work—that we could end human and non-human liver diseases within our generation. My name would forever be associated with the research for those cures. Charlie wouldn't perish because I would be able to save him. I could defeat death.

I also was young and stupid and gullible and arrogant and Vartag was a supreme manipulator.

Even as I hear them now, all these excuses seem remarkably hollow and disingenuous.

These excuses are now my bequest. And instead of being able to offer you some type of motivation to take Jaycee's case and perhaps save Cindy, my deception has only served to drive you light-years away from my last significant contribution to anything that really mattered.

How many times am I supposed to fail and be forced to witness the impact of my failures upon others? When will I have seen enough?

15

Simon hasn't aged well since I last saw him four years ago. The stroke and its aftermath—and perhaps something more—clearly have taken a toll on him. Simon had been a confident, energetic man with clear blue eyes that were a window to his mischievousness—"a real charmer," as my grandmother used to say. The eyes were a little dulled now, the speech slightly slurred, and the animation dampened by the metal of his wheelchair.

Still, Simon is genuinely enthusiastic to see David. They sit next to each other at a long black marble table in a huge boardroom that has more fine furniture and even finer art than I ever owned.

The table is now loaded with several towering stacks of documents. Simon signs the final page of the final document with a gold fountain pen and then places the document on top of a stack of others with an *umph* of finality.

"Done?" Simon asks hopefully.

David nods. "Done."

Simon wheels his chair away from the table to a shoulder-high armoire set against the wall. He opens the doors to the armoire, revealing a modern refrigerated wine cabinet. A bottle of red wine has already been decanted and sits waiting for him. Simon carefully takes the bottle and decanter and wheels them both over to the table.

David examines the wine label, which is yellow with age and written in French by hand. The only thing David recognizes from the bottle is the date. "Am I reading this correctly? Nineteen thirty-five?"

"Yes. The year I was born. Two years before my family and I left this city and Europe just ahead of those Nazi pricks."

"I didn't know you were originally from Paris."

"Yes. That's why I've always been waiting to come back. I will die here. I'm home." Simon closes his eyes and inhales, as if he's trying to capture every last nuance of the city he clearly loves before it is too late. I know that feeling.

Finally, Simon opens his eyes. "Would you be kind enough to get the glasses from the cabinet?"

"Of course." David retrieves the items and returns them to the table.

"Very few of these bottles left. It was my father's last and greatest vintage."

"I'm very fortunate then," David says.

Simon waves him off. "It is only a bottle of wine. The only loyalty it knows is to the one who drinks it. But it's the very least I could do to show you my appreciation for coming over here to take care of this. I know the timing is inconvenient." Simon squeezes the sides of his wheelchair. "But it was not possible this time for me to come to you."

"Well, it's a lot of business."

"Don't fool yourself. Max will take most of that credit for himself. I can't do anything about that. But I've impressed upon him and others on the executive committee the importance of your involvement."

Simon swirls the maroon-colored wine in the decanter. "I also want you to know again how deeply sorry I am about Helena."

"Thank you."

"She was very kind to spend time with an old fart like me while you were at the office working on my trial. I enjoyed our time together."

"As did she. She said you were a gentleman and a class act—the highest compliment she ever bestowed. I think you probably were the only client that she genuinely liked."

Simon beams at this and for a moment he is transformed into the man I knew before the stroke. It fades too soon as his face collapses in the frustration of his thoughts. "I don't understand it."

"What's that?"

"Here I am, sitting in this chair three-quarters of a century gone. I've done what I'm going to do. I will leave nothing behind me but money to be fought over. And yet your wife, half my age, is the one taken."

"I don't try to figure those things out anymore. I've learned that I'm not equipped for it."

Simon nods in sympathy. "She certainly did love her animals, didn't she?"

"Yes, she did."

"You have them all now?"

"Actually, it's more the other way around."

Simon pours a small splash of wine into his glass, swirls, and inhales. "Not just yet. Don't rush," he says to himself and pours the wine back into the decanter. "Will you be able to see any of Paris this trip? I'd love the company."

David shakes his head. "Being back here..." David doesn't finish his sentence. I believe he doesn't know how.

"Of course. I forgot. You honeymooned with Helena here, yes?"

"And proposed, too."

"It was insensitive of me to ask you to come."

"Please don't think that. It just shows me most clearly that I've still got a lot of work to do." David taps his chest by his heart for emphasis.

Simon appears to be lost in some memory. "There was so much of Paris and the countryside I intended to show her. Did Helena ever tell you about L'Île aux Chiens?"

"It doesn't sound familiar."

"That was number one on our list, but I guess..."

"No, we never did make it back here."

Simon smacks his forehead with the heel of his hand. "I'm so stupid sometimes," he says as he pushes a small button on a control panel that I now see is hidden in the side of the table. A young woman immediately enters the room with a pad and pen in hand. *"Oui, Monsieur Dulac?"*

Simon and his assistant speak briefly in French, and then she departs.

"Forgive me. I should've thought of this sooner." Simon is suddenly more excited than he's been the entire afternoon. "My driver will take us. We'll bring the carafe. This stubborn wine will be ready by the time we get there."

"But I—" David begins to protest.

"Do this thing with me. It would allow me to feel like I've made good on at least one promise, you understand?"

"Not really. You owe us nothing."

"There are different types of promises and they impose different types of debts. Please, David." Simon's voice is almost child-like in the request.

"Is it that important to you?"

"It is. Yes, it is."

In a small suburb north of Paris, Simon's Maybach limousine pulls up to a gothic wrought-iron gate set within a long ivy-covered stone wall.

Simon's driver, a large man who probably doubles as his bodyguard, quickly exits the car and removes a wheelchair from the trunk. While the driver helps Simon from the car, David wraps himself in his topcoat and wanders up to the gate.

The gate is a work of art. Interlocking angels of different shapes and sizes create a celestial panorama.

Just beyond the gate lies what appears to be a garden, now fallow in winter, and an old brick building.

David is still studying the gate's artistry when Simon, with a picnic basket and blanket in his lap, wheels past him. Simon pushes his chair against the gate, which opens easily on well-oiled hinges, and then he passes through, signaling David to follow. David jogs to catch up to him.

An elderly groundskeeper in an even older woolen coat and cap emerges from the brick building carrying a shovel. He is the only other person in sight. The groundskeeper tips his cap to David and Simon and walks down a path through the garden. David and Simon follow a few yards behind.

From a crest in the path, I can see that it continues through a cemetery at least an acre in size. There are rows of gravestones and small statues like the ones found in cemeteries almost anywhere in the world—including mine.

This cemetery, however, is different. All the statues are dogs.

David walks over to the first few gravestones as I look over his shoulder. The inscriptions on the gravestones are in French, but I can make some of them out. They are all about dogs loved and lost.

"L'Île aux Chiens?" David asks. "What does it mean?"

"Land of Dogs," Simon answers. "That is what we call it here. It is also known as le Cimetière des Chiens."

Many of the stones are very old with embedded images or aged black-and-white photos of the dog who lies beneath. A few of the graves have fresh flowers. A favorite food dish lies on one grave, and an unopened can of tennis balls presented with a bright red bow sits on another. Everywhere there are signs that someone once cared or still does.

David runs his fingers over the cut grooves in the gravestone nearest to him. His finger traces the image of the broad square face of a Newfoundland. The lengthy inscription on the stone is in French.

"What does it say?" David asks Simon.

"It's a quotation. Sir Walter Scott, I believe. 'I have sometimes thought of the final cause of dogs having such short lives, and I am quite satisfied it is in compassion to the human race; for if we suffer so much in losing a dog after an acquaintance of ten or twelve years, what would it be if they were to live double that time?'"

"Trust me," David says quietly. "Grief doesn't quite work that way."

Simon leads David toward a bench under a large tree at the far end of the cemetery. When they are settled, Simon carefully pours two glasses from the carafe and hands one to David. David sips the wine and I can see from the look on his face that it must be extraordinary. Simon is obviously pleased.

"To say it is the best I've ever tasted does not do justice," David says.

Simon smiles at the compliment. "Now, tell me what you taste?"

David takes another sip and closes his eyes. "Let's see. Chocolate...honey...smoke...peppercorns, I think." Then David shoots Simon a confused look.

"You taste something else?"

"Yes. But I can't place it. It's not so much a flavor as a..."

"Feeling?" Simon offers.

"Do you taste it, too?"

"Yes."

"What is it?"

"I didn't really know for many years. I couldn't find it in any other wine and my father, who crafted it in secret, was long gone. And then after my stroke I tasted a glass of this wine again and suddenly it came to me."

"What's that?"

"This wine was grown in the soil of the year 1935. We had survived one world war and we were better for it. The winds were beginning to carry the hint of a greater darkness from another land. We were afraid, but we were confident. We would be able to overcome grief and whatever came to our borders. There would always be another summer, more light, a chance to seek and obtain forgiveness, another love. I think what you taste is the flavor of hope."

Simon takes a soup bowl out of the picnic basket. He fills the bowl with a long splash of the precious wine and then hands the dish to David. "Put it on the ground over by that tree." Simon points to a large elm.

"Say again?"

Simon laughs at the confused look on David's face. "Just do it. You'll see."

David shrugs and complies.

By the time David returns to his seat, I'm amazed to see that feral cats have emerged from every direction of the cemetery—out of the bushes, over the stone wall, from behind trees and grave-stones. The cats, oblivious to David's presence, head toward the bowl. Soon five are jockeying for position to get a few laps of the wine. Others quickly join around the bowl.

David watches in amazement. "Only in Paris. Cats that like wine."

Simon shakes his head. "I don't think they drink it because they enjoy fermented grapes. I think they taste the feeling that you do. But who's to say for sure?"

As one cat is satiated, it moves off to make room for others. Soon the wine is gone, but the cats don't leave. Instead, they silently take up positions on the various graves and statues. Some clean them-selves; others stretch and bask in the winter sun. The cats have no fear of David or Simon and act as if they've come here to rest on these graves for generations.

"So much life among the dead," Simon says quietly.

"Here, perhaps, but not everywhere."

Simon shakes his head. "Don't make my mistakes."

"Which mistakes are those?"

"Pessimism, cynicism, fear. They will only lead you to a very small life."

I can still remember my last dinner with Simon. He was talking about losing his parents to the ravages of their despair following World War II.

"I was raised to believe that God speaks in the language of sacrifice," he told me. "You are expected to sacrifice because it is the measure of the depth of your belief. That is the God of Abraham and Isaac, of Job and of David."

"And now?" I'd asked him.

"I've seen too much sacrifice to believe that God is behind all of it, and I've seen sacrifice that has no indicia of the hand of God at all. Loss is not always part of some greater plan explainable by reference to the actions of a divine being with a divine purpose."

"That's not too comforting, is it?"

"No. Sometimes events that leave us bereft of anything but grief just happen for no reason other than happenstance—a car turns left instead of right, a train is missed, a call comes too late—and the real test of our humanness is whether, in light of that knowledge, we ever are able to recover. When we again find our way despite the inability to manufacture a deeper meaning in our suffering, that I think is when God smiles upon us, proud of the strength of his creation. Sacrifice today has become a crutch of the persecuted, an excuse to remain powerless. I can't imagine that this is how God would communicate to his children."

"So then how does God speak?" I challenged him.

"I know it is presumptuous of me, but I think God's language is juxtaposition. His—or her—voice is heard most clearly in the reconciliation of the contradictions and contrasts of life. God lives in the peaks and the valleys, the jarring transitions, not in the mundane, the safe, the smooth, or the repetitive. But that means there must be at least a certain amount of dissonance. Without dissonance, there is no need of belief, and without belief there surely is no God."

"I think you lost me," I'd said.

"Somewhere along the way, Helena, my life became very small. I worked so hard to eliminate the conflict—the fear, the tension, and yes, even the pain—that there was nothing left to force contrast and distinction. Belief—faith, if you will—was no longer necessary. And now I see, perhaps too late, that there isn't much God left in my life. I don't think that's coincidence. It frightens me."

"It's never too late," I told him with an optimism I subsequently lost in the excruciating days following my double mastectomy.

From across the table, Simon reached for my hand and kissed it.

Now, in response to Simon's caution, David says, "I believe those cards have already been dealt."

"It's never too late, my friend." Simon repeats my own yellowed and cobwebbed words to my husband.

David is so focused on Simon that he doesn't hear the grounds-keeper approach until he is almost upon them. The groundskeeper points to the cats and says something to David in French. David looks to Simon for translation.

"Philippe says that God's countenance must have shined upon these dogs in life because now he sends his angels to watch over them in death."

The groundskeeper points up into the sky and then, using his thumb and index finger, pushes his lips into a smile. "God... smiles, *oui*?" he says, and then tips his cap to David and Simon before moving on.

I lean over the wineglass in David's hand. I'm only inches from him now. I know I can't taste the wine, but some small part of me thinks that I might be able to sense its aroma. I want to know whether the dead can recognize hope.

David raises his face upward to the sky. The curious look on his face reminds me of my dogs when they sense something odd on the wind. "Helena?" David whispers.

At the sound of my name, Simon steals a sideways glance at his lawyer and smiles. I wonder: Was this the debt you really were trying to pay, Simon?

But too soon David's eyes cloud over with doubt. The moment between us is spent. Simon's gift, if that is what it really was, is defeated.

"I'd better get going," David says and rises from the bench.

Simon dropped David off at his hotel with many promises extracted for a longer visit in the early spring. Before he drove away, Simon gave David one last sentence of advice: "Don't live small."

David was scheduled to take the flight back from Paris that evening. My husband is many things, but spontaneous generally isn't one of them. So, when I hear David change his flight to the following day, I'm more than a little surprised. I watch him shower and put on a fresh shirt. When he catches his reflection in the mirror, he says to himself, "Are you ready?" I follow him out of the hotel and onto the streets of Paris.

David hails a taxi. As I hear him tell the driver the destination, it finally occurs to me what he's doing. We stare out the window of the taxi as it winds through the streets of Paris. His eyes are half closed and he hunches his shoulders against the jarring pain of memories recalled.

The taxi pulls up in front of the gates of le Jardin des Tuileries. David pays the driver and walks across the expansive gardens to a small bronze statue now half obscured by a bush that wasn't there last time.

The statue is of le Chat Botté—Puss-in-Boots—Perrault's clever feline.

David proposed to me at this statue.

When we got back to the States, I asked him why he picked the gardens and why that statue. It was such an ideal choice for me. I'd always loved the story of the cat who was able to speak and thereby both save himself and transform the life of his human counterpart. I also thought the image of the little cat in his oversize boots and plumed hat was too cute for words.

I expected David to offer some meaningful and romantic explanation. But it turned out that he first was going to propose to me at a little café, and decided at the last minute that it wasn't private enough. Then he was going to propose at our next stop—a bench under the Eiffel Tower—but decided it was too corny. Le Chat Botté was a complete afterthought, a small bit of trivia he'd recalled from reading Frommer's on the plane. I wasn't disappointed in his answer. Actually, I liked the fact that happenstance had brought him to the right place; it was comforting to know that life would support us if only we were listening.

Now David is here again.

I think I know why you've done this, David. When I was scared about what might happen to me at the end, you told me that the shadows thrown by a single candle flame often can be more frightening than total darkness. As usual, you were right. But since my death, it's you who has been living in the shadows, isn't it? You've been spending so much time and energy holding at bay the memories that threatened to creep into your consciousness when you're tired or just about to fall asleep that there's been nothing left except fear.

Tonight is your way of lighting candles. Tonight you want to see and feel the worst of it so that, if you can survive this, tomorrow you might begin to move beyond despair.

David takes a few deep breaths to steady himself and then begins speaking in a whisper to no one. "You know, Helena, I see many different possible futures. But all the good ones have you in it," he says as his voice cracks.

I feel the same way, I remember telling him that night.

David reaches into his pocket and pretends to remove something. That night, there was no pretending.

He holds the pretend object in his open hand and pushes it toward the empty space in front of him. I remember the feeling that night when I stared mute at the small jewelry box.

"I would really love it if you would marry me," he said then and repeats now.

I threw my arms around him and said, "Yes—yes, yes, yes!" But tonight when I reach for his hand, all I can feel is the ether that separates us.

David removes our wedding band from his finger. He stares at it for a few moments and then places the ring in his pocket.

I can't stop crying. I realize that something has changed in me these last few weeks. I'm no longer afraid of the details of a life that does not now, and will never again, include me. Instead, I'm greedy for the particulars of human interaction. I want to take in every look or nuanced sentence, each shoulder shrug or outstretched hand. These things suddenly are so significant to me, as if I now need them to anchor myself for just a while longer in David's world. I'm afraid to let go because then I'll need to face what lies before me and I know I will face it alone.

Catharsis sucks.

16

Following a poor night's sleep, David boards a plane headed back to New York City on the day before Christmas Eve.

In the darkened business-class cabin, David stares at his left hand, which is now devoid of any precious metals. He touches cautiously the spot where our wedding band once rested. It is almost as if he isn't certain the hand is his. Looking at his naked hand, I feel exactly the same way.

I don't know what precisely has changed in David, but something is different. He's lost more than just three-quarters of an ounce of gold. There is some air between us now, and we no longer feel like hot skin against upholstery plastic. While we're not free of each other by any means, I know that I'm no longer the black hole absorbing every particle of light that passes into his atmosphere.

Whether it was Paris, Simon's advice, anger at the discovery of my deception, or simply time, David appears to be developing perspective. He is no longer terrified.

I think perhaps he's starting to heal.

*   *   *

David's first stop immediately following his return from Paris is neither his office nor his home. Instead, he gives the driver the address for Joshua's office.

"You look like crap." These are Joshua's first words when he sees my husband.

"Thanks. It's been a long flight."

Joshua ushers David into his exam room, puts him in the spare chair, and closes the door. "How was Paris?"

"Interesting."

"Interesting in a painful sort of way?"

"Quite."

"Sorry. I know the city has special memories for you."

"You were Helena's adviser in vet school, right?" Joshua is taken aback both by the subject matter and by the absence of transition. Clearly, David is a man with something on his mind, and I know what it is.

"If you can call it that. She didn't need a lot of advising."

"Have you heard of someone named Jane Cassidy?"

"The name is vaguely familiar. Why?"

"She goes by Jaycee."

"Same answer. What's with the third degree?"

"Humor me. How about a chimpanzee named Charlie."

I can see that Joshua immediately recognizes the name. "Ah, yes. That one I know."

"Can you tell me what Helena's involvement was in his death?"

"What's this all about, David? You're really talking old, old stuff now. Did something happen in Paris?"

"Are you saying you don't remember?"

"No, I can remember, but I'd like to know why I should."

"Jaycee Cassidy, who claims to have worked with Helena, came by to ask me a favor. She said some things that, let's say, are surprising and different from what I'd been led to believe. I want to know whether I should help her, and before I do that, I want to know the truth."

"What did Helena tell you?"

"That she didn't know Charlie was being infected. That she never would have participated in such a thing."

"And Jaycee told you that was a lie?"

"Yes. And I think I'm entitled to know who the woman was that I married."

"You know who you married. You know precisely who she was. Trust your experience of her and let the rest go. Her past, the one that existed before you, became meaningless once she met you. It's certainly irrelevant now."

"No. Her stories about herself defined who she was. I want to know if they were simply stories."

"You sound like someone looking for an excuse to be angry."

David waves off Joshua's comment. "I'm not asking for therapy, just answers, okay?"

Joshua is kind enough not to call me a liar to my husband. "You need to understand that her father had just died. Vartag seduced Helena with the promise of answers to questions that had plagued Helena since she came to Cornell."

"Like what?"

"Her doubts. Are the animals that come into our care better for that contact? Do we make a difference or are we just making them better so they can live out their little lives as someone's playthings until that or another someone decides that they aren't worth keeping around? She didn't want to save things just to kill them. Vartag promised real consequence—that she could cure hepatitis and not only make Charlie well again, but spare future primates and perhaps humans from the same fate."

"That line worked on Helena?"

"Vartag was pretty convincing. I heard her myself. She had the credentials and the track record. It really was considered a big thing to be selected to work with her. Plus, Helena wanted to believe. That's pretty powerful motivation."

"But when Helena realized it didn't work? When she didn't get her answers?"

"It was too late. She came to me to resign her spot at the school. She thought if she could be led so easily by the nose into death, she shouldn't have the power to make the decision. I talked her out of it and convinced her to come to New York."

"So that part, at least, was true."

"I don't know what else she told you, but I'm betting that it was all true except for the one thing she couldn't bring herself to admit."

"I'm not so sure."

"Yeah," Joshua says. "I think you are. You're a trained litigator. You can smell liars. That wasn't her nature."

"But—"

"Stop it, David," Joshua snaps. "I can see that you're hurt, but you've got to try to understand the why of it. She did something she believed was so horrible that she felt she needed to hide it from the world—and probably even from herself. She did more than take a life; she caused an otherwise healthy creature she came to care about to suffer. The longer the secret stayed hidden, the bigger the secret became. She carried it with her to her grave without being able to seek forgiveness from the one person she loved above all else."

In this one thing, Joshua's words could easily have been mine. He knows exactly what the burden is like because he's lived with his own. And now he knows exactly what I need. "Now that you know, you'll have to find a way to forgive her."

"Forgiveness?" David repeats the word as I hold my breath for his answer. "Forgiveness is easy. Trusting who she was is hard."

I know who I was. I know who I was. I know who I was.

17

David, Sally, and Clifford exchanged presents just after sunset on Christmas Eve. Days earlier, David had invited them and Joshua to Christmas Day dinner, but said he had plans for Christmas Eve. I know Sally doubted the existence of David's "plans," but she didn't push him.

David gave Sally a day at the spa (Martha's suggestion), which she liked, and a pair of Tiffany porcelain pet food bowls for the new kittens (his own idea), which she loved. He also gave Clifford (with Sally's permission) the gift of a year of horseback riding lessons. Clifford was so excited that he couldn't stop talking about them.

Sally and Clifford gave David a framed photo montage of all our animals to put up in his office, "to remind you what's always waiting for you at home." It was exactly the right gift for him at exactly the right time.

Sally also left each of the animals one wrapped present under the tree and gave the three dogs a kiss on the forehead, holding a sprig of mistletoe above each one as she did so.

Now, standing at his front door on Christmas Eve, David helps Sally and Clifford with their coats and kisses Sally on the cheek. "Merry Christmas," he tells them.

"You sure you're—"

"Really. I'm fine," David says, cutting her off.

"You call me on my cell if you need anything."

"Thanks, Mom," David says with good humor. Sally smiles at him and then walks with her son down the steps.

After David is certain that Sally and Clifford are gone, he takes a stack of moving boxes from the garage and carries these back to our bedroom. The dogs take positions on the bed to watch David work.

Then my husband opens the doors to all the closets and the drawers to all the dressers and stands by the bed in the middle of the room. All my clothes are now in full view to him—my jeans, dresses, shoes, shirts, blouses, panties, socks, clothes that fit, clothes that got tight on me after I went on a junk food binge in the weeks following 9/11, and clothes that swam on me during and after my chemo.

David removes a pair of my jeans from the closet and, holding them close to his face, inhales deeply. Then he carefully folds the jeans and puts them into one of the boxes.

At eleven fifty that same evening, David stretches and surveys his work. All my personal items from the bedroom and the bathroom have been carefully packed, and he has just started on the living room. The dogs have fallen asleep.

David walks into the kitchen, pulls a bottle of Veuve Clicquot champagne (my favorite) from the fridge and two champagne flutes from a cabinet.

He calls for the dogs and all three of them follow him, the champagne, and the glasses out the back door and up into the barn.

The barn is silent as David enters. He yanks a bale of hay into the middle of the floor and drops down on it. Then he opens the bottle of champagne without allowing it to pop and pours it into the two glasses balanced on the bale.

Skippy jumps into David's lap and quickly settles into a comfortable half sleep while Chip and Bernie lie at his feet. Arthur and Alice peer into the barn from the adjacent paddock, curious about the late-night goings-on.

David checks his watch. It is now midnight. He lifts a glass into the air. "Merry Christmas." He takes a small sip from his flute and closes his eyes.

I remember another Christmas Eve in this barn. David, handsome in his tuxedo, and me in the one formal gown I owned, entered the barn holding hands and laughing at the behavior of the people at the party we'd just left. The dogs followed us.

In a long relationship, there are just some nights when you're more in love than others. Perhaps it is the way the women at a party looked admiringly at your husband, or the way your spouse always made sure you had a glass of champagne in your hand, or even the way he saved you from a boring conversation with a narcissistic jerk. Whatever it is, you realize that you not only love him, but you're proud to be with him.

This particular Christmas Eve, David was the love of my life and I couldn't imagine what I'd do without him.

"Christmas Eve, midnight, and about as close to a manger as we're ever going to get," David said to me, pointing to Arthur and

Alice and then nodding to the dogs. "If these guys don't talk now, then they never will."

I smiled back at him. "They've all been chatting with each other since we walked in. Don't you hear them?"

"Hmm," David said, playing along. "Perhaps they're mumbling."

I turned him to me and kissed him on the mouth. Then I tapped him lightly on the forehead. "Perhaps you need to listen to them a bit harder. Less head, more heart."

"I think I need a little more incentive," he said.

I kissed him again. "I love you, you know?"

I don't recall if David answered. He rarely spoke in those words, as if just by giving voice to his feelings he might put them in jeopardy. He counted on me to speak for the both of us and I was happy to do that for him.

Tonight, when I see David's eyes flash open in the barn, I wonder if my words are what he has allowed himself to remember. Who will speak for him now?

While David ponders the quiet of the barn without human companionship, Cindy sits alone in her Cube in the dark and empty laboratory at the CAPS facility. The lab—for so many months an ever-beating heart of activity—evidences only the silence of abandonment.

Cindy's head hangs to her chest. The shine of curiosity once inherent in her eyes has been replaced by loss, boredom, and hurt. She smacks her doll on the floor of the Cube again and again and it echoes through the hollow lab.

In a far corner of her cage, a pile of feces is visible. Humiliated, she refuses to look in that direction.

Cindy turns to face herself in the long mirror. With one angry scream, she pounds her fist against her own reflection until spiderwebs of fracture distort her beautiful image.

Can't you at least hear Cindy? Can't you see the images I cannot ignore? Try, David. Now that you know my truth and my shame, don't let this innocent being perish because of apathy. At least try to listen to her.

But David, trained for years to listen for the slightest inflection in a witness's answer, hears nothing in the barn he deems meaningful. He scoops Skippy up in his arms and, after one last look into the four corners of the still barn, turns off the lights and heads toward the house with the other two dogs following sleepily behind.

18

Christmas Day.

    The dining room table at our house is covered with the remains of a surprisingly festive holiday dinner for Sally, David, and Clifford. Although Joshua had been expected, he called to say he had an emergency at the hospital and would be late.

The candles on the table have already burned low. Gone from the room is almost all evidence of David's nocturnal activities; only one vestige remains—a vague purposefulness in his movements— but I acknowledge that even this may be only a projection of my imagination.

While David and Sally survey the damage David has created in the kitchen, Clifford sketches on a brand-new pad in the living room. Since David's gift to him, Clifford has taken to drawing detailed images of himself engaged in equestrian activities—riding, jumping, and even dressage. Sally is pleased at this development because Clifford had never before included himself in his own sketches. She believes that anything that makes Clifford more real to himself is a good thing. Makes sense.

The doorbell rings. "I'll get it," Sally announces and races to the door just ahead of Chip and Bernie.

In a few seconds she returns with a smile and Joshua.

"Hey Doc," David says, taking Joshua's outstretched hand. "About time you got here."

"Sorry. Two emergencies."

"I'm just glad you came," David says.

"We haven't had dessert yet, so let me fix you a plate of food," Sally offers. "David cooked, and I'm still standing—so far."

Clifford walks into the dining room and announces, "Merry Christmas, Dr. Joshua," and then in the same breath asks, "Can we go outside?"

Joshua looks at Sally for approval and she shrugs, another request from her son that she doesn't quite understand. "Fine by me then," Joshua says.

"Tell you what," David says to Clifford. "Why don't you take your mother, too, so I can clean up without her telling me what to do?"

Sally takes Clifford by the hand. "C'mon, let's put on something warm."

When Sally and Clifford are out of earshot, David turns to Joshua. "Something you want to tell me?" he asks, a hint of teasing in his tone.

"Something you want to ask?"

"Okay, I'll bite. What's up with you two?"

"I like her. Always have. I'm trying not to think too hard about it so I don't screw it up."

"You're entitled to some happiness, you know?" David says as he begins clearing the dishes from the table, stacking them into one pile.

"I could say 'Physician heal thyself,' you know?"

"But you won't."

"No, I won't."

"Just don't take her away from me. Not yet."

"Not possible," Joshua answers. "I think she really likes it here."

"And Clifford, too?"

"Hard to know with Cliff, but it sure seems that way to me."

"I like that kid. I don't understand him half the time, but"—David clears his throat—"somehow when I'm around him I feel more connected to Helena."

"That's a good thing, isn't it? Lies and all?"

David nods. "Sorry, you know, about being so short with you last time. You may be right; maybe I'm just looking for a reason to be angry."

The Joshua I knew would have been embarrassed by this conversation, but the Joshua before me now reaches out and squeezes David's shoulder. It's what a father would do.

David struggles for his next words. "Tell me something. Do you think Helena ever found those answers she'd been searching for?"

Joshua shrugs. "If you don't know how to answer that question, I'm afraid that no one does."

Sally and Clifford return, bundled in heavy sweaters and boots. Sally looks from David to Joshua. "So, what've you two been talking about?"

"You know, the usual. Peace on earth," David says.

"Goodwill toward men," Joshua adds. "And all that other seasonal stuff."

"Seasonal stuff," Sally echoes, nodding in a way that makes clear she doesn't believe them. "Right." She takes Joshua by the arm and pulls him away. "Boys." She sighs.

*   *   *

Once outside, Clifford leads Joshua and Sally to the woods in the back of the house. The three pass through a thin line of trees and approach a snow-covered field just turning dark under a deep purple sky. There, only twenty yards ahead of them, a huge stag with a full rack of antlers paws the snow for some hard-to-find greenery. The deer does not yet notice them.

Clifford motions for Sally and Joshua to remain where they are, hidden by the trees, while he approaches the stag. When Clifford is within ten yards, the animal sees him and stamps his foreleg, but doesn't run off. Clifford finally stops five feet in front of the deer.

"Just look at them," Sally whispers from her hiding spot, leaning against Joshua. She takes his hand and kisses the palm.

"What was that for?"

"Nothing. I just never thought I'd feel blessed again," she says.

Joshua doesn't answer. He can't. He's working too hard to stop his tears.

Our house—David's house, I must force myself to acknowledge—is quiet now. The dishes have all been washed and put away. The dogs and cats have all found their favorite spots to sleep off the bones and chewies, catnip and fake furry mice the holiday brought. Sally and Joshua left together in very good cheer, no longer needing to pretend to David that they did not want or need each other and not caring for the moment which it was. If their displays of affection mattered to Clifford, he didn't show it.

David, however, seems agitated. He turns on the television and, only minutes later, turns it off. He pours himself a glass of wine but doesn't drink it. He picks up the phone and briefly exchanges Christmas greetings with Liza and then Chris, but he's done with the conversations several minutes before they actually end.

Eventually, David ends up in the living room in front of the rows of shelves of my books. Although David had probably looked at these bookshelves every day, he has never opened a single volume—until tonight. He first pulls down a book by Schwartz, *Higher Primates.* He opens to the first page of a chapter, which is heavily highlighted and annotated in my longhand. He takes down another book, *Chimpanzee Society* by Costa, quickly fans through the pages, and sees more of my notes. Next, he grabs Howard's *Toward a Unified Theory of Communication,* and again finds my leavings.

Finally, David reaches for Ross's *Ethical and Religious Implications of Primate Vivisection.* I'm certain he cannot help but see that it is the one I've annotated the most heavily. David stops at one passage that I'd circled in red and then further set off with three large exclamation marks.

The passage ends with the following: "You will not find a respected developmental psychologist who believes that the state of consciousness is entirely unique to humans. There are degrees of consciousness of course, but the fundamental process is there in chimpanzees as well. You just may need to get down on your hands and knees and get dirty to see it in action."

David retrieves from his workbag my notebook. He must've been carrying it back and forth to work every day since that first meeting with Jaycee when she gave it to him, but he'd never opened it. Now he begins to read my careful, dense print. When he gets to my description of my first interactions with Cindy, he slowly moves his fingers over my writing so that he can feel the texture of the words written by my own hand.

"Why didn't you tell me?" he says. Then, notebook in hand, David slides down the wall to the floor. "Did you even try?"

No, David, not in life. But I'm trying now. I think I'm really trying now.

David reads page after page of my notebook right there on the floor until he cannot keep his eyes open any longer and he drops off into sleep.

David awakens a few hours later surrounded by my books. He still holds my notebook in his hands. He rises stiffly, stumbles over a few volumes, and heads for the window. It's snowing again, but not hard. These are the large snowflakes that seem to float down from the sky in gently swaying waves.

David quietly makes his way out of the house, careful not to wake any of the dogs. He even leaves his coat behind.

There is only one noise out there now—the sound of soft snow-flakes giving in to the unbending will of tree limbs that will let them fall no farther.

David listens to that sound for a moment and then does something I've never seen him do—not ever.

He prays.

I don't know if he asks for hope, connection, compassion, guidance, peace of mind, or simply a human ear. I don't know if he receives an answer.

What I do know is that as soon as it begins to turn light, David phones Jaycee and tells her—to her great relief and surprise and mine as well—that he will try to help her.

19

David's first act as Jaycee's counsel was something she probably would have objected to had she known about it: David requested an off-the-record meeting with Jannick and his lawyer. Jannick, without a moment's hesitation, agreed to meet.

Now Jannick is waiting for David and ushers him into a conference room on the third floor of the CAPS administration building.

"Should we wait for your attorney?" David asks.

"No need," Jannick says. "The US Attorney's Office has more important matters to deal with. I told them not to come."

"I was hoping we might be able to discuss Jaycee's case."

"It's ridiculous! Jaycee is not a criminal. Wrong, stubborn, and arrogant, yes, but not a criminal," Jannick says.

David is obviously relieved by Jannick's response. "If you feel that way, why is the case still being prosecuted?"

"You really think I want this? Even putting aside my own personal feelings for Jaycee, this whole matter is a distraction to our work."

"Then why—"

"Because that stubborn idiot wouldn't accept a plea deal and let it go. I got the US attorney to agree to a six-month suspended sentence. If Jaycee keeps her mouth shut and moves on, her record gets cleaned. But she wants this fight, she wants the grant continued, and she wants Cindy."

"She has a very strong connection to the chimpanzee."

"Too strong. It's damaged her objectivity."

"So you say, but Jaycee is absolutely certain that Cindy has acquired real human language ability," David says.

"She's wrong."

"How can you be so sure?"

"I know what the scientific protocol requires. The validity of Jaycee's work cannot be established through communication that exists only between one person and one chimpanzee. Jaycee herself wrote that protocol over four years ago precisely to avoid the risk of anthropomorphic tester bias, and on this she was correct. There's been no replication and—"

"Okay, then what if there was another person Cindy communicated with? Would that change your mind? Jaycee says—"

"She says a lot of things, but she hasn't come up with one person in addition to herself who can communicate with Cindy. If she had, that certainly would be an important fact."

"I believe there was another person."

"Where is he then?"

"She's dead. It was my wife, Dr. Helena Colden."

I can see Jannick making the mental connections and finally he leans back in his chair. "The woman with the doll," he says finally. "I saw her in the lab. Jaycee said she was an assistant. I'm very sorry for your loss. I didn't know your involvement in this matter was so personal."

"I guess I didn't, either, until a little while ago."

"Did you observe the interactions between your wife and the chimpanzee?"

"No."

"Why wasn't there film of it? Jaycee filmed everything. Why isn't there some proof of Cindy communicating with someone else?"

"I can't answer that. I asked Jaycee that same question. Either the interactions weren't captured or, if they were, the film can't be found. I don't believe that means it didn't happen. Jaycee wouldn't lie about my wife's involvement."

"I no longer share your confidence in her integrity when it comes to her bond with Cindy. She's stopped thinking like a scientist."

"I guess Jaycee would say, 'So what?'"

"Pardon?"

"Maybe the bond that you criticize is precisely why Jaycee was successful with Cindy. Perhaps Jaycee can communicate with Cindy only because she's stopped thinking like a scientist and started thinking like a—"

"—a what? A mother?" Jannick scoffs.

"No. I was actually going to say like a person instead of a scientist. Just a compassionate, nurturing human who cares about what happens to Cindy. Why is it so surprising that Cindy feels and responds to that?"

"Your premise is wrong, Mr. Colden. Those feelings are not mutually exclusive. You'd be surprised to learn how many scientists actually do care. That's precisely why the protocol was specific—to prevent the inference of meaning based on something other than objective, replicative action."

Jannick takes a deep breath and rubs his eyes. When he speaks again, his voice is tinged with sadness. "Look, this isn't just about me being cynical or jaded. There's a long history of language work with chimpanzees and bonobos. Jaycee wasn't the first. The meaning of that work has always been debated because of the problem of interpretation bias. Personally, I believe that a number of those primates were taught to some degree to communicate with humans using our language or some proxy for it. That's why I approved Jaycee's grant. But that's also why replication was a critical part of the protocol—to avoid the whole criticism of interpretive bias."

"But you just can't ignore—"

"What I can't ignore, counselor, is the fact that none of those earlier chimpanzees ever had a measurable human age equivalent, and certainly not one came close to a four-year-old. Obviously, in the absence of demonstrable replication, testing bias is a more likely explanation for Cindy's results than Jaycee's claim that in just four years she's opened an unprecedented bridge of human–chimpanzee communication. And frankly, even if there was another person, if she was just using Jaycee's programming, the bias is all through the code. I can show you examples where—"

"Can't you just give Jaycee a little more time to either convince you or convince herself?"

"I can't. I'm between my own rock and hard place. There are many within NIS who feel I've been too accommodating to animal welfare interests as it is and that as a result our research has suffered. Under my directorship, NIS has published only half as much peer-reviewed research as my predecessor. That means fewer new potentially lifesaving drugs, fewer surgical advances, a smaller number of new treatment protocols. I took a big gamble on Jaycee and now I'm wearing a lot of egg."

"But surely you're not prepared to sacrifice Cindy because of egg. You don't strike me as that kind of man."

"I hope I'm not," Jannick says. "But the truth is, we're all supposed to be on the same side. Jaycee came to us to do her work, we didn't go to her. We're not monsters. Do you know why chimpanzees are used in biomedical research?" David doesn't answer him. "We use them because chimpanzees are like us—remarkably like us in many ways. Research on a species that is similar to humans is necessary because it's more likely to generate results that are relevant. Otherwise you're just wasting time and life—of those humans that could be saved and those animals that must be sacrificed. This is the sad and inescapable paradox that all primate researchers acknowledge when they come to us—including Jaycee. Chimpanzees are not defective humans and they are not evolving into humans; they are perfectly fine as chimpanzees, and we can and must use them as chimpanzees."

"That sounds like a very well-rehearsed justification."

"What you hear in my voice is my own unease. This system isn't perfect. I realize that. But spend a day on the pediatric oncology floor of a major hospital. I've spent months with those kids and their families. Primate research is the best hope we have for that and many other types of diseases. We've spent decades looking for alternatives and haven't found anything even close to the research efficacy of the more developed primates. It's so easy to judge from the safety of the sidelines. Spend a day with those kids, look into their hollowed-out eyes, listen to their stillness, watch their parents beg for some miracle, and then tell me you wouldn't do anything humanely possible to save them—even if we must destroy some of these amazing creatures to do it."

I hear these words and I wonder, not for the last time, if I ever will be free of Charlie—we killed him because he was so like us. His proximity to humans made him relevant and signed his death warrant.

"Then just give Cindy to Jaycee or let her buy Cindy. You can afford to lose one chimpanzee," David says. "Giving up Cindy isn't going to bring all biomedical research to a shuddering halt."

"Release Cindy into the general public? After that chimpanzee attack in Connecticut a few years back? Did you see that poor woman? No hands, no face, disfigured beyond recognition. These are incredibly powerful creatures. Once they hit puberty, they become unpredictable and destructive. And why not? That's what they were meant to be. You can't undo millions of years of evolution by putting them in human clothes. We could never release a chimpanzee into the community at large now. Forget it."

"Then there has to be some other answer besides putting Jaycee and NIS on trial. I know you don't need the controversy and the publicity. Give me a way to save this chimpanzee and I will guarantee you that NIS will never hear from Jaycee again. No press releases, no television cameras camped out at the entrance, no protests. You can keep on doing whatever it is you do behind your closed doors. That's the deal—the life of one chimpanzee for Jaycee's silence."

While David negotiates with Jannick, Sally loads all three dogs into my Jeep and drives to the Agway. Chip and Bernie immediately lie down in the back. When he drove with me, Skippy usually liked to be my navigator and co-pilot. I see that, once again, Skippy sits in the front passenger seat and looks out the window.

I've noticed that Skippy's attitude toward Sally has become warmer and more comfortable since Clifford has become a fixture in my house. Perhaps Clifford has made Sally seem more permanent and, therefore, more safe. Or, perhaps, it is just about time.

Either way, I'd like to be able to tell you that I feel no jealousy toward Sally about the dogs, but it probably would be more accurate to say that I'm very happy that Skippy is happy and I wouldn't have it any other way.

After fifteen minutes of driving, Sally signals a left turn into the shopping plaza that houses the Agway, a pizzeria, a hardware store, and a pharmacy.

Once she parks, Sally lowers the windows a few inches for ventilation. Chip and Bernie evidence no interest in moving. As long as they feel safe, the two large dogs are more than happy to nap on a soft car seat.

Skippy, on the other hand, always likes to see and participate in the world—as if he's aware that every minute for him has more meaning because there will be far fewer of them as compared with other dogs. Sally takes Skippy in one arm and her purse in the other and, after checking twice to make sure that the car doors are locked, puts Skippy in the booster seat of an empty shopping cart and heads toward the store.

You can tell a lot about someone from the treats and toys they give their pets—if any. I'm pleased to see that Sally pushes her shopping cart right past the smokehouse section—the pig ears, hoofs, snouts, and bull penises—without any hesitation, although Skippy does lift his nose in the air for an appreciative sniff.

Sally opts instead for the insanely expensive Greenies and the boilable chicken-flavored Nylabones. She also buys a bag of all-natural dog biscuits and slips Skippy a few as they continue shopping.

Within a few minutes, Sally's shopping cart is almost full. "Just a few more things, Skip, and then we're gone."

Sally turns a corner and what she sees brings her to a hard, cold stop. It is a huge display—one that I'd never seen before—for MEMORIAL STONES FOR YOUR BELOVED PET. The display contains a sampling of a dozen or so "weather-resistant" resin "stones" in a variety of "traditional and modern designs" and "appropriate" colors to "honor your pet." The display highlights several suggested standard messages but, according to the accompanying flyer, "you can write one of your own for the low cost of $29.95 (up to a maximum of twenty-four words)."

Sally lifts one of the "stones" and weighs it in her hand. She then gently bangs it on the display table. The "stone" makes a flimsy, hollow sound. She tosses the item back onto the display table in disgust.

Sally stoops slightly so that she is now eye-to-eye with Skippy. "I'll make you a deal. You try to let me know as best you can when it's time and I'll make sure that no one puts some cheesy piece of plastic crap with some silly saying over you when you're gone. What do you say?"

She kisses Skippy on the head and then heads for the checkout counter.

Sally is rung up, paid, and heading toward the store exit in less than five minutes.

As soon as the store door opens, Sally's ears are hit with the distinctively sharp bark/yap of a Labrador in distress and the sound of bad, loud music. Four teenagers stand around Sally's car banging on the windows to get Chip to bark. Bernie, who does not have a fighting bone in his body, just whimpers. The music pours out of their nearby maroon PT Cruiser.

Sally plucks Skippy out of the shopping cart and, holding him under one arm, runs toward her car pushing the package-laden cart before her. Twenty feet from the kids, Sally releases the cart with a shove. The cart picks up momentum in the short distance and then slams into the two kids nearest to Sally. They go airborne and seconds later are moaning in pain on the ground.

The remaining two teenagers turn toward their attacker. The one closest to Sally is built like a linebacker, but has the blunt facial features of someone who pulls the wings off butterflies for fun. "You're crazy, you bitch!" he shouts at her, taking a step in her direction. In response, Skippy growls and shows his teeth. He actually bites the air a few times and his teeth click together. This freezes the linebacker in place.

"We were just playing around," one of the kids on the ground whines as he struggles to get to his feet.

Chip, emboldened by Sally's presence, snarls at the teens through the window.

"Playing around?" Sally says icily. "Okay boys, let's play." Sally puts her hand on the handle to the car door. Chip goes wild, scratching at the window with both front paws to get out. I don't think I've ever seen him this riled up.

"Don't let him out!" the second kid on the ground pleads.

"Don't want to play?" Sally's question is met with silence. "Then I just have one question for you boys. How fast can you run?" Sally slowly pulls on the door handle. The teenagers scramble for the Cruiser. Sally laughs as they all jump into the car like some circus clown act. The Cruiser peals out of the parking lot even before they've slammed the doors closed.

Sally watches the Cruiser until it's clearly gone for good and then opens her car door. "C'mon, boys. Stretch your legs." Chip and Bernie jump down from the car. Bernie seems more confused than concerned. Chip is panting heavily, but otherwise he's back to his normal self. Sally reaches into the shopping cart and gives each dog a biscuit.

I couldn't have done it better.

And with this realization, I can feel one more mortal bolt loosen.

By the time Sally has returned home with the dogs, David and Jannick have reached the outline of an understanding. NIS will drop all charges against Jaycee, and Cindy will be sent to a chimpanzee sanctuary in California where she can live out her life with the promise that she will not be used in any NIS studies. In return, Jaycee agrees that she will not disparage NIS, will not publicly discuss her work while at CAPS or Cindy, and finally will not attempt to publish any study about her work without advance written approval from Jannick.

"And if Jaycee breaks her promise," Jannick says.

"Cindy returns to 'government service.' I get it," David says.

"The question is whether Jaycee will get it."

"I still have to sell it to her, but I don't see that she has much of a choice. It's the only way to save Cindy. Jaycee gets a life for her silence."

David packs his papers and rises to leave. Jannick offers his hand and David shakes it. "It's not perfect, I know," Jannick says.

"Nope. But for today, I think it's good enough. I'll draft the papers and get a set to the US attorney."

20

That night, David made his arguments to Jaycee and, once she heard that Cindy would be safe, she reluctantly agreed to the deal David had negotiated. There was only one condition: Jaycee wanted to be able to say good-bye to Cindy. Jannick told David that this was a terrible idea and David agreed, but Jaycee was insistent. "I want to be able to explain it to Cindy," she told David. "I want her to know it from me."

The next morning, David and Jaycee drive to CAPS in silence. They meet Frank in the parking lot, and then all three walk to the entrance where Jannick is waiting.

To his credit, Jannick tries to maintain an air of professionalism. Jaycee, however, makes no effort at collegiality and refuses to shake his hand. Jannick wordlessly escorts them into Jaycee's old lab.

Thankfully, the Cube and Cindy have been cleaned for the visit, but now that much of the equipment is gone, the lab seems more like a morgue.

Cindy's demeanor toward Jaycee further accentuates the feeling. She is still, even as Jaycee approaches the Cube. It's as if Cindy doesn't recognize Jaycee at first, but then I realize that's not it at all. The word *betrayal* forms in my mind, and I can't get rid of it.

"Can I open the Cube?" Jaycee asks.

"I'm sorry, no," Jannick says.

Jaycee sticks her hand through the bars and begins to stroke Cindy's fur. A few minutes later, Cindy finally takes Jaycee's hand and puts it in her mouth.

"Be careful," Jannick says.

Jaycee ignores him. Cindy licks Jaycee's fingers and then gently places them on the side of her face. Jaycee rubs the fur there in slow, gentle strokes.

This is too much for Jaycee. She begins to cry.

Cindy reaches out through the bars and touches the trail of tears on Jaycee's cheek and then brushes away a wisp of Jaycee's hair.

Cindy offers her doll through the bars to Jaycee. Jaycee shakes her head. Cindy offers the doll again, more forcefully this time. Jaycee folds Cindy's hand around the doll and then covers it with her own hand. For a moment, human and chimpanzee fingers entwine. The fingers, to be sure, are different, but juxtaposed in this way, they seem entirely appropriate together. The divide just isn't that big; I can see that even without words, without language.

I glance at David to see if he notices what I do, but he's staring down at the floor, chewing on his lower lip.

Finally, Jaycee releases Cindy's hand, and Cindy slowly pulls the doll back through the bars of the Cube. Then Cindy turns her back to us.

Jaycee runs out of the lab and doesn't stop running until she gets into David's car.

*   *   *

A few days later, at ten o'clock on New Year's Eve morning, David and Jaycee wait on hard chairs in the downtown Manhattan offices of the assistant US attorney. They're waiting to sign the document that will bind Jaycee to her silence and secure Cindy's life.

At ten thirty-five, David and Jaycee are still waiting. David approaches the woman stationed behind a thick glass window. "Can you do me a favor and check with Mr. Cohen's office? The meeting was scheduled for ten."

"Of course," the woman answers as she lifts the phone and dials an extension. The woman speaks to someone in a tone too low to hear as she writes on a message pad. When she hangs up the call, she turns to David in embarrassment and says, "Mr. Colden, I'm sorry, but the meeting seems to have been canceled. I was asked to give you this." The woman tears off the message and hands it through the window to David.

David quickly reads the message and then, without a word to Jaycee and before I understand what is happening, grabs his brief-case and leaves the office.

Jaycee runs after him and catches David at the elevator. "What happened?" she demands. "What did they say?"

David ignores her until they get to the ground floor. He stops at the first newsstand he finds, grabs a copy of the *Daily Chronicle,* and flips through the first few pages until he finds what he's looking for. Jaycee stares at the paper over his shoulder. The headline in the middle of the page in large bold letters reads CAPTIVE CHIMP KNOWS HER ABC'S.

David hands Jaycee the message from the receptionist. It says, "Nice article in the *Chronicle.* Hope it was worth it."

Jaycee looks up from the note. "But I didn't—"

"'A source familiar with the project,'" David reads from the article, "'puts Cindy's age at four. But the future for this chimp is uncertain.'"

"Listen to me. I'm telling you it wasn't me," Jaycee protests.

"Then who was it? Jannick?"

"I don't know. Why would I leak the story now? It doesn't make any sense."

"That assumes that you're rational, and when it comes to your relationship with that chimpanzee, I'm not sure you are."

"What's going to happen now?" The panic is clear in Jaycee's voice.

"Now? Now the deal's dead. Now they're going to try to make an example of you. Now they'll do whatever they must to transfer Cindy back to the NIS general primate pool."

"So we're back to where we were."

"No, not we. You. I negotiated the best possible deal for you and you screwed it up. You played me. I'm done. I'm going back to my day job." David shoves the newspaper into Jaycee's hands and walks away.

"Why are you so quick to believe I'd lie to you?" Jaycee calls after him. "Because that's what Helena did?"

These last few words stop David's footsteps, but only for a moment. Then he walks toward the exit and into the cold New York air.

David tries to flag a cab going uptown, but they're all filled. He starts to walk toward the nearest subway.

"It was Frank!" Jaycee shouts from a hundred feet behind him. A few people turn to watch Jaycee as she runs toward David with her cell phone open in front of her. "Frank gave them the story!"

She catches up to David and, out of breath by this point, just gives him the phone.

David puts the phone to his ear and instantly hears Frank's voice. He sounds like he's been crying. "I'm sorry, so sorry. I thought it would help Jaycee. I talked to the reporter before she got the deal, weeks ago after the project didn't get renewed. When they didn't run the story, I thought it was just dead. Jaycee wasn't involved. I didn't know it would come out now."

David hangs up on Frank and hands the phone back in silence.

"Please. Help me," Jaycee pleads.

An empty cab finally stops next to them. "You really need to pick better friends," David says. "Get in."

David paces in Max's luxurious corner office while Max watches from behind his large desk.

"Look, I got Simon's business." David stops mid-stride and turns to face Max. "Now I need you to do a little quid pro quo for me. I want you to get this approved."

"You want? I want to not have ex-wives. *Want* is an irrelevant word." Max takes a hard look at David and then a deep breath. "David, I've always supported you."

"You mean when it suited your needs."

"Whatever. Do you really think this is wise? Are you asking yourself that? Your billables are not great at the moment. You're just now getting your life together."

"What life, exactly, is that? The twenty-four-hundred-billable-hours-a-year life? The life of profit allocations and the firm Christmas party?"

"No, the life that paid for your lovely house and feeds all those nice animals. The life that taught you how to be a lawyer. The same life that allows you to be a country gentleman instead of a schlepper."

"This isn't about hours or business generation. Don't try to hide behind that. I just brought in enough business with Simon to make my nut for each of the next five years."

"And what do you think Simon would say if he knew what you wanted to do?"

"I bet he'd respect my position and be proud of us for our skill."

"I seriously doubt that. Very seriously."

David reaches over Max's desk and grabs the phone. "Then call him and find out."

Max takes the phone from David and returns it to its cradle. "Simon is the least of your problems. We represent pharmaceutical testing labs and surgical equipment companies. We represent vivisectionists, or have you forgotten?"

"So what?"

"They're really going to love the fact that their law firm is defending someone who broke into a testing lab. And on the theory that it was justified to save a monkey from torture no less."

"She's not a monkey. She's a chimpanzee. And we have compelling proof that this particular chimpanzee at least has acquired human language and can use that language to express the thoughts of a sentient mind."

"Because she knows the symbol for Chiquita Bananas? Come on now."

"Look at the video. You can't make your case by distorting the facts—not with me."

"I've got an even better idea. Why don't we invite her into the summer associate program? We'll get her a cage here in the office.

She won't even need to go home. Think of the example she'll set for the others."

"Would you be serious?"

"I will if you will," Max says in a steely tone.

"I am serious."

"Then you are seriously out of your mind. In case you haven't noticed, there's no CRUELTY-FREE sign on the front door. And as sure as I am sitting here, some very large and very important company that we represent and that pays us lots and lots of money is going to end up on the opposite side of this issue and that, as they say, will be that—regardless of the outcome, which you must know will be a loss."

"There's no direct conflict of interest under the code. There'd be no basis for disqualification."

"There doesn't need to be any formal conflict or disqualification for clients to pull their business. You already broke the rules by representing her in negotiating the deal with the US attorney without the firm's approval. We'll overlook that one. But a public trial with press and television cameras? No way."

"I can't abandon her now. And you shouldn't ask me to."

"Don't act like you've got some entitlement to moral superiority. Don't pretend that you don't know what you are! You knew that all along. Helena understood that, too, and she was willing to take the benefits. So if this is about Helena—"

I've seen David and Max argue many times. Max lived on argument, and his contrariness was part of his management technique—he needed to be convinced. And so, although David occasionally lost his cool with Max, it always reminded me of a fight between siblings with Max playing the role of the older tormenting brother.

But with Max's last comment I felt the rules of engagement change.

"Don't you dare!" David shouts at him. "Don't you dare tell me what Helena did or didn't understand. You, of all people, you bastard. You led me by the nose all these years and I followed you like I was an imprinted duck. Helena was the only thing that kept my life from becoming four walls and a computer—and you'd be just as happy now that she's gone to act as if that part of my life never existed."

"I've no idea what—"

"Come on, Max, be a decent man for just once! Stand up for something besides profits per partner. There's got to be more. You can be more."

"You're becoming a cliché, you know that?" Max says condescendingly. "You go to Paris, have an emotional epiphany, and now the world is all Lifetime Television and the WE channel. Your naïveté disappoints me, David. I thought I trained you better than that."

"I'm not naïve. I'm just empty. Just like you. That was the gift of your training."

Max yawns wide. "Save the passionate speech for the jury. I'm not interested. Is there anything more you want to tell me about this or can we get back to real work now?"

David's eyes narrow to seething slits. "I'm going to the committee on this—with or without you."

Max leans back in his chair, rubs the bridge of his nose a few times, and then exhales slowly. When he speaks again, his tone is considerably softer and—had it not been Max—I would say warm. "I know it's been hard for you. I'm trying to help you here. Why don't you just let this sit for a little while? Take a week and then see how you feel. Don't jump into this. The repercussions for you here, frankly, may be profound and beyond even my abilities to alter."

"I don't have that kind of time. I might've waited too long already. I'll need to pick a jury in a week."

"Get an adjournment. No judge is going to deny that in a criminal case with the prospect of new counsel."

"I can't adjourn. I need some kind of order protecting Cindy pending the outcome of the trial. In less than two weeks, Cindy will be transferred and beyond reach. We need to go forward now."

Max shrugs. "You're making a mistake here, partner. Trust me on this. With or without me, the committee will never approve taking this on."

"I'm not sure their approval matters to me anymore."

Max looks at David as if these words previously have never been uttered in all of humanity. "You're bluffing," Max says finally.

David slowly shakes his head.

Max spins his chair around to an ornate wooden file cabinet. He opens the second file drawer and removes a single file folder. The folder contains a document about half an inch thick. Max pushes the document across the table to David. "I strongly suggest you read your partnership agreement before you decide to do something stupid. Empty or not, people have long memories."

David lifts the partnership agreement and weighs it in the palm of his hand. Then he gives Max a tight smile. "A lot's changed. It feels pretty light to me." David drops the agreement on the table and heads toward the door.

With one hand on the door handle, David turns back toward Max and is about to speak, but Max cuts him off. " 'He stops at the door and turns to his former mentor—someone whom he had once respected—to say something that will be both cruel and cutting.' Oh! The melodrama."

David's voice is barely above a whisper when he speaks next.

"You're so smart, Max. Always were. Always had all the answers. Played all the angles. So here's a question for you. What do you think it's going to feel like when you can no longer fool yourself into believing that all this is really enough? Maybe you're not there yet. I think you are."

"And I think you should watch your back," Max answers weakly.

"It's not my back I'm worried about. It's what I see in front of me that gives me nightmares. You're a sad, lonely, little man. And when those cigarettes finally kill you, the number of people who show up for your funeral will depend entirely on whether it rains that day."

Max's eyes glaze over for a moment, as if he's been punched hard in the face. Then he sucks his lower lip and uselessly shuffles some papers on his desk, avoiding David's stare.

When it becomes clear that Max isn't going to respond, David leaves Max's office and gently closes the door behind him.

Bless you, Max. Sometimes you never know how much something really means to you until you must defend it from someone's attack.

Two long hours later, looking tired and deflated, Max returns to his office and finds a note written in David's hand stuck on the end of his silver desk set.

Dear Max,
After careful consideration, I decided to handle this trial. I need to do this. I can't give you all the precise reasons why I do—I just do. To me that is not an irrelevant statement. I

will not embarrass you or the firm. Do what you need to do.
I understand you need to live by different rules.

Sorry what I said about you, but you really do piss me off
sometimes.

With affection,

David

Max crumbles the note into a ball and tosses it into the waste-
basket.

Skippy's cough pulled me away from Max and to Joshua's exam
room. When I heard that cough—a dry, non-productive rasp
that comes from trying to clear an esophagus compressed by an
enlarged heart—I understood that what had once been perhaps a
matter of months has become a matter of weeks.

Prince, the gargantuan vet office cat, saunters into the exam
room. Skippy was Prince's one known nemesis. When Skippy
would come to the office with me, as he did on most days, he would
spend the first several hours chasing after Prince under legs (human
and other), chairs, and desks until something or someone got
knocked over and Joshua or I decided to intervene. Then Skippy
and Prince would spend the next several hours glaring at each
other from a human-imposed distance, with Skippy usually emitting a constant, low growl.

I often wondered how much of these antics were just for the ben-
efit of those looking on or to give the two creatures something to do
with their day. Perhaps Prince was the Questing Beast to Skippy's
Sir Pellinore—an unattainable grail-like quest the pursuit of which
gave Skippy's life greater meaning.

The clearest evidence to me of the advanced stage of Skippy's illness is that he now makes no move toward Prince when the cat walks across his path at the animal hospital. Skippy doesn't even growl at the cat. Prince waits for a few more moments, clearly confused by Skippy's indifference, and then turns around and walks out of the room. I could swear that Prince's head hangs just a little bit lower, his tail slightly less spirited, from the encounter.

"I thought maybe it was just a cold," Sally tells Joshua.

"I wish it were. Did you tell David?"

Sally shakes her head. "He's had so much going on...And I wanted you to see him first."

"He's still eating, right? He hasn't lost any weight."

"I hand-feed him. He likes his eggs scrambled with a little cheese."

"I think it's going to need to be soon, but..."

One great myth of veterinary practice is that the veterinarian somehow knows "the right time." Part of that belief, I'm sure, is the client's understandable urge to escape the responsibility for taking the life of a loved one. In all the euthanasias I've performed, no "owner" ever asked me whether he or she could depress the plunger on the syringe that will kill the animal with whom they've shared their lives. Just once, I would've liked someone to move my hand off the syringe, say, "This is for me to do," and relieve me of the weight of even one additional soul.

The irony is that most owners care enough to hand-feed their creatures at all hours of the night, clean them of their own urine and feces, and carry them when they cannot walk on their own, but these same people will not—or cannot—make the ultimate irrevocable decision for their companions.

The other reason owners abdicate the decision is the mistaken belief that "the right time" to summon death can be determined by a review of objective medical factors—some combination of white and red blood cells, the amount of protein in the urine, or the results of a liver enzyme test. In my own practice, I tried never to predicate the decision to end a life on the cold reality of a test result.

Instead, I would ask my long-ago learned quality-of-life questions: How is the dog acting? Is he eating and drinking? Does he go to the door to greet you when you come home? Does your cat still like catnip, chase shadows, use the litter pan? These queries are all designed to get the answer to one question—what does your companion animal want you to do? Is the continuation of life too painful? Is defecating and urinating on itself too embarrassing? Does it still like life enough to want to live?

You've lived with this animal for years. You've laughed and cried with it, talked to it, eaten with it, and, more likely than not, shared your bed with it. What makes you think I'm better equipped than you to judge when your companion wants to end its life? Show me someone who wants their vet to determine the right moment for death and I'll show you a coward.

I'm glad to see that Sally is no coward. She bends down, holds Skippy's face in her hands, and looks deep into his dark eyes. They continue to be clear and alert. "Don't worry, Skip. We've still got a deal, right? No plastic crap."

Although Joshua doesn't understand Sally's comment, he knows enough not to ask. "For now," he says quietly, "we should increase his Lasix and digitalis again. That should keep his lungs clear and help with the cough, at least for a while."

Sally wills herself to form a smile. "I'll take what I can get."

21

When I find David again later that day, dressed in a pair of old jeans, work boots, and a wool coat, he is carefully maneuvering Collette into her pen. He shakes a bucket of food, and the pig seems content to follow him.

Once Collette is settled, David scratches her rump—a sensation that she enjoys. She expresses her pleasure with a short grunt and by rolling on her back to expose her substantial belly. David seems happy to oblige, getting down on one knee to do it.

With Collette safely away, David strides up to the barn. As soon as he's within those warm wooden walls, he takes a nearby empty box and begins packing away the most personal of my equestrian items. At this, Arthur lets out an angry snort.

David turns, and now horse and man face each other. "Still have a lot to say, don't you?" David says, not unkindly. Arthur just stares at him, confused, I believe, by David's tone.

"Look, I don't know why it was her time to go. I can only tell you that it had absolutely nothing to do with you. You didn't make

it happen. That's all the explanation I have. It's got to be enough."
David takes a tentative step toward the horse. "I know, I know,
practice what I preach. But at least I'm trying now." David takes
one more step. It is one too many. Arthur backs up and then bolts
out into the paddock. David calls after him, "I think we should try
couples therapy."

On his way back to the house, David spends a few moments
roughhousing with Bernie and Chip. It's the first time in a long
while that David has paid attention to them just as dogs instead of
additional cares that must be given food, water, and a safe place to
sleep. The dogs love the attention and show their appreciation by
knocking David on his ass as he laughs.

I can't remember when I've seen my husband more at ease in his
own skin. He's not between places or in resistance to where the day
finds him. He's made his decision—not only about Jaycee's case,
but I believe about me as well—and is no longer in real danger of
sliding ever downward on the cold, slick surface of self-pity.

David returns to the kitchen out of breath from play, the two
dogs right behind him. Sally and Skippy are waiting. When she
sees him, Sally smiles and her eyes crinkle at the corners.

"What're you so happy about?" David asks.

Sally pours David a mug of coffee. "I was just thinking about
this case. I'm glad you're doing it."

"You'd be well served by a little more cynicism," David says.

"No thank you. I've mastered that one already. All you get at
the end of a cynical day are the bragging privileges that come with
being right. I think I'd rather be happy for you at this point than
right."

"Okay, Miss Della Reese, just keep in mind that this is the hardest case I've ever had to bring in my entire career—which, by the

way, is now probably over. I've no legal support for the argument I need to make. But let's not stop there. I also have no associate help. I have no secretarial support. I have absolutely no idea what I'm doing and I have one week to do what my entire team and I usually struggle to do in a month."

"Well, then, what do you have?"

"I have the facts. I think I do have a damn good set of facts." David picks up my notebook from the table. "And I've got some ideas, if I can get someone to listen to them."

Sally looks around at the dogs and several of the cats who have now joined them in the kitchen. "I wouldn't say that's all you've got."

David follows Sally's gaze. "If only they could tell me what to say."

Since the die had already been cast with the article in the *Chronicle*, and the US Attorney's Office wouldn't budge on reinstating the deal, David and Jaycee decided to go all out in the local media. Jaycee was now telling her story to any reporter who would listen and, not surprisingly, there were many reporters who wanted to hear about the chimpanzee who could "speak" like a four-year-old and the scientist who was on trial for trying to save her. David hoped that the news stories could make Cindy politically radioactive and at least delay her transfer. Then, if the trial got national media coverage and if Jaycee won, Cindy would become an icon.

If.

David didn't want to be in the office when the fallout from Jaycee's first round of interviews hit the papers. So, by the start of the first full workday following his argument with Max, David converted the den into a makeshift office. His laptop computer, Cindy's file, my notebook, and several books that I recognize from the living room bookshelves are open on the desk before him. These objects compete for desk space with mugs of coffee in various stages of age—none of them hot—an ashtray filled with broken and chewed toothpicks, and several pads of paper.

David, a toothpick in his mouth, types slowly on the computer while Skippy rests in his lap. The increase in Skippy's meds has calmed his cough for the moment. The other dogs are sprawled asleep on the couch, and the cats sleep on books and papers strewn throughout the den. The animals now won't leave David. Go figure.

Far from fresh at this point, David rubs his eyes and then searches with growing frustration for a particular document on the paper-strewn desk.

The doorbell rings. David and the dogs ignore it and the muffled conversation coming from the front of the house as he continues his search for the document. He finally finds it, grunts in satisfaction, and starts typing again.

Within moments, Sally appears in his doorway. She looks grim. "It's for you," she says.

David doesn't even look up from his work. "Is it Jaycee?"

"No."

"Can you deal with it, then?"

"David," Sally says gently. "It's Max."

This instantly gets David's full attention, and he heads for the front door.

Max's tall, gray form literally darkens the hallway. I try to read his face—is it anger, disappointment, betrayal, jealousy? I get nothing off him.

"What's up, Max?" David asks, trying to sound unconcerned, his arms folded across his chest.

"Oh, I think you know. Some documents I needed to give you. You knew this was coming," Max says.

"You didn't need to come all this way to give me my expulsion papers. You could've just faxed them."

"Perhaps, but this is so much more fun. I get to see the look on your face, you arrogant little SOB," Max says, his voice ice-cold. He takes out a sheath of papers from inside his coat pocket and hands them to David.

Although David has tried to talk a good game, I see his hurt and fear. He wasn't really expecting this; it's too soon. He thought he'd have the opportunity to explain himself to the executive committee and hoped, in light of his personal circumstances, that they'd show some compassion or understanding, maybe cut his compensation for a year or something, but not this. Didn't they care about his years of service at all? The sacrifices he'd made? And if he was "out," how could Max allow himself to be the vehicle for delivering the message? But David knew the answer to that last question—it was always about the money. Always.

David unfolds the papers and begins to read. His brow quickly furrows in confusion. "What's this?" he asks, still reading.

Max can't help himself and cracks a smile. "You've never seen a new business committee report before?"

"Of course, but what..." David skips to the last page. There it is: his name and, under the section for "description of new matter," the phrase "pro bono criminal defense litigation of Jane Cassidy." At the bottom of the page are the signatures of all six members of the new business committee, including the familiar signature of one Max Dryer. David finally looks up at Max. "But this is an approval."

"Well, at least you can still read."

"But how..."

"You can be a self-important bastard, you know? But nevertheless, you do have a certain motivating style."

"You're telling me that I changed your mind?"

Max shrugs but doesn't answer. David pulls Max under the light in the hallway and then pretends to examine Max's face in exacting detail. Max pulls away. "What are you doing, you idiot?"

"Looking for evidence of moral fiber."

"So you convinced me. Big deal."

David shakes his head, smiling. "I've never convinced you of anything unless you wanted me to. So what really happened?"

Max puts his hand to his heart, feigning indignation. "Don't you feel the love?"

"I do. Except it feels a little like jailhouse love. Now come clean."

"Okay, you win. I admit it. You played me like a fish. There, I said it. Happy now? Actually, I'm very proud of you."

"Just tell me what it is you think I did. I want to know what made you so proud so I can appropriately repent to a higher authority."

"Don't be coy. You called Simon."

"Yeah, so? I wanted his advice."

"That may be what you wanted, but what you got was Simon calling every member of the executive committee and telling them the harsh economic consequences if the firm did not support you."

"I didn't ask him to do anything."

"Sure you didn't," Max says in a tone that makes it clear he believes otherwise. "I understand completely."

"No, really," David says, but decides that further protest is futile. "Well, whatever your reasons, thank you."

"It was getting too boring around the office without you anyway. Besides, you took my best lawyers."

"Say again?"

Before Max can answer, Chris walks in carrying two litigation bags. David watches her in mute shock. I think that Chris enjoys the moment.

"Anytime you're ready," Chris says, holding out one of the litigation bags.

Then Dan staggers in carrying even more books and papers. "I think I'm gonna puke," Dan mutters.

"He's carsick," Chris warns David.

"Bathroom?" Dan whispers.

David points toward the bedroom. Dan throws everything onto a nearby table and runs. The dogs run after him.

"By the way," Chris asks, "do you have a wireless network?" David shakes his head. "A cable modem then?" David nods. "Good. Go help Martha bring in the laptops and printers from the van."

"Martha?"

Chris pats him on the cheek. "Are you just gonna stand there doing the monosyllabic thing or are you going to help set up?"

At that moment, Martha walks in carrying two laptop computer bags. "Hey, boss."

David recovers from his initial shock and kisses Martha on the cheek. Then he points them all toward the den.

While the rest of the team heads to their temporary headquarters, Max hangs back to speak with David. "So, how do things really stand?" Max asks. "Now that our necks are stuck out under the microscope you put us under, it would suck to lose."

"I would say that our chances are somewhere between not good and really not good."

"It sounds to me like we may need to redefine success. Who's our judge?"

"Barbara Epstein," David says.

"Nice liberal woman. You could've done worse."

Before they reach the den, David turns to Max and smiles warmly. "I really want you to know that I will come to your funeral—even if it rains."

Max puts an arm around David's shoulders. "How comforting."

Max helped.

I don't feel qualified any longer to speak to his motives and I'm not even sure that motivation is an appropriate touchstone anyway. Motives get lost in the passage of time, subject to the ravages of memory and revisionism. What stays—and therefore what matters—is what you do.

Under this standard, Max gave a good account of himself and was good company in the process. I couldn't have asked more of him than that.

Once Max and David's team came aboard, events blurred before me. Part of this I'm sure is because of the speed with which things started to happen, but more important is the fact that, with Max, the group achieved a level of internal completeness that left little light for anyone outside the unit to absorb. Over the course of the ensuing days, it was as if I was watching one single living organism process raw materials into something completely new and unprecedented. The aggregation of the pieces clearly was greater than the individual parts. But that organism was both single-minded and stubborn.

Nothing got in the way of the preparation for Jaycee's trial during the week before it began—not other work, not the team's family obligations, not the ever-mounting evidence of Skippy's failing heart, and not grief.

The only real breaks were for eating and sleeping when necessary, talking to reporters when possible, and then reviewing the escalating news coverage of Cindy and the trial.

Of all the articles that had been written about the looming trial, only one made Jaycee gasp.

It was the one reporting that Dr. Scott Jannick had resigned his position as the director of NIS in order to "enable him to return to the research front lines." That same article revealed that the position of NIS director would be filled immediately by "a noted primate scientist."

I saw the words, but couldn't believe them. Jannick's replacement was Dr. Renee Vartag.

22

On the morning of the trial, Sally is up and about our house well before dawn because she hasn't slept: She's so anxious about Skippy—what is coming, and how Clifford will respond to another ending. She feeds the animals and ends up cooking breakfast at the stove while the two big dogs wait at her feet.

David bounces into the kitchen dressed for court—gray suit, red dot tie, black shoes. He's radiant. "Okay, then. I'm off to get my ass kicked."

Sally gives him a careful once-over. "Well, you definitely look like a lawyer."

"Are you sure you don't want to come and see the bloodshed?"

"Nah. I told you, I'd be too nervous." Sally gives him a peck on the cheek and a squeeze on his shoulders. "For luck."

"Thanks. Remember, I'll be overnight in the city." David gives Bernie and then Chip a quick rub on the head.

"Don't worry. Cliff and I will be here."

A shadow quickly passes over David's face. "I just looked in on

Skippy and he seems so tired. I wonder if he needs to have his Lasix upped. Can you take him in to see Joshua?"

I can hear Sally struggle to keep the emotion from her voice. "It must've been all the excitement. Lots of traffic this past week. I'll bring him over today."

"Okay. I'll call you when it's over for the day," David says as he grabs his overstuffed briefcase and coat. With a quick wave good-bye, he heads out.

Sally scoops scrambled eggs onto three plates. She places two on the floor for Bernie and Chip; she smiles as they instantly begin to devour the food.

Clifford must have heard the sound of voices because he stumbles into the kitchen in his pajamas, carrying Skippy in his arms. "Skippy is sick, Mama."

"Yes, he is." Sally carries the third plate over to Clifford and Skippy.

The boy gently lowers Skippy to the floor and sits down beside him. He tries to feed Skippy by hand, first blowing on a piece of egg to cool it off, but Skippy refuses to eat.

"Please, you've got to eat," Clifford pleads with him. It's one of the few times I've heard real emotion in the boy's voice while his eyes remained open and he was present in the world before him. Sally hears it, too.

Sally lifts Skippy into her arms and rocks him while she softly hums a melody. "I used to sing this to you when you were sick," she says to Clifford.

"What are the words?" Clifford asks.

Sally laughs softly. "I never learned them, but it still worked every time."

*   *   *

Although I know that Max is a spinmaster of the highest order, I'm still shocked by the throng standing in front of the courthouse when the taxi drops David off. Television news vans, with their live-feed satellite dishes thrust high in the air, line the street leading up to the courthouse, and reporters compete for room on the sidewalk. This case has become big news.

At least thirty animal rights activists on one side of the court entrance carry placards that say, STOP THE SLAUGHTER; THE QUESTION IS NOT WHETHER THEY REASON, BUT WHETHER THEY FEEL PAIN; and WE ARE JUST ANOTHER APE. They chant slogans that sound no less stupid to me than when I first heard them a decade ago: "What do we want? Rights for animals! When do we want it? Now!"; "No, no, we won't go!"; and "Compassion is the fashion."

On the other side of the court entrance, separated by five police officers and a barricade, a group of equally loud counter-protestors wave placards saying, GOD MADE HUMANS IN HIS OWN IMAGE; PEOPLE FIRST; and WHAT'S NEXT?

If David is intimidated by the crowd, he doesn't show it. He carries his briefcase and litigation bag up the courthouse steps where Max is talking to a group of reporters. Max offers "off-the-record statements" that he knows will nevertheless appear in print, but attributed only to "a source familiar with the court proceedings."

David ignores the reporters and gestures for Max to follow. Max excuses himself, telling the reporters, "No further comment until after the proceedings are over for the day."

Once inside, David says, "Nice job on the coverage."

"You've always got to have some clash," Max says. "Makes things interesting."

"Where's Jaycee and the rest of our crew?"

"Waiting inside the courtroom."

"How does Jaycee seem to you?"

"Nervous. Desperate, maybe."

"You think she'll do okay?"

"I think she'd throw you under the train and then step over your bloodied and comatose body to open the door if she thought that chimp was behind it."

"Good thing we're on the same side then," David says.

"So it seems."

They take the elevator to the seventh floor, where more people and reporters wait outside Epstein's courtroom. The reporters race toward David and Max.

"What do you put your chances at, Mr. Colden?" shouts one reporter. "Will Cindy testify on her own behalf?"

"We need to get into the courtroom now," Max says. "We'll be happy to answer any questions when we adjourn. Can't keep the judge waiting."

Max takes David by the elbow to prove the point, and they pass through the set of double doors and into Epstein's courtroom.

Spectators pack the benches; the courtroom hums. Up toward the front, past the mythical bar that separates the lawyers from the rest of the world, Chris, Dan, and Jaycee huddle together to discuss last-minute preparations and to calm their nerves. The table for the prosecution is still empty.

David takes the seat at the head of the defense table next to Chris, and Max sits behind them. David removes my notebook from his briefcase and places it directly in front of him. He rests his hand on the cover for a moment. There is absolutely nothing within its pages that can help David now.

"So, where are our adversaries?" David asks.

Before anyone can answer, the rear double doors of the

courtroom burst open with urgency and hostility. A short, bald, torpedo of a man in an ill-fitting suit—an "anti-Max" of sorts— storms into the courtroom followed by a much younger male and female attorney struggling to keep pace. Max greets the new attorneys with an exaggerated wiggling of his fingers. The senior lawyer scowls back at him. The two young lawyers, taking their cue from their boss, likewise attempt a scowl, except the look is comical on their young faces.

"Isn't that Alexander Mace?" David asks.

"None other than," Max says, clearly amused by the situation.

"Wow. Aren't you a little surprised they brought out the head of the criminal division for this?" David asks.

"What's the deal with him?" Jaycee asks.

"He's prosecuted international terrorists, organized crime families, and South American drug kingpins," David says.

"And now you," Max adds.

"They must be nervous," Chris says.

"Or, more likely," Max says, "they think the defense is so without merit they want to make an example of you by public humiliation. You know, dissuade other loonies from coming out of the woodwork to try to 'free Willy.' Mace has big political plans, and I'm guessing you're his first law-and-order soapbox."

Before David can respond, the court clerk enters from a door behind the judge's bench and calls out, "All rise!"

Two young female law clerks, who look like they just graduated law school, pass through the same door, followed by the court stenographer with her steno machine. Then the judge enters.

David and Max turn toward each other with the same *What the hell* look on their faces. The judge is not Epstein. The judge is not even a woman.

The judge is Allerton, and he looks particularly displeased. Actually, the only person in the courtroom who seems happy with this development is Mace; he grins at David and Max, and I imagine strands of saliva dripping from his canines.

The law clerks leave papers on the bench for Allerton and then find their seats in the jury box. The court clerk sits at a table just below the bench. The stenographer, a young woman with incredibly long fingers, quickly sets up her machine off to the side of the bench, between the judge and the court clerk.

After confirming that his various clerks and the court stenographer are seated and ready, Allerton sits in the throne in the center of the bench. "Be seated," he commands. The attorneys silently follow his order.

"Okay then. Counsel, as I'm sure you've noticed, I'm not Judge Epstein. Unfortunately, she was in a car accident last night and fractured her hip. She will be off the bench for several months. As chief judge, it has fallen to me to try to manage her case docket, so I'll be taking over the trial in this matter. I assure you that no one is unhappier than me about this turn of events. Nevertheless, here we are."

Allerton directs the attorneys to put their appearances on the official record, and David and Mace obey.

"And will we have the pleasure of hearing your dulcet tones in this case, Mr. Dryer?" Allerton asks.

Max rises and without a hint of irony in his voice says, "I am, of course, quite pleased to be in your courtroom, Judge."

Allerton makes a great show of reaching into his pant pocket and pulling out his wallet. "Thank goodness. It's still there." Mace laughs several decibels louder than necessary.

Max continues as if nothing has happened. "But I will have no speaking role in this case."

"And here I thought Christmas was over," Allerton says to Mace's obvious pleasure.

"Was that off the record?" the court reporter asks without looking up from her machine.

"Nope," Allerton says, looking directly at Max. "Let it all stay on the record." Allerton picks up a sheet of paper from the pile in front of him. "I have pending before me defendant's motion to produce. Talk to me, Mr. Colden."

David rises. "We want an order requiring that the government produce Cindy, the chimpanzee, in the courtroom during the trial. Dr. Cassidy has been accused of trying to steal government property. We believe that the evidence will show she was trying to save a life—a life that in all material respects is worthy of protection by application of the well-established defense of necessity. As part of that, we want the jury to see with their own eyes what this primate can do. It will corroborate Dr. Cassidy's own judgment about—"

"Last time I checked," Allerton says, "the defense of necessity was based on the necessity to save *human* life."

Mace pops up. "You are absolutely correct, Your Honor. The defense has only been applied to save a person—another human being. If you're not a human being, then you're a 'thing.' This lab specimen, according to the law, is no different than a house, a piece of land, a coin, or a chair. Necessity to save a 'thing' is no defense. It only goes to mitigating circumstances, not to whether she's guilty."

"I assure you, Your Honor," David says, "the law has never seen any property like Cindy. Once you learn about this chimpanzee, you will understand full well why Dr. Cassidy did what she did and why her conduct should be excused. It is our legal position that being human is not the same thing as being a person. Cindy is a person under the law even though she isn't human—she's in fact a non-human person. Personhood should be sufficient for the defense of necessity, whether or not the person is a human being. At least the jury should be permitted to consider it."

"I notice," Allerton says, "that your brief is pretty light on legal authority for that point. In fact, you don't have any authority for what you want at all."

"If you mean another case where a chimpanzee was held to be a non-human person, then you are correct," David answers. "Admittedly, we are in uncharted waters there. But we do have a whole slew of instances where non-humans have the rights of persons. Corporations are considered persons under the law, with the right to sue and be sued and other rights. Entire cities are considered persons under the civil rights laws. Then why not this one chimpanzee?"

"But, Your Honor," Mace begins, "if—"

Allerton motions for Mace to stop. David and Mace return to their seats. "I've heard enough. This is my ruling," Allerton says. "I'm denying, at least at this time, the defense's request that the prosecution produce the test subject at trial. I see no purpose in requiring the government to undertake the burden of producing the property in question to put on some sort of display for the jury."

Allerton's ruling is met with some booing from the benches. He quickly bangs his gavel. "Not another word!" Allerton yells at the crowd. "If you can't show this court some respect, I'll have you removed." The benches are instantly silent.

"I'm not done with my ruling," he says. "While I'm not going to require the government to produce the specimen, I'm not going to tell the defense how to try their case at this point, either. This is a criminal matter and the stakes are high—ultimately Dr. Cassidy's freedom. If she wants to testify about her work with this chimpanzee, it seems to me that the defense is right, in the limited respect at

least, that it is relevant to the question of her own motives in allegedly breaking into the facility—and that, in turn, may bear on the
difference between breaking and entering and criminal trespass, to
name just one example. It also goes to the issue of mitigating circumstances and I will allow the jury to hear some of it.

"But I don't intend to reach the broader question of whether
this chimpanzee is more person than chair and I'm not inclined
to allow the defense a great deal of leeway on that particular point
from the defendant's own mouth—PhD or not. The chimpanzee
is a chair under the law and in this courtroom and I intend to so
instruct the jury at the appropriate time.

"You have my rulings on the record for any appeals either side
may choose to pursue at the appropriate time."

David is quiet for a moment and then slowly rises. "About that
appeal, Your Honor," he says, "in light of your ruling, we request
an order from the court requiring that NIS make no change to
Cindy's existing condition—including that she not be moved from
her current facility—before the end of the trial without notice to
the court."

"For what purpose?" Allerton asks.

"So we can renew our application based on the evidence then
before the court and pursue an emergency appeal at that time if
necessary. As you know from our motion papers, once Cindy is
transferred back to the general primate population, the application
will most likely be moot."

Mace is back on his feet. "This is an outrageous request," he
says. "The primate is the property of the US government. We can
transfer it today if we want to."

"The issue," Allerton says, "is rendering moot any appeal by
defendant on my exclusion ruling. If there ever comes a time when

it is appropriate to bring the specimen into the court for whatever reason, that won't be possible once she's transferred. So the request of the defense is not unreasonable. But I don't like enjoining the government if I don't need to. Will NIS voluntarily agree to provide the court notice of any imminent change in the status of the subject?"

"I really don't see why we—" Mace starts.

"Because the court is asking the government to do so," Allerton says.

Mace huffs and sighs. "Then, only as a courtesy to you, Judge, I will do as you have asked and only until the case is submitted to the jury."

"Thank you. Now that we've got the preliminaries out of the way, let me be absolutely clear. I do not intend to allow my courtroom to be used to satisfy someone else's agenda—on either side. Here, there is one and only one agenda—and it is mine. And that agenda is for a fair trial. I will not tolerate any abuse of the court's processes to satisfy some other end, regardless whether that end is just or just idiotic. Have I been clear, gentlemen?"

David and Mace answer in unison, "Yes, Your Honor."

"Okay, let's take fifteen minutes and then we will pick a jury."

Once David and his team are together again outside reporters' earshot, Jaycee is the first to speak. "What the hell does all that mean?"

"It means," Max responds, "that you're still alive—for now."

"But he denied our request to produce Cindy," Jaycee says.

"We knew that was going to happen," David answers. "The request was just the way to get an order preserving Cindy's status during the trial. We didn't get that, but I think Mace's representation, given his long-term aspirations, has to be good enough."

Chris nods. "Mace wouldn't take the chance of screwing with Allerton on that one."

"So we got past step one," Jaycee says.

"Don't start planning the victory party just yet," David says. "Allerton's slicing it pretty fine on the necessity defense. He's going to cut off your testimony anytime you cross a very thin line between your subjective motives and whether, objectively, Cindy is a sentient being different from other government property."

Jaycee looks confused. "But the jury will still hear me explain what Cindy can do. Allerton said that."

"Yes," David answers. "But in the end, the jury will be instructed that it's not a defense to the crime. Without the ability to argue the legal point, your testimony about her may turn out to be just sound and fury."

"So what can we do?" Jaycee asks.

"The only thing we can do," David replies. "Tell the truth as clearly as we can and hope that it's enough to keep you out of prison."

"In that case," Max tells Jaycee, "I hope you packed your toothbrush."

David always told me that most cases are won or lost in the jury selection process, known as voir dire. This time, the process takes just over two hours of questioning by Allerton and the lawyers. At the end of it, the parties have a panel of three women, three men, and one woman alternate.

During the brief recess, Max tells David, "Not a bad jury, but I sure would've liked to have been able to excuse that last guy."

The "last guy," Juror Six, is a beefy head of production for one of the New York tabloid newspapers who worked his way up through the ranks. He played football in college, was married twice, had no kids, and no pets. Even I could tell that the guy hated being here.

David shrugs. "The question with him is really going to be whom he blames most for making him serve—Jaycee or the government for prosecuting her."

"Besides, you only need one to hang the jury," Chris adds. "We couldn't have done better than Jurors One and Two." Juror One was a single, thirty-seven-year-old female schoolteacher with two cats. Juror Two was a forty-three-year-old female nurse with two school-aged children and married to a pediatrician.

"Hopefully," Max says, "they're opinionated enough that they won't be swayed by Six."

"Let's see who they pick as the foreperson," Chris says. "If it's Six, that's a pretty good indication that he's taking control."

When the jury returns, they get their answer.

"Crap," David mutters under his breath. Juror Six is sitting in the first seat in the jury box, meaning that he's been elected foreperson by the others and will lead the deliberations.

"Nothing you can do about that now," Max whispers.

"Just stay on message," Chris encourages him.

Everyone takes their seats and Allerton enters the courtroom a few moments later. Once the courtroom settles following the "all rise," Allerton addresses the jury. "We will now hear opening statements, first from the government and then from the defendant. I remind you that opening statements are not evidence, but only brief summaries of what each side intends to prove with its evidence yet to come."

Mace walks the short distance between counsel table and the jury box and then stands directly before the jury.

When Mace begins to speak, his voice booms. "Ladies and gentlemen of the jury, my name is Alexander Mace and I represent the people of the United States." Mace says this as if he actually imagines the American flag is waving behind him when he speaks. He is pompous, self-righteous, and impossible to ignore.

"In short, I represent you—and every other law-abiding citizen. I represent the laws that the legislators you elected have passed to protect you and your families and your homes and everything in them. My job is to make sure that the laws are upheld and enforced. And that is what I am going to ask of you in this proceeding—uphold and enforce the law as it has been written and as the judge will explain it to you.

"Sometimes the laws that I am supposed to enforce are very complicated and require the testimony of experts to explain the who, why, and where of things. Today, however, my job is pretty simple. I'm charged with enforcing a rule of law that every child learns for the first time in nursery school—you can't take what isn't yours.

"The defendant in this case, Jane Cassidy, Dr. Jane Cassidy, broke into a government building with the intent to steal property of the United States government. You will hear witnesses who will testify that Dr. Cassidy, under cover of darkness, broke into the facility operated by her former employer and grabbed the item that she wanted. Then, with that item in her hands, she ran out of the facility. She was caught by two security guards a few feet away from a perimeter fence as she was trying to get back to her car. When she was caught, she still had the stolen property with her and even then she refused to give it back."

Now Mace looks directly at the foreman of the jury. "She took property that wasn't hers and that she knew wasn't hers."

Mace takes a step back and pauses for effect. "Property," he says. "We all have it in some form or another. Our houses, or cars, television sets, or computers. And we all work in places where we come into contact with property that isn't ours. Maybe it belongs to a co-worker or maybe to our employer.

"Our right to our own property is what allows us all to come together without fear that someone will take your possessions from you because they are stronger, or smarter, or just plain old sneakier, or that someone won't simply break into your house and take your possessions while you are here—at least not without thinking twice about the jail time he or she must serve if found out and convicted.

"Dr. Cassidy took property that belonged to someone else and that she knew full well belonged to someone else. Yes, ladies and gentlemen of the jury, this case is that simple. That is the beginning, middle, and end of this sad story. That is why you must find her guilty.

"Allow me to give you one warning. You will hear argument from the defendant that this property is different from a television or a computer. That's true. This property is a research subject—a chimpanzee that Dr. Cassidy had experimented on for four years. During that time, Dr. Cassidy was paid a handsome salary by the government institution she worked at and happily accepted all the compensation she was offered for her research expenses. Eventually, the decision was made that Dr. Cassidy had been given enough time on the government's dime and it was time to give someone else a chance. It's another rule we all learned in nursery school—share.

"Dr. Cassidy didn't like that decision, and who can blame her? Who wants to have to leave the warmth of the government bosom and be forced to get a job in the competitive world of the private sector, where there is no nine to five, no research associates to respond to your every beck and call? She disagreed with the decision so much that her last act was to steal from her employer.

"Now, the defendant may try to sway you with moving anecdotes about this chimpanzee in the hope that you will find her conduct excusable or justified. Don't allow yourself to be manipulated. Don't be used.

"Chimpanzees are amazing creatures. They can do amazing things. You may hear some of what this chimpanzee can do, and you would be right to be amazed. But there is at least one thing that it cannot do: It cannot choose to become something else under the law. This chimpanzee is property under the law. It is and has to be property because the only other thing it can be under the law is a human being just like you and just like me, and it certainly isn't that, no matter what games or tasks it can perform. That is the bright line the law has recognized ever since there was law. And you cannot break into someone else's home—or business—and steal their property, no matter how much you covet it or how much you self-righteously believe you can improve its existence.

"Some of you have dogs or cats at home that you love very much. I do as well. I ask you right now to take a moment and think about how it would feel if someone broke into your home and stole your dog or your cat and they did so with the justification that they knew what was better for it than you did. How will you feel when you get home today, expecting to be greeted by your beloved animal companion, only to find that he or she isn't there because it's been taken by someone else?"

Mace stops and lets each juror ponder that question for a moment. Some of the jurors shift in their chairs, uncomfortable with the images they've been asked to envision.

"Now remember that feeling when you hear the defendant testify. Thank you."

Mace returns to his seat and David is up before the jury has a chance to think about what they've just heard. David wears that boyish smile I love when he walks over to the jury box.

"Ladies and gentlemen of the jury, my name is David Colden. I represent that heinous criminal you just heard Mr. Mace describe to you. That's her," David says, pointing to Jaycee, who sits quietly with her hands folded in her lap, "over there. Now don't worry, ladies and gentlemen," David says, chuckling, "if she makes a move, those marshals are licensed to shoot." Jurors One and Two smile at David.

"I think Mr. Mace went to the wrong courtroom today. Whatever case he told you he was going to try today isn't this one. No way. Let me tell you now a little about this case. There was a crime committed here—but it wasn't by Dr. Cassidy. The crime is by those who would torture a thinking, feeling, caring, intelligent creature and expect others to sit idle amid the torrent of blood and screams.

"Dr. Cassidy is a world-renowned—that's right, an internationally respected—scientist. Her particular expertise is how different species have evolved—how species are similar, how they are different, why some learn language and some do not, and how that all came about throughout the history of time. She's written more scholarly articles and book chapters than could easily fit in a large bookcase. She's lectured at Princeton, Harvard, UCLA, and Northwestern. She's been honored with private and public grants for her research. And when you finally meet her directly, you will also see that she is one of the most compassionate human beings you will ever encounter.

"About four years ago, Dr. Cassidy met Cindy. When they first met, Cindy was just a baby, taken from her mother before she was weaned and left in a cold, dark place. Dr. Cassidy raised Cindy from an infant, she changed her diapers, rocked her and sang to her when she couldn't sleep, held her hand when they walked together. And Dr. Cassidy listened to Cindy when Cindy spoke to her, went to her when Cindy called her name, fed her when Cindy said she was hungry, and reached out for her at the end when Cindy screamed for help.

"And scream she did, when the only person who ever showed her any kindness and, dare I say it, love, was forcibly removed by armed security guards under the control of the United States government.

"That's correct, ladies and gentlemen, Cindy is not a human being; she is a chimpanzee. But she can communicate in our language as well as a typical four-year-old human child. You will hear and see conclusive scientific proof of that fact and, with it, the inescapable knowledge that Cindy is a vibrant, curious, funny, intelligent, and sentient being.

"It is a remarkable thing to see a chimpanzee use our language. Whatever else happens in this case, I hope at least that you will agree with that much.

"Surely, intelligent humans"—here David pauses to look at Mace—"knew the time would eventually come when we would understand enough about the natural world that we would be able to decipher the barriers that separate us, and in that process gain a better understanding of who we all are. Dr. Cassidy has been at the forefront of that understanding. She is no criminal—unless insight and caring have become crimes."

David paces the length of the jury box, giving the seven humans sitting therein an opportunity to consider what he has said thus far.

"So how do we find ourselves here? How is it that you've been taken from your jobs and your regular schedule to listen to the government try to prove that Dr. Cassidy is a criminal? That is a sad story indeed.

"The government decided to terminate Dr. Cassidy after four years, which is their right. They wanted to take her years of research, which it is true they paid for. Even that would not have brought us here today.

"But the government also decided that Cindy, this creature with the language skills of a four-year-old girl, would be ripped from the life she knows and returned to the government's general primate population, which is used for all types of invasive experiments. She could be infected with AIDS, or hepatitis, or forced to undergo experimental surgical techniques without post-surgery pain medications—experimental surgeries the likes of which, I assure you, will give you nightmares for weeks to come.

"Dr. Cassidy couldn't let that happen, not to this creature whom she had raised as an infant. Not to this creature who calls her by name and probably still awaits her return and rescue.

"It's not like she didn't try other means. Dr. Cassidy offered to purchase Cindy, but the government said no. She offered to do literally anything to save this young chimpanzee girl's life. The government said no. Then she tried to rescue Cindy from her fate, and here we are.

"One of the elements that the government must prove to you is that Dr. Cassidy was motivated by the intent to steal the government's property. The evidence will show that her only motivation was to save this chimpanzee—this conscious and communicative being called Cindy—from almost certain death. That is why you should find her not guilty.

"So now let me thank you for your attention and patience and finish this story where Mr. Mace finished his. A dog or a cat in your house."

David looks each juror in the eye as he continues. "Imagine that you've fostered this animal for four years of your life; that your home is taken from you and you're told you must leave the animal behind, alone in the house you've been evicted from; that you learn the animal will be subjected to excruciatingly painful experiments before it is killed. Now, finally, imagine that this creature isn't really a dog or cat at all, but something that acts, thinks, feels, and communicates with you like a little girl.

"There's only you. What will you let happen to her? What would you do?" David says so quietly that some of the jurors lean forward to hear him.

"Is she property? Perhaps so. But that is a limitation that is imposed by the law. You will see that this legal status certainly was not a limitation on Dr. Cassidy's heart. And today it need not be a limitation on yours.

"It has been said—and we have learned from history—that the only thing necessary for wrong to triumph over right is for good men and women to do nothing. Don't allow this wrong to prevail. Don't do nothing. Use your voice and set Dr. Cassidy free."

David finishes his opening, nods to the jury, and then quickly returns to his chair. There is a murmuring from the spectators, but it is quickly shut down by Allerton's gavel.

Allerton, poker-faced as ever, says, "Let's take lunch before the first witness." He then turns to the jurors. "I remind you that you've not yet heard a single shred of evidence. You should not discuss anything about this case among yourselves or anyone else. I will instruct you when it is time to begin your deliberations."

Once the jury is dismissed and Allerton is off the bench, David allows himself a little smile as he accepts compliments from Max, Chris, and Daniel. Then Jaycee steps up to him. "Thank you," she says.

"That's the easy part," David tells her.

Jaycee leans over to David and whispers so only he can hear. "I think Helena would've been proud to hear you speak."

David nods and walks out of the courtroom.

Proud? I don't think I've earned the right to feel pride. But I am grateful.

23

Following the lunch break, the government begins its case against Jaycee. The evidence is, as Mace had promised, straightforward and without any surprises. The guard whom Cindy bit testifies in short order to the elements of Jaycee's crime—that Jaycee had somehow broken into the building that used to be her lab, carried out the specimen chimpanzee, and was attempting to get to her vehicle with the specimen when she was apprehended. It takes less than an hour to put all the nails into Jaycee's legal coffin.

As soon as Mace is done with the witness, David rises to cross-examine.

"So, you saw Dr. Cassidy running toward the fence with the specimen?" David asks.

"Right."

"The specimen was a chimpanzee, right?"

"That is what I observed, sir."

"So what did you think was going on?"

"I don't understand your question, sir."

"You knew the woman was Dr. Cassidy, correct? You'd seen her before? Worked with her?"

"Correct."

"Well, did you think this was like a chimp-napping in progress or something? You get a lot of that?"

"Objection," Mace calls out.

There is some laughter from the benches, but Allerton quickly shuts it down.

"I'll withdraw the question, Your Honor," David says.

"Good thinking." Allerton gives David a cold *Stop screwing around* glance.

"When you told Dr. Cassidy to drop to the ground and release the specimen, I assume the specimen, now freed from her clutches, ran away, right?"

"Not exactly, no."

"How 'not exactly'?"

"Well, the chimpanzee was still in the area."

"Not just in the area, but actually clinging to Dr. Cassidy, isn't that correct?" David asks, raising his voice slightly.

"Yeah. I guess that's right."

"Dr. Cassidy was facedown on the ground with your weapon pointed at her and this chimpanzee actually was holding on to Dr. Cassidy, wasn't she?"

"As I said, yes."

"When you tried to separate the chimpanzee from Dr. Cassidy, the specimen bit you, right?"

"Yes."

"The chimpanzee was protecting Dr. Cassidy from you, isn't that right?"

"I couldn't tell you what was going through the chimpanzee's mind, sir."

"Do you know American Sign Language?"

"I do not."

"Pity, because if you did, perhaps you could've asked the specimen precisely that question."

"Objection!" Mace shouts.

"Sustained," Allerton rules.

David begins to walk back to counsel table, but stops in mid-stride, as if he forgot something. "One more thing. When Dr. Cassidy was being removed in handcuffs and you finally pulled the chimpanzee off her, what was the chimpanzee doing?"

"The chimpanzee appeared to be upset."

"Can you describe that?"

The guard pauses before answering that one. "The chimpanzee was screaming and reaching for Dr. Cassidy."

"Do you have any children, sir?"

"Yes, a girl."

David drops into a more conversational tone. "How old is she?"

"She's twelve," the guard says with obvious pride.

"Do you remember when she was four?"

"Of course."

David smiles at the guard. "I hear four-year-old girls can be a handful."

The guard smiles back. "That, counselor, is what you would call an understatement."

There is some laughter in the courtroom, and David waits for it to die down. "They can be stubborn?"

"Same answer." More laughter.

"Do you remember ever trying to take your daughter from her mother when she didn't want to go?"

"Oh, yeah," the guard says, playing up to the crowd now. "You never forget those screams."

At the word *screams,* the courtroom becomes still, David's point suddenly obvious. "But Cindy's screams didn't sound anything like that when you pulled her off Dr. Cassidy, I guess."

The guard looks down at his shoes, avoiding David's stare. That is enough of an answer for David. "Nothing further," he says.

After the guard leaves the courtroom, Mace rises to his feet. "The government believes it has made out the elements of the crimes Dr. Cassidy has been charged with. Indeed, we believe those elements are not disputed, subject only to the defendant's claim of mitigating circumstances. Accordingly, the prosecution rests its case at this time, but reserves the right to put on a witness to rebut any evidence of mitigation the defense may make."

"Very well, Mr. Mace. Mr. Colden, you have the floor."

All eyes in the courtroom turn to David as he rises from his seat and says in a strong, clear voice, "The defense calls Dr. Jane Cassidy."

Jaycee walks to the front of the courtroom and climbs up into the box next to the judge. "Remain standing while we administer the oath, please," Allerton says.

The court clerk comes over with a well-worn Bible. "Please raise your right hand," she says above some excited chattering from the benches and the shuffling of papers at the counsel table.

Allerton stops the clerk. "Hold on a sec, Bev." He turns to address the rest of the courtroom, and his demeanor is deadly serious. "I'm just going to say this once. The oath is a solemn vow. People have gone to jail for violating it. It is what truly matters in the administration of the law and justice in this country. The taking of the oath is entitled to at least the minimum degree of respect you can show—silence while the oath is being given. That means no talking, no whispering, no getting up and going to the bathroom.

I want complete and absolute silence during the oath in this courtroom. If that is unclear to anyone, you can leave now." Allerton waits a few seconds to see if anyone takes him up on his offer. He then nods to the clerk. "Okay, Bev. Go ahead."

Jaycee puts one hand on the cover of the Bible and raises the other as the clerk asks, "Do you swear to tell the whole truth and nothing but the truth, so help you God?"

"I do," Jaycee says.

"Be seated and spell your name for the court reporter," the clerk commands. Jaycee complies.

David, a slim binder in his hand, moves to the podium near the counsel table. "Good morning, Doctor."

David and Jaycee begin the Q&A that they've been rehearsing for several days now.

Jaycee, trying to maintain eye contact with the jury, responds to David's first question by reciting her impressive academic credentials, her employment as part of the research faculty at Cornell and Tufts, and her membership in the International College of Comparative Anthropologists. Then they move on to her work at CAPS.

"Why do you care about the use of language in your work?"

"Our language has always been relied upon as the great divide between us and every other creature. We have it; they don't. Historically, human language has been used as the proxy for sentience. So I set out to test the scientific validity of the premise that only humans can acquire and use human language."

"How did you go about testing the premise?"

"Frankly, with a great deal of difficulty. It's not like you can just put a microphone in front of a chimpanzee and engage it in a conversation. Chimpanzees and bonobos cannot speak as you and

I speak because they don't have the moving parts in their vocal apparatus that we do."

"So, why isn't that the end of the story?" David continues.

"There's a difference between *unspoken* and *unsaid*," Jaycee says. "Just because chimpanzees cannot speak doesn't mean they have nothing to say; the ability to vocalize thoughts is not the same as the ability to acquire and use language. We know this as a scientific fact because the ability to speak language is a relatively recent development in hominids. Chimpanzees share over ninety-eight percent of our genetic code, but they actually have ninety-nine point seven two percent of the specific gene that controls the development of human speech as we know it today. Evolutionarily speaking, they are a hairbreadth away from being actually able to vocalize human speech. The real issue from a research perspective is how to bridge the gap between how chimpanzees communicate and how we as humans listen."

"How did you plan to bridge the gap?"

"We started with the core concept that communication is merely the transfer of information in a manner that has meaning to the recipient. An animal communicates whenever he or she intentionally behaves so that another senses the behavior and reacts. We know that animals are great meaning makers—the dog that growls when you go near his food bowl when he is eating, the cat that purrs in your lap, the parrot that tosses food it doesn't like from her cage. Language is really just a systematic means of communication through symbols or sounds. Almost all animals use language. The problem is that when it comes to the issue of language, humans are incredibly narcissistic. Since we literally hold the key to their cages, our language is the only one that counts. So we needed to find a way to get Cindy to communicate in a language that counts to her captors even though she does not have the ability to actually speak."

"Objection," Mace calls out.

"Sustained," Allerton says without pause. "Dr. Cassidy," Allerton continues, "you will be better served in this proceeding if you keep to the facts and leave the advocacy and commentary to your counsel."

"Yes sir," Jaycee answers quietly.

"And Mr. Colden," Allerton says, "we're getting too far afield. Let's get back to the point here."

"Of course. Can you describe your methodology?" David asks.

"We got Cindy as an infant when we started. From day one, we treated her as if she had a concept of self, as if she could intentionally communicate and use language, and finally"—here Jaycee struggles to maintain her composure—"as if she were my own child."

"What was the process that you used to teach Cindy?"

Jaycee then explains the painstaking technical steps through which Cindy learned to communicate with humans: how Cindy was taught American Sign Language; how the interstitial linguistic programming was refined and modified for ASL and then adapted to the primate hand; how the ILP-programmed gloves were created and Cindy was taught to use them; and finally how Cindy was taught to use the lexigraphic keyboard to supplement the ASL and to take the place of non-manual markers.

While this testimony provides an important foundation for the evidence that would follow, it is also dry, impersonal, and abstract. David marches Jaycee through it as quickly as he can with one eye on the jury to make sure he's not losing them.

When Jaycee is done, David says, "Perhaps, Jaycee, you can give the jury a concrete example of what you've been explaining?"

"Of course. Take the sign for 'play.' You make the sign for two *p*'s—the tip of the thumb to the middle of the middle finger—and then swing the *p* back and forth." Jaycee displays the sign from the witness stand for the judge. "Because of the placement of Cindy's thumb in relationship to her other fingers, if she were to sign this, it might look like this." Jaycee makes the sign, but it clearly appears different. "She could be trying to sign the word for 'play,' but she also could be trying to sign any number of other words. When we put the gloves on her, and thereby compensated for differences in physiology, it was clear that she was in fact signing the word for 'play.' We ran the gloves back through the programming and Cindy's signs were converted into English words that appeared on my computer screen. Cindy also used her keyboard to add a mood or tone—like *play now!*" Jaycee says in a demanding tone, "or as a shortcut for a response—like a yes or no."

"Do you believe that you succeeded in having Cindy acquire and use human language?" David asks.

"I have no doubt that we did."

"Did you ever have Cindy independently evaluated?" David asks.

"Yes. Prior to the time that the project was terminated, we had Cindy's cognitive age equivalent tested by the Language Institute at Cornell."

"What do you mean by cognitive age equivalent?"

"It's just what it sounds like. Using an assessment of the subject's language acquisition and usage, the subject's skill level is measured against the test results of other subjects in various age cohorts and is then placed in a similar grouping."

David removes the document from a file folder and has it marked as an exhibit. He hands a copy to Mace, one to the clerk, and one to Jaycee.

"What did Cornell conclude?" David asks.

"When the project was terminated, Cindy, who was at this time four years and eight months old, had a cognitive age equivalent of a four-year-old."

The sound of surprise spreads throughout the benches. Allerton bangs his gavel once in annoyance. "All right now. Settle down."

David takes a moment for the room to quiet and to be sure that he has Allerton's attention. "Can you explain what that result means?"

Jaycee takes a breath and turns her face so that she is looking directly at Allerton. "It means that as compared with other humans and as measured by humans, based on factors such as vocabulary, arbitrariness, semanticity, spontaneity, turn taking, duality, displacement, and creativity, Cindy has the verbal mind of a four-year-old child."

This time there is a collective murmur from the audience that quickly expands to a dull rumble. Allerton bangs his gavel several times to establish order.

David turns to Chris and says, "Hand me the CD."

Chris takes out a small, square white envelope and gives it to David. He, in turn, hands the envelope to the court clerk, and she removes the CD and places it into a small computer/projector in the front of the courtroom. The clerk hands David a remote control. Mace watches David's movements, waiting for the correct moment to object.

"Dr. Cassidy, did you make a photographic record of any of your work with Cindy?"

"Oh, tons."

"What happened to those recordings?"

"I don't know. I tried to take a number of disks with me, but was

advised by Director Jannick that they were the property of NIS."
There is a noticeable stirring at Mace's counsel table.

"Are you aware of any photographic recording of Cindy that is not presently in the possession of NIS?" David asks.

"I'd saved a few files because I forwarded them to my home computer."

Mace stands. "We renew our objection to this evidence, Your Honor. Not only is this irrelevant, but any recording that Dr. Cassidy or her colleague made while working at CAPS is the property of NIS and was to be turned over to NIS before Dr. Cassidy departed. We cannot—"

"Your Honor, this is inappropriate," David challenges. "You've already ruled during the break that this tape could—"

"Objection overruled, Mr. Mace." Allerton doesn't even wait for David to finish. "Proceed, Mr. Colden."

"Thank you, Your Honor." David pushes a button on the remote control, and a large flat-screen monitor near the clerk's desk turns on.

A few more seconds pass, but nothing happens. David pushes another button on the remote control, but the screen remains blank. The court clerk comes over and tries to help get things going without success. The jury members begin to shift in their seats—the sound of impatience—and it could not have come at a worse time.

"It was working this morning," David says to Allerton.

"Another copy, perhaps?" Allerton offers.

"Just one moment, please," David answers and heads back to Chris.

She gives David another disk. "This is the original," she whispers. "I've only viewed the stuff we'll be using. The whole file runs for almost an hour, so you'll need to cut it off."

David gives the second disk to the clerk and holds his breath. Images soon appear on the screen—Cindy in the Cube, wearing her gloves, the large lexigraphic keyboard in her lap, Jaycee in front of Cindy and adjacent to her own keyboard and oversize monitor.

David had always said that the best type of trial witness tells a story. But he also knew that no matter how good the witness is, no matter how well the witness has been prepared, and no matter how interesting the witness's story may be, words cannot compare to a picture. Such are the limitations of human language.

David pauses the playback. "Can you tell us what we're looking at here, Dr. Cassidy?"

"This is the main CAPS facility that we occupied during the four years. That's me," Jaycee says with a trace of humor, "the human one. Cindy, you can see, is wearing the gloves I discussed and has the keyboard we designed in her lap."

On the monitor, Cindy watches intently as Jaycee signs to her, speaking at the same time. "Where is the milk, Cindy?" Jaycee asks. Cindy pauses for a brief moment on the screen and then pulls her lips back into what looks to be a smirk. She pushes several buttons on the keyboard and then signs. The words IN THE COW show up in large letters on Jaycee's computer screen. There is some laughter in the courtroom and even Allerton smiles.

David pauses the playback. "Can you walk us through the process that we just saw?"

"It's a typical communication-observation-response sequence. I sign the question to Cindy. Cindy observes the signing visually, thinks of an answer, and then, using the gloves and the keyboard, she responds. Cindy's response is translated through the program I testified about earlier, and then it appears on my computer screen. You'll note Cindy's joke. We found that she actually had a sense of

humor and, like her language skills, her sense of what was funny—
at least compared with my experience with my niece—was about
what you'd expect from a four-year-old girl."

David pushes PLAY on the remote. Back in the movie, Jaycee
signs and says, "Funny. Very funny. But what is the true answer?"

Cindy signs and the answer shows up on the screen as BOTTLE IN
REFRIGERATOR.

Jaycee signs and says, "Good, Cindy. Where is the refrigerator?"

Cindy presses a button on the keyboard and the word KITCHEN
appears in large letters on Jaycee's computer monitor.

"What color is the refrigerator?" Jaycee signs and says.

Cindy makes the ASL sign for "forgetting," which is taking
your hand and pretending to pull something out of your head. Even
before the words I FORGOT appear on Jaycee's computer screen, the
gesture on the film is unmistakable.

"Think again," Jaycee says and signs.

Cindy makes a gesture and it appears on Jaycee's screen as LIKE
THE MOON.

"Very good, Cindy," Jaycee says on the recording.

David pauses the playback. "What's that about?"

"That's Cindy's way of saying 'silver'—like the moon. Colors
tend to be a more abstract concept than we realize."

The recording jumps to another segment. Cindy signs and
punches a button on the keyboard. WHERE IS FRANK? shows up on
Jaycee's computer.

Jaycee responds in sign and voice, "Frank is sick today." Cindy's
head drops to her chest in response. "What is wrong, Cindy?" Jaycee asks and signs.

Cindy looks up at Jaycee, and her eyes express something I recognize all too well. Cindy puts a finger below each eye—the ASL

sign for "crying"—and then signs something with both hands. Jaycee looks confused and then checks her computer monitor. The monitor shows that Cindy has asked: WILL FRANK DIE LIKE MICHAEL?

David pauses the recording again. "Who was Michael?"

"He was another NIS chimpanzee at CAPS that Cindy used to have social time with. He was infected with hepatitis B and a few months later died from it."

"How did you explain that to Cindy?" David asks.

Jaycee shrugs. "I mean, assuming for the moment that Cindy is capable of rational thought, how do you explain it in a way that makes sense? I just told her that he got sick and went to sleep and could not wake up." The tremor in Jaycee's voice is a warning sign, so David quickly starts the recording again.

In the recording, Jaycee assures Cindy in sign and voice, "No, no. Frank is just a little sick. Frank is not dying."

Cindy signs back to Jaycee, and Jaycee reads off the monitor. I AM GLAD FRANK IS NOT SICK LIKE MICHAEL. Cindy's hand hesitates in midair, as if she is thinking about saying something else.

"What is it, Cindy?" Jaycee signs and asks.

After a pause that stretches for a few long seconds, Cindy signs and touches her keyboard. WILL I BECOME SICK LIKE MICHAEL?

In the courtroom, the recording goes blue and Jaycee covers her face with her hands. The courtroom is silent.

Whatever else my old friend might have done before, during, or since meeting Cindy, there could no longer be any serious question about the depths or genuineness of her feelings for this creature. Even the jury foreman seems disturbed by the scene unfolding before him.

David gives Jaycee a moment to compose herself before turning her over to Mace for cross-examination. In the process, he forgets to pause the video.

There is something else on this disk.

I suddenly come into view on the monitor.

I'd almost forgotten what I sounded and looked like in life. I think that's the way it's meant to be. How else am I supposed to withstand my present state of being if I must compare it with the deep, resonant colors that come only through breathing real air and touching anything that offers even the slightest resistance to my fingers? I so miss the feel of everything.

Nevertheless there I am on that screen, and I reel under the weight of the disconnect.

That day on the recording floods my memory. I'd just learned of my disease, but I was still optimistic that we would come through it without any lasting consequence. I also was thrilled to be with Jaycee and meet this remarkable animal called Cindy.

I still had hope and it showed.

"Will she come to me?" I say on the recording.

Jaycee appears next to me. "I think so. Give her the present."

I offer Cindy the doll I've brought. "Cindy? Would you like this?" I ask and sign as I hold the doll out to her. She takes it gently from my hand. For just one moment our hands touch. Then Cindy signs something.

The words THANK YOU appear on the monitor in the lab, followed by, WHAT IS YOUR NAME?

"My name is Helena," I say and sign.

Cindy signs again, and COME PLAY WITH ME immediately appears on the screen.

In the courtroom, David stands paralyzed before the monitor, the remote control raised but useless in his hand. I'm not the only one who has been jettisoned from the safe harbor of numbness by this video clip.

"I would love to," I see myself say and sign to Cindy on the screen. I approach Cindy, and for the next few moments of film we can be seen huddled together on the floor near her Cube.

"Mr. Colden?" Allerton asks quietly in the courtroom. Through some silent but shared language predicated on the syntax of grief and loss, Allerton knows the identity of this woman in the video. For Allerton, the missing explanation for David's involvement in this case has clicked into place. "Is there anything else you wanted us to see?" he inquires.

David doesn't respond. He can't. It's not just seeing my moving image and hearing my voice after these long months, it also is the fact that I've suddenly popped up in the middle of his courtroom— a place I would never be—like some misplaced but determined jack-in-the-box. My connection to Jaycee and Cindy is no longer amorphous and indeterminate for David, but instead is forever recorded and preserved in pixels, bits, and binary code.

I have become evidence.

"Mr. Colden?" Allerton asks again, his voice evidencing a measure of personal concern thus far absent from his demeanor during the trial.

Finally, Chris steps behind David, takes the remote control out of his hand, and, mercifully, pushes the STOP button. The monitor goes blue. "You're almost there," Chris whispers to him and squeezes his shoulder. "Just hold on."

"Do you need a moment, Mr. Colden?" Allerton asks.

At Chris's touch, David slowly comes back into himself. "Thank you, Your Honor. I'm okay."

"Do you have any more questions for Dr. Cassidy?"

"I think just one more," David says. Turning back to Jaycee, he asks, "Why did you do it? Why did you try to take Cindy?"

When Jaycee speaks, her voice quivers. This is by far her hardest answer, because this is Jaycee's truth. "How couldn't I? I tried every other way to save her. I tried to buy her, I offered to work for free, I wrote to congressmen. Nothing worked. With the end of the project, Cindy was going to be transferred to the general primate population. Once there, she can be experimented on, infected with diseases—just like Michael. I'm not married. I've no kids. Cindy was my life for four years. I raised her as I would my own daughter. I changed her diapers, I toilet-trained her, taught her how to eat, to express herself in our language, to care about what happens to herself and those around her. I just couldn't let them kill her. I needed to try something...anything to free her."

Jaycee finishes her answer just before her tears come. She makes no attempt to brush them away.

David turns to Mace and his voice is tight and low. "Your witness."

Mace, the confidence gone from his voice, says, "We'd like to take a few minutes, Your Honor."

Allerton looks at the large clock at the rear of the courtroom. "Make it quick, please."

"I messed up. I'm so sorry," Chris tells David during the break. "I didn't know Jaycee actually caught any of Helena on tape. I would never have..."

David still seems disoriented. It's as if the combination of seeing my moving image, hearing my voice, and watching me interact with Cindy means more to him than the simple sum of those parts.

I think the consequences of the trial have become more real for him, or maybe it is just that the reality of my absence has become inescapable.

I don't know if any of this is a good or bad thing though, or even whether it matters anymore at all, and this is what frightens me. "Jaycee said that she didn't have any," David says finally.

"She must've forgotten about that one."

"Well, now that we have it, I guess we've got to use it."

"What do you mean?" Chris asks.

David shakes his head. "I need to think," he says and walks away.

After the break, Mace began his cross-examination of Jaycee. Thus far, it has been difficult to sit through. In addition to the actual conduct for which Jaycee is being prosecuted (and which she freely admits), Mace also has established that: (i) Jaycee had formed a very strong maternal bond with Cindy that not only had the potential to cloud Jaycee's objectivity, it in fact probably did so; (ii) Jaycee would do almost anything within her power to save Cindy from harm; and (iii) Jaycee's work with Cindy was on the very far—and perhaps very, very far—edge of accepted anthropological theory.

And Mace isn't quite finished yet. I know where he's going. I think everyone in the courtroom can see it, including Jaycee. The entire cross-examination has been foreshadow; he will try to destroy any sympathy Jaycee has won among the jurors by discrediting the work that has consumed her for the last four years or by cracking Jaycee's professional composure. And Allerton will allow Mace to try because David opened the door by putting the merits of Jaycee's work at issue. I can tell by the way David begins grinding his teeth that we have come to a make-or-break moment, and the outcome all turns on whether Jaycee will be able to survive the coming attack.

"Now," Mace says, "let me direct your attention to the technology through which you say Cindy communicates. You gave testimony about interstitial linguistic programming, you remember that?"

"Yes."

"Can you explain to us the actual programming behind that concept?"

"Somewhat. Essentially, ILP, as I said earlier, involves comparing a normal physiology—or in this case, a human one—with an abnormal physiology, in this case that of a chimpanzee, and mapping the differences. Then you take the actions of the affected subject, again the chimpanzee, run it through that model, and the computer program will interpolate and predict the most likely intended action."

"Interpolate and predict the most likely intended action?" Mace asks quizzically. "That's the first time I heard you use the word *interpolate* in this proceeding. Can you tell us what it means?"

"Certainly. In general terms, it means to estimate between two known values."

"I see. So ILP is a program that estimates; it makes predictions."

"Yes, but with a high degree of accuracy."

"And how do you know the level of accuracy?"

"Because ILP has been tested and validated in a number of studies."

"Studies involving whom?"

"The vocally impaired."

"Humans?"

"Yes. Humans."

"Has any effort ever been made to validate it as against non-humans?"

"Not that I'm aware of. No."

"And as I understand your testimony, you're not using ILP in the manner for which it was originally created, correct?"

"I don't understand the question."

"Don't you? Really?" Mace asks in disbelief. "ILP as I understand it—and please correct me if I'm wrong, Doctor—was created to take vocal utterances and sort of fill in the blanks when measured against the human speaker's vocal impairment. Correct?"

"Yes."

"But you're not using it to fill in the words. You're using it in your research to estimate and interpolate American Sign Language utterances—basically, hand gestures."

"That's not accurate, sir." I can tell Jaycee is getting angry.

"In what way am I incorrect?" Mace taunts her.

"In some instances, the way in which Cindy signs is completely discernible. The ILP is just belts and suspenders."

"And in other cases?"

"As I indicated, in other cases the limitations of primate physiology require educated estimation."

"In how many cases is it necessary to estimate?"

"I don't know offhand."

"In the movie that we just saw, how many times was it necessary to estimate what the primate was attempting to communicate because of a limitation in physiology?"

"I couldn't say."

"Half?"

"I'm not certain."

"More than half?"

"I said I wasn't certain?"

"Every single time?"

"No, not every time."

"So somewhere between more than half and every time?"

"Objection," David calls out as he rises, "that mischaracterizes her testimony."

Allerton turns to Jaycee. "Can you give us a reasonable estimate of how many times there was a direct match between what the chimpanzee was signing and, for example, what I would find in an ASL dictionary? I think that's what Mr. Mace is getting at."

"I don't mean to argue with you, Your Honor," Jaycee says.

"But I sense you're about to anyway," Allerton answers to some amused laughter.

"I just want to clarify something. The reason why that's a very difficult question to answer is because very few people who sign do it exactly the way you would see it in an ASL dictionary. There are always small and subtle differences in the way someone makes a letter, for example. And just like humans, ASL signing chimps use facial expression and gaze direction to moderate the meanings of their signs. That's one of the reasons we also use the keyboard."

"So then," Allerton says, "the question seems to be how many times you relied upon the ILP with respect to what we just saw to interpret what the chimpanzee was attempting to sign?"

"I would guess maybe half the time," Jaycee says. I can hear David repeat in his head what he tells every witness—*Never, ever guess.*

Mace picks up on the thread before Allerton or David can say anything more. "So, you would guess—your word—fifty percent of the time?"

"Yes."

"Can you read ASL, Dr. Cassidy?"

"Yes, of course."

"Hmmm." Mace pretends to ponder. "Then can you tell me why it is that in every instance you appear in that recording, you needed to check the computer monitor to see what the specimen had said?"

Jaycee hesitates, trying to recall what the recording actually showed. "I always like to be sure, so I confirm my understanding."

"And the way you confirm your understanding is through a computer program that has never been validated for primates and was never intended for ASL?"

"Objection," David interjects. "Asked and answered."

"Sustained," Allerton rules.

"Dr. Cassidy," Mace begins again, "are you familiar with something called Lloyd Morgan's canon?"

"Yes."

"It is a canon of deductive reasoning, is it not?"

"It's supposed to be."

"What is it?"

"Never believe that animals think as you do unless you must."

"A derivation of the principle called Occam's razor, isn't it? All things being equal, one should prefer simpler explanations for behavior over more complicated ones."

"I believe that's what Occam's razor involves, yes."

"And you do know what anthropomorphism is?"

"Of course. It is the projection of human characteristics on non-human animals."

"Isn't anthropomorphism a serious risk in your business?"

"No more than speciesism is in yours. Do you know what speciesism is, Mr. Mace?" Jaycee snarls back.

Allerton leans over to Jaycee. "Please just answer the questions, Dr. Cassidy."

"I apologize. The answer to your question is no, I do not believe that anthropomorphism is a serious risk in a well-controlled study that employs principles of the scientific method like the work we did with Cindy."

"And the Cornell Language Institute study of Cindy," Mace says as he grabs the document off his desk, "specifically says, and I quote, 'the subject's language capacity and cognitive age equivalent assumes both'"—Mace pauses for emphasis—"'both that the interstitial linguistic programming is validated for primates generally and the subject primate specifically and that the modifications of the ILP to make it compatible for American Sign Language are valid and appropriate. We offer no opinion as to either assumption.'" Mace shows the document to Jaycee. "Do you see that in the report?"

"I'm aware of that qualification in the report, yes."

"So the assertion that Cindy has the language ability of a four-year-old also assumes the validity of your theory?"

"The qualification in the report says what it says, Mr. Mace. I didn't write it."

"Fair point, Dr. Cassidy. Let's talk about something you do have firsthand knowledge about. Who did the actual programming of the computer program that ran the ILP for the gloves?"

"My associate, Frank Wallace, was the actual programmer, but it was at my direction."

"Meaning that you directed him in what assumptions to include in the programming language?"

"Yes."

"And you assumed going into this study that Cindy was capable of acquiring and using human language, correct?"

"I guess that is a fair statement—based on my knowledge of the then-current state of the literature."

"Isn't it possible that the assumption that Cindy was capable of acquiring and using human language biased the ILP programming for the gloves?"

"No, it's not."

Mace starts to pick up the pace of his questions, ignoring Jaycee's responses and getting her to answer before she has thought through her response. "That, in fact, the computer modeling was biased at its inception?"

"Untrue."

"That when Cindy lifted her hand and moved her fingers, you programmed her gloves to interpret those random movements as words because you wanted to see words."

"Untrue."

"Words were the only thing that could save her."

"Untrue."

"And you so wanted to save her, didn't you?"

"Un..." Jaycee catches herself, takes a breath, and smiles at her interrogator. "That actually is true, Mr. Mace. I do want to protect her life. But because she is a living—"

"I have my answer, Dr. Cassidy, thank you."

David jumps out of his seat. "Your Honor, the witness was in the middle of her answer."

"You may finish your answer," Allerton tells Jaycee.

"Thank you. I was just saying that it's true that I do want to save her, but not by manipulating data. I want to save her precisely because she is a sentient being who not only suffers, and not only is aware that she suffers, but can tell you in her own words—yes, Mr. Mace, her own words using your language—that she wants you to stop hurting her."

Mace seems momentarily at a loss. He recovers quickly, but weakly. He says in a low, soft voice, "So you would have us believe, Dr. Cassidy."

"Anything else for this witness, Mr. Mace?" Allerton asks.

"I don't think so, but give me one moment, Your Honor," Mace says as he collects his papers from the podium. I get the distinct impression that Mace is waiting for the moment to pass, and that he has saved something else for last. When he lifts his face again, the overconfident leer on his face tells me I'm right. "Just one last thing, Dr. Cassidy. Do you own a car?"

"Yes."

"What type of car is it?"

"A Jeep Cherokee Laredo."

"Color?"

"Red."

"What's the license plate number?"

David jumps up. "Objection, relevance!"

"Where is this going, Mr. Mace?" Allerton asks.

"A little latitude, Your Honor. I only have a few more questions."

"Only a few more—in real-world terms, not lawyer terms, okay, Mr. Mace?" Lawyer jokes are always worth a few laughs from the benches. "Overruled," Allerton decides.

"New York X80 2PM."

"At any time after your arrest, did you return to the CAPS facility?"

"No sir," Jaycee says clearly.

"Are you absolutely certain?" Mace asks with an insinuation of incredulity.

"Yes. I'm fully aware of where I go, sir."

"I see," Mace says.

David tries hard not to squirm in his seat.

"Let me be more specific. Did you drive your car to the perimeter of the CAPS facility at any time following your arrest?"

"No."

"I remind you that you are under oath, Doctor."

"So I've been told, Mr. Mace."

Max leans over to David and whispers, "What the hell is this about? Is he just being an ass?"

"No idea," David whispers back, but I can see that he's nervous.

Up at the front of the courtroom, Mace turns to Allerton. "Then I've nothing further for this witness at this time."

"Okay," Allerton says. "Any redirect, Mr. Colden?" David, lost in his own thoughts, appears not to have heard. "Mr. Colden? Hello? Any redirect?"

David refocuses on the judge and then slowly rises to his feet. "Not at this time, Your Honor."

Allerton turns to Jaycee. "You're excused, Doctor." Jaycee steps out of the witness box and takes a seat behind David. "Do you have any other witnesses, Mr. Colden?" Allerton asks.

"Yes," he says. "We call the former director of NIS, Dr. Scott Jannick."

David's entire team simultaneously looks at him exactly the same way—*What the hell?* But if I know nothing else, I know my husband. I know what he has in mind. By some bizarre and convoluted series of events, he now has my last gift to him and to Cindy; he's not going to waste it, whatever the risks.

Mace is instantly on his feet. "Your Honor, this is entirely inappropriate. We've had no notice that Dr. Jannick would be called as a witness. He isn't even in the courtroom."

Allerton nods. "Have you made provision to have Mr. Jannick in the courtroom, Mr. Colden?"

"No. His testimony only became material once the testimony today was elicited."

Allerton looks at the clock. Four thirty PM. "I hate to end the day early, but I do think the prosecution is entitled to a minimum of notice before you call one of their own as a witness. We are adjourned until nine o'clock tomorrow morning."

As soon as Allerton is off the bench, Max goes to manage the press while David finds Jaycee.

"When did you decide to call Jannick?" she asks.

David ignores the question. "Why was he asking you about your car?" David asks.

Jaycee shrugs. "Fishing, I guess."

"The head of the criminal division of the US Attorney's Office doesn't fish."

"Well, he was this time, and whatever trick he had in mind clearly didn't work."

"Maybe, but the trial isn't over yet."

"Trust me, okay?" Jaycee says and quickly walks away.

Chris catches up to David. "What was that all about?"

"Do you know when it's time to really worry during a trial?" David asks her.

Chris shakes her head.

"It's when your client says 'Trust me.'"

Later that evening, David sits alone in his darkened office. I've been summoned here by the sound of my own voice and the light thrown by my own image. There I am on the computer screen, a ghostly vision from the past. And yet, here I stand, an ethereal phantom from the past. At least on the screen David can see me and hear my words; I carry the weight of history. He even tries to trace my movements with his fingers, so powerful am I. But here, I am nothing to him—not even vestigial.

When David hits the PLAY button on his computer for the sixth time, I am grateful that I can find my dear Skippy. He lies with his head on his paws between Clifford's legs in the bed that has become Clifford's when the boy stays at our house. Skippy's eyes are still alert, but his cough is persistent now.

One of my old photo albums is open before them, the one I called my Remembrance Album. It holds a photograph of every creature I'd ever lived with. On the inside front cover, I had written these words more than two decades ago: "On the pages within are those who came before; those who shared their lives with us all too briefly. These are the lives we honor. These are our beloved angels who have returned to God."

Clifford slowly turns through the photographs, pausing to point out each dog, cat, bird, or rodent to Skippy. When Clifford gets to the blank pages at the end, he carefully closes the album, kisses Skippy on the head, and turns out the light.

24

At nine o'clock the next morning, Jannick smiles at the judge and the jury from the witness box.

Following a few preliminary questions establishing Jannick's credentials, David requests and obtains permission from the court to treat him as a hostile witness. Jannick speaks clearly, calmly, and answers each question without hesitation.

"Did you, in fact, make the decision not to renew Dr. Cassidy's project for another year?" David asks.

"No. That was not my decision. I did, however, make a recommendation that the project not be continued."

"That recommendation was upheld?"

"Yes, it was."

"So, what will now happen to Cindy?"

"She will be returned to the general NIS primate population."

"Are there any plans for her once she gets returned?"

"Not specifically. But she will be available for suitable research projects."

"Suitable in what way?"

"Age, gender, sometimes weight, temperament—a whole range of possible factors."

"What are the current NIS research programs that she might be included in?"

"Objection," Mace calls out. "This line of questioning is clearly irrelevant."

"Your Honor, the prosecution has painted the picture that Dr. Cassidy was somehow emotionally disturbed because she didn't want Cindy to go back to the general primate population. The jury is entitled to know what awaits Cindy there. This is all about Dr. Cassidy's motive."

"Okay, Mr. Colden, but let's move it along."

"I certainly will try," David says. "The question, Doctor, is what are the current NIS research programs?"

"I can't recall all of them."

"Perhaps I can help. Hepatitis?"

"Yes."

"Carcinogenics?"

"Yes."

"Tuberculosis?"

"Yes."

"Ebola?"

"Not when I stepped down."

"HIV?"

"Yes."

"Brain stem trauma?"

"Yes."

"Spinal trauma?"

"Yes."

"Surgical technique?"

"Yes."

"Anything I'm leaving out?"

"I don't think so."

"Does NIS have any type of practice or policy regarding the use of post-surgical pain management?"

"We encourage our researchers to use the most humane practices."

"Is that a yes or a no?"

"We have no specific policy, other than to encourage the use of post-surgical pain analgesics where it is consistent with the protocol involved."

"Do you know how many of your researchers actually use post-surgical pain meds?"

"No, we don't keep track of that."

"You would agree, wouldn't you, that chimpanzees feel pain?"

"I would agree that chimpanzees experience nociception, which is the detection and signaling of noxious events through specialized nerves. I would also agree that they have the conscious perception of that nociception stimulus."

"How is that different from feeling pain?"

"People have different definitions of the word *pain* that often transcend the physiological response to noxious stimuli. I'm trying to be clear about my parameters."

"Do you believe that chimpanzees suffer?"

"Define *suffer*."

"*Suffer*—meaning the negative emotional reaction to perceived pain."

"I believe they have a response to pain as I defined it that is more than just physiological. I don't want to get into a semantical jousting match with you about the meaning of *emotion* or *spirit* or *soul* or *theory of mind*. You can affix whatever labels you like."

"In your experience, do chimpanzees understand when a painful procedure is about to commence?"

"We have documented certain physiological changes in anticipation of particular procedures—heart rate goes up, vocalization, blood pressure escalates."

"Vocalization? You mean they scream?"

Jannick nods. "That happens, yes."

"And when you say that NIS encourages the use of post-surgical analgesics 'consistent with the protocol involved,' what does that mean?"

"Analgesics are contra-indicated for certain research."

"For example?"

"Some areas of research are specifically designed to measure the effect of noxious stimuli. You certainly wouldn't want to use post-surgical pain meds in that context."

David reads off a sheet at his counsel table. "So, for example, in a study of a new design of hip joints for hip replacement, you wouldn't give post-surgical meds because...?"

"You wanted to assess the discomfort of the subject post-surgery."

"Dr. Cassidy was aware of the manner that NIS used primates in other experiments?"

"We had discussed it."

"And she advised you that she didn't want Cindy returned to the general NIS primate population because of those experiments?"

"That's putting it mildly, yes."

"Tell me something, Doctor. Have you ever had a hip replacement?"

"No."

"How about a knee?"

"Yes, a partial replacement, several years ago."

"Did you have pain?"

"Yes, I did."

"Are you sure you suffered pain following that surgery, or were you simply experiencing a conscious perception of nociception stimulus?" This question draws some isolated laughter from the benches.

"Objection."

"I'll withdraw the question," David says. "Dr. Jannick, are you familiar with the term *knock down?*"

"That's not a term that we use."

"But you have heard of it, haven't you?"

"Yes."

"Chimpanzees are stronger than humans, correct?"

"Generally, pound for pound, yes."

"So, the chimpanzees at NIS must be anesthetized for even the most minor procedures, including drawing blood?"

"Yes."

"How is this done?"

"The chimpanzee is darted with the appropriate amount of anesthetic."

"Before this happens, food and water are withheld, right?"

"Generally, yes. For the safety of the specimen, so it does not aspirate while under the tranquilizer."

"So that it doesn't choke on its vomit?"

"Yes, that's another way of putting it."

"The chimpanzees know when the anesthesia is coming?"

"I couldn't say for sure what they know."

"Okay, let's stick to what you do know. Does it sometimes take more than one shot to anesthetize the specimen?"

"Yes."

"Is the chimpanzee generally moving when the dart is fired?"

"Yes."

"Does the dart sometimes hit the chimpanzee in the face, or the anus or the penis or the vagina?"

"That has happened, yes."

"The chimpanzees hate these tranquilization episodes, don't they?"

"Hate is a human characteristic, Mr. Colden."

"Fair enough. How do the chimpanzees respond when they see the dart gun?"

"They vocalize."

"They scream?"

"On occasion."

"They urinate on themselves? Their bowels open?"

"This happens on occasion."

"Would you say they experience terror?"

"Again, a human characteristic."

David returns to his counsel table and takes out another CD. "May I use the court's projector for a moment, Your Honor?"

"What are you going to show us?" Allerton asks.

"One episode of what Dr. Jannick has just described."

Mace stands. "We object to these theatrics, Your Honor. It is patently irrelevant."

"To the contrary," David responds. "This is a well-known film clip taken by a former research assistant at an NIS facility. I don't think there's anything theatrical about it." David inserts the CD into the player at the front of the courtroom without waiting for Allerton to rule.

I've seen this clip before. The images at first are disorienting because they're taken from a shaky, low angle. A man in a green jumpsuit enters an area where five-by-five-by-seven-foot cages line the walls. Each cage contains a single chimpanzee. When the chimpanzees see the man, they begin to scream. The sound is deafening on the recording. The man stops before one of the cages. The chimpanzee in the cage, still screaming, tries to squeeze into the farthest possible corner. The man takes out a dart gun from a pocket in his overalls. The chimpanzee sees the gun, defecates on itself, and then turns its face away from the man, its body quivering. The man shoots, and in a few seconds the chimpanzee slumps to the floor, landing in its feces. The recording goes blue.

David stops the player. When he speaks, there is a tremble in his voice. "Is that the tranquilizing process you were describing, Dr. Jannick?"

"I don't believe that the reaction of the primate depicted is typical."

"But that is the process?"

"Basically, yes, but can I just say—"

"Thank you, sir. I think you answered my question. You don't believe that Jaycee succeeded in fulfilling her grant requirements, do I have that correct?"

"I believe that her work was very worthwhile, but I don't believe that the specimen, Cindy, actually acquired complex human language skills. I don't believe she can be analogized to a four-year-old human child at all. The initial research was promising, but it just didn't pan out."

"One of the reasons for your recommendation was that Cindy's communication with Dr. Cassidy couldn't be replicated, right?"

"Yes. Cindy would only communicate with Jaycee. That's a huge red flag because it often means the specimen is responding to particular non-language reward cues—like a dog trained to sit for a bone. It says nothing about the language acquisition capability of the species or the language actually acquired by the individual specimen."

"A dog trained to sit," David repeats. "I see. So if I showed you one German shepherd who got up on his hind legs, walked over to the phone, dialed the pizza parlor, and ordered a large pie with half cheese and half raw beef, how many more German shepherds would need to do that to convince you that your assumptions about German shepherds were wrong?"

"That's not the—"

"And if I could convince you about German shepherds as a breed, how hard would I need to work to get you to rethink Saint Bernards and poodles?"

"Objection!" Mace calls out above some laughter from the benches.

"Sustained," Allerton rules.

"It is not the fact that Cindy is only one chimpanzee that is so troubling, Mr. Colden," Jannick volunteers. "It is the fact that Dr. Cassidy is only one human."

"But you would agree that she is the one human that cared the most about this one chimpanzee?" David asks.

"Of course."

"Don't you think that matters?"

"No, in fact, I don't. I think it is the problem. Dr. Cassidy cares so much that she sees what isn't there."

"But isn't communication a process of creating meaning between the participants? Doesn't that require a willingness to share? To at least care enough to share?"

"Your whole argument presumes that this animal perceives a

unique emotional connection with Dr. Cassidy and is motivated by that relationship to communicate, but the only evidence of that connection is the very act of communication that you are trying to prove. It is one giant tautology."

"Actually, Dr. Jannick, I thought my argument only presumed that Cindy, like everyone else in this courtroom, would communicate the most with the person she liked the best. Mr. Dryer's ex-wives don't speak to him at all," David says, pointing to Max, who nods in agreement. "But that doesn't mean they can't. They just wisely choose not to."

The laughter from the benches is cut short by Mace's shout of "Objection!"

"Withdrawn," David says, having made his point. "You heard about the video clip from yesterday, right?" David asks.

"I heard about it and I've since reviewed it."

"You didn't know about that interaction before yesterday, did you?"

"No."

"Dr. Cassidy told you, however, that someone else had communicated with Cindy, right?"

"She did say that, but there was no proof of it."

"Now that you've seen it, you really can't deny that Dr. Cassidy succeeded in replication, can you?"

"Mr. Colden," Jannick says sympathetically, "I realize that this case has certain emotional connections for you—"

"Please just answer the question."

"I'm trying to. That snippet of interaction on the tape that I saw is not evidence of real replication, regardless of what you might want to believe. The replication that I'm talking about means demonstrable, spontaneous, context-appropriate communication under controlled conditions. I have no idea what the circumstances were on that video. For all I know, Dr. Cassidy could have been prompting Cindy behind your wife's back."

At Jannick's mention of the word *wife*, the courtroom stirs. I can hear the word whispered in the benches.

David speaks over the murmur. "You don't believe that, do you?"

"I believe what I see. I don't have the luxury of just following a tug on my heartstrings. My responsibility is—was—to administer a program critical for advanced research that can save humans from debilitating diseases and death. I was required to make difficult choices. I needed proof before I potentially sentenced thousands or tens of thousands to certain death because I stopped authorizing research on the one species that can give us answers."

"But you have doubts, don't you?"

"Of course I do. Every rational scientist does. Chimpanzees are beautiful creatures, remarkable, really. But I didn't make these rules. You want to make a complaint, do it during Friday-night services or Sunday mass. And if you've got another way to find cures, then I'd love to hear it. If not, then I suggest you step out of the way."

"Get out of the way so Cindy can be destroyed, that's what you mean?"

"Objection," Mace calls out.

"Sustained," Allerton rules.

"I have nothing further for this witness," David says.

Jannick addresses the jury directly. "If there was another way, believe me—"

"I said, I have nothing further!"

Mace rises before David returns to his seat. "But replication wasn't the only reason you recommended against renewing the grant, was it, Dr. Jannick?" Mace asks.

"No, of course it wasn't. I also had concerns about the methodology of Dr. Cassidy's research itself. While Dr. Cassidy claims that Cindy has a cognitive age equivalent of four, there's no way to rule out the issue of testing bias given the fact that the tester's hands are all over, so to speak, the method of communication."

"What do you mean?"

"It's in the ILP itself. Although Dr. Cassidy has indeed correctly stated that the ILP will estimate whether Cindy is signing a word within certain parameters, she neglected to tell the court that the estimate has an error frequency of at least ten percent and probably a lot more."

"Meaning?" Mace asks.

"Meaning that for every ten signs that we say Cindy makes, one will be not only wrong, but not a sign at all—Dr. Cassidy will see a word where one was not even intended."

"What's the impact of the error?"

"By my calculation, that alone could reduce Cindy's CAE by a year or more. Combine that with the fact that ILP has never been validated for a primate or for ASL and I think you start to see that Dr. Cassidy's work presumptively is of doubtful validity. Dr. Cassidy went into this project with the assumption that chimpanzees can learn and use human language, and she built the ILP already pregnant with that assumption. The program looks for an intention to make meaning where none may actually exist."

"Was there any other factor that led you to recommend that the grant not be extended?" Mace asks.

"Yes. I have to say that in the final year of the project, I began to get concerned about Dr. Cassidy's relationship with the primate. She seemed to be closing herself off from all other work and outside professional contacts. She stopped returning my calls, and others at NIS told me the same thing."

"What was your concern, Dr. Jannick?" Mace asks.

"Certainly her scientific objectivity was in jeopardy. This would not be the first time that a researcher crossed a boundary with a primate specimen, particularly in multi-year or open-ended research projects. It happens, and it never ends well in my experience. A grant is not renewed and the researcher takes the rejection personally; the specimen is somehow 'theirs' or there's some nefarious conspiracy to steal the researcher's work. There is actually a name for it—the Lefaber syndrome. I blame myself for not paying attention to the early signs."

"Thank you, Dr. Jannick," Mace says. "I hope we can now let you return to your other important matters."

"Anything further of this witness, Mr. Colden?" Allerton asks.

"Just one more minute," David says as he rises. "You are criticizing Dr. Cassidy because she assumed that the subject she was working with was attempting to use language."

"Correct."

"She went into this experiment to determine 'how' language was used and not 'if' it was used?"

"Basically, yes. The assumption of intention is embedded."

"Big deal," David challenges.

"Pardon?"

"I mean we always assume that humans are intending to convey some information to a listener when they speak, right? And that they are attempting to do so in a way that can be understood by the listener. Their intentions can be encoded in complicated and differing ways that often depend on context, but we assume they are trying to say something that will be heard, right?"

"I guess so."

"And there's a reason we make these assumptions: If we don't, we cannot study the language of humans—everything becomes random and, therefore, meaningless. Isn't that right?"

"It's not the same thing."

"Meaningless, Dr. Jannick. That's a pretty depressing and small view of the natural world, isn't it?"

Jannick ignores the question. "You're making a comparison that has no scientific predicate."

"All I'm saying is, why not come to the table with the same rules and assumptions for chimpanzees as you do for humans? Assume that they are trying to communicate—that they are trying to reach you—with all the tools they have in their non-human arsenal."

"We make assumptions for humans because we—"

"What? Because we are human, too. That's really what's going on here, isn't it? We just love to hear ourselves speak!"

"Objection!" Mace stands. "Mr. Colden is just badgering!"

"I'll withdraw the question," David says. "Let me ask you this. Taking everything that you've just said into account, if you had seen the video of Cindy and my wife before you made the recommendation to terminate the project, would this have caused you to consider extending Dr. Cassidy's work?"

Jannick waits a long few moments and then whispers an inaudible answer.

"I can't hear you, Doctor," David says forcefully.

"I said, 'I don't know,'" Jannick says a bit louder.

"But one thing you do know—once Cindy is sent back to the general primate population, you'll never know whether Dr. Cassidy was right, will you? All that work will be irretrievably lost. Potentially the most important breakthrough in primate language studies over the last decade. Lost," David says, and then repeats more slowly, "You will never know."

"Objection!" Mace calls out.

"That's fine, Your Honor," David says. "Dr. Jannick doesn't need to tell us the answer. I think he knows it."

The courtroom is silent in the aftermath of the exchange.

"Very well," Allerton says. "If there's nothing further, you're excused, Doctor."

Jannick pushes past the reporters waiting for him and heads quickly for the elevators. I don't know if David accomplished what he intended, but in Jannick's face now I notice an all-too-familiar countenance. He is haunted.

"Okay," Allerton begins. "What do we have—" Allerton's court clerk cuts him off with a note that he reads immediately. "Now?" he asks her. She nods. Allerton looks at the clock and then tugs on his nose. After a moment, he turns toward the jury. "We will adjourn for lunch. I need to take care of another matter. The joys of being chief judge." Allerton bangs his gavel and immediately disappears through the door behind the bench.

Ninety minutes later, Allerton returns to the courtroom to find the parties and the spectators waiting for him. "Do you have any other witnesses, Mr. Colden?" Allerton asks.

"No, Your Honor. We are prepared to move to closing argument."

Mace jumps up. "The prosecution has a very short rebuttal witness to respond to some of the defense's science claims."

"Approach," Allerton commands.

When the lawyers get to the judge's dais, David is first to speak.

"They already rested, Your Honor. I object to a new prosecution witness at this point. We've had no notice—"

"I did say that I'd give the government an opportunity to answer any scientific claims the defense made about Dr. Cassidy's work," Allerton says. "I think you clearly opened that door, Mr. Colden. And it seems we can hear the witness without unduly delaying the trial. Step back."

On the way back to his desk, David repeats one word under his breath—"Damn, damn, damn..."

"What happened?" Chris asks.

Before David can answer her, Mace calls out, "The prosecution calls in rebuttal Dr. Renee Vartag."

I hear the name just as the maw of my past opens and spits Vartag into the courtroom. Make no mistake; if you just wait long enough, all things do come around.

25

As soon as I see Vartag take the witness stand, I'm abruptly reminded of the words of my old friend Simon—"God's language is juxtaposition." I now realize that he was right.

It is not about one time and one place, this courtroom and this testimony. It is about the relationships between, among, within, and across a day, a month, a year, or a life. We've been granted—perhaps more so than any other living creature—the ability to derive meaning from contrast, discord, and dissonance. This is our gift and this is also our curse. The language of juxtaposition is more than merely jarring; it is agonizing.

A panoramic vista suddenly opens beneath me. I can't catch my breath as I see Skippy lying on Clifford's lap on my living room couch. Skippy's mouth is open, trying so hard to take in air. I hear a door open somewhere before I can see it. It is the front door to what was once my house, and Sally opens it for Joshua. He is more than somber. He carries a small doctor's bag.

Not yet. Please, not yet.

But I can't stay with Skippy. I have no control over this language. Now I can only see Cindy. She lies alone in her cage in the empty lab at the CAPS facility. Her large eyes are open but vacant. She holds to her chest the little doll I handed to her a lifetime ago.

Cindy stirs as she watches the door to the lab while it is unlocked from the other side. The door swings open, and a man dressed in a lab coat and carrying a clipboard enters. He looks familiar at first, but his face is obscured. Then it clears for me. It is Jannick, and he is accompanied by a woman. Jannick carries Cindy's gloves in his hand.

Cindy quickly moves to the far corner of her Cube and away from Jannick. I hear her whimper.

Then I'm back in the courtroom. Vartag takes the stand and recites her long list of credentials, honors, and professorships, culminating in her recent appointment as the director of NIS.

I swear she hasn't aged. Her confidence in herself appears to have grown over the years, if that is even possible. I wonder what it must be like to have so much faith in yourself.

Mace asks, "What do you think of Dr. Cassidy's work at CAPS, Doctor?"

"Not very much, I'm afraid."

"You've reviewed all of her work, as well as the decision not to renew the grant?"

"Yes."

"What was your opinion?"

"If I had been director at the time, I certainly would not have approved the grant. The premise of the study was flawed at its inception."

"In what way?"

"It's all really premised on an anthropomorphic syllogism: I am sentient, chimpanzees are like us, therefore chimpanzees are sentient; they can learn to communicate in human language because they are so like humans. The scientific truth is that, when it comes to communication and language usage, chimpanzees are not at all like us."

At the same moment, Jannick turns on the few pieces of computer equipment remaining in the lab and then approaches the Cube. He doesn't appear to notice the warning signs coming from Cindy.

"Dr. Jannick," the woman with him says, "I'm really not comfortable with this. This isn't my work and I don't know Dr. Cassidy's protocol. Can't you just do this?"

"I told you. I need a woman and a woman who knows ASL."

"But I don't know this animal."

"That won't matter."

"She seems agitated," the woman says.

"I assure you, she's been through this hundreds of times. She'll be fine once the gloves are on her."

In the courtroom, Mace lobs his next question. "But we do share so much DNA, don't we?"

"Dr. Cassidy is absolutely right that we have huge amounts of DNA in common. But there's also no doubt that it's the small disparities that are found throughout the genome that have made all the difference between us. Those minute fractions of DNA that Dr. Cassidy appears to dismiss as insignificant are why we humans have Shakespeare, Einstein, Clarence Darrow, Rembrandt, Lincoln, Kant, and the primates don't have even one example of a brilliant mind. There's a reason no one has ever found a poem by a chimpanzee. All of the achievements of modern humanity lie in that one or two percent divergence in our genetic code that represents millions and millions of years of evolution.

"I'm not saying chimpanzees are inanimate, but so far as we know, complex language is unique to humans. This skill has allowed us as humans to process profound amounts of information, and this, in turn, has resulted in a remarkable amount of knowledge acquisition in a minuscule period of time. Just look at the last hundred years, or even the last fifty. Look at how far we've come. But not any other species. Why is that? Because our ability to communicate in the way we do has propelled us in so many ways. Humans are unique. Period."

And then I am back in my home. Clifford watches as Joshua listens to Skippy's heart. After a few moments, Joshua looks at Sally and shakes his head. "No!" Clifford shouts. The sorrow in his voice momentarily cuts through all the other noise in my head. "Please," he begs. "Not yet."

Sally reaches for her son. "I wish I had the power to make him live forever," she says. "But the only power I have is to be there for you when he doesn't. I think Skippy is telling us he's ready."

Clifford pulls away from her and starts to pace with Skippy locked in his arms.

I'm not ready. Not yet.

And then I see Jannick open the Cube. "It's okay, Cindy," Jannick says in his most soothing voice as he signs. "I have a friend who wants to meet you." Jannick reaches into the Cube and takes Cindy's hand. In the process, her doll gets knocked to the floor of the lab. Cindy becomes still, her eyes wide.

Cindy's fear takes me back to the courtroom. "But Dr. Cassidy certainly seems convinced of the merit of her own work, doesn't she?" Mace asks.

"No doubt," Vartag answers. "It wouldn't be the first time."

"So, you've had experience with Dr. Cassidy's work before this?"

"Quite a bit, actually," Vartag says.

Before David knows what is happening, and before he can stop it, Vartag launches into our shared history at Cornell. When Vartag describes for the jury how Jaycee and I had killed Charlie, there is no place I can hide. David repeatedly objects, but Allerton doesn't stop her. When Vartag is done, the jury looks at Jaycee with a new skepticism—the type people specifically reserve for hypocrites.

"...and so I don't know where along the way Dr. Cassidy became so concerned about the long-term well-being of research primates," Vartag says, "but that certainly was not evident to me from her conduct during our prior work together."

The phrase *our prior work together* echoes in my head as Jannick begins to slide one of the gloves over Cindy's fingers. She struggles against him, and Jannick grabs her hand to keep it still. He accidentally twists her thumb. Cindy shrieks and bites into his forearm. He screams and tries to pull his arm away, but Cindy won't let go. The blood pools around her mouth.

The woman with Jannick screams for help as she tries to pull Cindy off him. "Call security," Jannick yells. The woman jumps for the nearest phone and dials. "We have an emergency in lab three!"

And then Clifford stops pacing and turns toward his mother, his face contorted in anguish. Beads of sweat suddenly materialize on his forehead. His hands begin to tremble and then he vomits on the floor near his mother. "I think I am dying, Mommy," he gasps.

"No, honey," she says as she leads him to a chair. "You're just feeling."

"It hurts, Mama. It hurts right here," he says, pointing to his chest. "What should I do?"

Sally takes Clifford's face in her hands. "We need to end his pain," Sally tells him.

"It's not time," he cries. With Skippy nestled between mother and son, Clifford weeps into his mother's hands.

I want to stay with them, but I'm dragged back to the courtroom just as Mace approaches Vartag with a folder. "May I have this marked for identification?" Mace asks as he hands one of the documents to the court clerk and two copies to David. They are color photographs of a red Jeep Cherokee Laredo. Although the occupant of the Jeep is lost in shadow, the license plate on the Jeep is clearly visible—X80 2PM. Mace gives the marked photo to Vartag. "Can you tell us what this is?"

"Yes," Vartag answers. "It's a photo taken by one of the new perimeter security cameras installed at the CAPS facility just after I took over."

"Do you know the date and time the photo was taken?"

"The security cameras are all date- and time-stamped. This was taken on December thirty-first at eleven oh five PM." The answer results in murmuring from the benches.

David looks like he's going to be ill. This is it. It's all over. The train is off the tracks now and hurtling straight toward him at inhuman speed.

"Do you recognize the vehicle in the photograph?" Mace asks.

"This is Dr. Cassidy's Jeep. You can see the license plate number very clearly."

Jaycee tries to hand David a note, but he ignores her.

"Can you tell where at the perimeter this was taken?

"Yes, it's from camera three, which is located at the very rear of the facility. I know this view. There was a fairly well-known gap in the perimeter chain link right about here. We repaired it and installed the surveillance cameras after Dr. Cassidy's arrest."

"Is there any legitimate reason why Dr. Cassidy would be at the perimeter of the CAPS facility at that date and time?"

"To the contrary," Vartag says, "she'd already been told that she was not permitted to return to CAPS without specific written authorization."

I can almost feel the blow. In the lab, Jannick hits Cindy hard in the face and she finally releases his arm. He crumbles to the floor next to the doll, his arm bleeding profusely. Two security guards run into the lab with their guns drawn. When they see Jannick, they point their weapons at Cindy, waiting for her next move.

Cindy's hands start moving so fast that I can only make out some of what she is saying. I don't need ILP or her gloves to recognize the words *No, go away, hurt,* and *sorry.* It is precisely the type of spontaneous, context-appropriate communication that Jannick, in his testimony, said did not exist.

Jannick must see what I do because his eyes become wide with realization. I think he tries to tell the guards to stand down, but instead it comes out as an unintelligible, mournful croak. The guards can't understand him; they must assume Jannick is pleading for them to shoot because their hands tighten around their weapons. Jannick struggles to lift his hands to wave the guards away, but he can't seem to get his arms to do what he wants. He is as helpless in the face of impending violence as the animals that had been in his charge. In the end, it is Jannick's words that have failed, not Cindy's.

Cindy begins to sign something else. *Not like…,* but I can't make out the last part of it. She repeats the phrase—*Not like…* Then I get it. From the look of horror on Jannick's face, I think he understands it the same second that I do. She's finger-spelling. *M-I-C-H-A-E-L.*

Not like Michael.

Cindy leaps out of the Cube. I know with every fading atom of sentience that Cindy just wants to retrieve her doll, but the doll is too close to Jannick. The guards only see another attack coming. They are blinded by the limits of their language.

I want to squeeze my eyes shut against what is coming and instead I see David open Jaycee's note. The note says, "Please don't let her die."

"Your Honor," Mace says as he reaches for another document, "I have Dr. Cassidy's bail-bond agreement. It specifically prohibits her from leaving Manhattan without the court's permission."

"I'm aware of that, counselor," Allerton says, giving Jaycee a disapproving look. "Continue."

"Did Dr. Cassidy seek your permission before coming—"

In the moments before David rushes to his feet, I abruptly feel his mind fill with my own confused and disjointed images—of the video clip of me playing with Cindy, of me in my hospital bed waiting for him to say good-bye, of Skippy and Clifford, of Sally and Arthur, and perhaps a dozen others. The scenes come too fast for me to keep them separate. These are the reflections of David's life— or, perhaps more accurately and generally, just of life. They culminate in a single word, and David now shouts it out: *"Objection!"*

At the same moment, miles away, Jannick screams "No!" Then the roar of gunshots.

"Grounds?" Allerton asks with one eyebrow raised. "I've already ruled this is relevant."

"Lack of foundation," David says.

In the courtroom, David tackles Allerton's doubtful stare. "Specifically, there is absolutely no evidence that Dr. Cassidy was the person in the car."

Mace looks like he wants to leap on David. "This is a preposterous attempt to obstruct my examination of this witness!" he shouts.

"May I approach, Your Honor?" David asks. Allerton motions for counsel to join him at the bench. After a moment's hesitation,

Max, perhaps sensing that David may need a friendly face, meets him at the front of the courtroom.

David starts in immediately. "There's been no testimony that the driver of the vehicle was Dr. Cassidy. This is rank speculation and it is extremely prejudicial before the jury."

"Oh, do get serious, Mr. Colden," Mace says. "It is her car. Who was driving? Santa going back to the North Pole? It is exactly the location that she broke in the first time."

"You didn't ask her whether she had lent her car to anyone or whether it was constantly within her control that night."

"She already testified that she had not been to the facility." Allerton turns to Mace. "Do you have any other photographs suggesting it was her driving?"

"We're still checking security tapes, but the occupant never got out of the Jeep."

"I guess," Allerton says, "it's possible that someone took her car and drove it all the way to the CAPS facility late at night for reasons not yet disclosed, Mr. Colden, but that sure seems unlikely to me."

"Unlikely or not," David answers, "that in fact is what happened."

"And how do you know that precisely?" Mace sneers.

David's face is a mask. "Precisely because I was the person she loaned the car to," he says. "It was me in the car."

"Come again?" Allerton says.

"It was me," David repeats. "We were prepping for her testimony at my house on New Year's Eve. I wanted to see the CAPS complex before the trial to get a feel of the place, and I wanted to do it without attracting a crowd. I used her car because I wanted the four-wheel drive to make the trip. There was snow on the ground."

Max coughs into his hand, but I can still see his smile.

Allerton examines David with evident skepticism. "I see," he says finally.

"I request that the court put Mr. Colden under oath," Mace demands.

"Do you have any other evidence that puts Dr. Cassidy at the facility at that time, Mr. Mace?" Allerton asks.

With great reluctance, Mace answers, "No. But Mr. Colden's story makes no sense. A middle-of-the-night run? On New Year's Eve, no less?"

"Perhaps, Mr. Mace," Allerton says. "But I suspect, depending on their particular circumstances, people have done more bizarre things on New Year's Eve. I'm not here to judge Mr. Colden's behavior. Mr. Colden is an officer of the court," Allerton continues, now staring directly at David. "When he speaks to the court in his official capacity as he is now, he is effectively speaking under oath, isn't that correct, Mr. Colden?"

"Yes sir."

"And Mr. Colden has made a factual representation to this court. If Mr. Colden had lied to the court, he knows I would seek to have him disbarred, isn't that correct, Mr. Colden?"

"Yes sir."

"He knows I would show no leniency, regardless of the circumstances—personal or otherwise, right, Mr. Colden?"

"Yes," says this man who teaches young lawyers the importance of the oath, the man who has always been so afraid of tarnishing his reputation for truthfulness, the man who has consistently chosen directness over dishonesty.

"Well then," Allerton continues, "Dr. Cassidy already has testified under oath in a manner consistent with Mr. Colden's representation. You have no contrary evidence. And I think we all can agree that the inference raised by the question is prejudicial to the defense; you are accusing Dr. Cassidy of breaking her bail agreement. If true, that allegation would throw her in jail. Absent some evidence—"

"But the photo…" Mace's protest trails off.

"Is not evidence of anything to the contrary. So I don't think it will be necessary to make Mr. Colden actually put his hand on a Bible at the moment."

"But," Mace stammers.

"But nothing, Mr. Mace," Allerton says. "Please step back, gentlemen."

The attorneys return to their counsel tables, but not before Allerton catches David's eye.

When David takes his seat, Jaycee tries to whisper to him, but he twists away.

Allerton turns to the jury. "I am sustaining the objection to this line of questioning. I'm directing you to disregard the photograph and any questions regarding the photograph. It was improper and should play no role in your deliberations. Do you have anything further for Dr. Vartag, Mr. Mace?"

Mace is silent for a long moment before he answers. "Can we take a brief recess?"

"Ten minutes," Allerton says.

I used to have this dream when I was sleep-deprived from being on call too many nights in a row: I was at the animal hospital and I needed to get to the operating room for an emergency surgery on a dog that was bleeding out. Every step I took moved me farther away from the surgery table. I could see the blood, but couldn't do anything to stanch the flow. I could only watch, helpless, horrified.

It's that same feeling now as I stare at Cindy. She crawls a few inches forward on the floor, the blood pouring from bullet holes in her neck and her chest. As she stretches out her arm, I can hear the sound of wind coming from her chest. She curls her fingers around the doll and pulls it close. Her lips touch the doll's face.

Jannick crawls over to Cindy. He checks for a pulse, and his blood mixes with Cindy's for just a moment before the guards help Jannick to a chair.

"Call an ambulance," one of the guards directs the woman.

The force of David's anger suddenly yanks me back to him. He grabs Jaycee by the elbow and moves her out of the courtroom and into a far corner of the hallway.

"I'm sorry," she says as soon as they are alone.

"That's it? You're sorry?" David hisses.

"I totally screwed up," she says. "I wasn't going to do anything. I just wanted to see her through a window. I didn't see any security cameras. They repaired the fence, so I just drove home. I didn't think they saw me."

"And you just chose to keep that from me? You lied to me, damn it." David can barely control himself. "What kind of game are you playing here?"

"If I told you, this would've been over before it started."

"And it should've been. What the hell were you thinking going back there?"

Her voice quivers. "Clearly I wasn't thinking, okay?"

"Are you just that stupid? The whole point of calling Jannick as a witness was to get him to question his decision in light of Helena's video. Now he'll think you're just a nut. Worse, you've confirmed his opinion of you."

"Maybe he'll buy your story that it was you in the car."

"Oh, please. I saved it from going to the jury, but Jannick will know exactly what happened. So will Vartag." David rubs his forehead as if he's trying to get rid of the memory of the lie he just told. "You broke the conditions of your bail and I helped you cover it up. Allerton could put you in Bedford Correctional right now if he knew the truth. I could be disbarred."

"But he doesn't know. And he won't, right?"

"You've manipulated me from the beginning, haven't you? Whatever it takes just to get what you want."

"Do you really know so little about yourself? I didn't ask you to lie for me."

"You didn't give me any choice."

"All you had to do was stay silent."

"So I can have Cindy's blood on my hands and yours, too? So Helena can spin in her grave?"

"No, so you can choose between ending a life and saving one. Welcome to my world."

"Maybe Jannick is right. When exactly was it that you stopped being a scientist? Before or after you rigged the ILP to save Cindy?"

Jaycee's head snaps back from that blow. When she looks at David again, her eyes are surprisingly bright and clear. "I hope Jannick is right. I can live with lying to some judge I don't give a damn about to save someone I love. That's what makes me human." Jaycee steps back from David. "How have you used the privilege of sentience, David? Tell me, what exactly is it that you've done to be worthy of being called 'human' anyway?"

David opens his mouth to respond, but nothing comes out.

"I thought so," Jaycee snarls. "When you can answer that for me, counselor, then you can judge me."

Jaycee brushes past my husband and back into the courtroom.

Until this very moment, I hadn't realized that Jaycee, David, and I, each in our own way, were trying to find the answer to the same question.

The thought is drowned out by the blare of sirens. I see an ambulance carry Jannick away. He is crying—whether from pain, regret, or humility, I will never know.

In the lab, the two guards shove Cindy's inert body into the confines of a small cage on wheels. Cindy's eyes are open, but there's no life within them now. Her fingers jut through the mesh of the cage as if even now she's looking for Jaycee's hand. Or, perhaps, mine.

The men begin to wheel her body toward the door. One of the guards drops back to the floor near the Cube. He picks up the doll that had been mine and then Cindy's. "What should I do with this?" he asks his companion, who answers his question with a shrug. The guard tosses the doll back into the Cube.

The men push Cindy's body through the laboratory entrance. The one who held the doll is the last to leave. He gives the lab a cursory once-over glance, turns off the lights, and then locks the door behind him. I am alone in the darkness of the lab as I listen to the echoes of their footfalls gradually fade away.

"So, anything more of Dr. Vartag?" I hear Allerton's voice in the shadows, but I do not return to the courtroom. There is no longer any point.

"No, not at this time." Mace's voice rings out all around me.

"Mr. Colden, do you wish to cross-examine Dr. Vartag?"

I hear that question and the space before me brightens ever so slightly. To cross-examine—to interrogate, reveal, uncover meaning.

I get it now. This must be it. David will destroy Vartag on the stand and, in that process, finally close this circle of torment and set me free. He will be my champion and give this whole story the meaning I've been seeking. This must be why I'm here, why Vartag has returned from my past, why David is representing Jaycee, why Cindy had to die, why I had to die. All so this could happen. So there would finally be meaning. Blessed, poignant meaning. Illumination. It all makes perfect sense. Beginning, middle, and now, end.

I am in the courtroom again, this time standing right beside David. The entire room pulses with anticipation. Spectators and specter somehow perceive the exact same thing.

David slowly rises to head toward the lectern in front of the jury box. Before he takes two steps, Max taps him on the sleeve. "This one is a true believer," Max whispers. "Careful, she can hurt you." David nods and then turns to face Vartag.

He smiles at this woman who has plagued my memory. Ha! We are coming for you, Renee, you twisted little bitch.

Vartag nods back at my husband, but it isn't a greeting; it is permission, the kind royalty might give to a servant to allow approach.

"You've been involved in animal research for thirty-five years?" David begins.

"Thirty-seven, actually," Vartag answers.

"So, how many animals have you euthanized over that time period?"

"I wouldn't know. I don't keep track of that—any more than I keep a tally on the number of human lives my research has saved."

"Hundreds of animals?"

"Oh, certainly."

"Thousands?"

"Certainly," Vartag repeats without any hesitation.

"Tens of thousands?"

"Perhaps."

"So many that you can't even keep count?"

"No, that's not it. It's just not a relevant figure."

"And why is that?"

Vartag shrugs. "Ten or ten thousand animals—it has absolutely no human pathological significance."

"Meaning," David says, picking up the thread, "if you must euthanize ten thousand animals to save a human life, then that is an acceptable result?"

"No, not only acceptable, Mr. Colden," Vartag says. "It would be a crime of science to decide otherwise."

"Even if those ten thousand animals are chimpanzees just like Cindy?"

"Oh, yes. Even if they've been trained to recite the entire Declaration of Independence. My job is to save human life. Chimpanzees will never be human. They weren't yesterday, they aren't today, and they won't be tomorrow. Nothing else matters."

David lets that answer sit for a full minute. "Thank you for your candor, Doctor," he says. "Good luck to you. No further questions."

Vartag walks out of the witness box and past the filled but silent benches.

Max was right. Vartag isn't evil or disturbed, or even, I must admit now, entirely unsympathetic. She is just convinced of the correctness of her own worldview.

My Grendel has become human, and through that transformation, much more powerful. She is so powerful that I can no longer delude myself.

There is no greater hidden meaning, no golden envelope with a mysterious life-affirming message, no silver key that unlocks a private passage. Angels do not flutter down with secret scrolls or sacred songs. There is only the continuous creation of endings. Nothing ever really gets saved. Not ever. Not Charlie, not Cindy, not David, and not me. My dream is my truth.

I suddenly feel so tired—like I've been treading water for days. I've nothing left and I'm out of time. My own pages have turned blank. All I can do now is bear mute witness to events that no longer have consequence, if ever they did.

A young man in a business suit, sweaty and out of breath, bursts into the courtroom. He scans the crowd, finds Mace, and whispers into Mace's ear. Mace's face turns ashen. "Are you absolutely certain?"

The young man nods.

"Anything else before closing arguments?" Allerton asks.

"Yes," David answers. "In light of the testimony presented, we renew our request that Cindy be produced for examination by the jury. The jury should see her."

Half the jurors nod in agreement, but the jury foreman looks at his watch and rolls his eyes.

Mace rises. "May we approach, Your Honor?"

Allerton sighs and nods. Mace and David join him.

"So." Allerton turns to Mace. "What's the matter now?"

"Your Honor," Mace whispers, "you had asked us...well me, actually...to make certain representations regarding the status of the property in question and to provide notice prior to any change in condition. I've just learned that there's been a change. The item in question...well, the chimpanzee..."

David drops all pretense of decorum. "What happened to her?"

Mace ignores him. "She attacked Dr. Jannick as he was preparing her for testing and she was—"

"She's dead?" David's question rings loud throughout the courtroom, followed immediately by a wave of confused commotion across the jurors and the benches.

"Please calm down, Mr. Colden." All of Mace's bravado is gone.

"Don't tell me to calm down! What happened to her?" David makes no attempt to lower his voice and Allerton doesn't admonish him. Everyone can hear them now.

"Answer the question, Mr. Mace," Allerton says in a steely tone.

"She was shot and killed during the attack."

Judge Allerton's heretofore calm and deliberative demeanor gave no clue that he had within him the volcanic eruption of rage that comes next. "WHAT?" It is one word, but it reverberates throughout the courtroom. "YOU MADE REPRESENTATIONS TO THIS COURT, SIR. YOU MADE REPRESENTATIONS TO ME! I ALLOWED YOU TO AVOID AN ADVERSE ORDER BASED ON THOSE REPRESENTATIONS!"

There is loud sobbing somewhere behind me. It is Jaycee. I want to weep with her, but I've no tears left. Chris moves to comfort her.

Over the sound of Jaycee's grief, Mace tries to stop the flow of Allerton's words. "This was an accident. I made those representations in good faith."

"GOOD FAITH? HOW DARE YOU USE THOSE WORDS!" Allerton lowers his voice, but only by a fraction. "You had us sitting here going through this facade while your client was acting in violation of the representation you made."

"Not at all. It was all in good faith. I was told—"

"Be quiet!" Allerton barks.

"I understand that you're angry, Your Honor, but—"

"You have not even begun to see me angry."

"But—"

"Step back!"

The noise level in the courtroom is now a dull roar. Allerton bangs his gavel against the top of his desk, but it has no effect. He smacks the gavel again, this time so hard that the head snaps off and careens somewhere behind him. "Quiet now, or I will have the room cleared!"

Allerton bellows to the court reporter: "On the record now! I still have pending before me the defendant's motion to require the prosecution to physically produce the allegedly stolen property in this courtroom for inspection. Having now heard the accumulation of the testimony, I've decided upon further reflection to grant that motion. Accordingly, I am directing the prosecution to produce in this court forthwith the property—a chimpanzee known as Cindy—to be examined by the jury."

Mace rises in response. "Your Honor, you know we can't comply with that order. As I've already indicated, the specimen is no longer alive."

"According to you, Mr. Mace, she's property. Why should it matter if she is living or dead? Produce her dead body, and I also want Dr. Vartag here to authenticate the body. She can explain to the jury how the chimpanzee became a dead chimpanzee. And tell her to wear a nice suit, because I'm also granting CNN's request for a live courtroom feed for this part of the trial."

Mace struggles to find his words. "A moment, Your Honor, please," he whines and then begins heated discussion with his colleagues at his desk.

"You have sixty seconds, Mr. Mace."

In half that time, Mace turns to Allerton and says somberly, "In light of your ruling and recent events, the United States government is withdrawing all charges against the defendant."

Some spectators in the courtroom cheer, but the sound is ridiculous following so closely the news of Cindy's death.

Above the noise, Allerton says, "That's the best decision you've made in this whole case, Mr. Mace." He turns to the jury. "You are discharged from further service. Thank you for your cooperation and your attention."

Then the clerk calls "All rise," and the entire courtroom— except my husband—is on its feet. There is a moment of silence while Allerton departs, and then David and his crew are surrounded by well-wishers and reporters. David ignores everything and everyone except my notebook. He slowly turns the pages as if he's looking for some clue to a solution he might have missed.

It isn't there, David. It never was.

David finally tries to stand, leaning heavily against the table. He takes several deep breaths and then straightens. "Maybe if I hadn't waited..."

"That's nonsense," Max says. "They just would've done it sooner."

"But we'll never know that now."

"No," Max agrees. "We never will."

"So much we'll never know," David says to no one.

Chris and Dan try to console Jaycee. It is all too much for her. Jaycee shakes them off and rushes out of the courtroom. The grief she will suffer for Cindy will be in private. David watches her go and doesn't try to stop her. Their reconciliation, if it ever takes place, will need to be another day; David, like me, no longer has the capacity to offer comfort.

One reporter calls to David. "Mr. Colden, the animal rights groups are already calling Cindy a martyr. They say that she'll do more for the cause dead than any decision in the case could've done. Can you comment?"

"Yeah, I'll comment," David says. "That's a very stupid thing to say. I came here to try to save a life, not lead a cause. I failed. We all did."

"Easy now," Max whispers to David.

Another reporter muscles his way through. "Are you going to pursue any claim for damages against NIS?"

Max steps in front of David to answer. "You bet your ass. Defamation, false arrest, deprivation of civil rights. I assure you that this is just the beginning. We are today creating a foundation to continue Dr. Cassidy's research, and I promise you that whoever is responsible for Cindy's death will be writing the first donation check—one way or another."

"Will you ask for an autopsy?" a reporter asks.

"I need some air," David tells Max and heads for the exit.

There is nothing left for me in the courtroom. I follow David outside and onto the courthouse steps. He uses his cell phone to call Sally.

"David?" Sally's voice carries the weight of tears.

As soon as he hears her, what is left of David's resolve begins to crumble. "We couldn't save her," David says, his lips trembling and his voice starting to crack.

"I know. I saw it on television. I'm sorry. I know you did the best you could. But you need to come home now."

"Home?"

"Yes. Skippy's waiting for you. It's his time."

It takes him a moment, but then David grasps what I already

know. "It's not supposed to be like this, Sally. What else am I supposed to learn? Hasn't it been enough?"

"You did all you could today. But you're needed here now. We need you. And as soon as possible. You understand?"

David gets home impossibly fast.

I see him as the front door bangs open—eyes red, tie pulled open, hair windblown, and clothes as wrinkled as if he had slept in them. For one last time, David looks to me like a little boy coming home after prep school, his uniform dirtied from a fight or a game of football.

The first thing David sees when he runs into the house is Skippy's little pointed black face as Clifford holds him over his shoulder. Skippy's eyes are narrowed in pain. A catheter runs from his foreleg. Clifford paces, his eyes open but distant. Sally matches her son stride for stride, trying to be in his world. Joshua sits nearby, his head down and his hands folded in his lap. I wonder if this, finally, is what Joshua looks like in prayer.

"He just went down fast today," Sally tells David. "We were watching coverage of the trial on Court TV and then he just started struggling to breathe."

"I gave him something to ease his breathing for now," Joshua adds, "but..." He just shakes his head. "He's finally giving up. I'm sorry."

"I know," David says. "Can I hold him, Cliff?"

Clifford finally acknowledges David. Their eyes meet, and Clifford holds David's pleading gaze for a few moments. Tears slowly roll down the boy's face as he nods. "He wanted to wait for you, for you to say good-bye this time."

David gently takes Skippy from Clifford and buries his face in the deep black fur at Skippy's neck, the place where he smells like autumn. "We won't let him suffer," he says and then lifts Skippy so they are now eye-to-eye. "You're almost home." Turning to Joshua, David says, "Okay, what do I do?"

"It's just an injection into the IV catheter," Joshua replies as he gets the materials ready. "Then it'll only be a few seconds. No pain."

"Can I hold him while you do it?" David asks Joshua.

"Of course."

David takes Clifford's hand in his and turns to Sally. "I want you both to sit with me." Sally nods because she doesn't trust herself to speak.

David slowly lowers himself on the couch with Skippy on his lap. Sally and Clifford join him. When I look into Clifford's eyes again, I'm startled to see love and peace and hope and trust and a thousand other emotions that I thought had abandoned me forever in the courtroom.

Bernie and Chip quietly approach the couch with their tails lowered. Chip nuzzles Skippy, who strains to lift his head. Bernie lies down on the floor next to David's legs and whines.

"After you left," Sally says about the two big dogs, "they spent the whole day near him. They know."

"So they won't just wonder where he went, like with . . . ?" David can't finish.

Clifford gently puts his head on Skippy's chest and closes his eyes. "They'll know," Clifford says. "They always did." Words come out of Clifford's mouth, but I'm no longer certain they're his. "I'm ready now," he says.

David gently rubs Skippy's ears and then leans over to one of them and whispers, "And on cool summer evenings we will sit among the trees and flowers and look for fairies in the moonlight." I know he is speaking to me. I know he is speaking to Skippy.

"I loved every moment," Clifford says for both of us.

Joshua, holding two syringes, gets on his knees next to Clifford. Joshua inserts a sedative into the catheter and presses the plunger. Skippy almost instantly relaxes in David's arms. "Are you ready? It'll only take a few seconds." Joshua is crying, too, and his hand shakes.

David kisses Skippy on the head. "When you see Helena, you tell her I said good-bye. And you tell her...tell her that she was right; I can hear them."

"It all mattered, you know? Each one," Clifford says finally and then becomes still.

Joshua inserts the second needle in the catheter and takes a deep breath. Just before Joshua depresses the plunger, David gently moves his hand away from the syringe. "This is for me to do," David tells him and pushes the plunger until nothing is left. By the time the syringe is emptied, Skippy is limp in David's lap.

Thank you, my love. Thank you.

Joshua feels Skippy's chest. His heart is still. "He's gone."

Sally throws her arms around David and her son. David at last gives in—to me, to Skippy, to Cindy, to the trial, to love, and to memory—and the sobs rack him and make his teeth chatter. "Oh, damn," he weeps.

Clifford rises and leaves the room. When he returns a moment later, he is carrying my Remembrance Album and a photograph. The photo is that one of me carrying Skippy through the New Hampshire woods.

Clifford takes a seat on the floor next to David and his mother.

He finds an empty page at the back of the album and inserts the photo. As he does this, he repeats my words: "On the pages within are those who came before; those who shared their lives with us all too briefly. These are the lives we honor. These are our beloved angels who have returned to God."

When the boy finishes, I no longer see David, Clifford, Sally, and Joshua as distinct entities. Instead, they appear to be one integrated whole. They've connected to form something entirely new—better than what they were before—in some ways that are measurable and in some ways that are not.

The death of one little black dog has brought them all together. And before that, a chimpanzee named Cindy brought David and Jaycee together; and before that a horse named Arthur brought David and Sally together; and before that a kitten named Tiny Pete brought Sally and Joshua together; and before that a cat named Smokey brought me and Martha, and then Martha and David together; and before that a chimpanzee named Charlie brought Jaycee and me together.

And a lifetime ago, in the middle of a dark and nearly deserted road, a deer pleading for a quick and painless death brought David and me together.

Jaycee had said that communication is merely the transfer of information in a way that has meaning to the recipient. It doesn't need to be spoken in words or even said out loud; it just needs to mean something. That deer in its last moments spoke to me and David just as clearly and just as deeply as Cindy spoke to me. The language was different, but not the strength of the voice.

They all spoke to me. And they all spoke in a way that mattered—a way that actually moved and changed me.

Watching Sally, David, Clifford, and Joshua so willingly share their grief and love, the pieces finally do make sense. I've been so foolish, running through the forest searching for some profound and eclipsing life meaning when it is the trees themselves that were bejeweled the whole time: Skippy, Brutus, Arthur, Alice, Chip, Bernie, Smokey, Prince, Collette, Charlie, Cindy, hundreds of cats, dogs, and other creatures whom I treated, made better, eased into death, or simply had the privilege to know. Each was worthy in his or her own right of being valued, each was instrumental in connecting us and then moving us onward in our own lives, and each gave much more than he or she got in return.

Clifford was right: Each one mattered. I was better for knowing any of them and blessed to have known all of them. I think I helped, but I know with absolute certainty that I cared.

I'm not empty-handed. I cared.

That is meaning enough.

26

I t's been seven years since I last saw David. I want to look upon his face again one final time.

When I find him, he is walking down a wooded path next to a large black dog. The dog is unfamiliar to me. Seven years is a long time in the life of a family.

I immediately see that the dog suffers from a bad case of hip dysplasia, meaning that its hips do not sit properly within their sockets. The dog walks with its hips pressed against David's legs for support. As a result, David and the dog must walk at exactly the same pace, one leaning against the other, which they do with great familiarity.

The two reach the end of the path and soon come to a small house. They climb the few steps to the front door. Next to the front door, a simple wooden sign reads:

DR. JOSHUA MARKS, DVM

DR. SALLY HANSON, DVM

David smiles at the sign, and his entire face lights up. I smile, too.

David and the dog enter what appears to be a veterinarian's office. Posters on the walls describe the benefits of heartworm prevention and canine oral hygiene. Four cats—one of whom appears to be an adult version of Tiny Pete—are nestled lazily together in a bay window.

A cheerful young woman, the office receptionist, says, "You're back early. How'd the conference go?"

"Good. We found a chimpanzee who tested at the level of a five-year-old. It looks like we finally may be ready to bring an action on a civil rights theory."

"Finally, a chimpanzee as a plaintiff. I really never thought it would happen."

"You need a little less head and a little more heart," David tells her with a smile.

Their conversation is interrupted by a stern voice coming from a room behind the reception desk. The voice unmistakably is Sally's. "Follow me on this one, okay?" Sally tells some unknown subject. "How would you feel if you were vomiting continuously for three days and nobody seemed to notice? I mean, that's just stupid! And you are not a stupid man, are you?"

"I'm sorry, Dr. Hanson," the unidentified man answers. "You're right. I'm really sorry."

"Don't apologize to me," Sally says. "I'm not the one who's been sick."

"I'm sorry, Bandit," the client says.

"Okay then. You sit right there. I'm going to take some blood."

The receptionist shakes her head in disbelief. "I continue to be amazed that her clients come back."

"People put up with a lot when you truly care about their animals."

Sally steps out of her exam room with a pug in tow. She sees David and runs over to hug him. "Damn, you've been gone a while."

"Miss me?"

"Yeah, but Joshua's really been pouting for the last two weeks without you. Take him with you next time, will you?"

"I would, but he can't bear to leave you."

"I know he paid you to say that. I've got to get back to work, but come by for dinner tonight? Clifford wants you to look over his college application essay."

"I'll be there," David says.

David walks to the rear of the office and stops so his dog can catch up. When the two are side by side again, they continue forward.

David and his dog come to a huge wall mural.

The mural has been painted in exquisite detail: Cindy, holding her doll, and with a book open in her lap, sits in the middle of a circle composed of humans and animals, including Skippy, Bernie, Chip, Collette, Arthur, Alice, a large stag deer, me, David, Joshua, and Sally. Cindy appears to be reading to us and we are all listening intently. The book she is reading from is *Ethical and Religious Implications of Primate Vivisection* by Stuart Ross. I know just from looking at it that this is Clifford's work and his vision. I can guess the passage Cindy is reading.

David smiles at the mural in a sad and knowing way as he passes it. I'm betting that he has the same smile every time he walks past.

Finally, David and his dog come to the back door of the clinic. Behind that door I can hear children laughing and a dog's playful barking.

David swings the door open to reveal a large grassy field enclosed by a picket fence. In the field, a dozen dogs of different breeds and sizes play with each other and humans of various ages. Several of the people seem to know David; they wave to him, and he answers in kind.

A small rubber ball crosses David's path, and a border collie chases it. A young girl of no more than eight runs after the dog. She stops in front of David so he can pick her up and swing her in the air. The girl throws her head back in laughter. David gently places her on the ground and she continues running after the dog almost without missing a step. Through all of this, David's dog stands proudly by his side.

A handsome young man jogs after the girl and the dog. He, too, stops in David's path. Jimmy has grown up; only the scar, the missing ear, and the crooked smile identify him as the teenager intent on saving a box of kittens long ago. David shakes Jimmy's hand.

"So, how's Cornell vet school's newest student?" David asks.

"You heard already?"

"Good news travels fast."

"I can't believe I'm going."

"You worked hard. You deserved to get in."

"But the scholarship... I don't know how to thank you."

"The foundation chose you because of the way you've chosen to live your life. We're proud to sponsor you."

The young girl who had chased the dog with the ball is now being chased by the dog. She's laughing even harder than before. "C'mon, Jimmy," she calls out.

Her laughter is infectious as Jimmy and David watch her run past. "I think you're needed over there," David says. Jimmy hugs David tightly for a long few moments, then joins the chase. David watches them, enjoying their play, before he continues down the path.

Five hundred yards from the field, David arrives at a modest house. The dog makes its way up the few stairs, nudges the front door open with a foreleg, and then walks inside the house for water and to rest.

This is where David lives now, surrounded by humans and non-humans who care about him and whom he cares about. He chose well. His life is not small.

If you were to ask David about the how and the why he came to be here, and if he was inclined to answer, he would offer you some vague explanation about me and Cindy and the need to protect those who speak in a language we are not prepared to hear.

But I think I know better. I know the real reason.

David took a life; he depressed a syringe plunger and killed another living creature. By giving death, he finally came to understand that his pain and his fears—the very things that prevented his connection to others and his better self—had no real meaning.

David, now without his dog companion, walks past the house to a small red barn with an attached paddock that has been carved out of an acre of forest. Two horses I do not know join him by the fence. He takes a face in each hand and scratches their chins.

There is a third horse in the paddock. He stands behind these two, neither moving forward nor retreating. This horse I know. My Arthur. David nods to him, respectfully. Arthur takes a slow step toward David and stops. He will advance no farther. Seven years and one step forward. David does not appear troubled by that calculation and neither does Arthur. It's as if they've both come to understand that—human or not—sometimes the heart just works that way.

David continues on into the woods. He soon comes to a six-foot-high stone wall with a rounded wooden door set within the masonry. David takes a key from his pocket and unlocks the door.

The door swings open, revealing an expansive, well-tended garden. Bold patches of floral color spread out in all directions. This place is oddly familiar, although I'm sure I've never seen it before.

Then the years fade away and I remember. This is the secret garden that David had planned for me, the garden that had been drawn in the blueprints David had received so many years earlier.

David enters the garden and closes the door behind him. A large stone bench shaded by an old oak tree sits in the center and across from several stone markers. I can read some of the names on the markers—SKIPPY, CHIP, BERNIE, COLLETTE, CINDY, ALICE, as well as a few others that are not familiar to me.

Max is here, too, as he wished. Wouldn't you just know it? His funeral took place on a cold, rainy, unpleasant day—and hundreds came. David gave the eulogy. Everyone cried, but no one louder than David (or so Max claimed).

And, yes, my name is also on one of the stones.

David sits on the bench and breathes in the scent of lilacs while he listens to the humming of the bees at work.

A cat walks out of the flowers and sits in front of my stone. My old friend Henry. He looks no different than when I left him. I cannot help but smile as he begins to clean himself, completely ignoring David. Seconds later another cat comes from a different direction and lies down in a patch of sun in front of Skippy's stone. He is followed by a third and fourth cat, who sit before the other stones.

In moments the garden is filled with more than a dozen cats— orange, black, long-haired, short-haired, tabby, and calico—who sunbathe in serene comfort and security.

My husband watches the cats in silence for a few minutes and then breaks into a broad smile. He says one word:

"Helena."

*　　*　　*

There is one last bit of information that I want to leave you with before I must go.

I was correct about what was waiting for me. Those creatures I'd been afraid to face in death actually were there in the end. All of them.

They looked into my heart with grace, mercy, and dignity and then lifted the weight I'd so long carried there. They were more forgiving of my humanness than you can possibly imagine.

Amen.

Afterword

O ne of the wonderful consequences of writing *Unsaid* is that I've had the opportunity to hear from readers about the impact animals have had on their own lives. Every experience is different and, yet, they are all profoundly moving. I would like to share with you a bit of my experience and how it resulted in this novel, in the hope that it will inspire you to return the favor.

When I met the woman who would later become my wife, I went from living in a small, dark apartment in Manhattan with a dead cactus to a house full of life. Amy, a veterinarian with a practice over an hour outside of New York City, had already managed to acquire a family of her own—horses, a pig, dogs, cats, birds, and even a chinchilla named Hopscotch. Like David in the novel, I was grateful to be able to share in that life, but also challenged by the needs of so many creatures I couldn't understand. Before Amy, the closest I had ever come to a horse was Gumby's plastic friend, Pokey—and even that relationship ended poorly, with Pokey being turned into a small puddle of goop when I left him too close to the stove. There was so much I didn't know about the animals I was suddenly living with and I appeared able to learn only through painful and/or embarrassing events—never open an umbrella around a nervous horse; cats will pee in your work shoes because they are angry, bored, or just because they're cats; the desire of a pig to cooperate with you is inversely related to how much you need the pig's cooperation; and when it comes to treats, dogs generally are not the best judge of when they've had enough (regardless of the impact on their digestive system).

I began to feel overwhelmed and resentful. I became, in the words of my wife and colleagues, "the complainer." Then I met Skippy.

Skippy is one of the animals in the novel, but he was a real dog—a small, black bundle of fur with a wise and handsome fox-like face. Skippy had been born with a badly malformed heart. He showed up at my wife's veterinary practice one day when Amy and I were at something of a crossroads. We had been debating whether to have children and we had also just learned that Amy was ill and perhaps very ill. I was so frightened of the idea of kids—that I wouldn't know what to do, that something would go wrong, that I would fail them somehow. The idea that my wife also was sick put my anxiety over the top. Fear is paralyzing; it closes your heart to all things—good and bad.

My wife operated on Skippy, but she couldn't fix him. She could only give him some additional time. We believed that Skippy likely would be dead within the year. No one wants a dog with that kind of lifespan, so he came home to us. That turned out to be a very good day.

We were blessed to have Skippy in our lives for three years. He used his time well—unafraid, present, loving, funny, loyal. He was a small dog, but he didn't live a small life. He helped us laugh at ourselves and then with each other with joy when we found out Amy was going to be okay.

But eventually, the day came when Skippy looked at us with those proud and intelligent eyes and we couldn't escape the fact that he was in pain. It was time to end his pain. Skippy died in my arms. I depressed the syringe that released the pink fluid that finally put his heart to rest. I needed to do that for him. I wanted to spare my wife the burden of one more soul.

When it was over, I was surprised at the depth of the loss I felt. The only way I can explain it is to tell you that something deep within me shifted. I realized I was so grateful for every minute with Skippy and wouldn't have traded the time with him for anything in the world, even though that time ended too soon. Then I understood that this was Skippy's last gift to me. By taking his life he taught me how important the act of living really is and how limited by fear I had become. The idea of having children suddenly wasn't so overwhelming. Without that little black dog I don't know if I ever would have made the leap of faith that brought me my two wonderful daughters.

I have come to believe in the power of animals. I believe they can heal, teach, and push us to be better people. I now live with twenty-nine creatures of different shapes and sizes and not a day goes by without learning something from them. I wanted to show Amy that I had started to understand the wonderful gift she had given me and also the blessing she brought to all those in her care, so I wrote her this story. After she read it, Amy thought the story might have meaning for others who both love their animals and struggle with the reality that we lose them too soon, so she encouraged me to share it. That was how the journey that is *Unsaid* began.

We also wanted to do something more. To honor the animals we have known, we started a not-for-profit animal sanctuary organization called Finally Home to help lost, abused, and abandoned animals (www.finallyhomeanimalsanctuary.org). A portion of the author proceeds from the book is going to that entity.

Was my experience with Skippy unique? This is the best part. The more readers I speak with, the more I learn that so many people who have loved and chosen to share their lives with an animal have an equally compelling story about how that animal has changed their lives. I can't believe this is just coincidence. I love that. It makes me believe in the inertia of good things.

In the novel, Helena says that animals were put here to help us redeem ourselves. I believe she is right.

If you would like to share your story with me, I'd enjoy hearing from you. I can be reached on my Facebook author page at www.facebook.com/neilabramsonauthor or via e-mail at countenancewrite@aol.com.

Reading Group Guide

Discussion Questions

1. *Unsaid* is about the healing power of animals. Have you had any personal experiences where an animal has helped you heal? Physically? Emotionally? Spiritually?

2. In the novel, one of the characters points out that there is a distinction between "unspoken" and "unsaid." Do you think there is a difference? What is it?

3. What characters in the book have left things "unsaid" when we first meet them? What remains "unsaid" by the end of the novel?

4. In the novel, Helena is unable to move on after she dies. Do you believe that her continued presence is voluntary or involuntary? In what way? What is the mechanism for her final release?

5. The novel ends with the word "Amen." Why do you think the author chose that word?

6. The novel points out an ever-present tension between specieism and anthropomorphism. Is anti-specieism always anthropomorphic? Is anti-anthropomorphism always speciest?

7. Is there an ethical way to use animals in invasive science research? What if the research causes the death of the animal?

8. Which characters in the novel are motivated by rejection? Which are motivated by the fear of rejection?

9. Cindy is limited in her ability to communicate with humans. In what ways are the human characters limited in their ability to communicate? What has caused these limitations?

10. Does Clifford's communication impairment result in his understanding more or less about the other characters? What does your answer lead you to conclude about the relationship between speech and understanding?

11. At the end of the novel, David insists that he be the one to inject the euthanasia solution that ends his dog's life. Have you ever made that request? Would you consider doing so?

12. Many of the human characters in the book experience grief. Do you believe that animals experience grief? Have you ever witnessed an animal displaying grief?

13. One of the themes of the book is that meaning only comes from juxtaposition and dissonance. If you could choose, would you "live small" in a numb and painless existence or seek meaning and purpose even though the price of that understanding is pain?

14. How would the story have been different if narrated by Clifford? If narrated by David?